"Volume 2 of Rosemary Curran's story of the Grimké sisters focuses on the careers of their Black nephews, who became leaders in the African American community, and on the full emergence of the American movement for women's rights, culminating in the first major national march for women's equality. Curran again richly limns the intellectual and emotional complexity of the sisters' lives as they face continued harassment and disregard in spite of their widely read publications and leadership. A significant addition to the history of the rights of Blacks and women in America."

   —THOMAS TRZYNA, author of *Pornography and Genocide: The War against Women*

"The second volume of Rosemary Curran's *Stony the Road We Trod* vividly animates the lives and families of the dauntless Grimké sisters as they become outspoken advocates of abolition and women's rights. With compelling detail and emotional depth, this historical novel draws us into American history and a mixed-race family in an era when racial and gender identities were being reshaped through the courage of women like Sarah and Angelina Grimké."

   —LINDA MIZEJEWSKI, professor of women's, gender, and sexuality studies, Ohio State University

"Based on skillfully dramatized, up-to-date research, Rosemary Curran brings to life in two volumes the intersecting stories of Sarah and Angelina Grimké and of their two nephews. The sisters' story reveals the arduous journey of rebelling against crucial values of their upbringing, becoming advocates against slavery and for women's rights. We see the fighting power, discipline and strength of their nephews who survive slavery and remarkably make their way to Harvard and Princeton Seminary."

   —Diana L. Villegas, scholar of Christian spirituality

"The abolitionist saga, the saga of women's rights, and the rising tide of the Civil Rights movement come alive in this very personal rendering of the lives of the Grimké sisters and their nephews Archibald and Francis Grimké. Curran has crafted a thoroughly researched and well-written historical novel detailing a complex period of United States history."

—ROSE GATENS, retired director, Center for Holocaust and Human Rights Education, Florida Atlantic University

"Rose Curran transports the reader to nineteenth century America in a compelling and sweeping family saga. With the backdrop of the Antebellum South and Abolitionist Northeast, the Grimké family sprang to life! The Grimkés were full of bold, remarkable people who tirelessly advocated for not only the abolition of slavery but also women's suffrage. Rose Curran masterfully portrays a dense and complex history in a superbly written narrative. I look forward to many pore publications from Rose Curran."

—LAURA GROSSO, international program manager

Stony the Road We Trod

– Volume II –

Stony the Road We Trod

—*Volume II* –

The Grimké Family's Journey
from Slavery to Suffrage

Rosemary T. Curran

RESOURCE *Publications* · Eugene, Oregon

STONY THE ROAD WE TROD, VOLUME 2
The Grimké Family's Journey from Slavery to Suffrage

Resource Publications
An Imprint of Wipf and Stock Publishers
199 W. 8th Ave., Suite 3
Eugene, OR 97401

www.wipfandstock.com

PAPERBACK ISBN: 979-8-3852-2223-0
HARDCOVER ISBN: 979-8-3852-2224-7
EBOOK ISBN: 979-8-3852-2225-4

VERSION NUMBER 06/13/24

For
Joel, Leah, Aimee, and Rob

And in memory of
Kathy Collins
my dear friend, who could never get enough adventures

"The rights of the slave and of woman blend like the colors of the rainbow...."
Angelina E. Grimké Weld

"I ask no favors for my sex. I surrender not our claim to equality. All I ask of our brethren is that they will take their feet from off our necks .... I know nothing of man's rights, or woman's rights; human rights are all that I recognize."
Sarah M. Grimké, *Letters on the Equality of the Sexes.*

Beware Lest He Awakes!

You are a nobler man
Because you have no tan,
And he a very brute
Because of nature's soot;
But though he virtue lack,
And though his skin be black,
Beware lest he awakes!

When called he follows you
With arm as strong and true
As though you were his friend,
And fights unto the end,
That you may safely live;
Then surely you must give
The laurel branch and crown,
And gifts of just renown;
At least you must and can
Call him your brother man!

Angelina Weld Grimké

Contents

Massachusetts

Massachusetts and Washington, DC

Preface to Volume II

STONY THE ROAD WE Trod is the fruit of close to ten years of research and writing, but its origins go back even further. Nearly forty years ago, my colleague at Wheeling University, Debra Beery Hull, and I wrote *Loving and Working*,[1] a research-based study of the challenges for American women of combining a meaningful career with a healthy family life that included children. It was a challenge that each of us struggled with personally—both of us full-time academic professionals, married, with pre-school children at the time. In addition to empirical research on professional women's attitudes, we examined the history of women and work and looked at role models, from biblical times to the present, of women who strove to combine a call to a public vocation and a commitment to a family or relational life. Among those we studied were the Grimké sisters, Sarah and Angelina, the abolitionists and proto-feminists, from a slaveholding family in Charleston, SC. Fascinated especially by the struggles of their later domestic life, I vowed to return to their story when my own family and career life allowed for it.

My goal has been to create an accessible story about this amazing family. There are already a number of excellent biographies available, but I wanted to bring their lives to a wider public audience in a more popular style. I was particularly inspired when I saw the film, *Glory*. Here was a compelling fictionalized history of the early Negro regiments of the Civil War—a story that I knew nothing about beforehand, and that greatly enriched my understanding of African American history. When I began the research for this book, I knew almost nothing of Sarah and Angelina's

---

1. Rosemary Curran Barciauskas and Debra Hull, *Loving and Working*, Bloomington: Meyer-Stone Books, 1989.

bi-racial nephews, the children of their brother, Henry, and his slave mistress, Nancy Weston. When I learned of their dramatic childhood stories and illustrious careers as advocates for civil rights and women's rights, I knew the story had to include them.

I will leave the reader to discover the themes of this book, but I will suggest here that there are several important themes interwoven. If it is a book about an unfinished historical and political struggle for human rights, it is also a book about domestic struggles, love and heartbreak, personal choices, and personal lives. In a way, it is a book about how these inevitably intersect. As a result, the story is told in two volumes, covering three generations of the Grimké and Weld families. I wrote it first as a series of screenplays and then decided to re-write it as a novel.

Writing Historical Fiction

There is an immense reservoir of personal documents from the Grimké-Weld-Stanley families: voluminous correspondence with each other and with many well-known names of the nineteenth and early twentieth centuries, as well as with lesser-known friends; personal diaries, newspaper articles, numerous published works, and unpublished manuscripts from each of the main characters. Although most are in collections at the Clements Library at University of Michigan or at the Moorland-Spingarn Research Center at Howard University, there are other sources that are scattered in a variety of other archive collections. It would take many years to read all of it. I had to content myself with a significant sampling of these primary sources, focusing on important turning points and events in their lives. I fear I may have missed something important, but I am confident that what I have read provides a reasonably full account of their lives and personalities.

One of the pitfalls of historical fiction, or in this case, "fictionalized biography," is telling a compelling story that is faithful to the facts, but not entirely bound by them. If I have erred in finding the right balance, it has probably been on the side of sticking close to the facts. I very much wanted to tell a *true* story—neither a glorified hagiography nor a sensationalized drama that ignored the ordinary struggles of daily life.

Obviously, when writing of nineteenth century characters, one does not have access to tapes or videos of their public speaking, much less of their private conversations. Very few of Angelina's and Sarah's speeches were recorded in written documents, except for Angelina's speeches to the Massachusetts Legislative Committee in February 1838 and at Pennsylvania Hall in May 1838, and a few excerpts that were reported in newspapers. In creating these speeches, I have relied heavily on their own written documents: their testimonies on slavery as published in *American Slavery as It Is* and their anti-slavery and women's rights pamphlets. I have sometimes put words written by Angelina in Sarah's mouth and vice versa. This seems justified because the sisters were in constant discussion of the issues and borrowed ideas freely from each other. It is not always clear which of them said or wrote a particular phrase or expressed a notion first. I have occasionally paraphrased or updated the language, and added sections that condense a particular line of thinking in a more oral style.

For their personal conversations, I have relied mostly on their correspondence and their diaries which reveal, as much as is possible, their personal thoughts and struggles. Necessarily, though, these have been supplemented with dialogue and descriptions that are my own creation. I have tried to maintain some semblance of the style and formality of mid-nineteenth century conversation and manners, while still making the characters humanly natural and recognizable to a twenty-first century audience. By far the majority of the characters and events in these volumes are historical. I have created a few minor characters and a few events where they are needed to fill out the story, but I have indicated that they are fictional in the notes. Only in one or two cases have I deliberately departed from what I knew to be factually the case, and I have also noted those situations, and my reasoning for those departures.

Additional Resources

Still, one is left with a considerable amount of interpretation of lives, where the historical record leaves us uncertain. Some of that interpretation may be controversial. In the Preface to Volume, I have indicated some of those challenges of interpretation or historical accuracy and on the website www.grimkelegacy.com I discuss these challenges and how I have dealt with them.

I found it fascinating to learn more about the practical details of nineteenth century life in the United States. I have recorded much of this historical detail in endnotes. However, because this is a novel, I have eliminated the more arcane or detailed discussions from the final version.

However, a version with the full, original endnotes is available at the website noted above: www.Grimkelegacy.com That website contains material to enrich the reading of the book including discussion questions, a family tree, timeline, notes on historical characters, and more.

Acknowledgments

I AM VERY GRATEFUL to the wonderful librarians at William L Clements Library, University of Michigan, who helped me find and use the Weld-Grimke Family Papers, including the recently added 2012 Addition, and to the kind and helpful librarians at the Moorland-Spingarn Research Center (MSRC) of Howard University which is home to the Grimké Family Collection, the Grimké-Weld-Stanley Early Papers, and the Angelina Weld Grimké Collection.

From the early days of writing this historical novel I have relied on colleagues and friends to read multiple drafts in various formats. Foremost among them were historian Rosanna Gatens Renn, Ph.D., former Director of the Center for Holocaust and Human Rights Education at Florida Atlantic University, and theologian and author, Diana Villegas, Ph.D. They have spent many, many hours reading and discussing this work with me from its early stages to the present day. Without their willingness to read, critique and advise me on this book over many years, and their constant support and encouragement, I know these two volumes would never have been completed. There are no words to thank them enough.

Other friends from various parts of my life also read and commented on drafts of the books at various stages. Among them were Mary Anderson, Judith McDonald, Sher Sellman, Debra Hull, and my dear, recently departed friend, Kathy Collins. In the last few months, English professor and author, Thomas Tryzna, Ph.D., read a quasi-final draft and offered invaluable encouragement and advice on publishing.

My immediate and extended family members have also listened patiently as I shared my enthusiasm for this story and my daily struggles to make progress and complete it. I am grateful that my son and daughter and their partners share my interest in the continuing struggle for African American civil liberties, for remedies to racism, and for women's rights and full equality in the workplace and in the home. My family, friends, and companions have honored my need to "keep writing" even when they (and I) might have preferred that I "come out and play" with them.

I am grateful for the guidance of the editors at Wipf and Stock, and for the opportunity to share this book with a wider audience.

It is perhaps not customary, but I also want to acknowledge my gratitude to the subjects of this work. I have come to love Sarah, Angelina and Theodore, Frank and Lottie, Nancy, Archibald, and "Nana." They were real people who, imperfect as they were, nevertheless laid the groundwork for immense progress in civil rights and in the status of women. To them, and to their friends and co-workers mentioned in this novel, we all owe profound thanks. As was said of Sarah at her funeral, "their deeds were wise and beautiful."

Charleston

1866

I

Nancy's Appeal

NANCY WESTON HOVERED OUTSIDE the school in Charleston that her boys—Archibald and Francis—had attended for several months after the war had ended. She watched as the first students came out the door from their afternoon classes. She summoned her courage and walked into the classroom where Frances Pillsbury had just finished teaching for the day. When she saw Nancy approaching, she rose and said, with genuine pleasure, "Mrs. Weston, so nice to see you!" But noticing the dark look on Nancy's face, she knew something was amiss.

Nancy greeted Frances politely, but immediately thrust her sons' letters into Miss Pillsbury's hands. "Please, ma'am, cain't you do somethin'? Frances read the letters quickly, and her face registered her obvious surprise and distress. She shook her head, then gestured for Nancy to sit down near the teacher's desk.

Frances took her own seat again and looked at the woman's worn face and thin arms with a rush of feeling for the sorrows she had seen. "No, this is not at all what we were told," she said. "Oh, Mrs. Weston, I'm so sorry! The boys should be studying and learning. They have so much to offer." She stopped to look over the letters again. "Hmmm. I really don't quite understand how this happened. I know Charlotte Forten thought it had all been arranged for them, you know, to be apprentices in law and medicine. Something went very wrong." She was frustrated not to have a focus for her anger.

Nancy spoke softly but firmly, "You see how the boys are puttin' a brave face on it, but I know they must be sore disappointed." She sighed and looked at her feet. "They had such hopes. And—well, ma'am—I know what my boys are worth—what they can do."

"As do I, Mrs. Weston." Frances paused to think for a moment, frowning as she contemplated the difficulties. "Hmmm, I have an idea. I think it is worth a try. I know of a new school close to Philadelphia; Lincoln University, it is called. It is for colored freedmen—young men like your boys, although most of them are probably northerners. There's a preparatory section as well as the regular university and I think that would suit the boys perfectly."

Nancy lifted her head and gave Miss Parker a skeptical look, but her heart welcomed any glimmer of hope. Frances continued with a tiny smile. "I have friends, my brother-in-law, Parker, and some of his colleagues, who can write on behalf of Archibald and Francis. They will need to be formally admitted. The school is free but there are some costs for room and board." Her brow wrinkled but she went on in a determined tone. "So, we will need to ask for some scholarship money. And the boys may need to work during vacations and summertime. Can they do that?"

Nancy's face brightened considerably, but she still looked anxious. "Oh, Mis' Pillsbury, d'you think it's possible? That would be so wonde'ful for them! You think they could go there? I—Well, I have no money. But, yes, of course, they know how to work—they *was* slaves."

Frances replied cautiously, "I don't want to encourage false hopes, Mrs. Weston—but I do think there's a very good chance. I will tell my brother how promising they are. I'll also say what good workers they are, and what admirable characters they have." She smiled fondly at the memory of her star pupils.

"And what about John, Mis' Pillsbury? Is he ready? Could he go, too? I—I know he's not quite so, uh, studious—not quite like the others, but . . ."

Frances was moved by Nancy's advocacy for her youngest son, although she feared that Johnny's future was less assured.[1] But she couldn't bring herself to dash Nancy's hopes. "I'll see what I can do, Mrs. Weston. I'll write this very evening. There's no time to lose for Archie and Frank. They've been through so much already."

The two women rose, and Frances extended her hand to shake Nancy's. "Thank you, ma'am. You cain't know how much this means to me." Nancy put her hands to her cheeks, as she looked directly at Frances. Her voice was just above a whisper as she said, "The Lord'll bless you for your great kindness, ma'am."

New Jersey
and Washington, DC
1839–1844

Twenty-seven years earlier

2

Mothers

Fort Lee, New Jersey 1839

SITTING IN THE GARDEN in the sixth month of her pregnancy, Angelina Grimké Weld could feel the flutter of the tiny being within her, and it fascinated her. She was tracing the ripples across her abdomen when her sister Sarah came out. She carried letters from their middle sister, Anna Grimké Frost and their brother Henry telling them of the death of their mother in Charleston. There was a tumult of feeling on each sister's part as they recalled both their mother's doting affection, her uncertain moods, and her horrible treatment of their household slaves.

Although there had been some letters back and forth, they had not seen their mother for over ten years. Even if they hadn't been banned from Charleston because of their anti-slavery writings and their two years of prominent public speaking against slavery, Sarah and Angelina felt certain that they would not have been welcomed by their slave-holding mother and siblings.

Later in the evening, Angelina's husband, Theodore, said, "Well, my dear sisters, it will not allay your grief, but I do have some hopeful news from Henry Stanton and Lewis Tappan." Sarah looked at him with interest and Theo continued, "Stanton writes to say that our book, *American Slavery as It Is*, is in a second printing—another 10,000 copies." He smiled and added, "They believe it will sell over 100,000 copies this year. Lewis says it will sell enough to pay both my salary, and our debt to him."

"100,000 copies!" Angelina brightened at the thought. "That could finally arouse popular sentiment for the cause of emancipation."

"Oh, Lewis said something about the Amistad case as well," Theodore recalled.[2] You know he is paying to house and feed the Africans while they await trial for taking over the ship? He is seeing that they are taught English, too. I've been helping a bit," he admitted.

"Lewis is amazingly generous," Sarah interjected, "despite his archaic views of women. Did I hear you say that John Quincy Adams has agreed to take the case?"

"Really? Is that true, Theodore?" Angelina asked. "I'm delighted to hear it. It is about time he acted more publicly on his views."

Angelina felt a small earthquake in her abdomen. "Look, Theodore, can you see? O Sai, I can feel it move. My heavens!" Theodore put his hand on her belly. "Nina, my love, I can feel it!"

The baby boy was born at the end of 1839 and Theodore asked to name him after his early mentor, Charles Stuart. Despite bearing the dignified name of Charles Stuart Weld, the baby boy cried and cooed and spit up his food as all babies do. On a spring afternoon Angelina carried her son around the garden to try to calm him. He had been fussing much of the day and she was at her wit's end. After Sarah finished planting some vegetables, she stood up and gazed at the mother and baby. "He sounds like he's hungry, Nina. Isn't it about time to feed him?"

Nina was irritated at the question. "No, Sai. I fed him two hours ago. He must be trained to wait four hours between feedings. And we mustn't feed him too much or he will get fat. Professor Combes says just a small amount at a time."[3]

Sarah knew better than to argue with her. "Here, why don't you rest, Nina. I'll try walking him a bit." There was a brief pause in the baby's fussiness as Sarah and Nina both looked at him. "Nina, isn't Charles Stuart a miracle! Isn't he lovely?"

Angelina smiled through her fatigue and frustration. "He is very beautiful, Sai. Much more lovely than Theo and I deserve." Charles started to fuss again, and Angelina continued, "But he has a restless nature like his parents. I can't seem to quiet him. And I'm so tired." Sarah carefully took the baby from Angelina and did her best to walk and soothe him. Charles continued to fuss for a while, but eventually quieted down. "Thank you, Sai," Nina murmured.

Angelina was ashamed to admit it, but she was relieved and eager for any activity that didn't involve feeding or walking the baby. Conveniently she remembered something, "Oh, I promised to go look in on the colored family that moved in north of the village." Angelina put carrots, apples and bread in a basket and picked up her shawl. "Will you be all right here with Charles, Sai? I won't be long, and I'll feed him when I return. Perhaps he'll cry himself to sleep."

"Of course, dear, Charles and I will be fine!" Sarah reassured her. She continued to walk the baby, and then played with him on her lap. The baby was temporarily pacified, but after a few minutes he began to bawl again. Sarah checked to make sure his bottom was clean and dry. It was. He continued to fuss while Sarah walked him.

Finally, no longer willing to deprive Charles of what he clearly wanted, she went into the kitchen and mixed some fresh milk and cereal for him, balancing him on her hip. "There, there, Charley, I know you are hungry. Let us see if food helps, or if you are just a fussy little one." She sat down and fed him, propped up in her arms. He gulped his food hungrily, eating all that Sarah had prepared. Sarah watched as his lids grew heavy between final bites, and he soon fell asleep.

She gazed happily at Charles as he slept, pulling up a chair to rock him very gently. Several minutes later Sarah heard footsteps and looked up to see Theodore entering through the front door. His face was drawn, but he brightened as he saw the peaceful scene. Sarah put a finger to her mouth to signal that the baby was sleeping. Theodore walked over to marvel at his sleeping son. They both moved away from the cradle so they could talk without disturbing Charles.

"You have a knack with him, Sarah. He was quite irritable this morning." Theo yawned, covering his mouth. "I confess I have not been getting much sleep!"

"I am the one who must confess, Theo. There is no magic involved— I have just fed him. It was an hour too early, and he ate twice as much as Nina told me he needs. She will be quite annoyed with me when she returns." Sarah looked anxiously at Theodore for his reaction, but then back at the deeply sleeping baby.

"Ah, you have broken the rules!" He looked at her with gentle amusement, and a conspiratorial smile. "But look what a good result you have had. I fear . . . "

The door opened and Angelina came in. She had hurried home, and she was agitated about her tardiness. Theodore swallowed his words and walked over to greet her, "My dear, here you are now!" He gave Angelina a welcoming kiss on the cheek which she received distractedly. She looked toward the cradle.

"Yes, I was in a hurry to get here to relieve Sarah and see to Charley's feeding. But I see he is asleep." She looked confused. "Did he cry himself to sleep, Sai?"

Sarah looked down guiltily, but knew she had to own up. "No, not exactly, dear, I'm so sorry, but I'm afraid I went ahead and fed him. It was early of course, but it just seemed—well, I could find no other explanation for his crying."

Angelina stared at her in disbelief, torn between annoyance at her sister and anxiety about her own maternal instincts. "But Sarah, if we don't adhere to the schedule, he will eat all the time. And he will eat too much! You know what Professor Combe says," her voice edged with anger.

Theodore took Angelina's hand, trying to calm her. "Yes, my dear, we know what Combe says, but look!" He gestured at the happily sleeping baby. "Look how sweetly he is resting. Perhaps he is not your average child," he suggested gently.

Angelina pulled her hand away, folded her arms and spoke testily, "Theodore, how can you say that. You know what we agreed to." Without looking at Sarah, she said, "Perhaps I should feed him again now, so that he stays on schedule."

"I'm sorry, Nina. But he ate quite a lot. Twice as much as you put out."

"What! And you let him?"

"But, Nina, perhaps he simply needs more food. Couldn't that be why he is so fussy? Look at how well he is sleeping now."

Theodore added, "Sarah may be right, my dear. You know how he cries at night. It doesn't seem . . . "

Angelina's face flushed with anger. Interrupting her husband, she said, "I can see I have no say in this matter. I am overruled! You two have decided—what does it matter what a mother think!" Angelina let out an anguished sob and rushed out of the living room and up the stairs to their chamber.

"It is entirely my fault, Theodore," Sarah murmured. "I only meant to soothe Charley's crying." She shook her head and added, "I must go beg Nina's forgiveness."

Sarah started towards the stairs to follow her sister, but Theodore stopped her. He spoke mildly, but she could hear the fatigue in his voice. "No, Sarah, I think it is better that I speak to her. We are both tired, and our tempers are short. I think she will see things differently tomorrow morning. Can you see to Charley for a little longer?"

"Of course." She walked over and gazed at the sleeping baby, then looked back at Theodore, "Thank you, Brother. But please tell Angelina how sorry I am. I had no right . . . " Theodore interrupted her with a gesture indicating that no apology was necessary. Sarah watched anxiously as he headed up the stairs.

Angelina sat in the small office off their bedroom amidst piles of Theo's books and papers. She looked in a drawer for a letter she had received a few days earlier. As she did so, a wave of nausea overcame her. She found the letter and re-read it, shaking her head in despair. She looked up as she heard Theodore's footsteps and saw him approaching the open office door.

"Nina, forgive me if I offended you, I only meant—"

Angelina looked silently at Theodore for a moment, trying to let her anger and sense of betrayal subside. "No, I do see that Sarah seems to have a way with Charles. Of course, it's easy if you give him everything he wants." There was a note of bitterness in her voice, but she tried to focus on her real concerns. "Theo, if we don't maintain the schedule won't he be spoiled, and grow unhealthy? And won't our lives be completely at his mercy?"

"Well, as for that, I suppose that children deserve to be tyrants for a while. They are helpless enough." Theodore smiled ruefully as he took a seat near her and rubbed her hand gently for a few moments. Tears began to run down Nina's face.

Theo continued, "Perhaps Charley is telling us something, my dear. If the child is hungry, how can he be happy? I wouldn't be!"

Angelina's face softened at Theo's last remark, but she was skeptical as Theo continued. "He is quite thin. Why not experiment for a few weeks to see if he thrives on a more flexible schedule? Sarah can help." For a moment Angelina seemed calmer, so he was surprised when she began to sob again.

"But Theodore, don't you see? I am terrible at this. I don't know how to be a good mother!" She sniffed and wiped her nose with a handkerchief. "And now—well, I wasn't going to say anything this soon—but it appears I am expecting again. How shall we manage? I am just so worn out!"

Theodore was surprised at the news, but he felt some relief since it helped to explain Angelina's unusual sensitivity. He pulled Angelina onto his lap and tried to comfort her. "Oh, my dear, that's wonderful news. Well, I had no idea. No wonder you are tired and anxious." Angelina wiped her eyes and moved to a more comfortable position. But still needing the reassurance of his closeness, she continued to share a chair with Theo, resting her head on his chest.

Theodore played with her curls for a moment, then added, "As for being a good mother—well, of course you are! You love Charley, don't you?" Angelina nodded weakly.

Angelina looked long at Theodore. She felt comforted by his understanding, but she had worse news to convey. She rose and walked onto the balcony. Theo followed her. "There's more, Theo. Our house here is so small—and with another child? We spoke of moving, but now with the division of the Anti-Slavery societies, your employment will end. How shall we live?"

"Not exactly end," Theodore objected. "But yes, I will get no pay for the work I continue to do." He paused briefly and frowned. "But I have a plan, Nina. I found a little farm over near Belleville that will be perfect for our growing family. Why the house has sixteen rooms! I can work the farm and we will be able to survive well with your modest allowance and with what Sarah contributes from hers."

At this Angelina's tears fell again, her face contorted with anguish. She raised her head and drew the letter she'd been reading out of her pocket. "But Theo, look, this is what I have been trying to tell you." She handed the letter to him.

Theodore took the letter and read it quickly, while he continued to run his fingers along Nina's arm. "Ah, I see." He spoke in a grave voice. "Hmmm. So, your Mr. Burton of Philadelphia has lost your capital for you—or most of it, it appears."

"He's not *my* Mr. Burton! He was our banker and invested our inheritance for us while we were in Philadelphia. He is very trustworthy, but there has been an economic slump as you know, and he seems to have lost it all." She sniffed. "Sarah recently moved her inheritance to a conservative bank, and it remains intact. That's fortunate, I suppose," Angelina said reluctantly. But we don't even have capital with which to buy the farm—much less to help support ourselves."

Theodore looked at the letter and read it over a second time. "Well," Theodore mused, "he promises to repay the full amount in time. And he says he will try to pay the interest at least—a few hundred dollars by the end of the year."

"So much for my financial independence! I wanted so much to do my part."

"*Our* part—we are partners, Nina." Theodore was mildly worried, but as was his habit in life, he refused to be bothered by financial insolvency. "It will all turn out fine. The Lord has never let me down in these matters." He gazed at the ceiling for a moment. "But I must have a paying occupation of some sort, with a growing family to support," he said cheerily. "So, shall we get the farm? I will simply have to ask Lewis for a loan again."

"I hate to be beholden to him. And will he be willing to help us once more?" Angelina pondered their situation, and added, "Sarah could help a little perhaps. She always offers to do more, but I hate to . . . "

"Lewis has never said no to me," Theo reassured her. "After all, I worked for a pittance for the Society. He knows that, and he knows I will continue to do what I can for the cause. I cannot join his new society, given its archaic views of women's role. But he respects our differences on that point."

Angelina recognized that Theodore's plan was the only practical course. She was immensely relieved that her own financial catastrophe did not seem to disturb her husband too much. She shook her head, and responded, "So we shall be indebted to one who denies our equality. Well, at least he is a friend of the slave, and is doing his utmost for the Amistad captives," she admitted reluctantly.

After a few moments of reflection, she gave Theodore a grateful smile. "Oh, Theo, a real farm! That will be wonderful! Think of the space for Charley to play! And perhaps a room in which Sarah and I can read and write when we have a few spare minutes? We must tell Sarah; she will be thrilled!" Theodore gave Nina a long, warm embrace; then they both hurried down the stairs to share the news with Sarah, the quarrel about Charley temporarily forgotten.

3

Householders

Belleville, New Jersey 1840–1841

THE WELD FAMILY MOVED to their new home at the end of the summer, in time to enjoy the brilliant yellow curtain of sweet birch trees that formed a wind break between the large, rambling farmhouse and the fields. With sixteen rooms the Belleville house was much more spacious than the Fort Lee cottage, although it was equally rustic and in need of repairs.

By early November, although the sun shone brightly, the air had grown chilly. The birch trees were nearly bare, but a few leaves still clung to the red oak in the front yard. Angelina came out onto the porch to stretch her back. It was obvious that her second child would be born soon. She moved her torso gently to relieve the painful ache in her back.

Theodore had finished mending a fence that their cow had broken through and was heading toward the house. "Did you have much trouble with the fence, Theo?" Angelina asked as they walked inside for their midday meal. Sarah joined them as they sat down.

"Not really. But there are other sections that are falling down, and we will lose our cow if I don't get them taken care of." Angelina's face clouded with anxiety. "And that's a small part of what must be done," Theo said in a tired voice. "There are the pumpkins and squash to be harvested and the late apples, and we need to plough under the back field."

He frowned and continued his list. "I shall need to buy a new plow before spring. This one keeps falling apart on me. Then we must have feed for the animals for this winter, and there's old Nelly who wants shoeing. I fear we haven't enough savings left to make it beyond next month."

Theodore rubbed his chin and studied the floor, then asked in an uneasy voice, "Sarah, can we spare fifty dollars—no, more like sixty-five dollars this month?"

Sarah was alarmed at the amount and didn't answer immediately. Instead, she asked, "Did you remember the pump handle for the well, Theo. I simply can't turn it anymore." She was apologetic as she added, "And there's the leak in the nursery upstairs. It will need fixing before the new baby comes."

"I can't do everything at once, Sarah," Theodore responded sharply. Sarah looked down at her plate. She was hurt by his tone but said nothing. "Forgive me, Sarah," Theodore said quickly. "I know you don't expect that. And they must be fixed. I'll see to them as soon as I can."

Sarah nodded and said, "As for the money, Theodore, well, we'll find it somewhere. She got up and found their accounts book nearby. She brought it back to the table and looked over the numbers anxiously. "We owe a payment to Lewis this month. After that we have about thirty dollars for food, writing paper, and lamp oil. Shall we put off the payment to Mr. Tappan?" She lowered her voice hoping Angelina wasn't paying attention. "Or I can make another contribution."

"Definitely not, Sarah," Angelina said impatiently. "You've done more than your share already." Sarah winced at Nina's testy response and shrugged in resignation.

Theodore jumped in. "Sarah, I believe Lewis can wait until we sell the winter and early spring produce. He understands that we are just getting started." Sarah nodded reluctantly.

Theodore scratched his head and frowned, "Is it the fifteenth of the month already? I promised to look over Henry Stanton's pamphlet and make suggestions, and I have a dozen letters to answer." He opened his hands in a hopeless gesture, "Well, they will have to wait. Every evening, I intend to get to that work, but I am so exhausted from the farm." He reached over to tousle Charley's hair. "And I'd so much rather play with Charley," he confessed.

As they got up to clear away the dishes, Theodore hoisted a gleeful Charley onto his back. But the adults remained quiet, each with their own worries. Angelina moved slowly, heavy on her feet. As she tidied up the kitchen, she stopped every few minutes to stretch her aching back.

Winter was long, harsh, and lean that year. Both Theodore and Sarah were glad for the reduction in farm work and for the dark, quiet days that provided a little extra time for writing and thinking. Angelina, first burdened by the final month of her pregnancy, and then shortly after the New Year, by the care for her newborn second son, did not reap much benefit from those dark months. The birth of Theodore, Jr. who would henceforth be known to the family as Thodie, was difficult. While the child seemed healthy, Angelina was left with several painful conditions that were not improving with time.

In the spring, their mood was lightened not only by the return of sunlight, but by a visit from Jane Smith and Elizabeth Cady Stanton, who had recently wed their friend and colleague, Henry Stanton. As they sipped tea and relished the rhubarb muffins that Sarah had made, Elizabeth began telling them about the London Anti-Slavery Convention that she had attended with her new husband. Lucretia Mott, William Lloyd Garrison, and Samuel May were also there.

"How many times we heard others say, 'Angelina Weld should be here'; 'Miss Sarah Grimké should be here,'" Elizabeth told them. "And by the way, Lucretia Mott has given me a long message for you. The essence of it is that she thinks you both have been withdrawn from the public arena long enough. In particular, she thinks that Sarah should speak again as she has no duties to prevent her."[4]

Angelina and Sarah looked at each other with amused chuckles. At that moment, Angelina was busy entertaining Thodie, and Sarah was keeping an eye on Charley, while also trying to serve tea. "Oh, my!" Angelina declared. "No duties to prevent Sarah, is it? Why yes, look at her. She clearly has nothing to do!" Jane joined in their mirth, but Elizabeth was perplexed.

Spring and summer meant arduous work on the farm, with little profit to show for it. Between farm duties, housekeeping, and childcare, the adults found meager time to pay attention to the anti-slavery struggle. They fell into familiar patterns and were too absorbed by their daily routines to think much about what they were missing.

One day Theodore took Charley by the hand and tried to match his long stride to his son's very short one as they headed out to the road to pick up the post. It was their second autumn at Belleville. Charley kicked up the flaming red oak leaves as they ambled along the path. Theodore sorted through the mail as they walked back toward the house, picking out one letter to read first.

As they neared the house, Theodore stopped short, his attention caught by the contents of the letter. Charley hugged his father's legs and tried to tug him along. Failing at that, he ran ahead to chase the geese who were visiting Belleville on their trip south. Paying more attention to the geese than to his feet, Charley stumbled and plopped down on his bottom. He looked around, not sure whether to cry or not. Theodore scooped him into his arms quickly and hurried into the house.

Angelina was seated in the parlor trying to finish some mending. Baby Thodie was sound asleep in the cradle that he had nearly outgrown. Theodore sat down close to his wife and spoke quietly to avoid waking Thodie, "Angelina, dear, I have a curious letter from Joshua Giddings. You remember that he was elected to Congress last year?"

"Yes, of course. What is it? Is it bad news?"

"Not bad, really. No, rather the opposite, but—well, perhaps you will not think so," Theodore frowned slightly as he plunged ahead. "You remember that they passed that infamous gag rule this fall? Members of the House have been forbidden to receive any petitions against slavery, or to introduce any anti-slavery resolutions on the floor. It is a clear violation of their right of free speech, both that of the citizens and that of the Congressmen."

"Yes, I heard, but how can they do that, Theo? It is despicable! Won't they try to fight it?" She was puzzled, "Surely this is bad news? Or is it something else? How does it affect us?" She looked up from her sewing in alarm. "Oh, no. Let me guess—"

Theo gestured to her to wait while he continued reading parts of the letter. She distracted herself by watching Charley return to his favorite corner and play with a toy wagon, complete with moving wheels, that Theodore had carved for him.

"Giddings says that he and his colleagues are determined to fight the gag rule by bringing in bills and resolutions that would open the issue to debate on the floor. Here's what he writes:

> We need information for our speeches, and guidance when it comes to strategy. We also need lobbyists to win over more congressmen to our side. We have discussed this among ourselves and can think of no better person for this work than you, Theodore. We can pay for your travel and your expenses while you are in Washington, and perhaps a very small stipend as well.[5]

Theodore watched Angelina to gauge her reaction. "Well, Nina, I am stunned. I hardly know what to think." Theodore was flattered at the invitation, but he knew that accepting it was not a foregone conclusion. He looked at Sarah who had just joined them.

Sarah spoke carefully. "Brother, it is surely a great compliment to you that they have asked for your help. It would be a wonderful work. But it does complicate things here, does it not? All the farm duties—."

"Oh, but Sarah, of course he must do it!" Angelina protested. Her quick response was not what Theodore had expected. She turned back to her husband. "Theo, you must! It is exactly what your talents and your work have prepared you for. Who but you have so much real information at their fingertips, and—and besides that, can be a voice of reason and persuasion?"

"Hmmm. Yes, it could be very worthwhile," he mused. He rose and walked around the room shaking his head and gesturing with his hands as he weighed his home obligations against the attractiveness of this new opportunity. Sarah looked down at her lap with a frown, also weighing the pros and cons. Angelina's eyes followed her husband, impatient for a response.

"But Nina, dear, Sarah is right that it is complicated. They say only a "small stipend" in addition to my travel and expenses in Washington. How would you and Sarah and the children be able to live on that?" he queried. "Even with a generous stipend, there is all the farm work to be done, and the repairs—then, there's the spring planting and the two children!"

Theodore's brow wrinkled as he examined his heart, realizing that while he took his family obligations seriously, he also felt resentful that the burden of his family and the farm conflicted with his excitement at rejoining the battle. He continued to pace around the room. Thodie woke up and began to cry until Sarah rescued him from the cradle and cuddled him on her lap. Theodore looked at Thodie tenderly, and said, "No. I would be mad to take this proposal seriously. It is impossible for me to leave this winter."

Angelina was annoyed with Sarah's hesitancy and her husband's wavering. "Theodore, you are denying a clear call from God to serve in a way that only you can do!" she said adamantly. "If you cannot see that, I don't know what to say. We will manage." She appealed to her sister's propensity for self-abnegation. "Sarah, don't you agree that we can give him up for this great work. It is a way we can contribute as well." She looked at her husband, "Through you, Theo."

Sarah let out a sigh of resignation. She spoke with just a trace of sarcasm. "Yes, we women must do our part at home. We certainly could not write, or do research, or persuade Congress as a man can." The point was not lost on Angelina who understood the unfairness that Sarah identified so clearly. But Sarah smiled wanly, knowing that pragmatically, anointing Theo as their proxy was the best they could do. Theo understood her point as well and responded to it directly.

"Sai, you and Nina and I know that you could do this work as well or better than I can. Indeed, I have no doubt you would do it better." He took a deep breath and frowned, "But, does that mean that I should refuse the work? I ask sincerely."

Angelina was alarmed at the prospect of him turning down the opportunity, and started to speak, but Sarah, appreciating that Theodore recognized the injustice of the situation, responded more quickly. "No, of course not, my dear brother. There is much to consider, but in the end, I agree with Nina that you *must* go." Theodore nodded his head in agreement, feeling considerable elation and gratitude. And Angelina felt an immense relief at gaining Sarah's clear acquiescence.

Sarah, on the other hand, had several minutes of well-hidden panic as she looked around the house and out the window at the farm, contemplating all the tasks to be done. When she finally spoke, she did her best to sound cheerful. "I believe you will be astounded at what we can manage here at home."

4

The Commission

Washington, D.C. 1842

IF A SENATOR OR Congressman had happened to be working late on New Year's Eve 1841, and if he had looked out an office window, he might have spied a figure in a worn woolen overcoat walking down the snowy street and into a boarding house directly across from the Capitol. The house bore a sign on the front door designating it as "Mrs. Spriggs' Establishment."

Theodore moved his satchel to his left hand and knocked on the door. A middle-aged colored man let him in. With one hand he took Theodore's coat and bag, and despite Theo's protest, he carried them upstairs. Theodore noticed that the man's left arm seemed to hang uselessly at his side. It made him wonder what his story was.

He walked into the dining room just after the other boarders had sat down to supper. About a dozen residents were seated at the table. They included Theodore's old friend, Joshua Leavitt, Congressmen Joshua Giddings and Congressman Seth Gates, all dedicated abolitionists. With them were another eight Congressmen from Pennsylvania and other free states.[6]

"There you are, old man! We've been guessing if you'd arrive in time for supper. I hope you are hungry—the food here is quite excellent," Giddings nodded appreciatively at Mrs. Spriggs who was supervising the serving of supper. He gestured to Theodore to sit in an empty chair, and then sank back into his own. Theodore bowed slightly to the gathering, murmured "Good evening, gentlemen," and moved to take his seat.

Before Theodore sat down, Mrs. Spriggs came over to greet him. "Welcome, Mr. Weld. How do you do? I hope you've had a good journey, despite this winter storm." She glanced out the window of the dining room with concern. Theodore followed her glance and realized that from this room they could see the whole of the Capitol Park filled with snow-covered trees and shrubbery.[7] She turned around and offered a friendly handshake to her new guest. Then noting his shaggy appearance, she muttered, "Well, I suppose you haven't had time to dress for supper."

Theodore was confused at first, then amused. "Dress for supper? Oh, oh, I see." He surveyed the others at the table, most of whom were dressed well, although not formally, for the evening meal. He looked at his frayed cuffs and his pantaloons still damp with muddy snow, and chuckled.

Mrs. Spriggs wondered for a moment if this man was a suitable resident of her well-respected establishment. But Theodore gave her his most self-deprecating smile, and said apologetically, "Yes, well, perhaps I do need to find a second suit of clothes."

Mrs. Spriggs shrugged and reassessed her judgment. "Hmmm. Well, no matter, sit down and warm yourself with some food and drink." Several of the men smiled knowingly, while a few looked at each other with raised eyebrows.

The men at the far end of the table resumed their conversation. Theodore took the plate of beef that his neighbor to his left passed to him, but he set it down without taking any. However, he gratefully took some of the boiled potatoes that were passed his way. He poured himself a glass of milk from a pitcher and reached for some steamed cabbage that was at hand.

Joshua Leavitt was sitting across from him. "Theo, you arrived just in time for the levee that President Tyler is holding for New Year's Day," Leavitt said cheerfully. We are all going over tomorrow. You'll come, won't you?"

"Should I? Hmmm. He is a slaveholder, is he not?"

"Yes, but so are many southern Congressmen, I'm afraid. This is not Ohio, nor New England," Leavitt replied evenly.

"Well, in any case, I suppose I should meet the—uh—'Accidental President'" They both chuckled at Tyler's nickname. "Joshua, perhaps you can dress me up."

Leavitt surveyed him with an amused eye, "I think it is hopeless, old friend, but we'll see what we can do. In any case, we have more serious matters to think about." He took a bite of his roast beef and continued,

"You've heard about the petition from Habersham County, Georgia, begging Congress to remove Mr. Adams from the chairmanship of the Committee on Foreign Relations?"

Theodore choked as he swallowed a large mouthful of potato, shaking his head vehemently. Giddings chided his friend, "The petition only arrived a few days ago, so he could hardly have gotten the news, Leavitt. In any case, while it is a dire insult to Mr. Adams—our Old Nestor—it appears that he has found a way to turn it to our advantage," Giddings suggested.

"I feel the insult for him." Theodore said once his mouth was empty. "A man who has served as president and secretary of state—and who was a secretary to our envoy to Russia when he was a mere fourteen years of age—to remove him from his chairmanship!" Theodore scowled. "Of course, it cannot succeed, but nevertheless . . . I wager it is vengeance for his success with the Amistad case." Theodore pushed his food around on his plate and his expression became more thoughtful. "But you say he'll turn it to an advantage?"

Several of the other men at the table were listening in on the conversation with great curiosity, and while he knew them to be generally sympathetic, Giddings was afraid to say too much. He replied, "Yes, he has an idea—and a good one, as usual. But he has invited us to dinner with him and Mrs. Adams tomorrow after the levee. So, I'll let him tell you about it."

Theodore answered enthusiastically, "Now there is an invitation I'm delighted to have! Angelina has met him, but I have not."

"Did he bite her head off?" Leavitt asked, then answered his own question. "No, probably not. He would be polite. But he *can* be irascible at times."

Giddings smiled quietly, "Oh, but it's nothing like the old days, Brother. He's mellowed a great deal. And I don't believe there is a more intelligent, well-informed man alive today than John Quincy Adams. You'll enjoy meeting him and Mrs. Adams, Theodore."

Theodore and his friends spent another half-hour in conversation about abolitionist news and national politics. Most of the other residents had finished their dinner and left the table. Leavitt offered to show Theodore to his room. The men climbed two flights of stairs and at the top Leavitt opened the door to a pleasant room with a large bed, fireplace, firewood, writing table, chairs and a wardrobe with drawers. Theodore's satchel was already there. Theodore stretched out on the bed and nodded approvingly, reluctant to get up again.

"Don't get too comfortable, Theodore. You must come and look at this view," Leavitt prodded him with a chuckle. Theodore roused himself and the two men looked out the third-floor window at the Capitol immediately across from Mrs. Sprigg's house. Veiled by lightly falling snow, it was an eerie but impressive sight. As he stared at it, Theodore felt his throat tighten with a solemn sense of pride and duty. He looked at Leavitt who nodded his head in tacit understanding.

By then it was nearly midnight, and Theodore's fatigue from the journey began to overwhelm him. Without further ado, he and Joshua wished each other a Happy New Year, and said goodnight. Theo poured water from a large pitcher into a basin, cleaned off his muddied pantaloons and hung them by the fireplace to dry.

Before he appeared at breakfast the next morning Theodore had considerably improved his appearance. He washed thoroughly and donned the cleaned-up pantaloons from the night before. Anticipating the levee at the President's House, he cleaned his boots and put on a fresh shirt. He even managed to tame his hair with a comb and some water. At breakfast, Joshua Leavitt brought down an extra coat for his friend to borrow. It was a little snug on Theodore, but preferable to his old one with the frayed cuffs.

At the President's House, there was a receiving line that curved from one room into another. Theodore felt decidedly out of his element, but Giddings stayed with him through the long wait, and introduced his friend to President Tyler. Theodore was unimpressed with Tyler but knew enough to keep his opinion to himself.

After visiting with his few acquaintances among the guests, Theodore wandered into the nearby East Room where the Gilbert Stuart painting of George Washington hung.[8] Theodore looked up at the painting and spoke to its subject with a quizzical frown, "What do you think of all this, George? Whose side would you be on in this battle for the soul of our nation?"

Leavitt found him just as he was muttering this and looked at him with amusement. "I don't think you'll find much enlightenment from that quarter, Brother," he said with a skeptical look upward. "In any case, it is time to go meet and dine with our sixth president. You will find him far more articulate when it comes to the evils of slavery than this one." Theodore returned Leavitt's wry smile with a nod. Joshua Giddings joined them as they left the President's House.

John Quincy and Louisa Adams[9] had planned a New Years' Day levee as well. It served as an alternative to those who were not eager to attend President Tyler's gathering. They knew the Presidential Levee would draw many southern members of Congress and their sympathizers. But Louisa was a celebrated hostess, and the Adams event was extremely popular. Their home had seen hundreds of visitors throughout the day. By the time, Theodore's party arrived, they could see that most of the earlier guests were on their way out, although a few lingered.

Mrs. Adams was tired from her long day of welcoming guests, and as the early guests departed, she excused herself briefly to give last minute instructions about supper to a servant in their small, simple dining room.[10] She then returned to the drawing room where several members of Congress and one woman were still standing together talking animatedly.[11] As Mrs. Adams was about to rejoin her husband, the butler announced the arrival of Theodore's party. "Gentlemen, The Honorable Mr. Joshua Giddings, Mr. Joshua Leavitt, and Mr. Theodore Weld," he declared.

Mrs. Adams hurried forward to greet the newcomers graciously. "Mr. Giddings, Mr. Leavitt, Happy New Year and welcome." She expected an introduction to Theodore, but waited patiently until Adams left the other men and came forward to greet the new guests as well.

"Mrs. Adams, Mr. Adams, I am pleased to present our colleague, Mr. Theodore Weld," Giddings said. Theodore bowed slightly and Louisa offered him her hand with words of welcome.

"Is it Mr. Theodore D. Weld?" Adams inquired, his bushy, white eyebrows raised.

"Yes, I'm afraid it is, sir." Theodore bowed formally and added, "Mr. Adams, I am deeply honored to meet you." He took in the former president's aquiline features and penetrating gaze as well as his balding forehead. Theodore had seen paintings of his presidential father and noted that the son was considerably better-looking even at his current advanced age.

Adams voice was gruff but admiring. "I know you well by your writings, Mr. Weld. Powerful rhetoric, and well-reasoned as well." He turned aside and coughed, then said, "Well, welcome to our home and Happy New Year." Somewhat to Theodore's surprise, Adams then took him by the elbow and steered him a few steps away, back towards his other guests, but still apart from them. "Tell me, how is your most illustrious wife?" he asked with a hint of a smile. "You know that we met in Boston a few years back? Her speech before the Legislative Committee was as compelling as anything I've heard in Congress lately."

"She is quite well, thank you, sir." Theodore said, heartened by his interest. "Perhaps you have heard that we have two sons now. Angelina and her sister Sarah are highly occupied with keeping them in line, and now that I am here in Washington, they will run the farm as well. Frankly, sir, it worries me."

"Ah, yes. My mother was often in that situation when my father was going about his diplomatic duties. I remember the three years he was away as our envoy to Paris and to the Netherlands during the war." Adams paused, frowning and thoughtful. "She suffered greatly from his absence, I know, but she ran our family and the farm with a fortitude that put us men to shame."

Theodore felt a stab of remorse as he thought of how he had left Angelina and Sarah in a similar situation. "I confess to feeling considerable guilt at leaving them, sir. But they both urged me to come."

"Don't worry, Mr. Weld, the mails are much better now, and you are not so far away. They will manage very well, I warrant," Adams reassured him, with a small, wry smile. "She is of the same blood as my mother, you know. My mother's mother was a sister of Governor Benjamin Smith of North Carolina and an aunt to the Rhetts. I believe Governor Smith was your wife's relation through her mother?"[12] Theodore looked uncertain, but Adams continued. "Well, that is too much to untangle, but the point is, they are of stalwart stock and are capable of a great deal without their menfolk."

Theodore nodded solemnly, not entirely convinced. Adams went on, "What is certain, Mr. Weld, is that you are needed here. Your talents appear to be precisely what is called for in this debate about slavery. I intend to make use of them."

"I hope I can be of adequate service, Mr. Adams. My abilities are limited, but I shall do my utmost," he said with appropriate modesty. Theodore did wonder to himself if he was up to the task. He was confident of his considerable abilities, but as he had confessed to Angelina, he felt his lack of much formal education amid the polish that surrounded him in Washington.

Adams looked toward his other guests and Theodore's eyes followed him to the group that had been engaged in a heated exchange. There was a lull in their conversation and several of the group walked towards them, eager to be introduced to Theodore. He acknowledged their greetings formally, if awkwardly, pleased to make the acquaintance of those loyal to Adams.

The remainder of the visitors to the levee took their leave of the Adamses prior to supper. However, Gates, Simonton, and his wife, Martha, were staying on to dine along with Theodore, Leavitt, and Giddings. Mrs. Adams gestured to the remaining guests, inviting them to the dining table.

The six guests sat down at the table with their hosts and a lemon vegetable broth was served. After the guests had exchanged polite inquiries as to the well-being of everyone's hometown and family, Giddings broached the sensitive issue of the petition.

"Mr. Adams, sir, I had hoped you would lay out your plan for us—how you intend to turn this insulting petition from Georgia to your advantage. I am afraid I don't quite see . . . "

Adams studied the faces of the assembled guests, as he interrupted Giddings. "Well, I believe all of us recognize that the gag rule is an unforgivable breach of our constitutional right of free speech. So, I shall speak freely about my intentions. I hope we shall not bore or shock our delightful companions." Adams raised his glass of cider to his wife and to Mrs. Simonton.

Louisa's glance was skeptical but tolerant. She commented drily, "My dear, I cannot think when the danger of boring or shocking our company ever stopped you from speaking your mind." She softened her remark with a hint of a smile, and then gestured to the server to bring in the main course of roast lamb and sweet potatoes.

Martha Simonton looked delighted. She smiled at her hostess' pointed remark, but said, "Mr. Adams, you know well that I am here because of my sympathy with this cause. I am all ears." Adams gave her a cool look, verging on a smirk. Louisa, fearing her husband would roll his eyes, distracted her with small talk.

Adams turned away, and Giddings spoke up, "So, tell us your plan, Mr. Adams."

"It is quite simple really. I will introduce the petition calling for my removal from the chairmanship of the Foreign Relations committee. Then—"

"But, sir, why would you introduce a petition which affronts you?"

"Well, someone must—it may as well be me. And in any case, the slaveholding congressmen will pounce upon it, as they do upon anything likely to lead to a discussion of slavery. They will move to table it." He looked at his plate of lamb with interest but hesitated to attack it.

Theodore caught his drift, and said, "And you, sir, shall claim the privilege of speaking in your own defense as a member of Congress?"

Adams looked at Weld admiringly. "Ah, you have accurately guessed my game, Mr. Weld! I would not like to play chess against you." He turned to the others, "Yes, I shall claim the right of privilege to speak in my own defense. And I feel confident it will be granted—grudgingly, of course. But the question of privilege overrides every other consideration."

"Brilliant, sir. They will have no choice but to hear you," Giddings commented as Theodore nodded his agreement. He nibbled at the lamb, found it delicious, and took a large gulp of the cider that accompanied it.

"And hear me they shall! I shall lift up my voice like a trumpet, till slaveholding, slave-trading and slave-breeding shall quail and howl under my dissecting knife. I shall deal my blows upon this triple-headed monster," Adams declared with considerable enthusiasm.[13]

"No doubt you shall," said Leavitt warmly. "Only I fear the uproar among the opposition. It will be a perfect Babel of retorts and recriminations,"

With a smile that betrayed his relish at a battle, Adams said, "Oh, Mr. Leavitt, you know that I am no stranger to opposition! I do not fear it."

With a knowing look, Louisa said, "No, I assure you he quite welcomes it. I supply the bandages on his return from the House chambers."

Adams tilted his chin to consider his wife's remark. After a moment he nodded sheepishly, and then continued, "But for this I shall need facts. Not sentiment, not exaggeration, not hearsay, but the clear, documented facts of the daily brutality and inhumanity suffered by our brethren in fetters."

Theodore spoke up eagerly, "Sir, I would like to offer my services to relieve you of the drudgery of gathering the requisite materials for your defense."

Nodding at Weld, Adams said graciously, "I thank you, Mr. Weld. That is exactly what I hoped for—and I accept your offer gratefully. You will do it far better than I could. Facts—and reasons, as well. The economic arguments, the political arguments, and above all, the moral and biblical arguments against this perverse 'peculiar' institution."

Theodore saw an opportunity to give credit where it was due. "Mr. Adams, perhaps you know that our sister, Sarah Grimké, wrote an extensive tract refuting the claim that the Bible permits, or even sanctions, slavery. To the contrary, as she points out, the spirit of the entire Bible is one of setting free and raising up the oppressed. You shall have the benefit of her scholarship and our family's lengthy discussions on this subject." Theodore went on, "The economic argument can be easily made based on the experience of Great Britain and the West Indies, and—"

Adams broke in, "Yes, that is exactly what we need. But enough said for this holiday meal. I shall be most in debt to you for your help." Adams dove into his neglected meal with gusto.

Louisa looked at Theodore with mild surprise. "Oh, Mr. Weld. I had forgotten that you share a household with your sister-in-law, Miss Grimké. We corresponded when her *Letters on the Equality of the Sexes* were published. I was glad to read her arguments as they eloquently expressed many of my own beliefs."[14]

"As they do my own," Theodore assured her warmly, forgetting his earlier insistence that Sarah's *Letters* were a distraction from the antislavery cause. He smiled at Giddings with quiet satisfaction as he contemplated the work ahead of him. He thought he might enjoy his time in Washington even more than he had imagined.

Several days later, Theodore found his way to the room in the Capitol that served as the fledgling Library of Congress.[15] With the help of the Librarian he found the documents and newspapers that would serve his purpose. He spent the next few weeks reading and taking notes there, and in his chamber until the wee hours of the morning. Leavitt, who slept in the room directly beneath him, accused him of pacing the floor at two a.m., and then rising at six a.m. for his calisthenics. It was true that Theodore's daily routine began before breakfast with running and jumping around Capitol Square even in the most inclement weather.

By the third week of January 1842, Theodore had provided Adams with reams of valuable materials and reasoned arguments against the institution of slavery. Adam's plan would circumvent the gag order against any discussion of slavery, by using his right to defend himself from the attempt to strip him of his chairmanship. On January 21st, Adams presented the Georgia petition, and the next day, his "defense" began. It would take several weeks.

When Congress was in session there was plenty of drama. Although he had been warned by Leavitt, Theodore was shocked at the number of interruptions that Adams had to endure. There was vehement pounding on desks, other congressmen berating and threatening him—sometimes shaking fingers within inches of his face—and food hurtled at Adams from the gallery. There were refusals to adjourn so that Adams would be worn out, but that did not stop him.[16]

Through it all, Theodore saw that Adams could take the material he had provided and turn it into oratory that was closely reasoned, powerful, and persuasive, if sometimes also devastatingly acerbic. Reporting to Leavitt after a session that his friend did not attend, Theodore exclaimed, "Adams rained blows upon the head of the monster!" He wrote the same to Angelina.

Theodore also read the current papers coming into the library and took it upon himself to let Adams know that his efforts were drawing attention. He buoyed Adams' spirits by reminding him that support across the country was increasing, at least outside the South. Back in his chamber after hours of listening to the arguments he had helped to craft, Theodore would try to read and reply to his letters from Angelina and Sarah. However, he regularly fell asleep from exhaustion before he had finished.

One day near the end of this period, Adams held the floor late into the night. There were only a few Congressmen still on hand, among them Giddings and Simonton. Most of the opposition had gradually slipped away, as a hoarse Adams continued to speak at a volume barely above a whisper. Simonton fell asleep at his House desk and began to snore. Giddings had to nudge him several times. Weld and Leavitt were still in the gallery, having once again missed supper at Mrs. Spriggs. As Adams slowed down, Giddings roused Simonton. Adams was ending his two weeks of "defense," which was really an attack on his accusers and on the institution of slavery.

As Adams finally stepped away from the podium with almost no voice left, Giddings and Simonton rose to congratulate him. Leavitt and Weld smiled and shook each other's hands heartily. Two Southern Democrats had stayed until the end as watchdogs for their party, but they left without speaking to Adams. On February 7, 1842, the Members of the House, exhausted and eager to hear no more of Adams' compelling rhetoric, voted 106 to 93 against the motion to censure their colleague.

Pennsylvania and Maryland

Twenty-five years later

5

Opportunity

Lincoln University, Pennsylvania, 1866

THERE WERE CHERRY TREES blossoming along the short path leading to Lincoln University's main building. Clustered around the main hall were several modest school buildings, all set in a hilly, wooded area west of Philadelphia. Less than six months had passed since Archie and Frank left Charleston, and it had been a lonely, desolate winter. When the boys reunited, Archie was dismayed to see that Frank had nearly caught up to him in height. Still slender, both boys had added inches and muscle since the War years of hunger and illness in Charleston. As a result, their thin arms and legs again stuck out from their pants and jackets.

The young men walked up the road to the brick Georgian building with their satchels, uncertain if further disappointment lay ahead. They were tired from their journey and anxious, so they had little to say to each other. After the boys presented themselves, a young man told them they were expected and asked them to take a seat. They waited several minutes. A few current students entered the office and looked at the boys with curiosity, although Archie feared it might have been amusement. Finally, the young man ushered them in to meet with the university's president, Dr. Rendall. They shook hands with the tall, severe gentleman in a rumpled coat, and sat down to be interviewed by him.

Dr. Rendall was unimpressed by the appearance of the scrawny, rough-edged boys. But he dutifully reviewed the recommendations he had received on their behalf. He asked them about their journey, their previous employment in the north, and their formal education. He listened skeptically to their answers delivered in deep South Carolina accents. Yet he could not deny that they spoke sensibly and articulately. The boys were escorted out to await his decision. They waited silently in the anteroom as Dr. Rendall left the office to consult with others about their admission. Frank's legs were shaking, and Archie looked gloomy.

Dr. Rendall returned with a young faculty member, and the boys jumped to their feet. Rendall nodded reluctantly at them and said gruffly, "Welcome to Lincoln University." Archie didn't dare look at Frank. He shook the President's hand vigorously, unable to voice the depth of his gratitude and relief, except for a faint "Thank you, Sir." Frank shook the hand of the other faculty member with equal enthusiasm and gratitude.

The young teacher led the boys into the hallway and through a door entitled "Preparatory Department, Lincoln University." The boys looked at each other in quiet amazement and Archie put his arm around his younger brother's shoulder to give it a tight squeeze.

As they began the preparatory program at Lincoln University, Archibald and Francis Grimké were chagrined at how much they had to learn. The first few months were grim. Most of the students were children of free northern Negroes and had considerable exposure to northern white culture. Many were kind, but others made fun of the boys' South Carolina drawl and enjoyed correcting their common deviations from standard northern grammar. It did not help that they were virtually penniless and still relied on the few clothes that they had brought from Charleston. There were wide gaps in the Grimké boys' general knowledge and in their grasp of northern ways. This earned them ridicule among the less charitable of their peers. Occasionally their teachers were the culprits. But Archie and Frank had lived free and confident as children, had endured the terrors and humiliations of slavery, and had survived the war through their own ingenuity. It was excellent training for the indignities of prep school.

They learned rapidly—not only what their teachers taught—but what was expected of them by their classmates. Within the first months they began to realize that in some areas of knowledge they were far beyond their age-mates, and the deficits in their background were swiftly remedied. By the end of the year, they had advanced to pre-college and college courses.

The boys' rare combination of desperation, determination, hard work, resilient character, and native talent conspired to guide them to academic recognition and social acceptance. Above all, they feared disappointing their mother's fierce hopes. In their darkest moments, they could depend on each other's counsel and encouragement. At the end of their first full year, they eagerly embraced the opportunity to earn money by teaching former slaves in a small rural community on the Delmarva Peninsula.

Maryland, 1867

Archie and Frank trudged along a dirt path, wiping the sweat from their brows in the hot, humid weather. The young men, now sixteen and seventeen years, wore their neat, but well-worn, everyday shirts and pants, the latter held up with suspenders. They carried their jackets in the heat and their shoes were gray with dust. They had knapsacks on their backs which held their Sunday shirts and pants, a few personal belongings, and some primers, slates and chalk.

As they approached the little settlement, they came upon the poorly maintained schoolhouse that was their destination. Frank opened the door that was hanging lopsided from its broken hinges, and they looked inside. It was filled with debris. Two of the windows were broken, and a few of the benches were upended or had missing legs. There was a chalkboard, but it was in poor condition, and there was no chalk.

"Not 'xactly what we were told to expect," Archie grumbled, with a discouraged glance around.

"Well, I've learned not to expect much," Frank said, but he shrugged and gave his brother a cynical grin. The boys discovered a small room off the back with two cots and a small stove. They set down their knapsacks and took a moment to appreciate the relative coolness inside the little building. Once they were cooled off Frank found an old broom in a closet and began to sweep while Archie picked up trash and tried to set the room into some semblance of order.

They had barely completed these tasks when they heard noises outside. Word of their arrival had spread in the little community, and a few of the children hurried over to investigate the new teachers. They hung around the outside of the schoolhouse, daring each other to peek inside at the two brothers. Archie turned and saw them, and with a grin beckoned them to come inside.

While the children were curious and friendly, the young men found that the local adults were wary and skeptical of them. But the adults soon found reasons to trust the newcomers who, they learned quickly, had been slaves like themselves. Two days after their arrival, Archie stood with a circle of ten mixed-aged students gathered around the blackboard where he did his best to teach basic vocabulary and spelling to those who already knew their letters and could read a little. The students were eager, but their attention span was short. Archie realized he would have to re-sort to all sorts of dramatic and comical behavior to keep their attention.

Frank sat with a group of younger students in the back of the school-house using a large slate and chalk to teach the students their letters. There was much giggling and poking going on, but Frank managed to settle them down with one or two stern looks. Before they could resume their shenanigans, he rearranged their seating so that the eight girls were mixed in between the five boys. It didn't eliminate the giggling, but it did minimize the elbowing among the boys.

The brothers were exhausted by the end of the three early morning hours when they taught the young people. They tried to rest during the heat of the day, although their quiet time was often interrupted by par-ents or children who had questions or just wanted to chat. They would usually eat an early supper with one or two of the families. Afterwards, in the cool of the evenings, they taught any of the adults who wanted to learn for another hour and a half.

The work was demanding and often discouraging. Inevitably there were misunderstandings with some of the adults, hurt feelings, and cau-tious reconciliations. But by the end of the eight weeks Frank and Archie had won the hearts of the community. There was sadness on both sides when the boys left to return to Pennsylvania. Archie and Frank would look back on that summer with considerable satisfaction. The students had made progress, and their young teachers had matured.

When the boys returned to Philadelphia in early September of that year, the local Freedman's Aid Society paid them the stipend they had agreed upon. It was enough to pay their room and board at Lincoln for another school year with some spending money left over. When Archie realized that they had succeeded in making their own living for the year, he felt a thrill of confidence. Frank, too, was heartened and proud.

New Jersey

1842–1862

6

Separation and Reproach

Belleville 1842

ON THE BELLEVILLE FARM, the snowstorms of January had subsided. The landscape was free of snow but still frosty and wintry. As Adams was delivering his blistering attack on slavery in Washington, the Belleville women were doing their best to make it through another lean winter.

Anna Frost had sent her housekeeper, the former slave, Betsy Dawson, to help her sisters in Belleville. With Mary Anna married, her household needs were less than theirs. Betsy was hanging laundry on the porch, even though it would dry stiff with cold there. Sarah had hitched up her skirt to gather eggs from the henhouse. She noticed a broken gate that she pledged she would repair that very afternoon.

Angelina was seated inside at the dining table writing a letter to her husband while Charley and Thodie played together on the rag rug near the fireplace. Angelina relaxed for a moment pleased at how well the boys were getting along.

She didn't notice when Charley grabbed a wooden box back from Thodie who had picked it up when Charley was not playing with it.[17] "No! Mine! Not for you, T'odie," Charley protested. Thodie began to cry loudly. Angelina looked up and sighed in frustration. At that moment, Charley pushed Thodie, whose angry wails could be heard down the Hudson to New York City, Angelina was sure.

"Charley, what have you done now? Are you hurting your brother? You are very naughty! You mustn't hit!" Thodie continued to cry loudly and tried to hit back at Charley even from his mother's arms. Charley was defiant and ran to the far side of the room. He began to cry and stamp his feet. Carrying Thodie who was still whimpering quietly, Angelina went over to draw Charley towards her, trying to be gentle despite her displeasure. Charley pushed her away.

"I want Auntie Sai! No Mama. Go 'way!" Charley stomped off to a far corner where he hid his head. Angelina was exhausted and sat down on a chair by the fire, trying to quiet Thodie. Thodie then slipped out of her arms and toddled over to get the toy box that was still on the floor. Like a flash, Charley saw him and ran over to claim it again. Thodie broke out in fresh protest.

"No, Charley, please stop!" Angelina pleaded. "You are being very naughty! Go stand in the closet until you can be a good boy.[18] Charley stamped his feet and refused to go into the closet. "Oh, my dear Lord," Angelina's minimal patience was utterly used up. "Betsy! Where are you?" Betsy, who was still outside, didn't hear Angelina, but Sarah heard her sister as she entered the back door. She had just finished the work in the farmyard, and she felt dirty and unkempt.

Charley saw a new opportunity for his version of justice, and called out, "Auntie Sai, T'odie naughty, not Charley!" He ran to Sarah as she came into the room. Sarah gathered up Charley, and gradually he quieted down, starting to suck his thumb. Thodie let out a few sobs, then fell asleep in Angelina's arms.

"My, what a lot of commotion. What happened, Nina?"

"Oh, the usual, I think," she answered. "Charley is not very good at sharing." She gave him a disapproving frown, and he looked back at his mother with a dark pout.

Sarah set Charley on his feet. "Charley, run along and help Miss Betsy, will you?" Charley ran off, glad to escape further scolding.

Angelina leaned back in her chair and sighed. "Sai, why am I so bad at this! They are always at each other."

Sarah was silent for a moment. She would do things differently than Angelina, but she knew it would not help to say that. Instead, she said matter-of-factly, "They are children, Nina. This is what children are like. You were like this as a child, too. I remember." She laughed ruefully, "They are selfish little brutes!"

"But shouldn't we train them to be good?" Angelina asked. "Mustn't we correct them when they are wrong? When they hit and fight?"

"Yes, of course, we must. But we need to be gentle and patient with them as well."

"But I am patient, Sai! At least I try to be," Angelina objected, hurt at the implication.

"Well, yes, I see that. It is just that distraction sometimes goes much further than punishment in keeping the peace between them."

Angelina suddenly felt very tired. "Peace? I don't remember what that is. I'm glad Betsy is here, but there is far too much even for the three of us—with the farm to run, the children, and the household." Angelina put her face in her hands and Sarah could hear how close she was to tears.

"And there is Theodore—in Washington, doing his important work—but how can I raise my sons alone? And run our farm?" She looked out the window at the barnyard and threw up her hands in a despairing gesture. "I know you do much more than I do, Sarah, but I just can't keep it up. I am so tired all the time, and I feel such—such, I don't know—" Her voice trailed off.

Sarah came over and sat in a chair near Angelina. She frowned, not knowing how to comfort her sister. Angelina looked at her and continued, "I love the boys, Sarah! You know I do. I just don't know what to do—and they run to you for everything, and only get angry with me!" As she said this her unhappiness overwhelmed her. She knew she resented Sarah's ease with them, and she felt it was somehow unfair. "But someone has to be firm with them," she insisted. "Theodore says—"

"Certainly, you love them, Nina! I know that. And you are still not fully well," Sarah reminded her. "It is normal for them to be unhappy with us sometimes—and for us to be irritated with them, too." Eager to reassure Nina, she added, "But more and more they come to you for comfort, too. Haven't you noticed?"

Shaking her head, Angelina betrayed the other source of her disquietude. "If only Theodore understood," she sighed, "but when I write to him, he just tells me how I fall short in raising and teaching them." She took out a letter from her pocket and showed it to Sarah. "Listen to this, Sarah. This just came from Theodore this morning. Well, he tells us all about Adams' speeches and how they are finally making inroads with the slaveholders—that is good news. But then he says,"

> My chief, indeed, my only painful concern about home is on account of dear little Charley. A weak, vacillating, irresolute, undecided course, pursued with him at this period, even for a few months only, MAY BE HIS RUIN.

"Yes, you see, Sai, he capitalized that part."

"Oh, dear, Nina. I see what you mean. He seems to blame us."

"No, never you, Sarah, he blames me!"

Sarah was taken aback at Angelina's resentful tone, but she just shook her head and listened as Angelina continued to read:

> Promptness, decision, uniformity, energy, firmness mingled with kindness, freedom from anything approaching to passion or impatience should be the great features of his management.
>
> Is he kinder and more considerate toward his little brother? Do you take constant pains to beget in him a love of serving and helping little Thodie, of sharing his good things with him? It is quite time to begin to teach Thodie these things, too.

"Honestly, Sai! How can he dare . . . ?"

"Yes, dear, I see what you mean." She took the letter from her sister to look at it more carefully. "It is all good advice—in theory," she said with a frown. "But he is not here to help us to be firm and constant. He does not know the daily trials we have. He doesn't lose sleep worrying about them and the farm as we do."

Angelina laid Thodie down, still sound asleep, on a blanket on the rug. She rose and went to look out a window at the bleak winter landscape. The broken gate was swinging in the wind. "Sarah, how shall we manage until the spring crops come up? We only have enough potatoes to last until March. The cabbages are rotting. We need to buy feed for Nelly, seeds, tea and honey. We must fix these gates, and we'll need to hire someone to help with the plowing and planting."

"I still have some money left, Nina, I can help," Sarah said softly.

"No! I absolutely refuse to take anymore from you, Sarah. Please don't offer again. I'll tell Theodore. He'll ask Lewis once more, I suppose, or perhaps Giddings can raise more for him."

Charley sidled back into the room, giving his mother a petulant look. He went straight to Sarah and curled up in her lap. Angelina looked at the scene of Charley with Sarah, but instead of trying to make peace with Charley, she shook her head in frustration, and walked upstairs to her room. After a few moments Sarah sent Charley back out to Betsy who had come into the kitchen. She picked up Thodie and laid him on the couch covering him with a blanket. Then she went to the table and began to write a letter to Theodore.

When Theodore received Sarah's missive, along with the usual letter from Angelina, Congressman Adams' long days of speaking had concluded, and Theodore's days were less hectic. He took the opportunity to respond almost immediately to Sarah's letter. It troubled him deeply. He walked restlessly around his room in a gloomy mood, pondering the best response. Finally, he sat down and unburdened himself.

> Your kind and most faithful letter, my beloved Sarah, I have read again and again, not I trust without profit to my soul. All pride and impatience which you lay to my account, yes—far more, IS MINE. The pride I have always been aware of; the impatience is a monstrous fungus growth of the last two years.
>
> For more than two years I have ceased to know myself. I do not necessarily agree with your opinion as to the wrong attitudes out of which my bad habits spring. But that the habits are bad, base, shameful to me, I know. Reform is possible and must be achieved.
>
> You say that I should continue my work here in peace—that it is more important than your difficulties at home. Yet, I feel the reproach of not being there to do my part. I miss my Nina and you and the children more than I can say, but you both insist that I stay. What shall I do? Pray, pray for me!
>
> Your Theodore[19]

Theodore wiped his brow and bowed his head despondently as he finished and sealed the letter. He looked around at the chaos of books, papers, and unwashed clothing in his room. He was overcome with loneliness and guilt and wanted to weep but could only feel a thick misery. Leavitt appeared at Theodore's door while he was still in a dark mood. Theodore invited him in, welcoming the distraction. He would go home soon, he decided.

He straightened his cravat, combed his hair, and pulled himself together. He picked up the letter to post it, then he and his friend headed out to meet with Giddings and Gates and plan their next strategy.

7

Struggles, Sorrows, and Fruition

Belleville Farm 1842–1843

THEODORE REPOSITIONED HIS SCYTHE to get a better angle on the summer wheat they were harvesting. Old Stephen, who had also joined their household, was helping as best he could, but his bad leg made it difficult for him to do more than work with the flail.[20] For the harvest they had hired a local farmhand to help. Theodore looked over to the adjoining field where the corn was beginning to ripen. He realized that it would need to be picked soon.

At a year and a half Thodie worked hard to keep up with his brother. He ran up to his Auntie Sai on his chubby little legs to show her a dandelion he had found. She was sitting on the porch shelling peas, but she stopped to thank him and take him onto her lap to give him a kiss. Nina, who was sitting nearby, glanced over at Sarah and Thodie and tried to quell the recurring lump of resentment that she felt as she witnessed Sarah's ease in winning the children's affection.

"Thodie, dear, come over to Mama. I want to show you these pictures with Charley." Thodie reluctantly slid off Sarah's lap and walked slowly toward his mother. He climbed onto her lap as Charley watched unhappily. In a flash, Charley pulled the book out of Angelina's hands and threw it down. Thodie grabbed at the chalk that Charley held, but Charley squirmed away.

"Charley, what is possessing you!" Angelina said, and in an instant of utter frustration, she raised her arm to slap his hands. She stopped herself just as he moved out of reach. Charley stomped his feet, and started to cry, saying "It's *my* book! Not T'odie's."

"It is not your book, Charley. Go to your room this instant. I do not want to see you until you can tell your brother and me that you are sorry."

Theodore, returning from the fields for their midday meal, arrived at the porch just as Charley, his face wet with tears, was running into the house. Theodore caught his son and swept him into his arms. "Whoa, whoa, whoa! What is happening here? Where is my big, happy boy?" he asked.

Sarah got up and went to help Betsy in the kitchen, eager not to be involved. Thodie wriggled away from his mother and sat up straight on the bench, confused and frightened, but silent. Angelina tried to explain. "He has been very naughty. I asked Thodie to come sit with us so he could see the pictures as well. Charley threw the book on the floor and stomped on it."

Theodore spoke sternly, "Is this true, Charley? You promised me yesterday that you would try harder to share with Thodie. Well, I'm afraid you will have to miss our meal—until you are ready to apologize." Theodore set Charley down gently, and Charley gave his mother and Thodie a dark look. He walked reluctantly to the boys' room, his lower lip in a pronounced pout. Theodore sighed deeply, looking away from Angelina as he sat down in the chair that Sarah had occupied.

"What, Theodore? You are accusing me, are you not? You think it is all my fault, and that I cannot manage the children! But what am I to do?" Angelina continued plaintively. "I feel that I have done everything you and Sarah ask to overcome my impatience and show the children more affection. Is it my fault that Charley is so willful and selfish? Or that Thodie defends himself when he is attacked?" She stood up shaking with anger and self-doubt.

"Angelina, my love, I don't mean to criticize," his voice still irritated. "It is just that I can't seem to find any peace in this house—it is always chaos and fighting."

"Well, then, you take care of the boys. You and Sarah—since you seem to have all the answers," she said bitterly. "Well, my appetite is gone," she said. "And, in any case, I promised to take some food and medicine over to the Towsons — that poor family down by the creek. Their baby girl is sick." Theodore looked at her uncomprehendingly as she headed into the front room of the house. She put on her cloak, gathered some things in a basket and left.

Theodore, Sarah, Betsy, and Thodie sat down to their meal. Stephen joined them as they were starting to eat. Theodore said very little, feeling vaguely guilty and forlorn. Sarah was also subdued, so Betsy did her best to chatter about the food and kitchen needs. Stephen managed to keep Thodie amused. After a few minutes Charley wandered out, whispered something in his father's ear, kissed Thodie, and sat down to eat with them.

Theodore worked past dusk in the fields, and he missed the family suppertime. When he came in Angelina was putting the children to bed. He washed himself, ate some bread and bacon in the kitchen, and went directly upstairs, saying very little. He was at his desk, writing in the dim lamplight when Angelina came up to their room. She could see how tired he looked, and she was ashamed of their fight. She walked hesitantly to her wardrobe, not knowing what to say.

Angelina slipped into her nightgown and took down her hair. "The boys are asleep," she ventured. Theodore looked up. "I read a story to them, and they sat together quietly. Thodie gave Charley a goodnight kiss." Angelina smiled wanly.

Theodore put down his pen and beckoned for her to come to him. She sat down on his lap, then put her arms around his neck and bent her head into his shoulder. "I'm so sorry, Theo. I am trying so hard—but I do not have a gift for playing with the children or entertaining them, or even for keeping the peace. Sarah helped to raise five of our siblings. I just never learned or cared to learn about these things." She hesitated, lifting her head to face him. "And I cannot bear your criticism. I know you don't intend it—but still, you seem to judge me so harshly at times."

"And you and Sarah have not failed to tell me that my vanity and my impatience often endanger my better instincts," Angelina continued. "I see that myself. Believe me, I am wretched about it. But sometimes it feels unfair. You even seem to think my works of charity are vanity—as though you resent my desire to help, and— and don't value what I *am* good at." She grimaced and continued, "Oh, sometimes I even miss the dreadful controversies of our public lectures."

Theodore's rubbed his bushy eyebrows with one hand. He didn't want to re-ignite their hostility, so he took a new approach. "I am beginning to feel that perhaps this—this, uh, mutual correction, is not the best way—in a family, at least?" His brow wrinkled as he thought it through. "Perhaps our faithfulness consists in bearing with each other's faults more patiently and quietly than we have done before. Yes, our faults are real, but we cannot be cured of them when we only feel the sting of harsh judgments of each other. What do you think?"

Angelina began to kiss Theodore's brow and face. She let out a sob. "Oh, yes, Theo, I only want to be the best wife to you and a good mother to our children."

Theodore lifted her chin and said, "Ah, but Nina, you are so much more than that!" He slid her off his lap as he stood up and dimmed his lamp, keeping one arm around her waist. Then he picked her up and carried her to their bed. She looked up at him eagerly as he traced his fingers along her face and neck. Slowly she drew him close, and they began to make love with a new urgency.

Washington, DC

In early January 1843 Theodore returned to Washington—once again in the middle of a winter snowstorm. Congress had begun its new session the previous day. He greeted his friends, Leavitt and Giddings, as the two men returned home from a day's work at the Capitol. Leavitt eagerly related all the latest congressional news before they went into supper together. Theodore felt his heart lift as he began to take up his favorite work again. But there was a nagging unease when he thought of the hardships for the family he had left behind in New Jersey. Especially since Angelina was pregnant again.

A month later, the family had settled into their winter routine without Theodore. Early in the morning Sarah carried a heavy load of firewood into the living room and started a fire in the large, chilly room. It helped to have Stephen and Betsy around, Sarah thought, but Stephen could only help with the lighter farm chores. Betsy was in the kitchen preparing their breakfast of corn mush, graham bread and fresh milk. Their apple and pear preserves were all gone so there would be no more fruit until late spring when there might be some early blueberries. But there was a steady supply of eggs.

Charley and his shadow, Thodie, came out of their bedroom sleepily with blankets wrapped around them. They watched intently as Sarah lit the fire. If all were going well, Angelina got a chance in the mornings for some solitary reading and correspondence upstairs in her room. She and Sarah had agreed to take turns caring for the children. Sometimes Angelina would look out her window and see her sister actively romping with the boys in the snow. One day with Sarah's help they built a snowman together and threw snowballs at each other. The boys chased Sarah until they all fell down in the snow; Sarah laughed as gleefully as the children.

When it was Angelina's turn, she walked around the farm with the children, then brought them inside to read together. Meanwhile Sarah could steal away to do her own reading and letter-writing. She loved spending time with the boys, but she knew that her thinking and writing time was easily the happiest part of her day.

One morning in late March Angelina waddled down the stairs trying to maintain her balance with a very enlarged belly. She was six months into her pregnancy, and it was the most difficult one yet. She had not felt the baby move for several days, and it produced a vague anxiety.

Angelina made little effort to read or write that morning. Before lunch she asked Sarah if she would mind the children a bit longer, and she struggled up to her chamber. Shortly after noon, she called out to Sarah. Sarah found her lying on her bed in premature labor, crying out with each sharp contraction. She wiped Nina's brow, trying to reassure her, but she could see that things were not going well. Sarah went part way down the stairs and called softly to Betsy, alerting her to Nina's condition, and asking her to watch the boys. Betsy quickly put coats and caps on them and herded them outside, to get them away from their mother's cries.

An hour later, Sarah wrapped the stillborn baby in linens and carried the tiny bundle down to Betsy who handed it to Stephen, instructing him to bury it somewhere close to the house. Sarah hurried back to help Nina who was still enduring painful contractions. Sarah gave her some powdered willow bark and held her sister's hand as her pain slowly diminished. When Angelina finally fell asleep, Sarah found a piece of paper and wrote to Theodore.

Theodore received the letter bearing the news of the stillbirth about five days later, on his return from a long day of work. He put his head in his hands and felt hot tears sliding down his cheeks. The decision came easily. He rose from his chair and threw his belongings into a small suitcase. He stopped at Leavitt's room to give him some books and papers and to say good-by. Leavitt, hearing about Angelina's condition, nodded gravely and promised to convey his regretful goodbyes to the others. Theodore then walked toward the new B & O train station a short distance from the Capitol.

Belleville Farm 1844

There was a late snow in New Jersey in March of the following year, but April brought a warm spell and blossoms began appearing in the orchard. A brood of baby chicks were underfoot in the farmyard. After two years of hardship and a year of diligent work, Theodore reflected, the farm was beginning to look in better repair, and he even dared to hope that they could realize a small profit by the end of the summer. Perhaps they could pay off much of their remaining debt to Lewis Tappan.

Angelina was seated on the porch with a blanket thrown over her shoulder as she fed her tiny newborn. She gazed down at her daughter who was latched tightly at her breast and felt a rush of gratitude. She had suggested they name the little girl after her sister, so she was christened Sarah Grimké Weld. Her aunt was thrilled, but they had all agreed to call her "Sissy" to avoid confusion. Angelina looked out contentedly over the farm noticing that Theodore and Stephen were maneuvering the old horse and the older plow into a far field.

Sarah came out with Betsy to help her hang up some of the linens and curtains for a spring airing. After a few minutes she left Betsy to finish the work and sat down with Angelina. "Oh, what a blessing it has all been." Angelina laid her head back on the chair. "Especially having Theodore here with us all the time. He says he thinks we will have a good crop this year." She put her sleeping daughter down carefully into the nearby cradle and murmured, "We shall see."

The children grew, and the months and seasons were marked by new challenges in their upbringing and education. For Theodore there was the ongoing struggle to make ends meet on the farm, and the frustration of work that did not suit his talents. He liked the hard, physical demands of farming, but he was restless for the public sphere in which he had thrived, and which he had now largely deserted. Angelina's health did not return to normal, and she seemed constantly fatigued and stressed by the demands of domestic life. Inevitably Sarah bore an increasing share of childcare and household tasks. She thrived on those duties, especially caring for the children, in a way that Angelina did not. But she also felt the loss of time for any intellectual life. Both she and Angelina carried on regular correspondence, despite the lack of time and opportunity for anything else.

8

The Snowstorm

Cazenovia, NY, February 1847

By the beginning of 1847, Sarah needed a brief change of scenery. Sissie would soon be three, Thodie had just turned five, and Charley was six. The boys could entertain themselves and each other for extended periods, so with Betsy's help, it would be possible for Angelina to manage them for a few days and take care of Sissy at the same time.

Theodore's parents were unwell and aging, so Sarah offered to go nurse them. They were living at the home of Theo's brother, Greenleaf Weld, in Cazenovia in central New York. She intended to combine the trip with a visit to her dear friends, Gerrit and Nancy[21] Smith, and their twenty-five-year-old married daughter, Elizabeth Smith Miller, in nearby Peterboro.

After Sarah had spent two weeks with the Welds, Gerrit arrived in a sleigh with Elizabeth, and her two-year-old son, Gatty, to take Sarah back to Peterboro. There was abundant snow on the ground, but it had been sunny and clear during the sleigh ride over. However, as they prepared to leave Cazenovia, Gerrit and his driver, John, looked at the darkening sky and began to worry.[22]

Sarah came out of the Weld home with Greenleaf Weld, who carried her small valise. Greenleaf surveyed the gathering clouds with a frown. In the freezing wind Sarah noticed his anxiety as she pulled her cloak and muff around her closely. She glanced at her friend. "Brother Gerrit, are you sure we can make it to Peterboro safely this afternoon? With Elizabeth and little Gatty here?"

Gerrit nodded cautiously. "Well, we have an excellent horse, and John is a fine driver. We should be safe. Nancy will have supper ready when we arrive."

With methodical care John completed harnessing the horse. Then he arranged the blankets in the sleigh and helped the women climb into their seats while Gerrit held his grandson. Gerrit handed Gatty to Elizabeth and seated himself next to John.

The sleigh made good time for the first hour, although there were a few minutes of sleet which dampened everything. It was a relief to Sarah and Elizabeth when the sleet turned to light snow. But the wind was still fierce, and rapidly the light snowfall turned into a blinding blizzard. The threesome huddled tightly under the blankets as the little remaining light turned to dusk.

The blizzard made the path forward almost impossible to discern. After several near accidents, the horse missed a curve in the road and carried the sleigh off into a deep ditch. The sleigh stopped at a precarious angle, ready to overturn. Gerrit and John jumped down and managed to get the sleigh onto more level ground. The women stayed in the sleigh, wrapping the blankets tightly around themselves and the baby. The snow enveloped them in a white whirlwind.

Just as the sleigh was righted, the horse took a step in the wrong direction and fell into another hole, the snowdrift coming up to his withers. John was reluctant to try to pull him out, worrying that the horse might have damaged a leg. They could barely see ten yards in front of them, and the forest ahead looked worse.

Gerrit walked a short distance to a clearing in the trees. As he scanned the horizon he saw a farmhouse about 300 yards away, barely visible through the thick scrim of snow. Returning to the sleigh, Gerrit took Gatty from Elizabeth and helped the women down. "There's a house up there—not an impossible distance if we go across the fields."

Sarah stepped down from the sleigh after Elizabeth, and immediately sank up to her hips in the snow. She let out an exclamation, "Oh, Gerrit! It is not possible! How can we walk?" She started to fall, but she managed to extricate herself enough to take a giant step forward.

"I'm so sorry, Sarah, but we don't have much choice." Gerrit said brusquely.

Sarah realized that he felt responsible for the quandary they were in. "No, please, Gerrit, I understand." She breathed deeply and tried to smile bravely.

"John, can you carry Gatty and go with Sarah and Lizzie?" Gerrit suggested. "I'll stay here with Trojan to make sure he is not hurt. You can return once the women and Gatty are safe. I'll unhitch him and we can dig him out. One of us can ride him to the house if his legs will work." John frowned at this division of labor, but he obeyed and reached for Gatty.

"Papa, is this the best way?" Elizabeth asked. "Gatty's frightened. I can carry him," she insisted.

"Lizzie, you will barely be able to make it on your own. Help Sarah if you can. Gatty will be fine with John."

Elizabeth looked distressed but reluctantly gave Gatty up. The baby cried loudly as he was exposed to the cold and the wind, and Elizabeth reached over to take him back, but John wrapped him tightly in his blanket and tucked him under his coat. Once warmed up his cries were reduced to an intermittent whimper.

The two women climbed over a low stone wall and set off doggedly across the uphill terrain, heading toward the distant farmhouse. John followed them with Gatty. Sarah plunged ahead and was soon separated from Elizabeth. She stumbled into a snow drift and again sank up to her hips. "Stupid as the horse," she thought to herself. She freed her leg by digging away at the snow with her lightly mittened right hand. Her left hand was still in her muff. Desperate to make progress, she tossed the muff away so that both hands were free. She climbed out of the drift, walked several yards, then stumbled again. Her mittens were wet through, and her fingers burned from the cold, but the muff was out of reach.

Sarah dug her way out of the snow once more, crawling on her knees until she could pull herself upright. She was breathing hard and had to stop to catch her breath. After another hundred yards Sarah clambered over a second fence. She looked around and saw that Elizabeth was struggling to get over the same fence thirty feet away. Sarah continued trudging slowly, watching out for drifts in the uneven ground and nearly falling several times. She found herself facing a third fence. Too exhausted to climb over it properly, she balanced her body on the top rail, pivoted and fell into the deep snow on the far side. Again, she struggled to find a way to get to her feet. She managed to navigate another twenty yards. Then she stumbled on a stump beneath the snow and fell flat on her face. She lay there with the coolness of the snow on her face, wishing she could just fall asleep.

She heard Gatty's whimpers before she saw John appear by her side. Still holding Gatty tightly with one arm, John offered Sarah his other arm. She held onto it and pulled herself up. The snow was still falling but she could now see the faint light of the lamp in the farmhouse ahead. Leaning on John, she willed herself to make it through the last hundred yards to the house.[23]

John knocked on the door, supporting Sarah, who was breathing hard and was close to fainting from exhaustion. He kept a firm hold on Gatty who had grown quiet. A homely old man stood on the threshold and listened closely as John tried to explain their plight. Seeing the strange, bedraggled party from a distance, the old man's daughter, the mistress of the farm, hurried over from the barnyard and urged them to come inside the house where they could find warmth and comfort. The woman took charge of Sarah, taking off her damp outerwear and helping her lay down on a couch. Elizabeth had just reached the door. Gatty held out his arms and his mother took him into her own gratefully. Sarah rubbed her frozen hands together frantically, but she was too dazed to speak for several minutes. She looked around for Elizabeth but only saw John.

"Where is Lizzy? Is she all right?" Sarah asked weakly. "Oh, there you are," she said as she turned her head and saw Elizabeth shaking off her snow-covered cloak. "Thank God! And I see Gatty has found his mother. Oh, his cries were so pitiful out there." Elizabeth looked at her boy now sitting contentedly on her knees. She ruffled his hair and looked at their driver gratefully.

"John, thank you—I don't know how we all would have made it without you!" Sarah said. She lay back on the pillows and with one deep breath she fell asleep.

After warming himself very briefly, John set out down the long hill to help Gerrit with the horse and sleigh. When the men returned, the mistress invited them to sit down to a hot meal of lamb stew and bread with her husband, their daughter of about four years of age, the grandfather who had met them at the door, and herself.

Sarah and the others ate hungrily. Towards the end of the meal, the grandfather got up from the dinner table and took the little girl by the hand. He sat in an armchair and read a story to her as the other adults remained at the dinner table. The girl was close in age to her niece, Sissy, Sarah thought.

As the conversation flowed around her, Sarah's mind wandered, and she found herself watching the old man as he carried his sleepy granddaughter into her room. The bedroom was just off the parlor, and with the door ajar, Sarah could see him putting on her nightgown and gently tucking her into bed. As he gave her a goodnight kiss, Sarah couldn't help smiling.

She rubbed her aching hands and shoulders as she reflected that she had not really felt any fear of perishing in the snow, although she now understood how it was possible to do so. Her energy had been completely absorbed in surmounting the obstacles and reaching safety.[24]

Boston 1848

About a year and a half after her trip to Cazenovia and Peterboro with its adventure in the snow, the household was on the verge of another change, and Sarah needed to think. She stole a few days to travel to Boston to visit one of her favorite correspondents, the practicing physician, Harriot Hunt. On the evening of her arrival, Sarah and Harriot entered her parlor after supper, intent on enjoying a long chat over tea. Sarah sank into a comfortable armchair, feeling more relaxed than she had in many months. She was tired from her journey but delighted to be in adult company. She surveyed the cozy parlor, filled with well-worn but handsome furnishings, warm colors, soft cushions and rich brocade draperies. As they were having their tea, Harriot asked Sarah about Angelina and the family. Then she got up and went over to a sideboard where there was a bottle of cordial.

"Sarah, I know that Theodore tolerates no strong drink in his home, but I am going to pour you a glass of cordial. It is excellent for your health. Think of it as medicine." She smiled conspiratorially at Sarah, who accepted the glass hesitantly. Sarah took a sip and nodded appreciatively as it warmed her insides. Harriot took her seat by the fireplace, facing Sarah.[25]

Sarah bit her lower lip and looked into the fire, then up at her friend. "Harriot, how can I thank you for welcoming me so warmly and listening to my woes! I felt I had to get away for a few days, although I miss the dear children terribly." Sarah paused and tilted her head to one side. "And I know I am desperately needed there, so I must return the day after tomorrow."

Harriet nodded, "Yes, I understand that you can't stay long—so we must make the most of our short time," she smiled.

"Tell me, have you heard back from Harvard yet?" Sarah inquired. "I was so glad to hear that you had written to apply to study with the Medical Faculty there."

Harriot shook her head sadly, "No, I have not heard anything—not since last year when they turned me down." She glared at the fire and rearranged herself on the couch. "But I shall keep trying. In the meantime, my practice seems to flourish. Many women seem to like having a woman physician." She shrugged philosophically, not wanting to dwell on her frustration.

"So, tell me about the school and about how Angelina is—I want to hear all!"

"Yes, well, the school is decided upon, and we shall welcome a few students next month—and perhaps several more in November." Sarah said matter-of-factly. "Little Sissy is not yet four and a half, but the boys are of an age to begin studying seriously, and Theodore and Angelina felt that we would all benefit from taking in a few boarders to study with them—perhaps several day-students from the area as well. Our niece, Mary Anna, and her husband have recently moved to the neighborhood, and they have a five-year-old son." She smiled at Harriot and added, "The house is large, as you know, and we have an out-building that we are fixing up with two classrooms."

"And how about you, Sarah? Are you content with this?"

"Oh, what else could I do, Harriot? I live for the children—and for Theodore and Nina as well—they are the blessed comforters of my poor, sad heart."

"Oh, my dear, are you really so sad?" Harriot inquired with an earnest look.

Sarah smiled bleakly and looked away for a moment, afraid to betray herself. "Oh, no. I try to be cheerful when I am at home. Should I not be happy when my loved ones are happy?" She stared into the fire again, looking less than happy. "Angelina thinks this is just the thing for Theodore—that his talents are wasted as a farmer. I agree on that point—he is a marvelous teacher."

"I don't believe you've answered my question, Sarah," Harriot chided gently.

Sarah sighed and looked even more troubled. "Nina is suffering greatly again from her prolapsed uterus—she can barely walk—and the hernia as well. And lately she has had sickening headaches." Sarah continued as Harriot nodded knowingly. "I fear she is depressed by this chronic illness. And I cannot bear to see her suffer. Is there anything you can suggest, Harriot?"

Harriot was thinking, but Sarah went on, "I only came now because Bridget is over her sickness, and Nina has designed a strap to relieve the pressure from her prolapse—and I was so tired that my temper was growing short." Sarah hesitated, unsure how much to confide. "To tell the truth, Nina and I have been impatient with each other, and I felt a little distance might help. The boys are so sensitive—they see when I am sad and ask me why. Can you imagine?"

"Oh, Sarah, I'm so sorry. And on top of this you are to begin the school year?"

"I don't know why I am telling you all this, Harriot—I have not uttered a word of it at home," she admitted. Pausing and looking away, "There are other things of which I must not speak, even to you."[26]

Harriot looked troubled by these words, but nodded understandingly, and said, "Yes, of course, just speak of what you can."

"I am trying to share in the family's eagerness to begin this work. Please forgive me." Sarah's voice started to break. She cleared her throat and went on. "I am to teach French, and to help with the young boarders. I shall enjoy the latter, but I do not enjoy the prospect of teaching. My French is rusty—I will need to study to keep ahead of the students." She managed a chuckle.

"You will do fine as a teacher, Sarah. You are so gentle with children."

"Yes, I love them dearly, but I'm afraid that affection is not what is called for in the classroom, Harriot. I fear I will bore them and," she confessed, "I really hate to discipline." She smiled, finding that her mood was considerably lightened by unburdening herself. "But let us speak of you and of our hopes for women!" Sarah said with genuine eagerness. "Tell me about the meeting in Seneca Falls."

Harriot was happy to take up their favorite topic. "I was only there for one evening session, of course, but I heard about it from others," she said. "It was rather an impromptu event—we only had a week's notice of it. But it was glorious, Sarah! Lucretia was the moving spirit, while Elizabeth Stanton seemed to be the organizer, along with Mary Anne M'Clintock. James Mott came to several sessions with Lucretia, as did hundreds of other women and dozens of men and children. "Oh, and Frederick Douglas was there!" she recalled excitedly.

"Oh, Harriot, how I would have loved to participate! I know they drew up a new Declaration of Sentiments. Did they speak of women's political rights? A right to vote?" Sarah asked.

"Yes, they did! It was a bone of contention between Lucretia, who thought it was too radical and would make us ridiculous, and Elizabeth Stanton, who insisted upon it."

Sarah was surprised to hear of Lucretia's caution. Her brow wrinkled with puzzlement, but she just nodded, and said "Hmmm, that's interesting."

"Frederick Douglas spoke in favor of women's right to the vote as well," Harriot continued. "He said he would not wish to accept the vote for his fellow Negroes without it also being extended to women. Isn't that amazing?" she smiled broadly.

As she was talking, Harriot had risen to pour some more cordial into their glasses. Sarah smiled impishly and raised her glass to Harriot. "Yes, it is, and I'd say that deserves a toast!" Harriot grinned and clinked her glass to Sarah's.

Then she continued her story in a serious tone. "Sarah, your presence was very much in the air there. I tell you truthfully. Elizabeth and Lucretia both referred to your *Letters on the Equality of the Sexes.* Many of its sentiments found their way into the Declaration. Nina's *Letter to Catherine Beecher* was mentioned, too, of course, but your writings were center stage." She looked Sarah in the eye and added, "You should be very proud!"

Sarah bowed her head modestly, but she couldn't hide her immense gratification at those words. "Thank you for saying that, Harriot. If it is only half true it gives me great satisfaction—if I had even a small contribution to this great work."

Sarah continued wistfully, "I had so many plans for this winter—to edit an article and to rewrite the *Letters.* I wanted to crawl into some quiet nook and rekindle my intellectual powers, and use them in reading, writing and thinking." She signed, "But that is not to be. Not now."

Sarah paused, rose from her chair and walked around the room, touching the velvety wine brocade of the drapes, and admiring a still-life on the wall. Abruptly, Sarah spoke again, "Harriot, I have been meaning to ask you. What are the views of Unitarians on eternal punishment? I heard that the Unitarians reject it, but I wanted confirmation that it is so."[27]

She nodded her head slowly, "I believe they do reject it, Sarah. I'll ask our minister if there is an official position, but I'm certain that none of my Unitarian friends give any credence to the notion of hell. I certainly don't!" she smiled.

Sarah sighed with relief, "I'm so glad to hear that! To me it is blasphemy against the mercy and justice of God. How could a loving Father be less merciful than we humans are?" Sarah paused, her face registering her anxiety. "The question has bothered me, Harriot, less on my own account than for the eternal peace of so many in my own family who are slaveholders. I believe it is sinful on their part, but they are not wholly evil. Surely God will show them mercy?"

Harriot nodded in agreement. "Sarah, your kind heart has taught you well."

Sarah leaned back in her chair, warmed by the cordial and reassured by finding her friend's views in harmony with her own. She yawned contentedly. Succumbing to the late hour and their fatigue, the two women rose, and Harriot took Sarah affectionately by one arm. She picked up a lamp and they headed into the entry way and up the stairs to their chambers.

9

An Interlude in Winter

Belleville 1850

By the second winter the Belleville School had attracted about ten students in addition to the three Weld children, and it was enjoying a modest reputation in the neighborhood. In fact, word of its rigorous but progressive educational approach had reached others who sought educational reform. Through Theodore's network of abolitionist friends, several had decided to come and see for themselves. On an afternoon in late January, Bronson Alcott arrived from west of Boston with his friend, Henry Thoreau, and two of his four daughters, Louisa and May.[28] Angelina came out of the house to welcome them.

So far it had been an exceptionally cold, dry January with just a little snow. The conditions were ideal for freezing the large pond that lay beyond the first field, within sight of the house. The dozen girls and boys had just rushed from their classrooms to try out the ice.[29] They ranged in age from the very young children just learning to skate to a few in their early teens. Charley was ten, Thodie had just turned nine, and Sissy would soon be six. By the side of the pond, Mary Anna Frost Haskell held an infant while her husband, Llewellyn, taught their seven-year-old, Lew[30] and his younger cousin, Sissy, to skate.

Angelina was about to apologize for Theodore's absence, when he appeared, hurrying out of the classroom building. He trotted up to greet Alcott and Thoreau and the girls. "Bronson, Henry, forgive my tardiness —I was deeply engrossed in preparing a class on *The Merchant of Venice*."

Shaking Theodore's hand heartily, Alcott responded, "Oh, you needn't worry. Angelina has been entertaining us—telling us all about the school, I am gratified to hear about your approach here—manual labor, healthy food, exercise, and a Socratic method of teaching. Bravo, dear sir!"

Theodore inclined his large head graciously to Alcott, "These are your ideas, Bronson—admirable ones with which I almost universally agree. Perhaps we lean a bit more toward traditional methods and discipline, but never corporal punishment, of course. How useless to teach children with violence!" Alcott frowned and nodded his agreement vigorously.

"But we should go inside where it is warm. The children will be in soon. I see you have brought two of your daughters," he said approvingly. His bushy eyebrows and direct gaze seemed fierce to Alcott's eight-year-old daughter, May, but his gravelly voice was kind and somehow reassuring.

After brief introductions, sixteen-year-old Louisa Alcott turned to Angelina and said, "Can we?" pointing to the pond. Angelina smiled and waved them off. Louisa and May were restless from their day of travel, and they wasted no time in running out to join the others at the pond. The Weld boys found them extra skates and they were on the ice in minutes. May took a few tentative glides to test the smoothness of the ice. Finding it deliciously slick, she skated over to join Thodie whom she thought must be about her own age. Louisa boldly set out to race around the ice with some of the older boys.

Back near the house, Thoreau was half-listening to their host, more intrigued by the brown leaves which still clung mysteriously to the branches of the red oak tree, and which, he noted, were decorated with bits of silver frost. "Henry, I suspect that you would prefer to be out walking—or perhaps skating with the children!" Theodore acknowledged. "But we need to hear from you, too. We have much to discuss!"

"Well, yes, I confess the pond does look tempting!" Henry laughed sheepishly but he joined the other adults as they retreated into the house. The previous summer Theodore had removed a wall on the main floor of the big house to create a large dining and gathering area for the school. The great room served as study hall, dining hall, dance floor or theatre depending on the need of the moment.

Angelina helped Sarah bring out tea for Alcott, Thoreau, and Theodore. Theodore related how they had tried to impose the Graham diet on the students only to find that the students complained loudly and wrote home to their parents that they were being starved. "That quickly made us aware that we could not insist on our way of life in every respect," Theodore chuckled.

As their conversation continued, the young people wandered in. Mary Anna, shivering from the post-sunset chill, appeared first with her new baby. The other children followed soon after. They put away their skates and hung up their coats, hats, and mittens on the hooks that had been assigned to each of them. Louisa, her nose red from the cold, chatted with Thodie and May. Close behind them, Llewellyn Haskell came with his son, Lew, and Charley Weld.

The youngsters could smell the cornbread that had just come out of the oven, and they clustered around the table as Sarah brought out hot cider and placed it in front of them, along with the bread. They filled their mugs, helped themselves to cornbread and honey, and drifted off into groups. Charley and an older friend found seats close to Theodore, Haskell, and Thoreau. They were soon deep into a debate about the color of Othello's skin. Thodie, May Alcott, Sissy, and Lew Haskell settled in a corner to play games. Thodie and Lew pulled out a checkerboard and began arguing over the rules. Disgusted with the boys' delays, May decided to teach Sissy her favorite clapping game.

Once the children had gotten their cornbread and cider, Sarah took off her apron and sat down with Bronson Alcott, Louisa, Mary Anna, and her baby. Louisa and Mary Anna gratefully warmed their hands on the hot cider, while Sarah rocked her niece's baby to sleep. Once the baby was settled in a cradle nearby, Sarah asked, "Louisa, I have heard that you like to scribble! I would love to read some of what you are writing."

Louisa was pleased, but looked down shyly, "Oh, Miss Grimké, it is nothing—just little stories for my sisters and friends. But I do love to make them up! You might disapprove—I like pirates and sword fights and lots of romance and melodrama." She bit her lower lip self-consciously and gave a little shrug. "Still, it is nothing like what you have written. My mother made me read your *Letters on Equality*. Well, she didn't exactly make me—but she gave them to me. And I'm so glad she did. They have given me such hope."

Mary Anna smiled sardonically at her aunt, before addressing Louisa. "Yes, Aunt Sarah was quite the rabble-rouser in her day. She made my mother squirm."

"Mary Anna, dear, what do you mean by 'my day'" Sarah objected strenuously. "Am I so old that I have nothing further to contribute?" Sarah admonished her niece with a tiny smile. Sarah was more disturbed by the comment than she revealed, and she sighed deeply. "In fact, I had hoped to do more writing this winter, but with the school, there is no hope of that. Well, now I am planning to write something about the education of women. Perhaps next summer. . ."

"Splendid!" Alcott slapped his knee with enthusiasm. "It is a topic on which my wife and I are deeply interested—forced on us I suppose by having four young women in our family! Tell us what you think, Miss Grimké."

Sarah obliged, "Well, you know perhaps, that there were many examples of highly educated women among the Greek and Roman heathens.[31] Women poets such as Sappho, Euridice who was the grandmother of Alexander the Great, Hortensia, and many others."

"But only the pagan women?" Louisa inquired, with a troubled look.

Sarah smiled, "Well, no, not only them. Constantine's mother, St. Helena, was educated, too, and a few others among the Roman noblewomen who became Christian. Yet by the Middle Ages, the education of Christian women was limited to that of the few exceptional nuns and abbesses." She pursed her lips and added, "We went decidedly backward."

Mary Anna looked puzzled, "But Aunt Sarah, you and Angelina have been able to educate yourselves! And you helped me with studies, too. Women are making great strides, are we not?"

"Oh, Mary Anna, if you knew how we have had to struggle—and still do—for the meager learning we have been allowed. Have you been invited to study at Harvard yet, my dear?" she asked with a small, acerbic smile. After a moment's pause, she shook her head, "And the abysmal situation of most women—it is disheartening. In much of the world, women are treated no better than donkeys!"

"No, I can't study at Harvard yet" Mary Anna retorted, "not that I would ever want to! But there is Oberlin you know. It is setting an example, is it not?"

Louisa looked at Sarah and said wistfully, "Well, I wish *I* could go to Harvard."

Sarah shared a regretful look with Bronson but then smiled indulgently at Louisa and Mary Anna. "For your generation or perhaps the next, yes, I do believe there is some reason to hope, but for most women it is still an utter impossibility."

"You see, I truly believe that education is the lever which raises humanity to a higher state," Sarah declared with great earnestness. "It is the tool for change and progress. Yet women have, for centuries—even mil-lennia—been denied a part in that. Their life's work was to make things comfortable for their "lords." Their intellectual powers have been stymied and crushed." Sarah looked away, embarrassed at the bitter tone she had slipped into.

"Do you not believe in marriage, then, Miss Grimké?" Louisa asked.

"No, no, my dear. Please don't misunderstand me on this point," Sarah insisted. "It is the evils of the current marriage system which are caused by man's usurpation of power over woman that I reject, not mar-riage itself. A true love marriage, one that is based on recognition of each other's equality of mind and soul is the holiest of things! She hesitated, looking at Bronson and his daughter with a curious smile. "And, Louisa, I believe you may have seen it, have you not?"

Louisa looked at her father uncertainly. He nodded slowly. "In truth, it is a difficult goal to achieve—this true equality. But my beloved Abby and I struggle to find the way.[32] He reached over and patted Louisa's arm gently. "You will have to ask her if we have succeeded."

Mary Anna glanced over at her husband who was holding forth with her Uncle Theodore and Henry Thoreau. She looked uncomfortable and skeptical.[33] "But isn't it rather idealistic, Aunt Sarah? As you say, a 'rare sight'"

"Well, I am hardly the best judge." Sarah shrugged and laughed. "But on education I can speak from some experience. It is because I have felt the denial of higher education so keenly myself that I know we must demand an equal education with men. We must equip women for social usefulness and financial independence. Thousands of women are perishing around us for want of something useful to do. Of this I am convinced."[34]

They spoke for several minutes about the practicalities of women's education and the importance of physical education for women. Louisa glowed. "I'm so happy to hear you say that, Miss Grimké! I love my books and my writing, but nothing thrills my soul as much as a good skate, or a walk in the woods, or a race with my sisters." Mary Anna smiled at her and asked Louisa about their home near Boston and her other sisters.

Sarah took the opportunity to lean towards Alcott and speak very quietly, "Mr. Alcott, I heard from your brother-in-law Samuel May that you and your family have given refuge to a fugitive slave at your home in Boston. I am so touched by your compassion and bravery."

"It is true—but we've only had one so far. They are the courageous ones. It must be so frightening for them to attempt this journey. We do . . . "

Alcott was interrupted as Angelina rose and addressed the whole group. "Come everyone! Betsy says that supper is ready. We can continue our wonderful conversations over our meal."

Betsy brought out dish after dish of hot and cold foods— squash soup, cabbage, cornmeal mush, and baked beans. To satisfy the hungry boys, there was also plenty of milk, cheese, bread, and even some sausages. Sarah and Louisa got up to help her set these on the long dining table lined with benches that they used for the family, the boarders, and now their guests. After supper, the younger children helped to clear away the dishes, and the older ones went to clean up in the kitchen under Betsy's direction.

When the clean-up was finished, Thoreau and the older boys pushed the dining table back to one wall. Mary Anna sat down at the old piano that the school had recently acquired. Mr. Haskell and one of the teenage boys took up their fiddles to play some dances.

The young people lined up to dance a Virginia Reel, although some of the boys were reluctant participants. Sissy pulled Aunt Sarah up to dance, and Theodore reached for Angelina's hand to join in. Henry Thoreau took Louisa as a partner and Bronson danced with his youngest daughter, May. Betsy came out of the kitchen to watch her favorite youngsters. Charley tried to get her to dance, but she chased him away with a "Get on with ya, silly boy!"

The musicians were imperfect, and there was much stumbling around and stepping on toes, but that just added to the laughter. New dances were tried and discarded, but the gaiety lasted until exhaustion set in, and the young people, at least those who were not already nodding off in a corner, sauntered to their beds.

10

Summer, Bloomers,
and the Children

Peterboro, NY Summer 1853[35]

IN THE SPRAWLING BACKYARD of the home of Gerrit and Nancy Smith,[36] their late-born son, Greene,[37] struggled to climb up an elm tree that grew over fifty feet tall. He followed Thodie Weld, who was about three feet from the top. Charley Weld stood near the trunk of the tree calling out directions to the younger boys. Thodie was close enough to the top that he could throw a piece of rope over the highest branch. After he got it over the branch, he adjusted it so that about three feet of the rope was hanging down to his hand, and the other end hung down to the ground.

"Thodie, it isn't straight," Charley yelled up. "You need to straighten it out."

"I know, Charley, I know! Greene's getting it. It's tangled in a branch."

Greene found a foothold about a foot higher and stretched his arm out to shake the branch vigorously so that the rope fell freely through to the ground. "I'm getting' it!" Greene called out. "See, I got it. Don't be so bossy, Charley. See, it's fine," he said as he teetered precariously on a slender branch. "I didn't want to disturb the birds up here."

At this moment Angelina walked out the back door of the Smith's large, comfortable farmhouse and saw the boys in the tree at the far end of the backyard. She picked up her skirt and hurried toward them, calling out in an anxious tone. "Thodie, what are you and Greene doing up so high in that tree. You come down at once—you're scaring the life out of me!"

65

"They are fine, Mama. We're just doing our science project," Charley explained calmly. "Mr. Youmans told us to measure everything we can. We measured the corn over there—and got an average height, and we measured the temperature of the creek—at three places!" Thodie and Greene clambered down the tree, poking each other with their feet and giggling as they came.

"Thodie, come here. What do you have to say for yourself?" Angelina asked in her sternest voice.

Thodie had a big grin on his face, prouder of his exploit than frightened at his mother's displeasure. He jumped the last few feet from a low branch to the grass. "I'm just great, Mother. See. It's like Charley said. Mr. Youmans told us that measurement is the heart and soul of science," Thodie pronounced confidently.

Angelina frowned, uncertain how to react. Charley continued to go about the task they had set themselves with great seriousness. He pulled down the rope and started laying it out on the ground so he could measure it with a yardstick and determine the distance from the top of the tree to the ground as indicated by the length of the rope. But it was too long for the width of the backyard. "Here, Thodie, I need your help," Charley called out.

Greene approached Angelina timidly, "I—I'm sorry, Mrs. Weld. We didn't mean any harm. I climb that tree all the time and I've never fallen. I thought—"

"Oh, never mind, Greene. It just gave me a scare to see you boys up so high." She was still torn between disciplining them and being impressed with their diligence. "Well, Nora has dinner almost ready, so you need to come in and wash up," she said with just a trace of irritation.

Angelina heard cries from inside the house. She turned to go indoors to find out what new crisis was happening there between Sissy and eight-year-old Gatty. The boys finished their measuring, and Greene and Thodie engaged in a friendly tussle over the yardstick. The boys' horseplay continued as they headed toward the back door of the house. Charley, who stood a head taller than the younger boys, was trying hard to show himself superior to their antics.

Nora, the cook, set a steaming bowl of stew on the table, fragrant with rosemary, onion, and a hint of garlic. There were fresh biscuits, too. Eventually all five children made it to their seats for their midday meal. Angelina sat at the foot of the table between Sissy and Thodie. Gatty's mother, Elizabeth Smith Miller, presided at the head of the table.

"I'm so sorry your mother's feeling poorly again, Lizzie," Angelina offered.

Elizabeth nodded thoughtfully. "She'll be down for supper, I think. She just gets so tired these days. She and Father—they try to do too much, you know." Lizzie's brow wrinkled with anxiety. "With Father in Congress last year, it was particularly difficult for her. I wish I could be here to help more often."

Elizabeth moved around in her seat to adjust the pantaloons of the bloomer costume that she had designed for herself about a year earlier. She smiled as she looked across at her much younger brother, Greene who was pushing a carrot around his plate as Sissy watched him with curiosity.

"But it's so wonderful to have you all here, Mrs. Weld," she continued. "The boys are having such fun together, even Gatty, though he's a bit young for the older boys. But he and Sissy seem to be getting on."

In a few minutes the children, having satisfied their modest appetites, were growing restless. Under the table Thodie and Greene took turns kicking each other. One of Greene's kicks went astray and hit Charley, who was startled and quietly poked Thodie in retaliation. Their mouths were silent, however, as they tried very hard to keep their antics hidden from Angelina and Lizzie. The two women continued their conversation, initially oblivious to the children's shenanigans. As the boys were occupied with their feet, Sissy stole a biscuit from Gatty's plate and stuffed it whole into her mouth. She was chewing it with obvious delight when Gatty looked around to see where it had gone. It wasn't until Gatty started to object loudly, that Angelina frowned and reprimanded Sissy. To Elizabeth she said, "Yes, well I'm afraid Sissy was teasing him a bit before dinner. Being the youngest, she's often the butt of the boy's teasing so she's learned all their bad habits."

"Oh, but they are lovely children, Mrs. Weld. You should be very proud of them. Of course, they misbehave sometimes, but don't all children?" She thought for a moment and then asked, "And how is your sister, Miss Sarah? I've missed seeing her this summer. I love talking to her. Oh, and I've made some bloomers for both of you," Lizzie added, excited to share her invention.

"Have you really, Lizzie? How marvelous! Yours look so comfortable. I can hardly wait to try them on."

Charley was no longer able to keep his impatience with the younger boys' antics quiet. With the latest kick, he cried out, "Ouch! Thodie, stop kicking."

Gatty decided it was time to assert his rights as well. He put on a pitiful face and said to Elizabeth, "Mama, Sissy took my biscuit. She ate it!"

Sissy's mouth was still full of the evidence which she attempted to swallow quickly. "Gatty gave it to me!" she lied.

"Did not! You took it!"

Elizabeth didn't know who to believe, but she beckoned her son to come over to sit on her lap. "Oh, Gatty, don't fuss so, my darling. We'll find you another biscuit." She picked an uneaten half of a biscuit off her plate and gave it to him.

Angelina finally noticed the children's hijinks. "Children, what is wrong with you? You can't sit at the dining table without causing chaos?" She looked at her younger son and said, "Thodie, apologize to Charley, please. And Sissy, sit up straight and don't tell tales that aren't true!"

In retaliation for Charley's telling on him, Thodie kicked him under the table one last time. "Mother, he's doing it again—can't you see," Charley objected. "Thodie, grow up!"

"Oh, my heavens, you are a sorry lot!" Angelina proclaimed. "Thodie, go to your room." Thodie slipped off his chair with a pout, heading up the stairs sluggishly.

"And Charley, you go into the library and read your book for an hour. Greene, can you take him there? I don't want to hear any more from you until teatime."

"As for you, Sissy, well, what shall I do with you?" she asked. Sissy hid her face and began to cry. Angelina leaned over and felt her forehead, then with a worried look she said, "Oh, dear, you seem to be feverish. I think you had better lay down and rest in my bed." Sissy nodded her head penitently and walked slowly upstairs to their chamber.

"Sissy never gets in trouble, Mama. You think she's such an angel, but she isn't," Charley said resentfully as he stood up to leave.

Angelina put a hand on her hip and gave him a stern look of warning. She knew she was losing what little patience she had left. "I want to hear no more insolence from you, young man. Do as I say!" Charley rolled his eyes at Greene as the two of them headed to the library.

Elizabeth was still holding Gatty who had fallen asleep in her lap amidst all the commotion. She carried him to the back parlor nearby and laid him on a sofa there. Angelina joined her in the front parlor, feeling frazzled and unhappy, "Oh, Lizzie, what shall I do about the children?" she said to the younger woman. "You see how naughty they are and how badly I manage them," she confessed. "You seem—well, it seems to come so naturally to you."

"No, I don't see that at all, Mrs. Weld! They are children—they are meant to be naughty. It is how they play and how they learn. But perhaps I am closer to my own childhood naughtiness," she said with a hint of a smile. "Well! Now we have some peace and quiet for a bit. Here, come with me to the sewing room and I'll fit your bloomers for you."

As they walked through the back parlor to the sewing room, Angelina asked quietly about Gerrit's coordination of the underground railroad in the area. "Your parents are so brave, Lizzie," Angelina commented. Elizabeth explained in a low voice that there was, indeed, a regular flow of fugitive slaves being housed near their home, enroute to Canada. "Do you know about Miss Harriet Tubman, Mrs. Weld? She is still bringing more slaves to freedom, even since the passage of the Fugitive Slave Law.[38] Father tells me stories about her incredible bravery. She brings some of them through here on their way north. It is so frightening for them now."

Angelina nodded, "Yes, it humbles me to think how little we have done when I hear the stories of her courage. But I understand that you cannot tell me too much, Lizzie," she murmured.

"Hmmm. Yes." Elizabeth said solemnly. "My mother supports these efforts wholeheartedly, but she worries constantly about someone being discovered. I suspect her headaches and fatigue are partly due to this worry."

A half-hour later Angelina stood on a slightly raised platform with her new bloomer costume on. Elizabeth had just put the last pin in the hem of the knee-length skirt with loose pantaloons below it. The two women looked in the mirror and both smiled broadly at the effect.

"Lizzie, you are so clever! How did you come up with this design? So much more practical than our long skirts!"

"Oh, it took great genius, indeed." Elizabeth laughed at the memory of her invention. "I was out gardening back at our home, and my skirts kept dragging in the dirt and getting in the way. Finally, in disgust, I ran into the house, got a pair of scissors and cut off the bottom eighteen inches of my dress." She shook her head, amused at the memory. "But of course, I couldn't wear it just like that. I'd seen pictures of Turkish women wearing these sorts of pantaloons, so I sewed up a pair of loose pantaloons like those and wore them under my dress. Et voila!" She gestured at Angelina's costume.

Angelina stepped down from the platform and walked around gingerly at first, but then with greater freedom, taking longer strides. "Oh my, Lizzie! I feel so free in these. What a liberation for us women. Sister Sarah will love them. But can you wear them only at home? What if you go to the village or to town?"

"I got a few disapproving looks the first time I went into town, but now the women mostly just smile at my eccentricity. They all know me, and know my unconventional views and habits."

"Hmmm. This feels a bit awkward," Angelina said hesitantly, tugging at the skirt.

"Yes, I'm not entirely satisfied with them yet. But, Mrs. Weld, you have no idea what a slave to fashion I am," Elizabeth admitted. "I went to my dressmaker and had her make up several pairs. I wanted them for my trip to Washington, DC to visit father when he was in Congress last year. I had one lovely suit of silk pantaloons and a silk taffeta skirt with a fur-trimmed cape on top," she said with a touch of pride. "Fortunately, my husband thinks they are wonderful!"

Angelina's brow furrowed and she looked at Lizzie seriously. "Why did you call them "bloomers"?

"Oh, that was a bit of an accident, too. I wore them on a visit to Elizabeth Stanton, and she insisted on showing them to her friend Amelia Bloomer, who put a drawing of them in her women's journal. So, they ended up being named after her—'Bloomers'! I don't mind. It sounds better than "Millers.""

After a half-hour of quiet in the library, Charley and Greene were restless. While the women were absorbed in conversation, the boys managed to tiptoe into the kitchen and set up a science experiment on the stove. Thodie crept down the back stairs from his exile and begged to be part of the action. But before Charley and Greene could caution him, he upset the apparatus on the stove and the boiling water from it burned his hand badly. Elizabeth and Angelina came to the rescue, but there were tears and commotion for another hour. Finally, they all settled down to a game of "I Spy" and the adults managed to restore harmony through the evening.

It rained heavily the next few days, and it would be difficult to say whether Angelina or the children found it more of a trial to be housebound. On the third day after Thodie's accident, Angelina sat in the bedroom she shared with Sissy, and watched the raindrops inch steadily down the windowpane. Angelina took up her pen and began a letter to Sarah.

> Dear Sister,
>   We all thank you for your good, long letter, but do tell me what makes you praise the children so? I could not read to them all your epithets of their nobility. I don't know what I wrote you, but my daily experience does not show me so beautiful a side of their characters.[39]

Angelina bit on the end of her pen, pondering how much to say to her sister. She knew her discontent had other roots than the children. But this time with them felt like enduring a bad toothache. She put her pen to the paper and wrote rapidly.

> Is it my fault? Very likely it is. Charley offers to help me sometimes, but he teases Thodie and Sissy so. They all blame each other when they are naughty and do not own up to the truth. Since the "science experiment" that I told you about, Thodie can only use one hand and needs to be helped to dress and undress.
>   He never means to be unkind to Sis, but his absent-mindedness often makes him do things that are annoying to her, or to Charley. Now Sissy is not feeling well and wants to be quiet. Charley sulks and Thodie whines.

Angelina paused again, staring out at the rain unhappily.

> Thank you for wanting to come, dear sister, but you know how I suffer when you look after my children. It is better that one of us be with them at a time.

When Angelina's letter reached Sarah back in Belleville, a week later, she started reading it eagerly. But as she read on, she was hurt and confused at Angelina's response to her offer to help. She put the letter into her pocket and walked despondently out to the back garden. "So, what am I to do, Nina?" she said aloud. "You tell me that you don't enjoy the children—that they are a trial to you," she continued in a quiet mutter, "but then you turn around and say you suffer when I am with them." She frowned again, shaking her head, "I believe you suffer to see that the children and I actually enjoy being together!" She wandered around the garden wondering how to respond. Eventually she returned to her writing desk and began a letter to Angelina.

On the same day that Sarah received Angelina's letter, Thodie lay back on the thick pillows of his bed playing with a kitten. One hand was still wrapped up from the burn and he had a sniffle, but he was more lonely and unhappy than sick. After several minutes the kitten slinked away, leaving Thodie alone. Thodie threw a book on the floor in frustration. Charley appeared at the door and Thodie greeted him eagerly. "Hey, Charley. Come play a game with me."

"Hi Thod, old man. I can't. I'm just getting my cap. Greene and I are going to cut some wood out back. It's not raining so much right now. Can't you come? You don't look very sick."

"Mother says I mustn't. She thinks I overdid things on Saturday—you know, with the hammering and all. It's just this cold of Sissy's I've got. Say, Charley, can you just help me get over to your bed so I can look out the window. I'm so tired of being holed up here by myself."

Charley sighed with annoyance, but he did his best to accommodate his brother. Once he was settled on the other bed, Thodie told Charley, "I wrote a note to Aunt Sai, asking her to send me something to amuse me. I said, 'I can't tell you what to send, because it will be more fun if it's a surprise.'" He grinned as he thought about it. Charley was barely listening. "Then I said to her, 'Send yourself if you can. You will do better than anything else.'"[40]

Charley finished arranging the pillows and blankets and said, "Well, it would be nice if Aunt Sai came. We do have jolly times with her. But," Charley continued, "I don't think Ma wants her to come. I heard her say that to Mrs. Miller—something about Aunt Sarah being needed at Belleville. But I don't know why." He shrugged. "Well, I have to run. Greene's waiting. See ya later, Thod."

That evening Angelina stood at the window of her chamber reading Thodie's letter to Aunt Sarah that he had given to his mother to mail. She read it a second time and looked away with anguish as she reflected on his words about wanting Sarah to come. Angelina came to a decision and sat down to begin a letter to Theodore which she would send with another one to Sarah.

> My dearest Theodore,
>   I have seriously considered what you said about it being best for me to have this time alone with my children.[41] But I am under such very trying circumstances that I see no comfort or advantage resulting from it. I think Sarah should come to relieve me as she wishes to do.

In any case, I shall see you and your dear parents in a few days. I will stay here for just a day or two after Sarah arrives. . .

It was early September and at Belleville Theodore was enjoying the fact that the first of the apples had been harvested that afternoon. He went to pick up the post and found Angelina's latest letter. He read it quickly and headed back to the farmhouse. Sarah could see that he looked pensive as he came up to the porch where she was peeling the new apples. He handed Sarah Angelina's separate letter to her. "It appears you are being called to Peterboro after all, Sister." Sarah took the letter with a puzzled look and began to read it to herself.

> Dear Sarah,
>   I am enclosing a note to you from Thodie. He wants very much for you to come. He is feeling ill and despondent again and says only Auntie Sai can cheer him up.

Sarah smiled to herself at Thodie's sentiment. Although she had appreciated the few weeks of quiet time, she missed the children greatly. She read on.

> So, we shall change places after all. I think that is for the best. I will stay till you arrive with Edward on Monday, then return with him on Tuesday. Sissy was pleased with the things you sent, and looks forward to seeing you, too.
>   Please bring the two jackets for the boys, and that warmer dress for Sissy when you come. Tell Bridget I shall have wash to do when I get home.[42]

Sarah put down the letter and glanced over at Theodore who was picking some squash from the garden. She was pleased at the prospect of being with the children, but unhappy about the obvious resentment on Angelina's part. She recognized that the tension between them had been simmering for months, perhaps years. But with Angelina's previous letter it had been put into words. The humidity of the afternoon suddenly seemed oppressive. For a reason she couldn't identify, she felt humiliated, and she had no idea how to shake it off.

The trains to central New York had improved greatly by the early '50's, and it was only a six-hour trip to Syracuse. Although it wasn't particularly comfortable, Sarah loved the chance to sit and watch the rolling hills of central New York pass by. The orchards were weighed down with ripe crimson apples, and the hillsides were a mixture of late summer green and the brilliant yellow and muted orange of early fall. From Syracuse Sarah transferred to a local train, getting off near Cazenovia. Greenleaf Weld's driver, Edward, picked her up in his wagon and took her the last lap to the Smith's home. Thodie, Sissy and Greene swarmed out of the house to greet her. There were abundant hugs all around. Sissy took Aunt Sarah's hand to lead her to the porch while Edward took her baggage inside.

Angelina, who was wearing her bloomers, pointed to a chair on the porch and they both sat down. "You've had a long trip, Sarah. You must be exhausted."

"Ah, but not so long when I'm looking forward to seeing my dear children here!" She took Sissy onto her lap, and Thodie stood close by, eager for his share of attention. Sarah reached into her small travel bag and found a book she had brought and handed it to him. As he reached for it, she saw his scars and said, "Thodie, let me look at that hand of yours! Oh, my! Does it still hurt." Thodie shook his head with a grin. Sarah looked over Sissy's head and said, "Greene, look how you've grown! But where's Charley?" she asked with a puzzled look.

"Well, as you can see, Sissy and Thodie are doing much better," Angelina replied, "but now Charley is sick. Honestly, I can't keep up," she sighed. "A neighbor has invited us for dinner tonight, but Charley isn't well enough." She hesitated, "And I thought you might prefer to stay home with him, since you've been traveling. Nancy is resting, but she'll join you for supper."

A flicker of disappointment passed over Sarah's face at this plan, but she hid it quickly. "Well, certainly. Yes, that's fine. Charley and I will get on very well. And I will be delighted to have some time with Nancy. Gerrit is back in Washington, DC, is he not?"

Angelina nodded. "Yes, and heavily involved with the Free Soilers' efforts to fight the extension of slavery. He has done so much for the slaves, especially for the fugitives.

Then Sarah noticed Angelina's bloomers and studied them approvingly, "And look at you, Nina! Oh, my, you're actually wearing them."

"Well, yes," Angelina said, glad for a shared enthusiasm. "Did I forget to tell you? Lizzie made them for us. It was her invention, you know. There's a pair waiting for you in your room."

"Wonderful! Let me see." Sarah examined the pantaloons and exclaimed, "Oh, how ingenious. I can hardly wait to put them on! But where is Lizzie?"

"She's with her husband in Cazenovia, but she and Gatty are coming back with us this evening. I'll leave tomorrow, so you'll have plenty of time with her then."

Sarah was up early the next morning, eager to don her new bloomers. She had some trouble figuring out how to put them on, and she felt self-conscious as she descended to breakfast. But the children were used to seeing them on Angelina and Lizzie, so they paid no attention.

After breakfast she followed the children outside and was soon engrossed in a game of hide and seek with all of them. As they ran back and forth, Sarah marveled at the freedom of movement she felt with her bloomers. The children were all laughing at the sight of their aunt, her hair falling out of her bonnet. She grabbed Sissy and Thodie into a hug, laughing with them.

Angelina came to the back door and observed the merry scene. "Oh, Nina, we were looking for you to join our game," Sarah said gaily. "These bloomers are delightful—I feel free as a child!"[43]

Angelina's retort was cool and sarcastic, "Well, you must not have looked far. I was in my chamber packing, as I said I would be at breakfast." She was ashamed of her resentment. "It doesn't matter. I had to pack, and now I must leave. It's eleven a.m."

"Already?" Sarah lifted her eyebrows in surprise. "Oh, my." She called out, "Children, come and say good-by to your mother."

The children straggled toward the front yard, clowning as they made their way. Nancy Smith and Lizzie came out of the house to say good-by as well. Angelina shook hands with the older boys. She hugged Sissy and Thodie, but her manner seemed restrained. When Angelina and Sarah exchanged formal kisses, Angelina avoided meeting Sarah's eyes. She climbed on the wagon and took a seat.

They all waved as the wagon rolled down the driveway to the road. Sarah frowned, troubled by the deepening chasm between her and her sister. Increasingly she felt that she could not comprehend what Angelina was thinking or feeling, and it was a new experience for her. Sissy grabbed Sarah's hand, and she welcomed the distraction as she walked back into the house with the children.

I I

Separation

Belleville Fall 1853

THEODORE KNELT BY THE side of Sissy's bed as he finished reading a story to her. He tucked her in and kissed her goodnight. As he came out of the bedroom, he saw Angelina alone at the dining table, looking over their bills and making a list of things needed for the school year.

"May I talk to you, dear?" Angelina asked gravely. "I need to figure out these accounts. We only have eight paying students this year, plus our three children and the two scholarship students who can't afford to pay anything.

"Hmmm. Yes, I guess that is right," Theodore frowned. "Thirteen seems like plenty for us to teach, especially when they are at such different levels. You said Gatty was coming this year, along with Greene. Did we count them?"

Angelina nodded; her brow furrowed.

"Well, Gatty and the other little ones will be with Sarah—at least for part of the day," Theodore mused. "We've let Miss Peabody go until next year when we'll be at our new school at Raritan Bay, so that is one less salary. But you and I will have to manage all the older ones, won't we?"

Angelina shook her head in frustration, "These accounts are in such a muddle! Sarah does them differently than I would. She's lent the school so much money—and here, it looks like she's crossed out our debt to her. But we must pay that back." Theodore shrugged his shoulders as though it mattered little.

"Theodore, she goes around in those old clothes and writes on tiny bits of paper, ekes out a little here and there for her charities. Yet she keeps wanting to mix her finances with ours. It drives me wild, Theo! It's like. . .like she's throwing water into a dried-up riverbed."

"But she wants to help, Nina, my love," Theo said gently. "She wants to feel like she is part of the family. Is that so bad?"

Angelina felt a rush of anger at his denseness. "Don't you see, Theodore—that's exactly the problem. She thinks she can buy her way into our family; into our children's affections!"

"Oh, my dear, is that fair?" Theodore objected. "She *is* a part of our family. And her contribution is from her kindness of heart." He was confounded by his wife's outburst, and added, "Well, the children—that is another matter entirely."

Angelina was annoyed at her husband, and ashamed of her own feelings, so she changed the subject. "Well, we must improve the quality of the food for the boarders you know. Some of them are such little gourmands," Angelina said.

Theodore chuckled. "My dear, let us do our best to muddle through this year. Next year we shall have a real school with a separate dormitory for the students and for our family, and space for more paying students."

"Yes, and we must start out well," Angelina said firmly, "with first-rate housing, and first–rate teaching. With a good reputation we can attract the brightest students from the best families in the area and take in scholarship students as well. You have so much to offer them, Theo!"

Sarah was just returning from a visit to Theodore's sick father who had recently moved close by. She shook out her umbrella on the porch. Theodore and Angelina did not hear her footsteps, but she could hear their conversation from outside.

"As do you, Nina. It will be a wonderful school—a first-rate affair, as you say."

Angelina hesitated, "I don't know what Sarah wishes to do. I think it is better if she doesn't teach, don't you? I mean, if we want to build up our reputation for excellent teaching." Her voice trailed off for a moment, as Theodore looked at her with even greater puzzlement.

"Oh, Theo, I do wish she would just separate her pecuniary affairs completely from ours," Angelina said in a bitter tone. "If she could just establish herself independently, there are so many things she could do on her own. She says she wants to write again." Angelina continued, "I'm just so tired of this constant tension—of never feeling like my home, or my children are truly my own. I'm tired of her total dependence on us!"

On the porch outside, Sarah was frozen in place, unable to grasp or believe what she was hearing. Her chest tightened. Angelina's voice grew more impatient, "You simply don't understand what it is like for me to try to share everything with her—even Charley and Thodie and Sissy. Even you, sometimes!"[44]

Theodore felt a cold fear coming upon him as he pondered her words. He was amazed that the sisters' relationship could have deteriorated this far and chided himself for not having understood it. "Nina, what are you saying? I know it is difficult sometimes, but you can't be serious! What would we do without Sarah? We need her. You need her, the children need her—and I need her to help teach in the school." He looked with consternation at his wife, "And how could we forego her intellectual and spiritual companionship with us?"

Angelina began to sob, but her anger outweighed any penitence she may have felt. Sarah, having overheard the conversation, tiptoed back off the porch and stood desolate in the rain. She understood immediately that things had reached a crisis. However, to spare all of them embarrassment, she noisily announced her return, coughing and pounding her feet on the porch.

Angelina quickly wiped her eyes, with a look of fearful chagrin on her face. She glanced back at Theodore, but he was studying the floor, and she could only assume that Sarah had heard little or nothing of their conversation. Sarah entered and hung her wet cloak and umbrella up in the entryway. She looked over, noticing the accounts lying on the table and smiled wanly.

"Well, I can see you are having a serious talk here," she commented coolly. "Theodore, your father is resting well, and Cornelia says hello, but she seems even more lonely and despondent since your mother died."[45] Theodore nodded wordlessly. "I'm very tired," Sarah declared. "I think I shall just go off to bed." She walked quickly toward the bedroom she shared with Sissy.

Sarah undressed in the dark room, and stood for many minutes by the window, struggling with the decision that was forming in her head. Finally, she lay down, and after a few painful sobs, her unhappiness gave way to an exhausted sleep.

Sarah slept deeply until just before dawn, but she woke with a deep dread of the day ahead. Sissie was still sleeping. Sarah got up quietly and began putting her personal books and notebooks in a satchel. She walked into the front room to start the fire, but the room was still chilly when

Angelina came downstairs. Angelina pulled her shawl around her and looked at Sarah with curiosity.

"You'll be glad to know that I have made my decision, Angelina. Since I am not a 'first-rate' teacher, you can easily replace me at school this year," Sarah said acerbically. "I shall leave soon. I no longer wish to be a burden to you and Theo."

Angelina was stunned. She was embarrassed when she realized that Sarah must have overhead part of the previous night's conversation. But if she was unhappy at Sarah's having heard it, she was not particularly dismayed by the outcome. "But—this is so sudden," she commented at first, then added coldly, "Oh, I see. You were eavesdropping on our conversation last evening."

Sarah was incredulous that Angelina could make her the villain in this piece, and she was roused to an anger that was unfamiliar to her. "Sister, I was doing no such thing! You didn't hear me when I arrived home, and I couldn't help overhearing your conversation from the porch. You made your feelings very plain." She felt a surge of righteousness as she continued. "I only wish you had the courage to speak truthfully to me, face to face, rather than discussing me with Theodore behind my back. This was not loyal nor worthy of you, Angelina."

Angelina raised her voice in defense. Although she could not deny the justice of the accusation, she was certain that she had been wronged as well. "Sarah, do you not realize how many times I have tried to speak to you? How many times have I appealed to you to let me be a mother to my own children, and urged you not mix your finances with ours? You refused to hear it!"

Sarah looked around and said, "Shh, Angelina, we'll wake the children and Theodore. Let's go into the kitchen." Angelina followed Sarah to the kitchen, still glaring at her. Sarah retorted, "Well, now I *do* understand, sister, and I will do as you wish. Do you really feel that my teaching will hurt the reputation of the school? I don't love being a disciplinarian, but I love the children, they learn, and they love me. I don't see how that can be harmful to our school."

Sarah paused and gave Angelina a challenging look as she asked, "I am curious if Theodore shares that view?" Sarah was certain that this conflict was more about Angelina's jealousy of her relationship with the children than about her teaching.

"Well, it doesn't really matter, does it? Since you choose to leave us," Angelina said turning away. "But since you ask, no, I don't think he

fully shares my opinion on that point. But he thinks only of what is convenient, not of the long-term future of our schools." Sarah looked away
again. She was aghast at Angelina's hardness and apparent indifference to
her decision to leave. She had still nurtured a hope that Angelina would
beg her to stay.

When Angelina's silence became unbearable, Sarah said, "Well, then
I will gather the rest of my things. I think it is better that you say nothing
to Theodore or to the children until I am gone. If the children ask, I'll just
say I'm going away for a bit," Sarah added. "You can explain to Theodore."

Angelina looked out toward the back garden and said nothing.
She knew that she did not really want Sarah to change her mind. After
a pause, she turned and looked back at her sister. "So where will you go,
Sarah? Do you have a plan?"

"Oh, I will manage somehow. I—I haven't had time to plan. I'll send
a note ahead to Harriot Hunt and go stay with her for a few days. Then
perhaps I'll visit Anna and our friends in Philadelphia. I may even go to
Washington, D.C. to do some legal research on laws affecting women.
Oh, I will need some cash, however," Sarah admitted reluctantly. "I'm
afraid I only have two dollars in my purse. I suppose you could pay me
some of what the school owes me?"

Angelina was taken aback, but she saw the justice of this. "Well, yes,
of course, Sarah. Uh—how much do you need? It's just a bit sudden. I
don't know how much we have on hand."

"Oh, I can get by with eight or ten dollars until I get to Philadelphia.
I believe there is that much in the cash drawer. I just need train and coach
fare. I'll bring food from here, and perhaps some from Harriot's for the
trip south."

Angelina rummaged in a kitchen drawer for the cash that they kept
on hand. She frowned when she saw how little it was. "Oh, dear. There's
only $12.50 here. Will eight dollars be enough?"

"Yes, it will do. I will get an advance on my annuity when I get to
Philadelphia."

The sisters stared at each other, Sarah searched Angelina's face for
some sign of sorrow or compassion, but she found none. It was as though
she no longer knew the person in front of her. She looked away in bitter
sorrow. "I'll go finish my packing," she turned to go, then turned back to
say, "I will write the children soon and explain my actions as best I can. I
will say nothing of our differences." She sighed deeply, her lips quivering.

Then she muttered under her breathe. "I cannot imagine my life without them."

After the children were up and busy with their day, Sarah went to ask Stephen to take her to the train station. When he came around with the wagon, Sarah handed him her satchel and valise. Stephen loaded them in the wagon and helped her up. Sarah looked back at the children, but the sight of them left her with such an immense grief that she turned away and gazed stonily at the road ahead.

Angelina, who had watched from the door, went back into the house with an exhausted sigh. There was relief in the sigh, but there was an uncomfortable remorse as well. She wondered how she would explain this sudden exodus to Theodore, and she feared his reproach.

Late that day, Sarah deposited her belongings at Harriot Hunt's home in Boston's West End. Since Harriot was still seeing patients, Sarah decided to walk up the hill, past the State House to Boston Common. The walk brought bittersweet memories of Angelina's triumphant days of testimony at the State House fifteen years before. Although she had missed most of it because of sickness, she remembered it as a high point of Angelina's public career. It was also the week, she recalled with pain, that she had received the devastating letter from Theodore. Although she knew she had since earned Theodore's profound admiration and affection, his blunt assessment of her speaking ability still rankled. She pushed down that memory, unwilling to compound her current self-doubt.

She was cheered, however, by the crimson and yellow symphony of trees scattered throughout the Common. Most were still holding onto their leaves. The late afternoon sunshine slid through the unburdened branches and cast long, mottled shadows toward the northeast. Sarah sat on a bench in a quiet corner of the Public Garden where the weeping willows dipped into the pond, their sad, bent boughs matching her own mood.

She found it necessary to take stock. Her assessment was brutal: she was alone, sixty years old and, although still healthy and vigorous, beginning to feel her age. What did she have to show for her life? A poor speaking career, a few pamphlets, and a painfully close attachment to children who were not her own. She sat pondering all this for a long time. Then, unable to imagine a happy future, she rose slowly to walk back to Harriot's home. She made her way listlessly up Beacon Street, over the hill along Bowdoin, and down toward the West End.

Once again after their evening meal, Harriot and Sarah settled by the fireplace in the comfortable parlor. Sarah had some mending in hand. Harriot began apologetically, "Sarah, dear, you have been quiet since you arrived. I'm sorry I've had so little time to spend with you, but my practice has grown large, and it seems to be the time of year when everyone gets sick."

Sarah nodded understandingly, and gave a tight smile, "Of course you are busy, Harriot. I shouldn't have imposed on such short notice. But I had nowhere else—"

Interrupting Sarah gently, Harriot said, "Oh, no, my dear. I didn't mean it that way. I'm so glad you've come. I just feel badly that I had to be gone all day and not get home until supper." Harriet gave her friend a worried look, "Come, tell me what has happened with Angelina. I know some of the tensions between you, but not the whole story."

"I really don't think I can speak of it, Harriot." She paused on the verge of tears; still too hurt and confused to say very much. She looked away, then at her sewing. Harriot waited patiently. Eventually Sarah continued, "I just never thought it would come to this. I knew Angelina was unhappy about the children. She thinks I mean to turn their affection from her, when exactly the opposite is true. In fact, I have always urged them to go to her rather than to me in their troubles." Sarah frowned and shook her head slowly. "But, of course, they were with me a great deal when they were little, because Angelina was often sick, and well, truthfully, she sometimes didn't seem to have much patience for them."

"Yet she resents your closeness to them?" Harriot asked.

Sarah shrugged, "So it appears. Of course, I love the children dearly, but I only wanted to be their loving aunt, not their mother. It has seemed to get better as they have gotten older. There are more things she enjoys doing with them now, but still . . . " Sarah hesitated to say more, but the words kept pouring out. "Well, she always wants to teach them something, to make them better people. Of course, that is wonderful. But sometimes they just need to play. Or be hugged! Oh, look how much I've told you. I don't mean to . . . " Her voice trailed off.

"No, I completely understand, Sarah. You nurtured and comforted them, and she guided and taught them; and the children need both. But somehow it has made it difficult for dear Nina," Harriot observed. "And could it be that both of you would prefer to be doing the other great works that you are so capable of doing?"

"Hmmm. I hadn't thought of it exactly that way, Harriot," Sarah mused. "Yes, certainly, Angelina misses being more publicly active. We both do our bits of charitable work, but nothing like those years just before her marriage. She misses that time, I believe. She had ambitions for a greater public role." Sarah's brow wrinkled with thought. "As for me, well, I have no desire for the limelight or public forums, but I would have liked to keep up my writing. And we have missed so many of the important meetings among the younger women."

"Can you do that now, Sarah?" Harriot asked gently. "What are your plans?"

Sarah's face contorted and she could not hold back her tears. "I feel so ashamed, Harriot! I was so blind not to see how much pain I was causing Nina! And now—look at me! I'm sixty years old, and the movements have passed me by."

Harriot came over to sit next to Sarah on the settee, trying to comfort her. Between her sobs Sarah managed to say, "I don't want to teach. And though the public advocacy for abolition was essential in those years when we lectured, now the real decision-making is in Congress and in the political arena." Sarah wiped her nose with a handkerchief, and dried the tears on her cheeks, adding, "And the younger women have taken hold of the quest for women's rights: Elizabeth, Abby, Lucy Stone, Susan Anthony—and yourself, Harriot."

Harriot chuckled a bit, "Well, I'm not that much younger than you, Sarah. And you know that you and Lucretia have been our inspiration."

Sarah calmed herself and smiled faintly at Harriot. "I appreciate that thought, Harriot. But now I must find a new way to be useful—something that I can do better than others. I'm still trying to figure it out. Perhaps I can do something on women and the law. I can still write."

Then she frowned as she thought about it, "But that will not earn me any money. I can manage only very minimally with my annuity. I've lent much of it to Theodore and Angelina, so the principle has declined. If I need to set up housekeeping on my own, it will be difficult." "But truly, Harriot," Sarah added, "it is not the financial part that makes me anxious—or even finding work to do. It is the prospect of living alone. Already I miss the children desperately. And everyone at Belleville. I have been lonely there at times, but never like this."

Harriot put her arm around Sarah's slight frame and drew her close. Sarah leaned her head into Harriot's shoulder, glad to be comforted. She was embarrassed by her confession, but she felt deeply grateful for Harriot's kindness.

12

On Her Own

Washington, D.C. 1853

SARAH ENTERED THE FRONT door of the boarding house where she was
lodging, stomping her feet and shaking the snow from her cloak. The
three law books she carried slipped out of her hands. She managed to
hold onto the precious copy of Lamartine's *Jeanne d'Arc* that she had been
so happy to find in a nearby bookstore. She picked up two letters on the
mail table that were addressed to her, put them in her volume of *Jeanne
d'Arc,* and then picked up the law books from the floor.

Reaching her sparely furnished bed chamber, she shivered as she
hung up her cloak. She hurried to light a fire in the fireplace. She lit the
oil lamp, and seated herself close to the fire, picking up the letters that
were on her lap.

Two weeks earlier at Belleville, Angelina stood staring into Sarah's
bedroom. She went in, packed the few belongings that Sarah had left behind in a box, and set it in the closet. She went out to find Stephen to help
her take down Sarah's bedstead and carry it out to the barn for storage.
Sissy's small bed remained in one corner. With Bridget's help, Stephen
brought in a small desk and an old armchair to create a study corner for
Sissy and the boys.

When Sissy wandered back to her room from the classroom building, she took a long look at the changes, and ran into the kitchen unable
to hide her distress. Bridget set her on a chair and knelt to speak to her
consolingly. When she had calmed down, Bridget whispered a suggestion

in her ear. Sissy wiped her cheeks, nodded, and looked for some writing paper in a drawer. She sat down at the small desk in her room and began her letter as usual with "Dear Auntie Sai."

Sarah looked over the two envelopes. Although she dreaded it, she began with the letter from Angelina.

> Dear Sarah,
> We hope you are well. School is fully underway now with our twelve students. Mary Anna had to have her breast lanced, and Anna will not leave until she is a great deal better. I know you must have been disappointed not to have found Anna at home in Philadelphia.
> I'm sorry that you regretted our taking down your bedstead. With all the changes I felt it was best to make room for a desk and some of the children's things.[46]

Sarah put the letter down and looked out the window with a resigned sigh. She opened the other envelope addressed to her in Sissy's childish cursive. It warmed her like a hot cup of tea on a frigid morning, and a smile slowly smoothed out the grooves of pain on her face.

> Dear Auntie Sai,
> I hope you are well. I cried so hard when Mama told us you were gone. Why didn't you say good-by? At first, I thought it was just for a week or two. But when Mother told me that you would not be home for Christmas—and perhaps not for a very long time—well, I just couldn't stop crying. Bridget asked me why I was crying so much, and I promised her I would try not to cry anymore.[47]
> I just wish you were here to teach us. It was much more fun than with Miss Peabody. Mon francais es tres mauvais. Tant pis! Next year I will be in the upper school, and mother and father say we will have more students—more girls, I hope! I miss you very much, dear Aunty, and long to see you again. Your loving niece, Sissy

Although she was cheered by Sissy's affectionate letter, Sarah couldn't shake the heaviness in her heart. She contemplated her unfamiliar room for a few minutes, then half-heartedly, reached for one of the law books. She paged through it and found what she wanted: a treatise on domestic law in the United States.

In Belleville, school was again in session after a short Christmas break. Angelina sat in a corner of the large front room, correcting a pile of student copybooks. Theodore held court at the other end of the room, vigorously chatting with several of the older boys about the meaning of a passage from *The Tempest* that they were reading. Thodie sat by himself at the dining table, sketching rather aimlessly and looking depressed and lonely. Gatty came by and teased him playfully, but Thodie pushed him away moodily.

After her schoolwork was completed and the children were settled down for the night, Angelina sat at the writing desk in their bedroom. The house suddenly seemed very quiet. Angelina looked over at Theodore reading in an armchair nearby. She raised her pen to begin another letter, "My dear Sarah. . ." After the usual greetings and family news, Angelina wrote,

> I'm glad that Gatty wrote to you, although I do not know what he meant about the rooms being cold and the fire always going out. We've never had so little vexation or complaints from the scholars as we have had this year. All seem to be doing well, and as to myself, it is certainly the happiest winter I have had since my marriage.

Angelina sealed her letter and put away her writing things. She put on her nightgown and sat on the edge of their bed while she took down her hair. Theodore looked up from his reading and spoke softly to her. "Have you been writing to Sister Sarah, my love? She must be so happy to get your letters, and news of the children and all."

Angelina looked away, feeling a moment of remorse. "I'm afraid I don't really have much to say to her these days."

Theodore looked at her quizzically. "Is that so? Hmmm. Well, it seems that you have needed this time apart."

"Theo, I don't know if you can truly understand what a relief it has been to me—not having the resentment and tension, the constant interference! I know it is partly my own fault but . . . "

Theodore lay aside his book and gave her his full attention. "Yes, I try to comprehend your feelings my dear, but sometimes—well, I do miss Sarah's companionship, and so many things great and small that she did for us." Theodore bit his lower lip, not sure what line to take. "The children have adjusted quite well, but Thodie seems dejected at times. And

Sissy—well, one day she's happy as a lark, and the next day she's moping around like Thodie. Perhaps we can . . . "

Angelina interrupted Theodore quickly, and spoke sharply but with real anguish, "Theo, I'm not ready to talk about this yet. I don't know what to think. I am struggling; but the thought of her returning—I just can't imagine it."

Theodore rose and came over to sit next to her on the bed. He wrapped his arms around Angelina's waist. She started to turn away, but he nuzzled her neck, and she relaxed a little. "Let's go to bed, my darling," Theodore suggested. "It will come clear in God's time."

New York, 1854

Sarah remained in Washington, D.C. through the fall but after Christmas she moved to New York City where she found an inexpensive boarding house in the less densely settled area just north of Gramercy Park. She liked the quiet there, although it was a long walk to the city center in Lower Manhattan. As she sat with Angelina's latest letter in front of her, her face crumpled as she read the sentence describing Angelina's happiness since her departure. She paused in her reading, looking away to regain her composure. But she forced herself to read on.

> . . . All seem to be doing well, and as to myself, it is certainly the happiest winter I have had since my marriage. I shall feel young again if my mind can be relieved of the heavy load it has had to carry in secret, silent bitterness for many years . . .

Sarah cried out in indignation at this. "Oh, Nina, could you not have spared me such cruel remarks!" She sunk into her chair "How could you more plainly say what a horrible burden I have been to you!" she thought.

After a few minutes of self-pity, Sarah roused herself and walked to her window, looking past the city's edge to the snow-covered fields up north. There were a few fences in her view. It brought to mind her journey through the snow and over the fences after the sleigh accident. Sarah knew she was angry—perhaps more so than ever before in her life—but the anger stirred her and jolted her to a realization. She could no longer be a passive onlooker to her life, nor could she blame her sister. It was time to face forward and take steps, although she could barely see where she was going.

The following month it seemed that spring had suddenly arrived. New York's Washington Square was alive with early blossoms and tiny, flittering birds. Young people had brought out blankets and rugs to picnic on the grass. Sarah felt a rush of contentment as she walked through the square enjoying the light and sun and warmth after what had seemed like an unendingly bleak winter. Sarah made her way to a newsstand near the corner where Fifth Avenue ran into the Square. She read the main headline: "Wisconsin Supreme Court Declares Fugitive Slave Law Unconstitutional"[48] and hurriedly gave a few coins to the newsboy.

She found a bench near the entrance to the Square in the shadow of the red brick Georgian homes that were being built on the Square's north edge. Sarah read the lead story eagerly and with great satisfaction. But her eye was caught by a smaller headline at the bottom of the page: "Over 300,000 copies of *Uncle Tom's Cabin* Sold Last Year," it declared. Sarah smiled broadly at this. "Oh, Mrs. Stowe, well-done!" She knew that Harriet Stowe had spent hours poring over a copy of *American Slavery as It Is,* using material in it as background for her book.

Sarah took a letter from a publisher friend out of her pocket and re-read it. Folding it up and replacing it in her pocket, she rose from the bench with new energy. She remembered seeing a stationery store up Fifth Avenue and she walked there quickly. She wanted three notebooks, but as she counted her money, she decided to buy just two. If she were careful, it would be enough.

She continued up Fifth Avenue and then turned down Twenty-Third Street to reach her boarding house. She walked upstairs to her chilly room, lit a fire, and immediately sat down at the old, heavily scratched desk. She situated one of her fresh notebooks under her writing hand. With her copy of Lamartine's *Jeanne d'Arc* opened to the first full page, she arranged her French dictionary in front of her. As she began to translate, she wrote rapidly at first, but slowed down as she searched for unfamiliar words in her dictionary.[49] Many hours later, having missed the boardinghouse supper, she closed her notebook for the day, sat back in her chair, and smiled with a satisfied air.

13

Return

Belleville April 1854

ANGELINA HAD A HARD time concentrating on her students' essays, so she picked up a shawl and asked Sissy to join her for a walk out toward the pond and the corn fields. The fruit trees near the house were in blossom and some were beginning to send out their fresh green or maroon leaves. They chatted about Sissy's schoolwork and friends, but soon the ten-year old tired of the sedate walk. She asked if she could join her classmates who were playing a ballgame in a field nearby.

Angelina's prolapsed uterus still prevented her from walking with complete comfort, but she had designed an undergarment that helped her to go about her normal activities with minimal awkwardness. She tired easily but she had learned to pace herself better, and although it went against her grain, she now accepted help from others for tasks that proved beyond her strength.

Left to herself, Angelina surveyed the farm, the school building, and their home with a sigh of contentment. As she walked, her head was full of pros and cons, and her heart was equally uncertain. The sun went down and strangely, the dusk seemed to bring some clarity. Angelina went into the house and stopped to gaze into the room that she still thought of as Sarah's old bedroom. A few of Sissy's playthings lay on the floor, but otherwise it seemed empty.

Theodore washed up from his late afternoon chores and came into the house through the back door. He walked over to his wife and stood quietly behind her. She turned and spoke a few words to him. He looked at her and nodded solemnly. His face revealed his approval and gratitude at her decision, and he wrapped his arms around her tenderly.

After supper with the noisy gaggle of school children, Angelina excused herself and went immediately up to their chamber. She sat down at her writing desk to compose her letter.

> My own dearest sister,
>   I thank you from my heart for reading my long letter; it cost me a great deal to write it. I felt that I had had deep-rooted feelings which you did not suspect, and yet which it seemed to me you ought to know. I felt self-condemned, mean, and hypocritical in concealing them from the one who most had a right to know them.
>   The conflicts through which I have passed have been terrible, but I do not blame you. Somehow, I finally feel that my heart is changing. We shall still have our differences but with God's grace, we can find our way together.
>   We miss you terribly, dear Sai, and we all feel this to be your right place—the home of your heart. We want you to share in our new endeavor at Raritan Bay. Please, dear, agree to come back to our home—to *your* home. Your Nina[50]

It was late afternoon about a week later that Sarah found Angelina's letter waiting for her when she arrived at the boardinghouse after an outing. She took it to her room, sat down, and read it carefully by the fading daylight from the window. She stood up with the letter in her hand and walked around the small space looking troubled and thoughtful.[51]

Sarah glanced at the notebooks with the translation of *Jeanne d'Arc*. She knew that if she left off now, it could be years before she would be free to work on it again. But she smiled quietly as the full import of the invitation to return dawned on her. She went to supper in a jubilant mood and her fellow boarders were amused at how uncharacteristically gay and talkative she seemed. After supper she set aside her *Joan of Arc* notebooks and took out a piece of writing paper. She stared at it for several minutes with her pen poised above the paper before she began to write.

> Dear Nina,
>   I read your letter with both grief and joy. I have already said how much I regret and suffer from the pain and tension I have caused you. I need to know myself better, but I find that I need you and Theodore and the children to learn the lessons I must learn.

So, yes, of course, I will hurry home. I have been overwhelmed with sadness at the separation from the children who
have been the brightness of my life these last ten years. Without
our family and the children, existence has no charm for me.[52]

I suspect there is much in both our hearts that we must confess to each other.

Your loving sister, Sarah

By the time Sarah returned to Belleville in May 1854, plans were
well underway for the Weld family to join the Raritan Bay Union, a uto-
pian community that had recruited Theodore to organize and head a
progressive school on its site. The Union was located near the bay south
of Perth Amboy, New Jersey. The school would be known as Eagleswood.

Angelina thought that visiting the site would afford Sarah some
reassurance about the move, as well as give them some time together.
After a brief discussion, Sarah agreed. They checked the train timetable
and arranged to make the thirty-mile trip from Belleville. The sisters arrived in the afternoon on a clear spring day. They were both wearing their
bloomers for the adventure.

Angelina and Sarah climbed up a small rise next to the new stone
school building under construction.[53] They looked out at the expansive
view of the beach and the bay below them. Angelina took Sarah's hand
and squeezed it happily. "Isn't this a magnificent site, Sarah? Look, there's
a pier down there that just needs a little repair work to be safe. Theodore
says he will insist that all the students— girls and boys—learn to swim,
and perhaps to row as well."

Sarah continued to have some anxieties about their move. But nevertheless, she smiled quietly. She liked the idea of the girls learning to row,
and she sincerely wanted to share Angelina's enthusiasm. "It *is* beautiful,
Nina. I couldn't agree more. Sarah remained thoughtful for several moments. Since her return, she was determined to express her fears as well
as her appreciation of their new situation, so she added, "To be honest, I
find it hard to imagine living in that large— well, that hotel." She gestured
back at the stone construction that would house several families of the
Raritan Bay Union: themselves, other teachers, and dozens of students.

"You know how much I treasure the privacy of our own little family
circle." She paused stifling a sigh as she said, "But the children are growing up, and everything will change. I can see that we must all adjust to
that." Angelina took Sarah's arm silently as they strolled. It was a warm

afternoon, and the sisters walked to a cluster of rocks near the bay, where they could sit down.

"Oh, thank heaven for these bloomers," Angelina proclaimed. Sarah chuckled as the two of them arranged their pantaloons. Nina reflected on Sarah's last remark, "Yes, things are changing, and I know that leaving Belleville is a disappointment for you, Sarah. I feel sad that we ask so much of you—to embrace the dream that Theodore and I have, which is not really your dream."

"But it is what I am choosing, Nina. I chose to return to your family—to our family. I know I need my own pursuits as well, but I must find a way to do those within our family circle. I simply cannot live that lonely life of this past winter. I confess my weakness, but I should perish without the company of you and Theodore and our dear children." Sarah realized suddenly that her last phrase might offend, and she apologized. "Your children, Nina—I do know that they are yours and Theodore's. But you must forgive me, bear with me, for loving them so much."

She looked appealingly at Angelina. She felt so vulnerable in confessing this. Angelina responded hesitantly. "Sarah, there are times when I feel humbled in the dust, because I never have been willing to share my blessings with you equally. When I look at all the sorrow and disappointment you have met with in life, I feel ashamed and confounded at my ingratitude."

Sarah took Angelina's hand and looked out over the bay with some anxiety and sadness in her voice, "I blame myself, Nina. I know I have— well, sometimes expected too much, I suppose. It has been hard to know the boundaries."

"Oh Sai, I do not feel that you need any self-defense. You never meant to do me any wrong. You have only lived out your own beautiful and generous nature." Sarah listened quietly, want to give Nina the chance to speak frankly. "But I couldn't surmount my feelings," Angelina continued. "All I could see was that it seemed unnatural that a wife and mother should ever be willing to share the affection of her dearest ones with any other human being. My heart refused its assent. It was impossible for me to see things from your perspective."

"Now I recognize that these feelings were ungenerous and, given how much we depended on you, very unfair. Oh, how many nights I laid awake and prayed that God would give me a right heart." Angelina paused in her long speech, and looked up, "I am weary of this conflict which has lasted fifteen years. Do you think we can truly bring it to an end, Sarah?"

Sarah looked directly at Angelina, searching her face for signs that she was sincere about repairing their relationship. Seeing the earnest humility in Angelina's eyes, she responded with clear-eyed truthfulness, "We shall struggle on, Nina. Our painful feelings may not be healed immediately. But perhaps as we turn our efforts outward again, to the larger world, we will once more find those common hopes that have made our bonds deeper than those of blood. And those, I suspect, will make our differences dwarf in comparison." Sarah smiled at the prospect.

Angelina nodded her head in solemn agreement. "Yes, you have said it well, Sai, as always." She was silent for a moment, then thinking about Sarah's last remark, she asked, "So you have a new project, I believe? Tell me what it is."

"I am working on a translation of Lamartine's *Jeanne d'Arc*. It is a labor of love that I have long had in mind. I shall try to find time to continue it amidst my teaching duties here." Sarah rearranged her bloomers and looked at the clouds gathering over the bay. "Theodore wants me to teach French again here at Eagleswood. So, these two endeavors will work well together."

"And there is so much to discuss with you and Theodore—about the fugitive slave situation, the call for emancipation, and what is going on among our women friends," Sarah went on, feeling a new enthusiasm. "But most worrying of all, whether war is now inevitable." Angelina shivered as the sun set behind them, and as she and her sister contemplated the latter possibility.

That evening, the two women left the house after dining with their hosts. They again walked down toward the bay under a moonless night sky that was startlingly clear. "Sarah, look at the stars tonight," Angelina said. "Brrr. It's chilly out. But so magnificent! Can you imagine? What is it all for? It is so superfluous to us, and yet so wondrous."

Sarah wrapped her shawl around her tightly. She was still somewhat preoccupied with a suppertime conversation on the plight of fugitive slaves. Angelina continued to muse. "You know Theodore has given me some science monographs to read—about astronomy and about that man, Darwin. It is all so strange." Her voice trailed off, sounding troubled.

"Yes, I read some articles about these new theories when I was away," Sarah's interest was engaged. "I find it both disturbing and strangely fascinating."

"Do you think it is possible the world is more than 6,000 years old—as we have been told by the scholars of sacred scripture?" Angelina frowned.

"Well, Nina, you know what I think of those so-called 'scripture scholars.'" They looked at each other and laughed heartily, like naughty schoolgirls. Sarah looked up and studied the wide swath of sky visible between the arching trees on the perimeter of the property. "But yes— these stars." She bent her head to one side to see them better. "We are so small, and they are so far away. They say they are like our sun, only thousands—maybe millions of miles farther away. If the universe is so vast—well then, perhaps time is vast as well."

"Does it frighten you?" Angelina asked. "It frightens me sometimes. Where are our certain truths, then, Sarah? What can we stand on? Our lives here on this earth are so short and even you and I—we are not getting younger. I'm so tired sometimes, and discouraged, and I wonder. . . Oh, Sarah, my doubts are so terrible. I wonder if there is a purpose. I wonder, even—oh, I tremble to say it—even if there is eternal life awaiting us."

Angelina looked at Sarah with tears coming to her eyes, "I know— well, certainly I *believe*—that we are living the best we can, Sarah, but does it matter? Finally, does it matter?"

Sarah heard the anguish in Nina's voice and took her sister's arm, leaning into her shoulder, and gently rubbing the back of her hand. "Yet on a night like this I feel so much awe and peace," Angelina confessed, smiling as she wiped away her tears. "Yes, I am afraid. But it all seems right. The world seems, well, so much larger than our cares."

"Yes, my dear, I think I know how you feel. I had so much time to think and read and be alone this past year," Sarah paused. "I was very lonely at times." She gazed down at the bay, away from Angelina, trying to hide the pain she still felt.

"Oh, Sarah—I'm so sorry for all that. How could I . . . ?"

Sarah interrupted her gently, "No, no, Nina, it wasn't your fault. And what I was going to say was that despite the loneliness, I learned so much. I learned to let go of certainty." She looked at Angelina to see if she understood, then continued to explain as best she could. "Nina, I'm just so grateful. We have been given this life—this conscious life—to seek to understand and to love this world and each other. Last year—well, after all the sadness— I was so deeply touched by the beauty and variety and immensity of the world, and by the kindness of so many people."

Angelina glanced at Sarah with grudging admiration, and said, "You have a gift for seeing the good in people, Sarah."

Sarah continued, "I still feel great sadness and—yes, guilt—for our enslaved brethren. And I feel dread and horror at the—the violent upheaval—that is likely to come before slaves can claim freedom and justice. I worry about our Charleston family, both for their safety and for their guilt. Yet, amid all of that I have felt peace as well. What a gift we have been given, Nina! To live consciously, to do justice as much as we can, and to love each other mercifully, as Micah the prophet said."[54]

"And to walk humbly with our God," Angelina finished the scriptural reference, nodding her assent. "But Sarah, tell me. You haven't really answered my question. Sometimes I wonder. Do you—do you still believe in God and in our Holy Redeemer?" She spoke with a quaking fear that her doubts about Sarah's true beliefs would be confirmed, and that her own doubts would be doubled.

Sarah paused for a long moment as she contemplated her answer. She turned and looked at Angelina, taking both her hands, and giving her an amused look, "Oh, my dear sister! You are my godchild—but I do believe you are the one worried for *my* soul!"

"But let me answer your question. Yes, I do, Nina. I do believe. But not in the God of our childhood or the God of those clerics who condemned our speaking and had the audacity to tell us to stay in 'our place'!" Sarah allowed herself an unladylike snort in disgust. I do believe in the God who has given us this immense sky and ocean and life itself, however it has come to be, whether over millions of years or in six thousand." Her lips turned up in a tiny smile, and she said, "Does that matter, I ask you?"

Sarah and Angelina fell silent as they found their way down the dark path to the smooth rocks near the bay. They sat themselves on the rocks as they had in the afternoon. Sarah frowned as she struggled to form her words as truthfully and simply as she could. "Nina, you have heard me say that I am convinced that there is one truth—and that ultimately Scripture and science must converge upon it. We are discovering it, year by year, don't you think?" she asked rhetorically.

"But I do believe that the Spirit still comes upon us so that 'our sons and daughters shall prophesy' as Joel foretold. I have been doubting and unfaithful in so many ways, Nina. But when I have trusted in that Spirit— in that inner light guiding us with a 'still, small voice'—then I have not gone wrong, at least not for long." She paused and added, "And that gives me serenity."

"Oh, Sarah, I envy you that. You always get there before me. I am still unsure, but I sense that you are right. And what you said gives me peace as well, and strength."

Angelina sneezed from the chilly evening air and hugged her arms across her body as she shivered. "Come, my dear, let us go in before we catch pneumonia." Sarah hated leaving the stars and the bay, but she nodded, knowing there would be many other such nights ahead of them. It was a lovely place, she conceded to herself. They retraced their steps back to the house, arms around each other's waists for warmth and comfort.

14

A Picnic

Eagleswood School July 4, 1861

ALTHOUGH THE IDEALISTIC RARITAN Bay Union survived for several years after Sarah and the Weld family joined it, it was the Eagleswood School under Theodore's direction that grew and thrived. In its idyllic setting at the south end of Perth Amboy, one could look across the river to South Amboy or across the bay to the forested South Point of Staten Island. The large lawn stretched from the old mansion and the new school structure to the beach and a reconstructed pier.

On the morning of the Fourth of July, a bevy of students were busy decorating an outdoor stage with red, white and blue streamers. Other students cleaned up a large barge and some smaller boats on the beach, while a third group of younger students set up chairs in front of the stage and carried tables onto the expanse of grass between the school building and the bay. The thirty or so students were all between 12 and 17 years of age. It was nearly an even mix of girls and boys, and there were several colored students among them.

Theodore wandered out to watch the preparations which seemed to be going smoothly with very little intervention from the teaching staff. With him was a British journalist from *Fraser's Magazine* and several others who had been invited to come over from New York.[55] They were there to observe and enjoy this patriotic celebration by the young scholars, just as the country was about to break apart its body in the battle for its soul.

Thodie was not among the busy students.[56] He was laying listlessly in his narrow bed with a few neglected books sitting nearby on a bedside table. The room was somewhat darkened with heavy curtains. Sarah entered the room quietly, carrying a tray with coffee and a bowl of corn mush. Thodie looked up at her blankly. "Thodie, dear. I thought you might still be asleep." The young man looked away indifferently. There was very little evidence of the sweet, mischievous boy that he had been seven years earlier. He shook his head and coughed a bit. "No, I'm awake, Aunt Sai. What's all the racket out there?"

"Happy Fourth of July," Sarah said cheerfully as she took a seat near his bed, balancing the tray of food on her lap. "Did you forget? The students are getting things ready for the festivities."

"Oh." Thodie stared at his feet that he had disentangled from his blankets. He slid up a bit on his pillow, although he remained more lying down than sitting up.

"Here's some breakfast for you. Can I help you eat?" Thodie looked away. He showed no interest in the food, nor did he thank Sarah for bringing it. Sarah spoke very tentatively, "We thought you might want to come out for the speeches—or at least for the boat races later?" She managed a weak smile, "It's a lovely day—I don't think you'd be too cold—or too warm."

"No."

Sarah moved some of the books and set the tray down on the nightstand. She reached over to gently caress Thodie's forehead, but he turned his head away. "Your mother and father hoped . . . " Sarah's voice faded.

Thodie was annoyed, "Tell mother and father to go jump in the . . . " But seeing Sarah's distress, he regretted it. He shrugged penitently, and said, "No. Sorry, Auntie. Just tell them I'm too tired. And I don't like all the flies." Thodie managed a wan smile at Sarah. Sarah knew better than to push him, but she sighed quietly.

"Yes, I know—I'm such a disappointment," Thodie glared at the wall.[57]

"Oh, darling boy, of course not! We just want—well, you are sick, and we just want you to be better." Sarah got up and looked at Thodie with a neutral expression. "I'll go now. But I'll check in later to see how you are, or if you've changed your mind." She leaned over and gave Thodie a kiss on the brow. He looked at her with bemused tolerance as she left the room.

Shortly before noon, the thirty-some students, half-dozen faculty members and about a dozen parents and other guests seated themselves in front of the brightly decorated stage to listen to the student recitations and speeches. Theodore and Angelina sat in the front row, while Sarah sat a few rows back with Sissy and Charley who were home from school in Boston for a summer visit. Lizzie Smith Miller and her husband, Charles Miller looked on proudly as their son, Gatty, rose to speak from the podium. His speech weighed the evils of violent conflict against the merits of a just and necessary war. His measured tone seemed beyond his sixteen years. Lizzie thought about how proud her father, Gerrit, would be of his grandson and namesake, and she wished he had come with them. Gatty concluded,

> So, I leave you with this thought. War is a great evil, and we know that our northern brothers are dying on the battlefield and in the hospitals. We know, too, that our southern compatriots who have strayed from the fold of our Republic—are losing their lives daily. So, what is this war for? How can any outcome be a victory?
>
> Only the liberation of four million slaves can justify a war of such horrible proportions. Their lives, their chance to live as free, industrious, and dignified human beings, only this—not any abstract notion of the "union"—can justify this war. And to this cause, we will dedicate our voices and our lives![58]

There was enthusiastic applause as the young orator ended his address. Theodore stood up from his seat in the front row and addressed Gatty. "Well done! Well done, young Gerrit. We applaud your fervor as well as your eloquence!"

He turned to face the audience, and added, "But now, as is our custom, you must answer questions from your fellow students. This is the true Socratic method by which we may all learn. So—first question?"

Theodore looked around, and after a moment a young woman of about fourteen years raised her hand timidly. Theodore nodded at her, saying, "Yes, Ellie, bravo!" And she stood to ask her question.

"Gatty, we are indeed impressed with your rhetoric," she said hesitantly, "but what makes you think that this war will affect slavery when President Lincoln and his cabinet have repeatedly said that it is a war for the Union alone, and will not affect the condition of the slaves?" She sat down hurriedly, as students around her nodded their agreement with her question, although others frowned at it.

Gatty was enjoying himself and ready with an answer.

> An astute question! Let us recall that first war of Independence whose outcome we celebrate today. It began as a war over the tax

on tea! But that war over tea grew quickly towards its true goal, the right of citizens to be represented. And that led to the right of our citizenry to our independence from that oppressive and tyrannical rule of England over its colonies. No appeasement on the question of tea would have stopped our revolutionary forefathers from fighting for their ultimate goal.

We hear much about how the coming together of those states was cemented by the blood of our forefathers. But what, I ask you, will be cemented by the blood of this generation? Will it only be to regain the broken walls of Fort Sumter?

The audience grew serious and hushed once again as their fellow student laid out his case eloquently.

Will it only be to return to the Union those states which continue to abuse and enslave our negro brothers and sisters? Will it return to the Union, the territories that tar and feather colored freedmen?

Are we giving up the best blood in our land that our flag may again unfurl over the lash, the chain, and the auction block? Already the blood that has been shed leads men to avow that "this war will end slavery." This prediction is growing from a wish to a resolve. This war *shall* end slavery!

Many in the audience, including Ellie, nodded their heads in approval, and there was further applause. Gatty stood aside from the podium, trying to maintain a solemn modesty as he looked out toward his beaming parents.

Sissy Weld moved to the front of the assembly where a pianoforte had, with great difficulty, been placed. Angelina shepherded two students into position to march up the center aisle bearing the American flag and a New Jersey flag. Just before she sat down at the piano, Sissy gestured for the audience to stand. She led them in singing *Viva L'America*[59] as she accompanied them on the piano:

Noble Republic! Happiest of lands,
Foremost of nations, Columbia stands;
Freedom's proud banner floats in the skies,
Where shouts of Liberty daily arise.
"United we stand, divided we fall,"
Union forever—freedom to all.
Chorus
Throughout the world our motto shall be
Viva l'America, home of the free.[60]

The student body and guests joined loudly in the second verse and a repeat of the chorus. As it ended, they began to break into happy groups of students, parents, teachers and guests, with Angelina, Sarah, Charles and Sissy Weld among them.

Theodore walked up to shake hands with Gatty and the two flag-bearers. He stayed to chat with Lizzie and Charles Miller who had come forward to hug their son. Sarah Douglass, her hair now streaked with white and gray, had come up from Philadelphia for this celebration, and she had brought with her another young colored woman, Charlotte Forten, whose family she knew in Philadelphia. Sarah came over to greet her friend, and to meet the young woman.

"Oh, I'm so glad you came, Sarah!" Sarah Grimké exclaimed as she kissed her friend on both cheeks. She stood back and said, "And this must be Charlotte Forten. I'm delighted to meet you. I knew your mother, you know, God bless her, and your aunts, Harriet and Margaretta, when we were living in Philadelphia. I believe you were a wee one—or perhaps not born yet?"

Charlotte looked pleased, and said, "Miss Grimké, I'm so honored to meet you. Please, call me Lottie, though. That is what my family and friends call me."

Several students came up to ask for direction from Sarah about the next events, but before she excused herself, she said, "Lottie, I heard you were a teacher up in Salem. We have so much to talk about! Sarah, why don't you two join Sissy and the others. I'll be there as soon as I can."

The students were watching a regatta of large row boats that had gathered on the Staten Island side of the bay. They focused on one boat that was heading back toward Eagleswood. As it drew near, those on the shore could see the group of young women rowers dressed in long blouse-like tops which came to their knees. Below their tops they wore brightly colored stockings and boots. The six Eagleswood girls had set out early that morning to join the July Fourth Regatta at Staten Island, and they were headed home.

As the boat approached the Eagleswood pier most of the students had gathered near the beach to greet their return. A group of boys had donned their bathing costumes right after the ceremonies, and they plunged into the chilly water and swam out to meet the boat, escorting it for the last ten yards to the dock. The girls pulled in their oars and waved their hats to the crowd of their peers as they drew near. One of them held up a large red ribbon they had won at the Regatta. The girls debarked with much gaiety, smoothing their costumes and shaking water out of their boots. The boys got out of the water and ran into the building to dry off.

Within minutes the boys had arrived back on the lawn with dry clothes and wet hair. The rowing crew had also hurried to dry off and change into their best summer dresses. They soon joined the other students in the line to get food.

Sissy had taken her place at a table with Lizzie Smith Miller, Sarah Douglass and Lottie Forten. Aunt Sarah had made sure they were served plentiful portions, and she joined them once the serving was well underway. At another table nearby, Angelina and Theodore sat with Charley Weld and Lizzie's husband, Charles Miller.

Lottie was in intense conversation with Lizzie and Sarah Douglass. She told them of her hopes to travel to the Sea Islands of South Carolina to teach the former slaves abandoned by their white owners. Lizzie was fascinated with their story and wanted to know more.

As a pause in the conversation, Aunt Sarah turned to speak quietly with her niece. "Are you enjoying your music lessons, Sissy? And how do you find Cambridge? You know we miss you so much here, my dear!"

"Oh, I love it, Auntie Sai! I miss you all, of course, but Charley is close by. We see each other about once a week." She gave her aunt a confiding smile and said, "I've begun volunteering with the Massachusetts Women's Suffrage Association, just helping them get organized. But I love the other women there, especially Lucy Stone and Julia Howe. And I do like being on my own!" she added.

Lizzie overheard this remark and turned to grin at Sissy. "I can't believe you are on your own already, Miss Sissy! I must say I'm quite dismayed to hear Gatty tell me how excited he is to be "on his own" at Harvard next fall. You must keep an eye on him, too, Sissy. You are the elder by a year, and you know how boys are."

"I shall, Mrs. Miller," Sissy replied, flattered to be considered the responsible elder. "Oh, Auntie Sai, I wanted to thank you for sending me *Les Misérables*. I have enjoyed it so much, although it is a struggle at times. I'm reading it in French with Monsieur, my tutor. He corrects my abominable pronunciation."

"Your mother and I began *The Hunchback of Notre Dame* a few weeks ago," Sarah said. "Such a tale! Your mother couldn't finish it."

Lottie jumped into the conversation eagerly, "Yes, Hugo can draw such horrific characters, can't he? And also, heroic ones. I do think he has a wonderful sense of the human conscience and human devotion and affection. Jean Valjean embodies those qualities so profoundly."

"I very much agree," Sarah rejoined. "But I don't believe he can sound the depths of a woman's heart. I don't believe a man could ever have written *Jane Eyre*, for instance.[61]

Lottie nodded thoughtfully, "But could Miss Brontë really understand Rochester's mind, do you think?"

Sarah looked at her appreciatively. "No, maybe not entirely. But perhaps as much as Shakespeare understood Portia." They all chuckled, and Sissy said to the group, "Well, Portia is Aunt Sai's favorite Shakespearean character, so perhaps it is not a fair comparison."

Sissy smiled as she stood up from the table. "So good to see you, Mrs. Miller and Miss Douglass! And very happy to meet you, Miss Forten," she said warmly as she departed to seek out her friends among the older students.

Sarah Douglass stood up as well and said, "Sarah, I need a walk, and I'd like to show Lottie around the grounds. Will you excuse us for a few minutes?"

Sarah answered, "Of course, dear. We'll visit more later."

She turned to Lizzie, glad to have some private time with her. "Lizzie, I want so much to come and visit your mother and father in Peterboro. How is your father doing now? He was so ill after the failure of John Brown's raid. I believe he was nearly in despair. What did you think?"

Lizzie bent her head and let out a deep sigh. Sarah saw that her eyes were beginning to tear up. "I don't like to talk about it, Sarah. I don't really know what his involvement was. They say he knew about the raid ahead of time and helped with money.[62] I don't believe that. But truthfully, I don't know. I do know that when they hung John Brown, Mr. Hazlett, Mr. Stevens and the others, my father went out of his mind. I believe he was ready to harm himself if my mother and my husband hadn't taken him to the asylum." Lizzie's tears were falling generously onto the table, and she did little to stop them.

Sarah put a hand on Lizzie's gently. "Yes, I knew a little from your mother about how difficult it was—for all of you." She hesitated and then asked hopefully, "But he is much better now, isn't he? He is such a generous and courageous man."

"Yes, he's doing better. But I don't think he believes he is courageous. He wanted to come today, especially to hear Gatty's speech." She smiled with motherly pride as she looked over at Gatty with a group of students around him. "Well, Father didn't say this, but I think he couldn't quite face it, knowing that Albert Hazlett and Aaron Stevens' bodies had been brought here to Eagleswood for burial. It was just such a dark episode for him. For all of us. But now that the war is underway, he feels hopeful for the slave again. So, he's back in politics wholeheartedly, supporting Lincoln, but using all his powers to pressure the President into emancipating the slaves."

Sarah's face brightened, "Angelina and I have been circulating a petition for Emancipation. So far everyone we have asked has agreed to sign it. I believe we have nearly a thousand signatures already, just in our neighborhood here. But perhaps it will happen before we even have a chance to present it," she said in a mood of stubborn optimism.

Lizzie confirmed Sarah's hopes. "Yes, Father says it could come as soon as this fall—what we have worked for and hoped for—for so long. Especially you and Angelina and Theodore." Lizzie was thoughtful for a moment, summoning up her resolve. "Sarah, I would like to go visit the graves of John Brown's companions. Can you show them to me? And after that I'd like to go see Thodie. Is he any better? It makes me so sad," her voice trailed off.

Sarah smiled gently as she rose. "Of course, dear." Lizzie got up and Sarah took Lizzie's arm. The two women walked toward a small grove a short distance from the school building where two headstones marked the grave of the two men hanged along with John Brown.

At the next picnic table, Theodore's raspy voice was becoming exasperated. "But Charles, you cannot be serious about objecting to Harvard allowing army recruitment on your campus! Now that we have finally engaged in the war that may definitively end slavery, why would you not wish to encourage your fellow students to join the Union Army?"

Charles responded with equal heat, "Father, I am astonished that you do not regard my view on this matter as correct. And in fact, the only view consistent with honor. To serve in this army is to support this government and its right to force men to engage in warfare. This is a position which you have long taught me no government has the right to exercise over the conscience of its citizens."

Theodore was nearly roaring now. The students and guests nearby look over to see what could arouse this man they knew as their wise and genial head of school who, despite the passionate rhetoric of his younger years, usually seemed the epitome of calm, rational discourse.

"But Charles," he thundered, "this is the war to end slavery. This is the war to restore the conscience of our nation; this is an awakening, a religious revival of our nation, better deserving of this name than anything before it! Have you gone mad? Have your southern friends at Harvard utterly destroyed your reason?"

Angelina pressed her hand on Theodore's arm to calm him down. Charles looked away angrily and retorted, "Whatever my opinion is, you will attribute it to some mental disorder, Father. But it is a delusion on your part to deny the rightness of my view." Charles was embarrassed by the public setting of their argument, and he lowered his voice. "Were you in my place, I know you would scorn to receive military instruction from a government which you did not support. Particularly if that government were to forcibly require you to act against your own conscience."

Angelina disliked taking sides between her husband and her son, but she was as appalled as Theodore by Charles' stance towards the war. She spoke quietly but with equal fervor. "Charles, you speak of principles, of conscience. But this war is not, as the South falsely pretends, a war of races, nor of regions, nor of political parties. It is a war of principles," Angelina insisted. "Our nation is in a death-struggle. It must either become one vast slaveocracy of petty tyrants, or wholly the land of the free. How can you not wish to be a part of this revolution? Your father and I agree that you should not be forced into a war in which you do not believe. We agree that no government has the right to overrule your sovereign conscience. However . . . "

Charles interrupted, "Then why do you harass me? Why do you and Father not let me choose to act upon my own conscience?"

Angelina's voice was both perplexed and pleading, "But why would you not *choose* to fight, Charles? Why not join in this great battle? Look at the negro men who have generously come forward to join the Union army, despite the multiple wrongs they have suffered, and even though they are not allowed citizenship."

Charles stood up in anger, ready to end this acrimonious debate. Angelina continued to look up at him, while Theodore looked away in a mood of grave disappointment. Angelina reached her hand out to Charles' arm to keep him from leaving. "Yet they stand up to fight for their brothers in chains," she continued. "Whatever Lincoln and his Cabinet intend to accomplish with this war, God's design is to deliver from bondage his innocent people!"

Charles was hurt and disgusted with his parents' apparent unwillingness to understand his viewpoint. "Well, I am no match for the two of you! I'm afraid I only see your hypocrisy. You taught me to think for myself, and to hate violence, and—and now you are ashamed of me because I do not choose to embrace war."

Charles walked off, trying to ignore the looks of the nearby guests and students who were glancing at each other with raised eyebrows. For those close by, especially the younger students, this serious family squabble seemed to dampen the good feelings of the day. Angelina put her head in her hands in distress at this chasm between their lifelong commitment and the attitude of their eldest son. After a few moments she raised her head and looked at Theodore. He shook his head and shrugged hopelessly.

After their visit to the graves and a short, heartbreaking attempt to engage with Thodie, Lizzie and Sarah joined the others for the closing event. It was growing late, and they had picked up their shawls against the evening chill.

Sissy was seated at the piano again. Lizzie joined Gatty and her husband. Sarah had missed the argument with Charles, so she was puzzled by Angelina's troubled air as she came up to her sister. Sarah Douglass and Charlotte Forten came down to the lawn from their walk around the grounds, as most of the other remaining guests and students gathered around the piano in the twilight for a final song.

Sissy began playing, and the words of the Star-Spangled Banner rang out over Raritan Bay. They had timed it well. As they sang "And the rockets red blare, the bombs bursting in air," they could hear and see the fireworks being set off from barges across the bay near Staten Island.

Massachusetts

1868—1874

15

Revelation

Hyde Park, Massachusetts 1868

WITH SISSY AND CHARLES studying and working in the Boston area, and with a change of ownership at Eagleswood Academy, the Weld family had decided to move to Hyde Park, just outside of Boston. They invested in a large, gracious home on Fairmount Avenue. Offered for sale by an acquaintance, it was part of a cluster of new homes that wandered up the hill just across the river from the town center. The town had a reputation for its open-mindedness and enlightened views, so the opportunity seemed exceptionally attractive to the aging, but still vital, Weld household.

Sissy walked through the front door and into the hallway, shaking the mud off her boots.[63] She carried a bag with some books and newspapers in it. Susan, their new housekeeper, came out to help her with her coat and boots.[64] Sissy called out gaily, "Hello, everyone. I'm home!"

"Thank you, Susan," she said, handing her a bonnet as she struggled to remove her overshoes. "It's so cold and damp out there—mud season in Boston!" As she hung up her coat, she turned and smiled at the housekeeper, asking "How are you, Susan?"

"I'm jist fine, honey. Good to see you home!"

Aunt Sarah called out from the main parlor just off the hallway.[65] "Sissy, is that you? Come in dear and give me a kiss!" Sissy came into the parlor, carrying her bag. She bent over to give her Aunt Sai a kiss on her pale cheek.

"We were so delighted to hear you would come home today," Sarah said. "Here, come sit down with me."

"Hello, Aunt Sai. Oh, it's so cozy in here. I do love this house!" Sissy said as she dropped into an armchair close to Sarah.

Sarah looked around the comfortable parlor. "Yes, I do, too, Sissy. I'm quite ashamed of how much I love it, after our years of puritanical asceticism," she said drily. They both chuckled, and Sarah asked, "Well, how are your studies, dear?"

"Just fine. I'll tell you more, but here—I've brought you and Mama some copies of the Boston Commonwealth and the National Anti-Slavery Standard." She pulled the journals out of her bag and set them down on a lamp table.

"Thank you, dear, that's very thoughtful. Now, tell me how things are going! We haven't seen you since New Year's Day."

"Well, I'm studying hard—and I'm very happy! Piano and music-theory are fine, my French pronunciation is finally improving, but Mr. Stoughton's course in Modern History is quite dull. I want to take an advanced geometry course, but I can't find anyone to teach it to me. They all say it's useless for women to learn. But I love geometry, Auntie Sai, it's so interesting—and logical!"

"Yes, isn't it curious how men can love knowledge for its own sake, but when women express such interest, they are told they should only concern themselves with what is 'useful'" commented Sarah. "But tell me about your friends, my dear. We haven't had a good talk in many months," she looked over her spectacles at her niece with a conspiratorial glance.

"Yes, I shall." Sissy looked around. "But where are Mother and Father? I don't hear them about."

"I believe they will be home for supper. They are helping Mr. Lewis conclude the affairs of Lexington Academy."

"Ah, yes." Sissy frowned. "Mama and Papa were so sad when the school burned down. Papa, especially. I gather that Mr. Lewis didn't have the heart to continue. But I suspect you are not so sad, Auntie?"

Sarah was amused at Sissy's perceptiveness. "Well, it means a loss of income for the three of us, but you are correct. I, for one, do not miss the trip to and from Lexington twice a week. We all have reading and writing we want to do, and Theodore will continue to lecture occasionally.

"Oh, here, my dear! I wanted to show you the final print of my translation of Joan of Arc." She picked up the elegantly bound copy of her translation of Lamartine's *Joan of Arc* that was lying on a nearby table and handed it to Sissy.

"Oh, this is lovely, Aunt Sai. And I saw a very warm review of it in the Boston paper last week. You must be so proud of it."

"I am, Sissy," Sarah confessed. "The publisher assured me it is selling well. But, as you know, it was a labor of love—I have felt a certain kinship with dear Joan." Sarah's face darkened, "What a strange life she had—so short—and a brutal, unjust death." Sarah shook her head to cast off the bitterness of those thoughts.

"Aunt Sai, have mother and father heard from Thodie?" Sissy asked tentatively, fearful of broaching a tender subject for them all.

Sarah sighed and turned sad eyes to Sissy. "Hardly a word. We know he is established at the farm in Maine. That is where he felt he would be more at peace. He does work there, and from what we hear, he seems to be doing much better." Sarah sighed, "It is a quiet, undemanding life, and it seems to suit him. He was so anxious here—" Her voice faded away to her inmost thoughts. Then she added, "I miss him, but he was so unhappy and paralyzed with self-doubt—and your parents—well, you know. It was just always difficult." She paused and added, "This is better."

Sissy nodded, and she and her aunt shared several moments of silent regret. Then Sissy introduced a more cheerful subject. "You asked about my friends in Cambridge, Aunt Sai. I do not lack for good company—I see my friends, Nettie and Isabella, often. And there's Lucy Stone and Julia Howe at the Suffrage Association. They are older than me, of course, but I so enjoy talking to them."

"And, well, there's a Mr. Hamilton, who took Nettie and me to a lecture on women's education at the Unitarian church last week. Uh, Mr. William Hamilton is his name." Sissy tried to look nonchalant, but she blushed just enough for her aunt to notice.

Sarah took off her spectacles and looked at Sissy with more than usual interest. "Oh, really? And this Mr. Hamilton, who is he and how do you know him?"

"Umm. Well, let me think," Sissy said, biting her lower lip. "I suppose Mrs. Howe introduced us. He's studying for the ministry. She goes to the same church as he does. He's—-well, he's tall—and very intelligent, and he has been kind enough to take Nettie and me to several events."

Sarah smiled teasingly at Sissy, sharing her evident happiness. "Yes, well, this is exactly what your Aunt Anna warned us against—letting you live alone in Cambridge—that hotbed of free thought and dangerous associations!" she said mischievously. They continued to chat amiably until Theodore and Angelina came in.

Theodore and Angelina came in, tired from their day, but happy to see their daughter. After kissing Sissy and asking about her trip out from Boston, Angelina's eyes fell on the newspapers sitting on the lampstand.

"Oh, yes, Mama, I brought those for you and Auntie Sai," Sissy said eagerly. There are some interesting articles . . . " Her voice faded as she noticed her mother's preoccupation. Angelina had picked up the paper and was deeply involved in reading an article on the bottom of the front page. Her face paled and she looked like she might faint.

"Mama, what is it?" Sissy asked, wondering what could distract her mother so thoroughly. Angelina looked at her daughter blankly and announced that she was going to her room.

Theodore objected with an uncomprehending frown. "But Nina, Sissy's here and . . . " Before he could say more, Angelina fled with the newspaper under her arm.

Sissy looked down, clearly disappointed at her mother's apparent indifference, but also puzzled. Theodore turned back to Sissy and Sarah. "What can be the matter with her, Sarah? I know she's tired, but she seemed fine when we came in." Sarah shrugged, no longer surprised by her sister's sudden changes of mood.

Angelina came down to dinner later, but she was inattentive to the conversation and her questions to Sissy were distracted and repetitive. When Theodore joined her in their chamber that night, he read the article that had disturbed her, but he couldn't fathom her state of mind.

"Well, yes, the boys are named Grimké," he said, "so perhaps they came from your brother's plantation. But they seem to be young men to be proud of. Look here. It says they are excellent debaters," pointing to a line in the article. "I don't understand your distress, Nina." Before Angelina could answer she got up and walked hurriedly over to the wash basin where she threw up repeatedly. Theodore was perplexed, but it was not the time for questions. He walked to her side, poured out water, wiped her face and drew her gently into his arms to comfort her. After he helped her into bed, he brought a damp cloth to lay on her forehead and held her hand as she fell sleep.

They saw little of Angelina on Saturday, and although Theodore recognized the issue she was struggling with, he was surprised by the severity of her reaction. Early on Sunday morning, Sissy stood in the front hall, dressed in her winter coat, bonnet and boots. Theodore, Sarah, Angelina and Susan were all there to say good-bye.

Angelina gave Sissy a good-by kiss. "My dear, I'm so sorry I was sick yesterday and couldn't spend more time with you. But I'm feeling stronger today. You must come back next Sunday when Charles will be here, too."

Sissy shrugged, nodded, and gave her mother a cool look. She said warm good-byes to the others. She felt crestfallen at the mysterious behavior of her mother when she had so looked forward to the few days at home. Although she'd had good conversations with her father and with Aunt Sai, she couldn't shake her disappointment at her mother's remoteness.

As the door closed, Angelina gestured to Theodore and Sarah to join her in the parlor. Before they all sat down, she gave the newspaper to Sarah to read. Sarah skimmed it quickly and looked up at Angelina, puzzled but also mildly annoyed.

"And this is what has made you so morose and indifferent to Sissy's visit?" she asked unsympathetically. "I'm sorry, Nina—I just don't understand. It's a very uplifting story."

"But, Sarah, look! Their name is Grimké. How many Grimké families do you know?"

"None but ours. But it seems to me there are two possibilities here. Either they were slaves out at Cane Acres and took our family name—as most of the freed slaves have, or . . . " She paused, with a slight smile, "Or or . . . "

"Yes, or . . . !" Angelina pounced on the word. "Or they are children of one of our brothers. They are the right age—it could have been—well, it never would have been John. He is the soul of propriety. But Henry?"

Sarah's expression was puzzled, but not disturbed. She looked at Theodore for his reaction, but he was looking down, not wanting to impose his thoughts on the sisters. "Yes, Henry. It could be," Sarah said, frowning thoughtfully. "Well, Selina died in 1843, so he was alone. And he had grown into quite a fair master from what we heard. I could imagine . . . "

"But Sarah," Angelina's voice was impatient and almost shrill, "the shame of this—we have always been so horrified at the way white masters treated their female slaves. We were indignant about the mulatto children. And now, our own brother! And he never said a word of it—no hint. Nor did John, or Montague or Eliza or Mary or Henry's own son, Tom, while he was with us at Eagleswood. So how would we have known? And now, what are we to think?"

Sarah moved over closer to take her sister's hand and look into her eyes. She spoke firmly, "Nina, dear, I understand your feelings. I admit it is a strange, new feeling for me, too. But what have *we* to be ashamed of? And how can we judge Henry? We know almost nothing yet—whether our guess is true—or what the circumstances were. But if they are his— well, his children—then they are our nephews," Sarah said plainly. "And it appears that they are very accomplished young men." She looked at the ceiling straining to remember any hints that Mary or Eliza may have dropped in one of their letters. "I wonder who their mother is?" she murmured.

At this point, Theodore intervened, "Angelina, dear, and Sarah, too. I believe we need more facts—don't you think?" Angelina was still troubled, but she had calmed down. She looked at Theodore pensively, then at Sarah. She stood and walked around for several minutes. Theodore and Sarah exchanged anxious looks.

When Angelina spoke, she surprised them both. "I—I'm so ashamed. As always, you two see things so much more clearly than I do. If I am truthful, I must admit that the prospect of family relations who are colored—well, it is that hateful prejudice rearing its ugly head in my own heart. I thought I was free of it. You see how awful I am, Theodore," she looked pleadingly at her husband with tears in her eyes. "I was just so taken aback—and so confused! I couldn't see past the shame—the embarrassment. I couldn't see the boys themselves, whoever they are."

Theodore, who had somehow been spared this insidious awareness of color and caste, nevertheless understood its unconscious presence even among the white abolitionists. He had thought the sisters mostly free of it, but now he recognized the ultimate test of Angelina's convictions. He stood up and took her gently into his arms.

After a moment breathing deeply into his shoulder, she looked up and said, "Yes, I must write to them. I want to." She paused trying to strengthen her resolve. "I shall write to them today and simply ask them who they are, and what is their relationship to the Grimké family." She lifted her shoulders. "And we will see." She smiled weakly and sat down, exhausted from her struggle.

Two weeks later, Frank strolled out of the main hall at Lincoln University, heading towards a bench in the grassy field. He was reading the letter from Angelina which he had just picked up from the mail table. His brow was wrinkled with curiosity, but as he read, one side of his mouth curved into a half smile.

Archibald walked across the grass toward Frank and surprised him from behind. Frank was startled and gave his brother a friendly punch. Then he handed him the letter to read. After Archie read the first few lines, the two of them looked at each other. Frank was still stunned and not sure how to react. Archie, grave and cautious, put his arm around Frank's shoulders as they headed back to their dormitory building, each nursing their own thoughts.

After supper that night, Archie sat down at the desk in the small room the boys shared. Frank looked over Archie's shoulder as he wrote, nodding approvingly at his brother's clear prose.

> Dear Madam,
>   I am very happy to hear from Miss Angelina Grimké of Anti-Slavery celebrity. I am the son of Henry Grimké, your brother. Of course, you know more about my father than I do; he was a lawyer and was married to a Miss Selina Simmons. She died, leaving three children, viz. Henrietta, Montague, and Thomas.
>   After his death he took my mother—who was his slave and his children's nurse—as his mistress; her name is Nancy Weston. I don't think you know her. By my mother he had three children also, Archibald, which is my name, and Francis and John . . .[66]

Angelina watched the mail anxiously for several days before the envelope appeared bearing a return address of "Archibald Grimké." She opened the letter in the entryway with great trepidation, calling out to Sarah in the parlor nearby as she did so.

Angelina sat down next to her sister as she read Archie's opening words. She grabbed Sarah's hand as she continued to read. Sarah couldn't restrain herself, "Then they are indeed our nephews, Nina. How strange and yes, disturbing. Yet how fitting and wonderful!" She paused to digest the news, then added, "I don't remember the mother—Nancy—do you?"

Angelina shook her head. Despite her determination not to panic, she was still much more disturbed by these revelations than Sarah was. "I don't either," Angelina responded. "Eliza might have mentioned her name in talking about the children's care after their mother's death, but I don't really recall. I wonder how much she and Mary knew?"

"Well, it is exactly what I would expect from our Charleston family— a code of secrecy—those mulatto children just fall from the sky!" Sarah grimaced. "But what else does he say, Nina? He seems very articulate. How were they treated? How did they get to Lincoln?"

Angelina continued to read out loud from the letter,

> Our father died about sixteen years ago, leaving my mother, with two children and in a pregnant state, in the care of his son, Mr. Montague Grimké, in his own words, as I heard, "I leave Nancy and her two children to be treated as members of the family."

"And were they?" Sarah interjected, knowing the certain answer.

"Let me finish, Sarah!" Angelina objected, as she read on,

> My poor mother, a defenseless woman, crippled in one arm, was thrown upon the uncharitable world, for Mr. Montague Grimké did not do as his father commanded. He informed my mother [in 1860] that he wanted me and that she should send me to his house.
>
> His mandate was irresistible; it was a severe shock to my mother. But this was only the beginning of her sorrows, thus he kept on taking her sons until she was rendered childless.

"Oh, Sarah, how could he? It seems that the boys were made his slaves again!"

Sarah's lips were pressed tightly together, and her eyes were steely. She was close to tears, but more of anger than of sympathy. She looked up at Angelina. "Yes, it confirms our worst fears, Nina. I have not heard much good about Montague."

Angelina nodded, "I knew Selina, his mother, of course. I used to talk to her about slavery. She was a good influence on Henry, I believe. But Montague! Well, I suspect he was a victim of that evil system. How else could he enslave his own blood brothers without a second thought!"

She looked grim. Then two photos dropped out of the envelope she was holding, and her face brightened. "Look, Sarah!" She examined the photos and held them up for her sister to see. She finished reading the letter out loud.

> I hope, dear Madam, you will excuse this badly written epistle. Perhaps you would like to see our pictures; they are enclosed. I shall hope to hear from you soon.
>
> Most respectfully yours, Archibald Henry Grimké

Angelina studied the photos for a few moments, then handed them to Sarah who gave them equally eager attention. "Francis looks just like Henry!" Sarah exclaimed with a smile.

"Sarah, what shall we do?" Angelina asked, her voice still tight with uncertainty.

For a second summer, Frank and Archie agreed to teach former slaves in rural Maryland. On their way back to the city, the young men spent considerable time talking about their prospects for the future. They were deeply involved in their university studies, but the world beyond Lincoln University looked daunting.

Although they had now met their father's sister, Angelina, and her son, Charles, their meeting at Lincoln University had been somewhat stiff. They had the uncomfortable feeling that they were being sized up by both mother and son. Still, their aunt had invited them to visit their home in Boston, and they had agreed to do so in the fall, when their summer work was completed. But they didn't know what to expect. They wanted to show their desire and readiness to be educated gentlemen; but they also wanted to prove their self-sufficiency. Their knowledge of the sisters' abolitionist work led them to hope for a civil relationship with their aunts, but they knew better than to expect more.

After they had returned to Philadelphia and been paid for their summer work, Frank asked where they might buy gentlemen's clothing in the city. They were directed to a men's clothing store in the center of town. When they found it, they gazed at the elegant suits, top hats, boots and canes in the window. Both white and colored gentlemen were entering and leaving the store, but neither Archie nor Frank felt bold enough to go right in. Archie procrastinated by reading the sign that said, "Best Fashion for Men: Ready-made and Made-to-Order Suits and Shoes."

Frank said, "Ok, Archie, let's see how much we will have left after we pay Lincoln."

Archie pulled the money out of his pocket, and with their heads together they counted how much they could spend. Archie was worried that they would spend their entire savings, but after counting and subtracting, Archie nodded, satisfied that they could buy what they needed. "But we will have to be careful with our spending money this fall, Frank." Frank nodded his understanding and grinned at his more prudent elder brother. They walked into the shop and emerged an hour later with bundles and boxes. They were solemn and seemed to have grown several inches in stature.

In late September, Aunt Sarah was sitting in the parlor of their Hyde Park home. She looked up from her reading as Angelina entered the room. Sarah noted with dismay that her sister again looked drained with anxiety and older than she had seemed the previous spring. After Nina's trip to Lincoln with Charley, she had spoken highly of the young men. Still, her feelings were conflicted. The war that had scoured the heart and soul of the nation was over, but Angelina knew its fearful work was far from completed. Like the nation, her body was wasted, and her internal organs were impaired. She often felt divided against herself.

"Sarah, where is Charles Stuart?" Angelina asked. "He promised he'd be here to help us greet our young nephews.[67] Oh, I'm so worried. Do you think they will be able to find their way on the streetcar? And from the streetcar here? Perhaps we should walk out to meet them?"

"Nina, you have assured me that they are very capable young men. I think they will be able to find their way here. They've been in Boston before, have they not?" Sarah spoke sternly, but she softened it with a smile, aware of Angelina's high anxiety about whether this visit would go well.

"Charley went out to buy a paper," Sarah said in a gentler voice. "He will keep an eye out for the boys if they arrive early. I believe Theodore walked out with him. And Sissy is coming on the streetcar, too."

Angelina sat down, frowning, and trying mightily to calm herself. "I know I shouldn't worry. But I want to make sure they know how welcome they are!" Angelina's face relaxed for a moment. "Oh, Sarah, if you could have heard their stories! How much they have been through. I felt so ashamed—so ashamed of the South, of Charleston, of our relations."

"Yes, dear. I know. You have told me the stories many times! I see how it has affected you all this summer. I understand your compassion for their struggles." Sarah tilted her head and added, "Yet, I don't quite understand your sense of shame and guilt. We did all we could to advance the day of their freedom."

"But, Sai, it wasn't enough! It wasn't soon enough to spare them weeks of horror in the workhouse, months of indignity and mistreatment in Montague's household, years of hiding in a filthy cellar." She paused and murmured, "It's never enough." Angelina put a hand to her temples "Oh, my head!"

Sarah rose and went over to her sister. She put her hand on Angelina's arm and said, "Nina, please. Stop berating yourself. We did what we knew how to do—what God asked us to do."

Angelina looked unconvinced. She murmured "Nephews. . ." But she shook her head, closed her eyes, and struggled to calm herself. After a few moments she said, "I believe there are a few blooms left in the garden. I'll go gather them for this room." Sarah smiled and nodded approvingly. As Angelina left, Sarah looked after her with concern.

Charles and Theodore returned, and Sissy arrived shortly after. Angelina had come in from the garden and stood by the window, looking out for their visitors. Charles was telling his father about politics in France, and Sissie was fidgeting excitedly.

Archie and Frank walked up Fairmount Avenue to the Weld home, checking the address and directions against a letter. They stopped at the corner to adjust their top hats and cravats, and dust off their new boots. Archie straightened Frank's cravat, and Frank dusted something off Archie's jacket. With serious demeanors, they approached the front door.

The sisters were dressed in their simple, well-worn and rather drab clothing, while Sissy was in a well-cut light blue gown with navy trim. Charley was the most fashionable, wearing a charcoal day suit with a light blue fleur-de-lis patterned waistcoat that he had had tailored in Paris.

Suddenly, Angelina called out from the window, "Oh, my, Sissy, look!"

But it was Sarah who hurried to the window. "Oh, I see them!" Sarah declared. "My—look at them—well, they are quite handsome and grown-up as you said, Nina!" Sissy joined her aunts and exclaimed at the young men's fancy dress. "Top hats! Oh, my! And canes, as well," she giggled.

The doorbell rang and Susan hurried to answer it, but Sissy was already there. Charley also got up immediately and walked to the foyer. "Oh, Angelina, look how comely they are—so handsomely dressed!" Sarah exclaimed.

Angelina thought again of how she and Sarah and Theodore had struggled and suffered to see a day like this. Yet she had never imagined emancipation to be so personal. She looked at her own son and daughter who were eagerly waiting to meet their young cousins of a different complexion. Theodore came and took his wife's hand as they walked toward the foyer. She gazed gratefully at Theo—he who had no doubts—and she felt an unexpected elation as her daughter opened the door to her nephews.

"Oh, please do come in! Welcome!" Sissy said enthusiastically. "Let me see, you must be Archibald, and you must be Francis? Am I right? I'm Sissy—your—well, your cousin!"

Archie and Frank were both gratified and amused at Sissy's eager welcome. They smiled quietly, but they remained formal and awkwardly reserved. Archie found his voice and said, "Miss Weld, we are delighted to make your acquaintance."

Sissy said, "It's "Sissy." Please call me that! Or Miss Sissy, if you prefer. I'm not much for formalities," she added with an engaging laugh.

Charley stepped forward and shook their hands vigorously. "Archie, Frank, so good to see you again," he said. "We are so happy you could make it here. Come in, come in."

"Oh, this is Susan, our housekeeper." Archie gave her a slight bow.

Frank was disarmed by Sissy and shook the hand she extended to him with a friendly nod. "Miss Sissy—delighted!" He realized with chagrin that she was nearly as tall as he was.

Archie turned back to Charles and, with a little bow, said, "Charles, it is our pleasure to be here!" The young men turned to enter the parlor just as Theodore and Angelina reached the threshold. Theodore shook their hands vigorously and patted them on the shoulders. Angelina extended her hand to greet Archie, followed by Frank. Frank noticed with relief that her smile was warmer and more relaxed than it had been at Lincoln University. He could sense a change in her.

Then both young men turned toward their Aunt Sarah whom they had not yet met. Sarah beamed radiantly at them, almost enraptured. Angelina said, "May I present my dear sister, Sarah, of whom you have heard so much. She has been so eager . . . "

Her voice trailed off as Sarah came forward spryly and embraced each of the boys tenderly, taking them by surprise. She held them at arm's length in admiration. "Ah, it is true, then! Francis, you take after our dear Henry—your father!"

"And Archie," she said, turning to the elder brother, with tears in her eyes, "I cannot look upon you without thinking of my brother, Thomas."

Frank and Archie were stunned by her effusiveness and their faces betrayed their sincere gratitude at her welcome. Archie uttered their carefully prepared words of appreciation. "Miss Grimké, your graciousness in welcoming us is equal only to your fame—and your sister's—in the cause of freeing the slave. We are many times and many ways in your debt."

"And we hope to do honor to the Grimké name, dear sisters!" Archie concluded his speech in a manner that Sarah thought bespoke both true humility and dignified confidence.

Theodore interrupted with a cough, "Hear, hear—enough of these formalities! We are eager to hear of your trip here, your studies and your plans. So much to discuss!" He gestured for the boys to sit down, and the young people all found seats. Susan brought in tea which Sarah poured, while Sissy passed around the teacups and some gingerbread.

"You must be tired and hungry from your journey," Angelina said. She had, indeed, relaxed as she realized that the challenges of this visit were mostly in her imagination. It dawned on her that the boys themselves, with their grace and genuineness, made it easy to imagine them as part of her family, despite their fancy clothes. "We hope you will join us for supper after we have had a chance to talk," she said kindly.

Much later, Archie, Frank and the rest of the family rose from the supper table after hours of exchanging individual stories and sharing the pieces of their country's history that they had personally witnessed. As Susan came in to clear the table, she whispered disapprovingly to Sissy, "What they doin' with them top-hats and canes and shiny shoes! How can they afford that? Don't they know we simple folk here?"

Sissy was amused at Susan's disapproval and said, "Well, I believe they know that now!" She spoke quietly to their housekeeper as she gazed at the young men retreating to the parlor. "But Susan, don't you admire their elegance and fashion. I'm sure they worked very hard for it!" Susan pursed her lips and shook her head skeptically as she piled dishes up her arms.

As the others re-entered the parlor, Theodore cleared his throat and spoke to Archie and Frank in his gravelly voice. "So, you are determined to join the law course at Lincoln, now that you've finished your college course?" He tilted his head back and gave them a quizzical gaze. "There are other choices available now, you know."

Sarah piped in eagerly, "Yes, we have heard good things about Cornell University. They seem eager to welcome promising young freedmen like yourselves. Our friends tell us—"

"Yes, we know there are other opportunities," Archie said quickly. He looked away, trying to disguise his embarrassment, "But we have very little money, and there are scholarships at Lincoln that have been promised to us." He looked over at Frank, and said, a little sheepishly, "And we feel at home there."

"Yes, expense is a concern of course," Angelina nodded, "but we want to help."

"Yes, we want to do all we can, but, well, you see, we don't have a great deal ourselves," Sarah said apologetically. "We have this lovely house now, but our incomes are very limited, especially since Dr. Lewis' school closed after the recent fire."

"But we didn't expect—that is, we want to be independent. That's why we thought it best to stay at Lincoln." Frank protested adamantly. He had hoped to avoid this conversation, and he felt immensely awkward about it. He knew Archie viewed it differently.

But Sarah waved her hand to dismiss his objections, "We promise to send you all that we can! I have a little extra from the sale of my translation of *Joan of Arc*," Sarah said with undisguised pride. "And I am going to dedicate that to your education, to give you a start at least."

"Of course, we are grateful for any ways you can help us," Archie responded with a quick look at his brother. "But we value your counsel and friendship above all."

Theodore answered drily, with a knowing look at Charley and Sissy. "Well, I'm sure your aunts will have plenty of counsel for you! Of course, we will all do what we can." He cleared his throat with a little cough, "But we also believe firmly in the value of manual labor and of earning one's way. We hope you will consider the resources of your own bodies as well."

Archie felt a surge of resentment that this man whom he so admired would think they were unwilling to work. He stifled his desire to remind his uncle that they had been slaves, and said only, "Yes, sir, we have, and we shall. As you know, when we arrived in the North, I worked as a farmhand and Frank worked in a shoe factory. It wasn't what we had expected, but we did it. And we spent the last two summers teaching a community of former slaves to earn our keep at Lincoln." In an earnest voice, he added "We do know how to work, sir!"

Sarah shot a look at her brother-in-law and immediately jumped to the young men's defense. "Certainly, you do, boys! We can see that you have all the industry, good sense, and intelligence of the best of our brothers." She hesitated only a second before adding, "And of your mother as well, I am sure!"

Frank ran a finger across his mouth as he pondered how much to say. "There is another school being started in Washington—primarily for negro students, but they expect to admit some white students as well. I believe it is—Archie, what is the name?" He bit his lip and frowned as

Archie looked at him blankly, "Oh, yes, Howard—Howard University," Frank recalled. "Perhaps in another year or two, we would be ready to apply there."

Theodore nodded his head in measured agreement. He admired the frankness and dignity of both young men, and Sarah's remark reminded him to restrain his life-long temptation to urge moral improvement on others.

The conversation about schools and financial means continued for several minutes in the parlor, but as darkness fell the serious talk gave way to lively chatter. Charley and Theodore conversed comfortably with Frank, while Angelina, Sarah and Sissy chatted with Archie. The formality fell away quickly as laughter and teasing and genuine curiosity about each other took its place.

16

The Women Vote

Hyde Park, Massachusetts Winter 1870

THEODORE WAS IN A jovial mood as he and the three women of his household entered the ballroom of the Hyde Park Hotel. He greeted neighbors he knew and joked with them about the "subversive" speaker they were about to hear. Lucy Stone had been invited to give a lecture on women's suffrage, a topic dear to the family's heart. Angelina, Sarah and Sissy walked directly over to greet their fellow abolitionist, and now suffragist, before her speech.[68]

"Thank you for coming to our small town, Mrs. Stone," Angelina began before getting straight to the point. "You asked us about serving on the Board of Officers of the Massachusetts's Woman's Suffrage Association. Sissy gave us your note." Lucy smiled at Sissy, whom she knew from Sissy's volunteer work with the Association. "Of course, we would be honored to serve," Angelina said quickly.

Lucy's smile grew broader, "Oh, I knew you would say yes! Thank you, Mrs. Weld! And Miss Grimké, you, too, I hope? You know, don't you, that when I was only nineteen, your *Letters on the Equality of the Sexes* echoed the certainties of my own heart and gave me the courage to speak out? In fact, forgive me, but I will rely on many of your arguments in my speech today."

Sarah was deeply pleased by Lucy's tribute, but she only said, "How could I refuse your invitation, my dear? This is now the cause nearest to my heart. We must do all we can to further the education and preparation of women for their full rights as citizens." She took out a handkerchief and wiped her nose, red from the chilly weather. "When do we meet?" she inquired.

"Next Monday, already. Can you make it? At 10 am. We're meeting at Julia Howe's home. Do you know it?"

"Oh, my, yes, indeed. We shall be there," Sarah said, looking at Angelina, who nodded her agreement. "But now, you must go and take a moment of quiet before your speech."

Lucy looked grateful and with a slight bow, she turned and walked slowly to a seat by the speaker's dais. The women joined Theodore who had found seats for them in the third row. Angelina looked over her shoulder and was pleased to see about forty women and girls, and perhaps thirty men, now gathered in the ballroom. As Lucy began her speech, the audience was quickly drawn in by her modest manner and cogent arguments for women's right to the vote.

There were strained looks among husbands and wives when Lucy spoke of refusing to take her husband's name when they married. And there was some agitated shuffling of feet when she noted that because of the language of the Fifteenth Amendment which was in the process of being ratified, the eventual enfranchisement of women would include all women, that is, former slaves and free colored women as well as white women, if they were born in the United States. When she finished her lecture and took her seat, the applause was gratifying, if not thunderous. The women sitting near the Weld household murmured approval and began to chat among themselves.

Sarah spoke to a woman friend on one side of her, while Nina made approving comments to Sissy on her other side. After a few moments, Mrs. Stone gestured that she wished to speak again, and the audience quieted down.

"Ladies and gentlemen," Lucy began, "I welcome questions now that I have laid before you the reasons why we women should enjoy the vote on an equal footing with male citizens. Please share with us your thoughts. Miss. . .?"

A young townswoman had jumped to her feet, "Vanderbeck, ma'am. Miss Margaret Vanderbeck."

"Mrs. Stone, you have answered our critics admirably, and I can only add that now it is up to us to put women's suffrage into action. I suggest, well—what if we were to make a demonstration, right here in Hyde Park, of participation in the voting process." She looked around at the audience eagerly.

Several older women shook their heads doubtfully and others tittered with amusement at the young woman' earnest enthusiasm. But immediately, Sissy jumped up and said, "What a grand idea, Maggie! Let us do it thoroughly. Shall we not draw up a slate of candidates for our local election. Then we can all come together on the day before the regular election and have an election of our own."

She looked down at her father for reassurance, and seeing his faint smile, she spoke out loudly and confidently, "I hereby move that the women of Hyde Park illustrate their commitment to women's suffrage by a demonstration vote in the local election of 1870."

Maggie Vanderbeck and several other young women called out "I second the motion!" Angelina looked around to gauge the mood of the audience and saw faces reflecting everything from amused delight, to doubt, disapproval and shock. But many in the room seemed to be giving the idea serious consideration.

Angelina felt a restless movement by her side. The ballroom grew quiet as the gathering noticed their eminent citizen, Theodore Weld, rise slowly. He began to speak in the familiar voice that was raspy and low, but still strong. "Mrs. Stone—I shall call you Madam Chair, since you have inspired us to move into the mode of formal deliberation."

He cleared his throat. Angelina looked up at him with affection, and Sissy watched her father with a solemn look of expectancy. "Madam Chair, I shall speak to the question before us, and to the larger issue which it represents, if you will pardon me for doing so." He coughed a little and cleared his throat again. "It has long come to my attention that human rights are indivisible." He turned and gave a slight bow to Nina and Sarah, and there was a ripple of amusement and approval in the assembly.

> If a right to self-governance is due to the white male of our species, it is due to every adult human, whether white or black, red or brown, male or female. Do we not all bleed human blood? Do we not suffer human ailments? Do we not all have a stake in the laws and leadership of our government since it pertains to our pursuit of life, liberty and the pursuit of happiness?
>
> Mrs. Stone has amply made these points, so I will not belabor them further, except to say that this motion to demonstrate the truth of our equality before God is most fitting. What is the use, you may say, of an action that can, at present, only be symbolic. And I answer you that symbol is everything!

Theodore, relishing the use of his full rhetorical skills, paused for effect, then continued.

> In the days of slavery, we treated escaped slaves with the dignity they deserved as free beings, although before the law they were not free. We acted as was right, despite the backwardness of the law.
>
> So, too, we should act as is right, and let the onus of disregarding the votes of women fall upon the government which is not yet enlightened on this point. Women shall vote! First in Hyde Park, then in Massachusetts, then throughout our great nation. And the day will come when women's vote will be counted. Dare I say, they will hold the highest offices—throughout our civilized world!

Theodore's oratory once again hit its mark, and the audience broke out in loud applause. Several of the younger women call out "Hear, hear!" and there was an echo of "Hear, hear" from several of the mature women in the audience as well.

Sarah watched as a dozen skeptical men and women quietly left the hall. To them it was evident that the "radicals" were taking the day. Then she saw an unfamiliar young man rise to speak. Lucy Stone recognized him as a Mr. Fitzhugh.

> Madam Chairman, none of us can equal Mr. Weld's eloquence. I only wish to add that I heartily endorse his view of the question. I would propose that we follow through on this proposal with due ceremony. Let us draw up a slate of candidates next week, as suggested, and let the men who are present here, and others who wish to join in, all convene here on March 7th, the day before the town election. We will escort our ladies to the polls at the town hall and honor them as prototypes of the future we hope for.

An older gentleman called out "I amend the motion to state that we proceed as Mr. Fitzhugh has described." A chorus of seconds to the amendment rang out. There was a moment of silence, then Sarah struggled to her feet.

"I call for the question!" she said firmly. Her spectacles were sliding down her nose, but her happy expression discouraged any ridicule, and touched those who could see her face.

Lucy Stone had listened quietly to these proceedings with growing satisfaction. "Yes," she declared, "And we must first vote on the amendment. All those in favor of the amendment to proceed with the nominations and elections with due ceremony, signify by saying 'aye.'"

A loud chorus of "ayes" rang out.

"And those opposed signify by saying 'nay.'

An older gentleman who had fallen asleep, woke up just in time to call out "nay" in a loud voice. Those around him looked at him with various shades of disgust and amusement. His distressed wife whispered something to him. "Oh, I see. Excuse me, Madam Chairman, I meant to say 'aye'—Yes, I was just joking," he said with an attempt at a chuckle.

"Noted, good sir," Lucy replied with an inscrutable look. "I believe the amendment has passed unanimously. So now to the main question."

The enthusiastic assembly all voted "aye" to the main motion. The few dissenters had by then exited the hall. The younger women jumped to their feet in excitement, embracing each other, while the older women and men shook hands or simply nodded their heads with thoughtful approval. Few of them had come to the lecture with the expectation of revolutionary action, but the prospect of this dignified symbolic demonstration pleased them.

Sarah rose to her feet next to Sissy, who almost crushed her aunt with a hearty hug. Theodore looked at Nina with a satisfied smile and kissed her on the cheek.

March 7, 1870, started out with a glimpse of pale sun, but dark clouds approached from the northeast and by noon, heavy snow was falling. At the hotel forty-two pairs of women and men gathered, and by a quarter past noon the first few couples emerged from the front door of the hotel and headed around the town square where Fairmont Avenue, River Street and Central Avenue converged.

The slight, young Mr. Fitzhugh accompanied a rosy-faced Margaret Vanderbeck at the head of the parade. But Sarah, leaning heavily on Charley's arm, was nearly abreast with them. Angelina held tightly onto Theodore's arm, and Sissy followed them on the arms of her fiancé, William Hamilton. The women were bundled up in warm coats, woolen bonnets and muffs against the snowstorm, but the weight of the wet snow didn't seem to dampen their high spirits. The men also sported woolen scarves around their necks, but their ears were red and exposed under their dress hats. The women carried paper ballots which they folded inside their muffs or pockets to protect them from the snow.

A smattering of curious townspeople and local shopkeepers watched the parade of men and women processing gaily toward the town hall despite the severe snowstorm. Some of them—those who were already dressed for the weather—followed the group to the hall, chatting amiably with their neighbors and acquaintances in the makeshift procession. There were a few jeers and catcalls from young rowdies along the street, but the onlookers who hadn't read the local paper were just puzzled at the spectacle.

When the parade entered the town hall, they saw that a ballot box had been set up on a small table to receive the women's ballots. The mayor of Hyde Park was standing expectantly behind it, looking on with a benign expression. Margaret Vanderbeck stood aside and, with a gracious gesture, deferred to the distinguished elders of the town. Angelina, Sarah, and Sissy let go of their companions' arms and walked alone to drop their ballots into the box. Angelina was solemn, but Sarah's smile was blissful. Sissy could not restrain herself from exchanging a triumphant grin with Margaret and with her fiancé, William. The first three women were followed by Margaret and three dozen other hopeful and determined women. To one side the organizers had placed a large box of flower bouquets. As the men separated from their female counterparts, they picked up one of the bouquets, and as the women left the ballot box their escorts handed them a bouquet of flowers.

The group remained in the hall watching the procession until the last few women cast their ballots. As they did so, applause rang out and a shout went up among the younger women.

"Hurray! Hip, Hip Hurray! The vote for all women!"

The applause continued for several minutes, although the bouquets the women were holding made it awkward. Although their initial reaction had been curiosity about this foolishness, many of the onlookers from town were moved by the solemnity, and they joined approvingly in the applause as well.

Sissy and William broke away to talk to several other young people and to celebrate the moment with hugs and congratulations. Sarah whispered to Angelina, "We did it!" and her sister returned her beatific smile as many of their local friends gathered around to congratulate the sisters and each other.

Theodore was happy to cede the spotlight to his wife and sister-in-law. He and Charles stood off to one side and watched the women celebrate the moment, although he looked every bit as pleased as they did. As they walked home afterwards, Charley had his head down with his hands deep in his pockets. Sissy grabbed his arm and asked, "You look grumpy, Charley, aren't you happy for us women?"

Charley gave her a look that was somewhere between pitying and amused. "I wish I could share your excitement, Sissy, but I fail to see how you can be so satisfied with this symbolic act—an empty gesture really—when the reality is so preposterously impossible. Men would have to approve the female vote, and I can't see that they ever will. Not the men I know, at least," he added glumly.

"Well, Father would, and William would!" Sissy proclaimed, although her brother's pessimism affected her deeply. "And it was white men who ultimately gave the vote to colored men," she insisted stubbornly. Her brother rolled his eyes with a cynical smile, "Yes, and please note that they were all men."

Sissy kicked a stone with her boot, her gay mood disturbed. It was 1870, she thought. Surely in her lifetime—in twenty years, perhaps? She shrugged and took her fiancé's arm again, deep in thought.

Sissy married William the following November in a quiet ceremony at the Presbyterian Church in Hyde Park. Their first daughter was born in Hyde Park and named Angelina Grimké Hamilton after her grandmother. Soon after they moved to Springfield where William hoped to work as a minister.[69]

Now in their late sixties and seventies respectively, neither Angelina nor Sarah was in the best of health. Although they kept up correspondence with a few old friends, including their nephews at Lincoln, and they paid close attention to the women's rights organizations, their small remaining energy was focused close to home. Theodore still lectured occasionally but traveled less than in the past. Thodie was settled at the farm up in Maine, while Charley remained with his parents in Hyde Park. Angelina missed her daughter, but Sarah mourned the loss of Sissy's lively companionship even more sorely.

17

"Her Deeds Were Wise and Beautiful"

Hyde Park, Massachusetts 1872

ON ANOTHER WINTRY DAY nearly two years later, Sarah put on her worn woolen coat and bonnet and wrapped a scarf around her neck. She walked briskly down the hill and went into a clothing store near the town center. Sarah waited for other customers to leave, then spoke gently but earnestly to the shopkeeper. He looked puzzled, and shook his head in annoyance, but Sarah would not be put off. After a few moments, the shopkeeper frowned, nodded slowly, and went to a back room. He emerged with several articles of clothing that he had not been able to sell or that were slightly damaged.

Sarah happily stuffed the clothes in a large sack and shook the man's hand in gratitude. As she left the store, she noticed that snow was beginning to fall. Sarah looked up at the dark sky but decided to soldier on and complete her mission. She stopped at several other establishments, including one or two residences. At one she was turned away empty-handed, but at the others she came away with several more pieces of good, used clothing.

Sarah examined her sack with great satisfaction. She hoisted the sack up and held it with both arms, struggling with its weight as she walked across the river and up the hill to the Weld home. By that time the snow was coming down heavily. Angelina looked out the window as Sarah's tiny frame paused to catch her breath halfway up the hill. The enormous sack obscured her face. Angelina hurried to open the door and to help Sarah carry in the sack.

"Sai, what were you thinking? Why do you always choose the coldest, wintriest days for your charitable work!" Angelina spoke in an exasperated tone, but Sarah knew she was more anxious than angry.

"Nina, I'm not a clairvoyant, you know. I didn't realize it was going to snow." Angelina helped her take off her coat which was heavy with snowy dampness. "Besides," she said with a shrug and a smile, "I like the snow."

Angelina helped carry the bag into the parlor and Sarah opened it, exclaiming, "Look what I have, Nina!" She began taking things out of the sack. "Look, dear, look at what Mr. Spring gave me from his shop. Why these things are brand new! They are just things he had made up and no one ever came for them—or they didn't fit quite right. I'm not sure." She took more clothes from the sack.

"And then Mrs. Weitz was so kind—she gave me all these things from her husband. He passed away last year you know. Of course, Mrs. Engels had nothing for us! She's quite the old bat, isn't she?"

Angelina couldn't help smirking at Sarah's last remark. "Old bat" aptly described Mrs. Engels bird-like beak and screechy voice. Despite her annoyance at Sarah's imprudence, she shared her sister's delight in her "haul." Angelina held up several articles of clothing to examine. "Yes, I see. These will be wonderful for the freedmen in South Carolina and Florida. They are suffering so much these days. I'll help you bundle them up and we'll get Theodore to take them to the Pillsbury's. They'll know best how to get them south."

Sarah began to shiver. She started to cough with a deep wheeze and couldn't stop for several minutes. She sat on the edge of the couch until the coughing stopped, then moved to the armchair near the fire to warm up.

Angelina was alarmed. "But Sarah, you simply must be more careful about the days you go out. These things can wait until the weather warms up a bit. Now, listen, we've had a wonderful letter from Archie—and a note from Frank as well. We'll read them as we have tea."

"Tea, yes—that's a happy thought," she said as she sank into the chair with relief. "Well, so are the letters, of course!"

Angelina disappeared momentarily into the kitchen and brought out the tea herself with a plate of dark bread and jam. Sarah arranged herself comfortably for her tea and for the letters.

"Now, let's hear!"

In their spartan room at Lincoln University, Archie caught up with his correspondence by a dim gaslight. There was an envelope and an opened letter from Harvard on his desk, dated January 31, 1872.[70] Frank was sitting on his bed reading a book. Archie finished the letter to his aunts and looked it over with satisfaction. He handed the letter and envelope to Frank to add a note.

Angelina set down the tea and pulled out the letters to read as Sarah poured the tea, added a little honey, and spread jam on the bread. "You can read the details, Sai, but the main thing is—well, can you guess where Archie has decided to continue his studies next fall?"

"I don't want to guess, Nina. Just tell me, please. He plans to continue studying law, does he not? At Cornell?"

"No. Well, yes, law—but close by in Cambridge, at Harvard Law School! Can you believe it? He has written to them, and he just heard back that he has been accepted for the fall term."

"Well, the excellence of his record and his recommendations have certainly earned him this spot." Sarah wrinkled her brow and put a finger on her cheek. "Hmmm. I wonder if Wendell Phillips put in a good word for him." She turned her gaze back to Angelina and said quizzically, "But I didn't know they had any colored students there yet?"

Angelina looked over the letter, frowning, then smiled as she read on. "No, they have not, Archie says. He will be the first—or one of the first at least.[71] Oh, I'm so proud of our boys. One of the first young men of negro heritage to be admitted to Harvard Law. And one who was himself a slave!"

Sarah allowed herself a brief smile, but then said solemnly, "I hope it will not be difficult for him to break this new ground." She pondered for a moment, then concluded, "But, no, he is such an able and charming young man. His manners are so perfect in every way. He will make friends and succeed fully." She nodded her head emphatically. "I am confident! And what does Frank say? Does he tell us his plans?"

Angelina unfolded the note from Frank and looked it over quickly, then tilted her head and nodded approvingly. "Frank says he is determined to make a try at law school at Howard." She read on, "But he sounds a bit hesitant. I wonder—"

"I wonder, too," Sarah rejoined. "For a while it seemed that Archie was the more devout of the two young men. I thought that he might consider the ministry, but now I understand that he is ably suited to the law."

She shook her head remembering her own impossible ambition to be a lawyer. Then she continued, "But Frank—hmmm," she mused. "He is so thoughtful and sensitive. There is a depth there. I would not be shocked if he changed his mind about the law."

"Well, for now their course seems determined, and their prospects excellent. They have not entirely heeded our advice—but they have chosen well." Angelina sighed deeply, thinking of her own children with some anxiety and a little disappointment.

"What is it, Nina?" Sarah asked.

"I don't know. Charles Stuart and Sissy have struggled to find their ways—especially Charles. But now he seems to be ready to settle into a life of teaching and scholarship."

"And Sissie seems happily joined with William. I only hope her considerable talents are not consumed by housewifely tasks, and children, of course!" Angelina's face darkened as she dimly recognized the divided loyalties she had never successfully resolved. Sarah looked at her sister thoughtfully for a moment as she contemplated the ambivalence underlying Angelina's remark.

Angelina continued, "If only our dear Thodie—" Tears fell from Angelina's eyes.

At the mention of her troubled nephew, whom she loved like a son, Sarah sat stonily silent for several moments, a bitter look on her face. Then she moved over to comfort Nina.

That year Sarah's health began to deteriorate, and although she slowed down considerably, she insisted on doing what she could to be useful. She turned eighty in November, but she claimed to have forgotten how old she was. Shortly after the first of the year in 1873 Sarah went out again on a cold, windy afternoon.[72] Angelina was away with Theodore so she knew she would not be scolded. She wore her winter coat, muffler, hat and gloves but the temperature had fallen well below freezing. After a few minutes outside she began shivering, and she tried fruitlessly to warm her hands against the cold wind. She carried about fifty copies of John Stuart Mills' pamphlet "On the Subjection of Women" which she was eager for every woman in town to read. "And every man, too," Sarah said to herself, but her hopes on that score were realistically low.

In the effort to keep her hands warm, she dropped several pamphlets on the ground. She bent over slowly and struggled to pick them all up, chasing a few errant ones down the street. When she arrived near the town center, she began offering the pamphlet to the women she met along the way. She walked slowly and offered the pamphlet to several small groups of women, and to a few individuals. In her kindly, wispy voice, she said simply, "Please read this," or "Please read this—you will enjoy it!"

"Please read this—it tells our story!" she continued with quiet insistence. Sarah was familiar to most of the townspeople and nearly all the women and a few men accepted her gift more or less willingly with a smile and a "thank you." A few rolled their eyes or exchange amused glances once she passed by. A few discarded the pamphlet immediately, but many of the women began looking through it with interest.

Sarah left copies with merchants she knew, and with some of the women shopkeepers. After about an hour she headed back from the town center toward home. She handed all but the last copy to the people she encountered on her way.

As she crossed the bridge on Fairmount Avenue, she stopped for a moment to watch the winter sun setting over the Neponset river. She handed her last copy to a young man coming from the other direction. He took it politely and passed on. But when he read the title, he looked over his shoulder at her with amused curiosity.

Sarah pulled her coat and muffler tighter around her in the deepening cold. Then she looked down at her empty hands and smiled with profound satisfaction. "I believe my work is done," she said under her breath as she headed up the hill.

The summer passed uneventfully for the sisters, and despite a constant cough and a failing heart, Sarah rose each morning and carried on with her routine of reading, corresponding, and doing whatever charitable works she could manage. But when winter came again, an illness sapped her remaining energy, and she could barely rise from her bed. One afternoon, Charles Stuart sat with her, reading a book she had requested. At eighty-one, Sarah's tiny, thin body lay hidden under a thick quilt, her outsized head propped up on several pillows. Her fatigue was evident, but there remained a sweet glow on her face.

"Auntie, shouldn't you rest now," Charley asked at the end of a chapter. "You look so tired."

"No, dear—I'm well enough today. Thank you for reading to me. You can put that away." She paused to find strength, then said faintly, "But I want to write a short note to Sarah Douglass. Can you write it for me?"

Charley put away the book and took up a piece of stationery and a pen from the nearby desk. "Of course, I shall, if you aren't too tired." He got up and reached over to tenderly adjust the quilt which had slipped off Sarah's shoulders. "There—now you'll be warmer!" He sat down again and asked, "All right—what shall we say?"

Sarah coughed deeply, cleared her throat, then summoned her small reserve of energy to dictate:

> Dearest Sarah,
>
> By now you have heard of my recent illness. The first two weeks are nearly a blank.[73] I only remember a sense of intense suffering, and that the second day I thought I was dying.

Charley wrote quickly with a furrowed brow, looking up at her as he finished each line. Sarah paused, already exhausted from the effort to speak, but after a few moments she continued serenely.

> But death is so beautiful a transition to a higher sphere of usefulness and happiness, that it no longer looks to me like passing through a dark valley, but rather like merging into sunlight and joy.

It was a long sentence, and Sarah coughed violently, gasping for breath. Charley rose and offered her a glass of water, helping her to drink it. He was worried as she quieted herself, and then continued faintly. He had to lean closer to hear her words.

> When consciousness returned to me, I was floating in an ocean of divine love. Oh, dear Sarah, the unspeakable peace that I enjoyed! Of course, I was to come down from the mount, but not into the valley of despondency. My mind has been calm, my faith steadfast. I am lost in wonder, love, and praise at the vast outlay of affection which I have received.

Sarah moved her head slightly and looked affectionately at Charley as she dictated the next lines.

> Charles Stuart has been like a tender daughter, and all here have been so loving, so patient.

"Oh, Auntie, I can't write that! I've done no more than Mother and Father and Susan have."

"Well, I'm sorry you must," Sarah said softly, "You are only my secretary—not my editor." She managed a wry chuckle at his embarrassment. "Please sign it, 'Your loving friend in Jesus, Sarah Moore Grimké.'"

Charley signed and sealed the letter then stood and gazed at Sarah with anxious sadness as she fell into an exhausted sleep.

Sarah died quietly two days before Christmas, and four days later, the Unitarian church in Hyde Park was filled with those who came to remember the quiet radicalness of her life, and to mourn losing the warmth of feeling she had bestowed on each of them. Her family filled the front rows of the church: Angelina, Theodore, Charley, Sissy and her husband, William Hamilton, and their baby daughter, Angelina Grimké Hamilton.[74] Archie and Frank came and sat with Susan, who had forgiven them their fancy dress. They sat in the second row just behind the immediate family. Thodie, still too ill to face this large gathering, was notably absent.

Sarah benefitted from the fact that many of her colleagues and friends were younger than she, and thus survived her, although many were aging as well. Mixed in among her Hyde Park neighbors and friends, were her long-time confidantes and friends, Sarah Douglass, Harriot Hunt, and John Greenleaf Whittier. Among her abolitionist colleagues from the Boston area were Wendell Phillips, William Lloyd Garrison and his son, William Lloyd Garrison, Jr.

Elizur Wright and his daughter, Ellie, were there.[75] Frederick Douglass arrived early and sat with Lucy Stone and Julia Howe. Sarah's dear friends, Gerrit and Ann Smith, came with their daughter, Lizzie Smith Miller, who was accompanied by her husband, Charles Miller, and their adult son, Gatty Miller. Catherine Birney, son of James Birney, and a former student of the sisters was there. It was a grand gathering of people who, if they had not already changed history, were about to do so.

Angelina had asked that the service begin with the church choir singing a favorite hymn, "Nearer my God to Thee." As the congregation gathered and quieted down, the words settled on their ears with comforting sweetness.

> Nearer, my God, to thee, nearer to Thee!
> E'en though it be a cross that raiseth me,
> Still all my song shall be,
> Nearer, my God, to thee.

It felt completely natural for the congregation to join enthusiastically in the refrain, as they were certain that the words perfectly described their sister Sarah.

The plain pine coffin Sarah had requested, was open. It was surrounded by abundant evergreens and holly branches. She appeared placid and serene. The pastor, Rev. Francis Williams, addressed the group. "We have come to lay to rest our sister, Sarah Moore Grimké." Angelina looked tired, sad and almost defeated. Theodore's eyes glowed with tears, but the sorrow was tempered with a pride in his sister-in-law that brought joy. He held tightly onto Nina's and Sissy's hands. Rev. Williams continued:

> To the last, while her mind could plan, her pen could move, and her heart could prompt, she was busy in the service of human-ity. With her might and beyond her strength, she gave herself in constant nameless deeds of kindness to those in need in our own neighborhood.[76]
>
> Nor did she forget those far to the south. Her deeds were wise and beautiful: help to the poor, sympathy with the suffer-ing, consolation to the dying. She has finished her course of duty; she has kept the faith of friendship and sacrifice.

Sarah Douglass wept openly. Archie looked over at her solemnly, wishing his own tears would come as freely. Frank stood with his arms folded in front of him, frowning thoughtfully.

"We will more truly live because she has lived among us. May her hope and peace be ours," Rev. Williams concluded.

There was a brief organ interlude as William Lloyd Garrison rose to speak. The music continued softly in the background. His eulogy went on for nearly a quarter of an hour, describing Sarah's importance to both the abolitionist movement and the cause of women's rights. Then he summarized,

> In view of such a life as hers, consecrated to suffering humanity in its manifold needs, embracing all goodness, animated by the broadest catholicity of spirit, and adorned with every excellent attribute, any attempt at panegyric here seems as needless as it must be inadequate.

It was Charley's turn to be moved to a profound sense of loss. It was not her public deeds he remembered, but her tender hugs when his very young self had needed comfort, and her tolerant empathy as he struggled through adolescence. He bent his head, letting tears fall freely as Garrison continued.

> Here is nothing to depress or deplore, nothing premature or startling, nothing to be supplemented or finished. It is the con-summation of a long life, well-rounded with charitable deeds,

active sympathies, toils, loving ministrations, grand testimonies, and nobly self-sacrificing endeavors.

"She lived only to do good," Garrison observed, "neither seeking nor desiring to be known, ever unselfish, unobtrusive, compassionate, and loving, dwelling in God and God in her."

Garrison took his seat and Lucy Stone arose to add a few words.

Neither do I have any eloquence equal to the goodness of this woman. Sarah has been a mother to us all. She was a mother to many of you when the battle was being waged to free the slave, but then she became a mother to us who struggle for the rights of women.

Lucy took her seat amid nods of appreciation from many in the congregation. There was a long silence, broken by a few muffled sobs and some blowing of noses. It was a welcome interlude. After several minutes, Theodore struggled to rise and come to the front of the church. "I wish I could say a few words . . . " His voice broke and there were tears streaming down his face. "But I—I can't . . . " Theodore turned his face away from the congregation and took a few moments to compose himself.[77]

Our dear Sarah must be laughing to find me dumbstruck! I want only to echo what has been said here, of Sarah's self-denial, her tender love for us, her family, and her simplicity.

He started to choke up again, but managed to pay his last tribute, putting his hands on her coffin.

She wanted, you know, to be buried in this plain, pine coffin—so that—so that the difference in cost could be given to the poor.

He struggled back to his seat next to Angelina who put an arm around his back and a hand on his left arm. As the organ played a hymn, the pallbearers carried out the coffin. Theodore and Angelina left their pew arm in arm, and lead the congregation out into a sunny, December day, to greet their families and friends.

18

Archie Makes His Mark

Boston and Cambridge, Massachusetts 1872–73

ON A FALL DAY in 1872, Harvard Yard was dappled with lush afternoon sunlight streaming through the red and yellow leaves of the American elms, the maples, and the few old oaks that were scattered across the green. A slight, young colored man, Archibald Grimké, walked along one of the crisscrossing paths of the yard, carrying several books and looking very serious. Several other young men were chatting with each other at the end of the path nearest the law classrooms. Noticing Archie walking alone, one of them called out as he approached.

"I say, Sir, are you joining our law class? I believe I know who you are," Henry Cabot Lodge said jocularly. "Do I have the honor of addressing Mr. Archibald Grimké, a famous name here in Boston?"

Archie looked up. "Why, yes—uh—" Archie replied, stunned to be known by name, but pleased, nevertheless.

Lodge extended his hand in greeting. "Lodge, here—Henry Cabot Lodge, that is. Quite a mouthful!" he added in a mocking tone.

"Mr. Lodge, I'm pleased to make your acquaintance," said Archie, shaking his hand vigorously.

"Oh, just call me "Lodge" or "Henry" if you prefer. We're informal here. But I'm amiss in introductions. Here, these are my friends and our fellow law scholars, Mr. Cyrus Heizer and Mr. James Wolff.[78]

Heizer, looking like the rugged athlete that he was, towered over Archie as he welcomed him cordially. Wolff also extended his hand to Archie, giving him a generous, open smile. "Well, I guess we're in for it now, aren't we? Two years of books—no fun, no girls, no drink—just the dismal law to warm our beds at night!"

Archie was disarmed by James' easy manner and returned his smile with a wide grin. He was relieved to find another colored person among his classmates. "Can it be so awful?" Archie asked. "Well, we must do our penance, I suppose."

A bell struck the hour from the clock tower. "Ah, there it is. The death knell," Lodge commented. "Come brothers, let us prostrate ourselves before Lady Justice—a harsh mistress, they say! But she is blind and may yet prove merciful to us!" Chuckling, the young men entered the law school hall together.

Wendell Phillips liked to get acquainted with the young law students from Harvard. He had a particular interest in the progress of young Mr. Grimké and the other colored member of that year's class, James Wolff. He had fought for their admission to his alma mater. Thus, it was that several weeks after their first term began, he hosted a dinner for some of them at his home in Boston.[79]

Archie arrived at the front entry of the Phillips home on Common Street, anxious about his first formal evening in Boston society. He was dressed in his good dress suit, his winter coat, and a top hat, but he had dispensed with the cane. He handed his hat and coat to a servant as he came in. He felt awkward when he looked around and realized that he was among the first to arrive.

Wendell Phillips came forward to welcome him warmly, introducing him to his wife. They chatted for several moments, but when the couple moved on to the next guests, Archie stepped into the parlor where he stood alone, uncertain what to do with himself. A waiter with the fair skin and stark blue eyes of an Irishman, offered him a glass of punch. He was still not used to being waited on by others, but he accepted it gratefully as he watched the bevy of guests coming through the door.

Lucy Stone arrived, shepherding an attractive young woman in her early twenties. Archie's glance lingered on the young woman for a moment. She was laughing gaily at something Lucy Stone had said. Archie was happy to see Parker Pillsbury come in, the brother-in-law of his Charleston teacher, Frances Pillsbury. He noticed that Frederick Douglass had arrived and right behind him, Archie saw his two friends from Harvard Law, Henry Lodge and James Wolff brushing snow off their coats. Archie relaxed and started to walk towards Henry and James as they were being greeted by the Phillips. But Parker Pillsbury saw Archie immediately and waylaid him with a wave of his hand.

"Archibald, good evening!" Pillsbury said heartily.[80] I was hoping you'd be here. Here is someone you really must meet."

"Mr. Pillsbury, good evening. I'm delighted to see you as well. How are your brother and sister-in-law? They did us so much good in Charleston," Archie added fervently. He shook Pillsbury's hand, genuinely glad to see a familiar face.

"They are well, thank you! We are happy to finally have them nearby," he commented. Pillsbury turned to Douglass. "Frederick, may I present to you, Mr. Archibald Grimké. It is a name you must know well. Archie, Mr. Frederick Douglass." Archie bowed deeply. He had seen the distinguished gentleman at his Aunt Sarah's funeral, but they had not been introduced. He remembered his abundance of bushy hair with a streak of silver running though the top.

Archie was momentarily at loss for words, but he enthusiastically shook Douglass' extended hand. "Uh, Mr. Douglass, sir, I am—indeed, I am so very honored to meet you, sir!" Archie felt very young and uncertain face to face with one of his heroes, but he managed to add, "Your life and your writings have inspired me beyond what you can imagine."

Douglass looked intently at Archie, sizing him up quickly. He noted the young man's decent suit of clothes, his direct gaze, and the self-possession underlying his diffident manner. He was favorably impressed. "Mr. Grimké, I believe I saw you at Miss Sarah Grimké's funeral. She was your aunt, as I understand it?" His regard was kindly but grave.

"Yes, sir. Her brother, Henry, was my father, but he died when I was quite young. I was raised by my mother who had been his slave."

"Hmmm. Quite a familiar story, isn't it? In fact, my own situation was similar, although I did not long have a mother's care. She was sold away from me." He spoke matter-of-factly, but his downward look told Archie that it was still a painful memory. "How did you come to the north?" Douglass asked.

Their conversation was interrupted briefly by a servant offering them punch, and when the two older men had each taken a cup, Pillsbury jumped in to answer the question. "My sister-in-law, Frances, taught him in Charleston just after the war." He looked at Archie with some personal pride as he added, "His exceptional abilities as well as those of his brother, Frank, impressed her so much that she found a way for them both to continue their studies at Lincoln University in Pennsylvania."

Archie started to demur, but Douglass nodded and said, "Ah, yes, I see. Somehow you learned to read—as I did—despite all odds—and that was the key, was it not?"

Archie tilted his head thoughtfully and nodded. "It was my father who first taught me." He had always taken his ability to read for granted since he had been taught his letters as a toddler, but he knew he was an exception, and he understood Douglass' point. Douglass was pensive for a moment, then gave Archie a knowing look. "And your aunts took you in. That alone is quite amazing. But then, again, not at all surprising from what I know of their character."

Before Archie could agree, Douglass continued, "Miss Sarah—what a loss for all of us. I believe it was her writings that confirmed my own view that the ballot box must not be denied to anyone because of their color—nor because of their sex."

Archie looked at Douglass with new appreciation and nodded vigorously. "A view I certainly share, sir, and—"

Douglass interrupted, as Pillsbury moved away to speak to other guests. "And how are the Welds? Your Aunt Angelina and Theodore?"

"Uncle Theodore is very well. He is nearly eighty you know, but he is still quite vigorous. Fortunately, I see him often." He paused, biting his lower lip as he recalled his last visit. "But Aunt Angelina suffered a severe stroke shortly after Aunt Sarah's death. She can only move about with difficulty. She depends on Theodore and their son, Charles Stuart, and their housekeeper for everything. Theodore is totally devoted to her. Well, they all are," Archie added after a pause.

Douglass replied, "Yes, now I recall. I had heard she was taken ill. I was so sorry to hear it. What a golden voice she had in those early days of barnstorming for abolition! I heard her speak once," Douglass continued, "And Theodore. Well, of course!"

At that moment William Garrison and his son came up to join them. "Frederick, my old friend, how glad we are that you were in Boston for this occasion. I see you've met the Grimkés' young nephew and protégé." Turning to the young man, Garrison asked, "Archibald, how are you? Have you met my son, William?" Will, about ten years older than Archie, grabbed Archie's hand in a firm grasp. He asked him about his law studies and how he was finding Harvard, while the older gentlemen caught up with each other.

The room had grown warm with the animated conversation. Archie was enjoying talking with Will Garrison when Wendell Phillips' strong voice called out, "Ladies and gentlemen, our supper is served. Please join us in the dining room."

The guests begin to pair off to walk formally into the large dining room. There were about twice as many men as women, so several of the men walked in together. Archie looked around for one of his friends, but his eyes fell on the young woman who had come in with Lucy Stone. She appeared next to him and seemed to be without a dinner partner. She gave him an amused grin. "Don't be shy, Mr. Grimké. You see, I know quite well who you are! May I?" She boldly tucked her hand into his arm to be escorted to dinner.

"But I'm afraid you have the advantage of me, Miss—? You see I don't believe we've been introduced. As I understand these things, I may escort you, but I may not speak to you." They both laughed at this absurdity.

"Yes, isn't it ridiculous!" She hesitated and looked at him saucily, "Miss Bradford, if you *must* know. Nelly Bradford.[81] I hate all this formality. But Lucy Stone has told me all about you. Still, you must tell me yourself. I love to hear people's stories." The guests settled into their seats at the table, and Archie pulled out a chair for Nelly to sit next to him. He turned and shook hands warmly with James Wolff who was on his other side, but whom he had not yet greeted. Careful observers, Wolff among them, noted that Archibald and Nelly carried on an animated conversation, punctuated by frequent laughter.

There are years of great wars that divide history, and then there are the years when apparently small decisions, minor but insidious, shape the centuries that follow. Most of us are oblivious to those barely perceptible foreshocks, but there are those who sense the seismic shifts and feel the colliding plates in their bones. The chipping away at Reconstruction was such a case.

In the spring when an exceptionally warm day lured them from their law studies, Henry Lodge proposed a Saturday afternoon expedition to the upper reaches of the Charles River. Archie, James Wolff, Henry Lodge, Cyrus Heizer, and several young women walked gaily west along the Charles River from Cambridge towards Watertown. Nelly Bradford was among them.[82] They carried a picnic hamper and blankets.

As they settled down to their picnic by the riverside, there was earnest conversation about the chaotic state of national politics, including news of corruption in President Grant's administration, and what it would mean for the Republicans in the next year's election.

"Perhaps a woman will run again, like Victoria Woodhull," Nelly Bradford suggested mischievously.

"Well, she was a joke," Henry said disparagingly. "She wasn't even old enough to be president. And Frederick Douglass didn't really acknowledge his nomination as her vice president. No, we need to think seriously and realistically about the future of the Republican party, or the gains of Reconstruction could be lost."

Archie looked worried. "Yes, I hear rumors. My brother Frank tells me that there is much unrest in the southern states, although the northern newspapers don't report it. Colored men are afraid to vote, and land, rightfully owned by them is taken away. Legal titles mean nothing and, even in counties where they are in the majority, former slaves and free colored are intimidated. It's—it's frightening."

James chimed in, "Is it really that bad, Archie? I hear about colored legislators and more colored children in school, and successful farmers. Aren't you rather gloomy, Sir?"

Nelly glanced at Archie to see his reaction, but he only shrugged and said, "I hope I am wrong but . . . "

Henry rejoined, "I don't think you are wrong, Archie, and that is why we need to elect a liberal Republican, no matter what! The Democrats are determined to placate southern landowners and white farmers." Cyrus nodded in agreement.

"Well, for that you would certainly benefit from women's suffrage" Nelly replied seriously. But she smiled and said, "At least women are honest and don't do back-room deals." This earned her shrieks of laughter from the other women as well as dismissive snorts from the young men.

"Oh, heavens, Nelly" one of the women said, "Surely, you don't believe that!"

The conversation passed to lighter topics, punctuated with laughter and good-humored teasing. Archie was happy to put aside his troubled thoughts and when he wasn't admiring Nelly's lively eyes, he looked out contentedly at the boats sliding by on the Charles. The young women waved their hats at the boaters as the men stretched out on the grassy slope, freeing their minds briefly from the affairs of the world and the sophistries of Lady Justice.

Massachusetts and Washington, DC

1875—1913

19

Frank in Washington, D.C.

September 1875

FRANCIS GRIMKÉ AND REV. John Reeve came out of Reeve's office at his church as their visit concluded.[83] Reeve shook Frank's hand vigorously, with one hand on Frank's shoulder. "Francis, I know you have struggled to come to this decision, but I feel that it is the right path for you. Of course, personally I am delighted. You will make an excellent minister and colleague. I think you will find Princeton Theological Seminary very much to your liking."

"Thank you for encouraging me, Reverend Reeve," Frank said. "As you know, your example has inspired me. If you'd told me five years ago that I would end up studying for the ministry, I would have been as much amused as shocked! Piety was always my brother Archie's strength," Frank admitted with a chuckle as he headed toward the door of the rectory.

"I hope that my two years of law study will not be entirely in vain. Howard University was good to me. But the law —there is so much speciousness in it. And I don't really want to send people to jail. I want to help change their hearts." Frank gave a self-deprecating shrug. "I fear that I have wasted some time."

"Not at all, my dear boy! I am confident that this is all part of what the Lord intends for you. The discipline of the law and its importance in the political realm will strengthen your mind for the work ahead."

They reached the outside door, and Reeve lowered his voice, speaking gravely. "Frank, I'm worried about how things are going in the South. It all looked so hopeful a few years ago—but now the Republicans are questioning the principles of Reconstruction, and the Democrats have regained control of the House. And even of many offices in the South."

"There is talk that our government could pull back the federal agents and leave southern justice to the workings of the white population—many of them deeply embittered. That must not happen!" Reeves shook his head in distress. "The stories I am beginning to hear from our brothers who make it up here to Washington are disturbing, to say the least."

Frank had heard the rumors, but he was unsure of their veracity, so he asked with a frown, "What kind of stories, Reverend?"

"Land lawfully bought by ex-slaves is being taken back by white landowners; tenant farmers are unable to command fair prices for their goods; and when colored farmers *do* succeed, any pretext is sufficient to punish them for such effrontery. You've heard of the Klan?"

Frank listened intently. Some of this was news to him. "Yes. But I thought President Grant put an end to that. Surely it can't be that serious, can it?" He turned and looked at his mentor with uncertainty. "Now, with the right to vote, can we not elect our own local officials—our own sheriffs? In many counties, colored people are the majority, aren't they? Why we have fourteen colored men in Congress! I heard recently that a half million colored people are attending southern schools. Isn't this good progress in so short a time?" Frank asked.

Rev. Reeve stared at Frank gravely, hating to dampen his youthful optimism. "I wish you were right, Frank, but that is not what I hear. However, let us not dwell on trying thoughts today," he said with a weak smile. "When will you be back from Princeton? I look forward to more discussion then."

"I expect I'll be back by early summer. I may spend Christmas in Boston with Archie if I can afford the fare." Reeve gave him a pat on the shoulder as Frank headed out into a sunny afternoon in Washington. As he watched him leave, Reeve's face grew solemn, pondering the inevitable struggles awaiting his young friend. "Lord, hasn't he been through enough already?" Reeves thought.

Frank sniffed at the brisk autumn air that seemed to be a spicy mélange of wood smoke, damp leaves and sweet herbs. Occasionally he caught a whiff of local cooking—bacon, garlic, aromatic stews and roasted vegetables—coming from the neighborhood homes. He walked from the north end of the District down Georgia Avenue to where it became Seventh Street, then along Seventh towards the center of town.

Ahead of him to the southeast he could see the Capitol Building. Frank's mind was clouded with what he had learned from Rev. Reeve, but as he walked the sights and smells of the city improved his mood. He smiled at the children playing on the street, dwelling on his own hopeful prospects for the future.

Near the Mt. Vernon market above the intersection of Seventh Street and New York Avenue, Miss Charlotte Forten came out of the market area and turned west away from where Frank was walking south. She paused, remembering that she had forgotten to buy peppers. She turned back to Seventh Street as Frank was approaching. She saw him before he saw her. At first, she was unsure if he were the young man she had known nearly nine years earlier. But the cocky tilt of his head made her quite certain of who he was. As she approached, she stopped abruptly.[84]

Frank glanced up and recognized her, a look of surprise and delight quickly crossing his face. He took in her well-tailored, conservative dress, high-heeled boots, and the erect bearing that made her look taller, although, he reckoned, she barely cleared five feet.

"My stars! If it isn't that poor, pathetic excuse of a boy, Francis Grimké!" She was smiling broadly, at least as happy to see him as he was to discover her. She looked him up and down approvingly. "Well, I think your fairy godfather came and turned you from a frog into a handsome prince. I am amazed!"

Frank laughed at her reluctant compliment. "Miss Forten! Look, you are smaller than me! So, I think you must no longer take that air of superiority which ill becomes you!" They shook hands heartily, Charlotte giving Frank a small, mocking curtsey.

"Yes, sir. But don't forget, I am your elder. Well, never mind, I see I must treat you with all due respect." She shrugged in surrender at the prospect. "But what a shock! What brings you to Washington?"

"Why I have been here nearly two years now. I've been studying law at Howard University." He hesitated, then asked with an interested smile, "And you?"

Charlotte was impressed, but not enough to forget that he was her junior in nearly every way. "Hmmm. Well, that explains it. You have been studying hard, I hope? That was not an auspicious beginning you had in New England, was it?" Then her brow wrinkled in puzzlement. "But how have we not met before?"

Frank responded with a wry smile and a shrug of his shoulders. Charlotte frowned and answered her own question, "Well, I'm not often in this part of town so it is not so surprising that our paths have not crossed. I'm working at the U.S Treasury Department. Are you a rich merchant yet? We will come after you for tariffs, you know," she said with a hint of a smile.

Frank laughed ruefully. "I am rich in friends and family. Do they tax those?"

Charlotte approved of that remark and her tone changed. "Francis, I do want to hear everything about you. How are you doing? You do look so well, and so—so, grown up! And how is Archie?" she continued, wanting to make up for lost time. "Oh, and please, call me Lottie. That is what my friends call me."

Frank began. "Well, there is so much to tell. Archie is very well." He looked around and pointed to a place in the square, "There's a bench over there, Miss Forten—uh, Lottie, that is. Can you sit for a few moments?"

Charlotte glanced anxiously at the lowering sun, but she nodded agreeably. She and Frank walked over and took seats on the bench, each talking animatedly and listening carefully in turn. Frank's eyes rested on her intently for a moment, but he looked away quickly, embarrassed at the turn his thoughts had taken. After thirty minutes, Charlotte rose to leave, knowing that another chance meeting was unlikely since Frank was leaving town. She felt a twinge of sadness at that, as she wished Frank well at Princeton Seminary. Frank started down the street, but he turned and looked after her for a long time as she walked away.

20

Nelly

Boston, May 1876

DESPITE THE DEMANDS OF law school, Archie was not one to neglect his social life. During the year after their introduction at Wendell Phillips' soiree, and the subsequent picnic with their friends by the Charles River, Nelly Bradford and Archie had become frequent and fond companions.

On a day in mid-May Archie walked into the Common, heading up toward a bench near the Statehouse. He took off his jacket, surprised at the warmth of the spring weather. He sat down on the bench and looked around expectantly. The Common shimmered with sunlight sliding off the newly leafed trees and pouring onto the crocuses and daffodils that surrounded him.

Several minutes passed until Archie looked impatiently at his watch. Frowning, he stood up and put his coat back on now that he was cooling off. He looked around, then sat back down with his head hanging in moody dejection. Nearby, an elderly colored woman fed the birds from the bench where she sat.

Nelly Bradford hurried down into the Common from the Beacon Street side then walked hastily up the path with her precariously perched hat flying off her head in the wind. She grabbed it before it flew away and held it in her hand. Several curls escaped from the loosely fastened bun on top of her head. Archie turned his head and saw her coming up the path. His face brightened. Nelly waved her fashionable flower-covered little hat gaily, then attempted to pin her hair back in place and fasten her hat properly. She called out from twenty yards away. "Archie, I'm so sorry! Am I very late? Did you think I wasn't coming? I'm so glad you are still here!"

"No, no—of course I knew you would come!" he said, and though he knew it wasn't quite true, he forgot his uncertainty now that she had arrived. They shook hands eagerly, Archie beaming at her.

"But if you hadn't, I thought I'd ask that gentle lady over there to come to the Athenaeum with me." He nodded toward the elderly, colored woman nearby. Nelly pretended to look hurt, "Well, if you'd prefer—I could take her place feeding the birds!" They both laughed lightly. Archie offered his arm and Nelly tucked her hand into it as they walked up the hill toward the Boston Athenaeum.

"Nelly, I'm very glad you suggested the art gallery here. I heard from Henry that they will soon be moving into their new building on Copley Square—the Boston Museum of Fine Arts it will be called. Quite an imposing name."

"Yes, it looks like it will be very grand," she responded. The opening gala is next month. Would you like to attend?"

Archie looked at Nelly with surprise. "Seriously? But don't we need an invitation?"

"Yes, but my parents have one for themselves and guests."

"Well, then, certainly. I would be delighted!" Archie said with only a brief hesitation. "But Nelly, you need to instruct me. I've read a bit, but I'm not well-versed in fine art. I know what I like but—"

"Oh, there's nothing to it, Archie. Some people are so pretentious about it. Just look carefully and see what interests you. What you like and what moves you. That's all there is to it, really. At least that's what I think."

"And *you* are not shy with your opinions, my friend. I admire that about you." Nelly accepted the compliment with a wry look.

"But wait—before I forget," Archie added, "I have an invitation for you as well. Aunt Angelina and Uncle Theodore have invited us to dinner next Sunday evening. Can you come?"

"Oh, my! I'm dying to meet them both. I've heard so much about them, even before I met you. And now that I know how kind they have been to you and your brother, I could not imagine not liking them."

She stopped walking and frowned, "Oh, dear—is that the 24th? It's my birthday! Well, no matter. My parents won't mind if we celebrate it a day late."

"Are you sure?" Archie said with consternation. "Of course, Aunt and Uncle would love to celebrate your birthday with you! But I don't want to—"

"No, it's perfect. What a lovely birthday present for me. It is settled then," Nelly said, enormously pleased. They had arrived at the door of the Boston Atheneum and Archie opened it for Nelly. The attendant who directed them to the art gallery looked after the young couple with curiosity.

Early on the evening of May 24th, Theodore and Susan helped Angelina down the stairs to the parlor just before the dinner hour. Angelina's face was lined with fatigue, and she grimaced with pain as she descended the stairs. Paralyzed on one side she could only move slowly with great deliberation. She carried a cane which allowed her more independence once she was on level ground. Her mouth was drawn down slightly on her paralyzed side, but her voice was still clear and distinct. Theodore helped to settle Angelina in a chair in the parlor.

Theodore had for some time allowed his white beard to grow to his chest and, coupled with the bushy white eyebrows above his kind eyes, his resemblance to Saint Nicholas was startling. There was a knock on the door and Susan went over to usher in Archie and Nelly. Archie introduced Nelly to Theodore and then to Angelina who remained seated. Nelly greeted the stalwart elder couple with courteous respect tinged with awe.

Angelina was immediately taken with the young woman and said, "Now, Miss Bradford, please sit here next to me, and tell me all about yourself. My body is rather worn out, but I still hear very well."

"You are very kind, Mrs. Weld. But please, call me Nelly."

Angelina peered at her with a slightly amused look. "Nelly, then! Archie has spoken of you with much enthusiasm. But he makes up in fervor what he lacks in detail." Nelly blushed a little and looked down with a pleased smile. Angelina and Nelly were soon in an animated conversation about women's progress and the right to vote, while Archie and Theodore caught up on political news.

After a few minutes, Theodore turned the conversation to a more personal concern, saying, "Archie, Wendell Phillips is keeping me informed of your comings and goings which appear to be plentiful. He is my spy, you see."

Archie laughed, "Well, uncle, you couldn't have a better one! We often walk together of an evening. He lives quite close to me, you know. He listens to me carefully, and so I value his advice."

"Hmmm, yes indeed. And your law studies? I hear you are doing well," he said. Then he frowned and added in a teasing but fatherly tone, "Although from what I know of your social life, I am not sure how that is possible."

Archie was used to Theodore's tendency to expect moral perfection, so he answered carefully. "I admit my head has been turned a bit by the wonderful friends I have made. And it has been difficult to pass up opportunities for serious conversation and for meeting the most interesting people in Boston. Did I tell you I met Frederick Douglass at Mr. Phillips' home?" he asked. "And of course, I met Garrison and his son, Will, and Lucy Stone—and Nelly," he said glancing over at her appreciatively as she chatted with his aunt. "It is like a feast of rich food, and I am not yet persuaded to manage my diet," he said light-heartedly.

Theodore looked at him with tolerant skepticism. Archie's face grew more sober, realizing he needed to reassure Theodore more straightforwardly. "But, sir, I assure you I take my studies very seriously," Archie continued. "I graduate in a month, and next fall I will begin as a clerk in the law offices of William Bowditch. Mr. Phillips and others have persuaded him to take me on, and I'm ever so grateful. I wish only to do honor to my parents and my aunts and yourself—to be worthy of the Grimké name," he said.

Theodore's piercing eyes bore through him. "So, you will stay in Boston for the time being?" He nodded toward his wife. "You know that Angelina believes you would do well to return to South Carolina and help your colored brothers there."

Archie's face darkened for a moment, but he said patiently, "Yes, I understand her thinking about that. I hear from Frank about how badly things have been going in Florida and the Carolinas, especially since last year with the panic and all. So many of our brothers have come north because their legal rights have been consistently denied them: their right to a fair trial by their peers, to the proceeds of their own property, and even their recently won right to vote."

Then Archie spoke earnestly and imploringly, determined to make his benefactors understand. "But, Uncle Theodore, Aunt Angelina of all people should understand how impossible it would be for Frank and myself to return to that scene of our oppression." Archie glanced over at his aunt to make sure she was fully engaged with Nelly. "The system of slavery may be overturned, but the system of white privilege and power endures." Archie looked away, trying to disguise the bitterness he felt. "Uncle, she could not bear to live there, as a privileged white woman! And yet she thinks Frank and I could be happy in the city where we were so recently enthralled, starved, and scourged?"

Theodore listened intently and his compassion overcame his moralism. He answered slowly, "This is a compelling argument you make, Archibald, and I, for one, am convinced by it. You have every right to find your new life here in New England. Your aunt can be insistent in her opinions, but I know she wants your happiness above all." Theodore glanced over at the women who were still chatting animatedly. He looked sidewise at Archie with a sympathetic chuckle. "And your friend here, Miss Nelly Bradford; I can see how she could be quite a distraction."

Archie scratched his ear in mild embarrassment. Fortunately, Susan appeared to call them to supper. The four sat down at the table, and after she had served the dishes, Susan sat down with them. They bowed their heads for a moment's grace, then conversation continued as Theodore gave Nelly the third degree, but in a genial way that she enjoyed.

Angelina looked at Archie with proud contentment, her fatigue and discomfort temporarily forgotten. She asked him about his latest news from Frank and inquired when his brother might visit Boston. At the end of their evening together, Archie and Nelly said good-by to their hosts, promising to see them again later in the summer. They left the house with Nelly's hand in Archie's arm. After Theodore showed them out, he returned to the parlor where Angelina sat. She felt very tired but peaceful. Turning to her husband, she asked eagerly, "So, Theo, what did you think?"

Theodore couldn't resist teasing her a bit and said, "Whatever do you mean, my dear? I thought it was a nourishing meal."

Angelina rolled her eyes with mild impatience. "You know exactly what I mean, Theodore. What did you think of Nelly? Do you think Archie has serious intentions? He's still quite young and not well-established yet."

"Ah, Nelly!" Theodore pretended surprise. "Are you match-making, my dear? Well, she seems like a sensible young woman, intelligent, and pretty as well."

"Yes, I agree—and she seems to be very fond of Archie. I believe they are an excellent match."

She looked down, uncomfortable, as she raised the inevitable issue of race. "I hope she is not toying with him, Theo. I hate to ask this," she hesitated, "but do you think she would seriously consider marrying a man of colored descent?"

"Hmmm, since you put it that way—would Archie seriously consider marrying a woman of pale, puritan descent?"

Angelina frowned at him. "Theodore, you and I know, as much as we hate color prejudice, that this is not a laughing matter. Could they be happy together?" Angelina pondered her own question, and answered it, "I believe they could be. I believe they are! And it should be their choice. But what about her parents?"

"Nina, you are right to be concerned, of course. However, I know her parents, John and Jane Bradford, and they are ardent abolitionists. I suspect that Nelly's attitude exactly mirrors that of her parents. And, well—their own friends are all abolitionists and free-thinkers. They have little to fear from this segment of Boston society."

Angelina sighed, and looked uncertainly at her husband, as he came to help her get up to their bedroom. "I hope you are right, dear. She seems like a lovely girl, very self-assured, and very committed to women's rights, of course." Angelina's face brightened, "You know what she said to me? She said that Archie has manners so exactly right that there is nothing to remark about them."[85]

Angelina struggled to get to her feet with Theodore's help. "Theo, do you remember how ill-suited we once seemed to be? And yet, in other respects, how perfectly matched. We had our dark times but look how well it has turned out." Angelina looked at Theodore fondly, then leaned her head into his shoulder. He embraced her gently, kissing her on the forehead before helping her up the stairs.

Archie worked diligently through the summer but continued to enjoy outings with his friends and a full social life. It was a golden time for him. On an afternoon in early fall, he was sitting on his favorite bench in the Public Garden, contemplating how to prepare a brief for the Bowditch firm, but distracted by other thoughts. There were clouds gathering and a chill in the air.

He had just decided to head back to his lodgings when he saw Nelly hurrying toward him. She looked distraught and her eyes were red. Archie was very pleased to see her, but as she drew close, he noticed her distress.

"Archie, I hoped I'd find you here! Everything is in a muddle—I'm so unhappy!"

"Yes, I can see that. Dear girl, what *is* the matter? Can it be so bad?" Archie took her hands in his own, gently squeezing them, then drew his away, not wanting to be overly affectionate in public.

"Come, can we walk a bit? I need to think," Nelly said with a deep sigh. They headed out toward the Charles River and walked along it for several minutes until they found a secluded bench. Archie waited for Nelly to speak. Finally, she looked over at Archie, "It's my father—well, my whole family, really. His business—it is taking him to western Pennsylvania, and he wants us all to come along." She started to sob, "Archie, I don't want to leave Boston. I don't. . ." She looked at Archie to see his reaction. He looked stricken but also puzzled. Nelly continued, searching his face. "I don't want to leave my friends here—or you, Archie, for you are the best among them!"

She looked away, embarrassed at her confession. Archie glanced around to make sure there was no one close. He took her hand quietly. "And you, dear Nelly—you are my good fairy! How can I live without my dearest companion here." Archie frowned and asked, "Why must you go? Can you not stay here with friends, or in a boarding house?"

"My father won't hear of it. I did ask him. But the truth is, I love my parents. I would miss them terribly. I just don't want any of us to have to leave." She turned her face up to his imploringly, "Oh, Archie, what shall we do? I don't see any good outcome."

Archie was distressed and deeply conflicted. After a moment he said earnestly, "Nelly, you know that if I were established—if I had my own practice and were worthy of you . . . " He stammered a bit, "You know—in two years perhaps."

"Shhh. Yes, I know. I understand. This is no time for you to make promises, to me, or to anyone." Nelly bit her lips. She was crestfallen. She knew that she had secretly hoped for an engagement, but she also realized the impracticality of it. It was part of her distress. Nelly wiped her eyes where tears had begun again. She looked bravely at Archie and said, "I believe we are the best of companions, but it seems we must part. I think we must trust in God that our future will be what it will be. You have been a gift to me, Archie. That will never be taken away."

"And we can write, can we not? I am a very faithful correspondent," Archie assured her.

Nelly looked down, trying to swallow her sadness and the tight pain she felt in her heart. She spoke quietly, resignation in her voice, "Yes. If you aren't too busy." Archie lifted her chin and kissed her gently on the forehead. She smiled up at him, and they held each other in a sad but comforting embrace.

21

A Meeting of Mothers

Christmas, Hyde Park 1876

ARCHIE STOOD ON THE platform of the Readville station of the Boston and Providence Railroad Line restlessly awaiting the arrival of a train. His ears were filled with the dissonance of Christmas chimes, noisy conveyances coming and going on the main street outside, and loud chatter around him. He tried to distract himself by watching the other local citizens anticipating the arrival of loved ones for the Christmas season. He shared their eagerness, but he affected a nonchalance that he thought better befit his dignity as a newly established lawyer. He had not seen his mother since he left Charleston over ten years earlier.

As the train chugged slowly into the station, his impatience overcame any pretense to dignity, and Archie eagerly jogged down the platform toward the passenger compartments looking for Frank and their mother. Likewise, Nancy Weston, now close to sixty, looked out the train window hoping to catch a glimpse of her eldest son. Her face was creased like a mosaic, but serene.

Frank retrieved their suitcases from an overhead compartment, jostling with other passengers who were reaching for valises and bags filled with Christmas delicacies for their hosts. Once he had their bags, Frank waited politely until other passengers got off. When the aisle was nearly empty, he helped his mother stand up and walk to the door of the train.

Frank held on to his mother as they navigated the steep steps to the platform. He looked around for his brother and saw him searching frantically for them at the far end of the train. Archie turned and seeing them, darted through the crowd at a run. He swept his mother's slight frame into a bear hug, then holding onto her, he greeted Frank with a hearty handshake. He kept one arm around his mother, laughing as joyfully as a child on a carousel. His mother leaned away so she could survey him properly. Then, pleased and proud, she nodded approvingly at her grown-up, well-dressed son. Archie reached out to take her bag from Frank.

Although it was only a mile and a half from the Readville station, Archie paid for a private cab to carry them to his simple two-room lodging in an establishment in Hyde Park. He showed Frank and his mother the living room which included a table, three straight-backed chairs and a sofa, the adjoining kitchen area with a coal-burning stove, and the small bedroom with a single bed made up. Archie set his mother's things in the bedroom where he had placed a vase with holly and evergreens. He had also draped some evergreen boughs around the windows in the living room in an attempt to brighten up the very plain interior.

"So, Mother, this is home! Not even as large as our little house on Coming Street," he said apologetically, "but fine for me, even during a Boston winter."

Nancy surveyed the place approvingly. "Archie—and Frank—y'all know that I'd be happy in a thatched hut as long as you two was there." She reached out to embrace Archie again as she held onto Frank's hand. "Oh, my boys! What a joyful Christmas this shall be!" Her voice, the boys noticed, was hoarse and weak, despite her evident pleasure in being with them.

"But Mama, you must be so tired—and hungry," Archie observed. "Look here, I'm not much of a cook, but I have some cold ham and some bean soup that I made up last night, and some good bread. And I bought us a special treat for Christmas eve.

He walked over and uncovered a fruitcake he had purchased, eager to show it off. Nancy smiled broadly at her eldest son. "My stars! Well, I 'spect that's more for you than for me," she teased. "But it does look right delicious. Thank you, son."

Frank broke in to say, "We did eat at Hartford, Archie, but that was at least four hours ago. I'm famished." The three of them ate their Christmas eve meal with relish, and the brothers caught up on their news. Nancy listened carefully but said little. After eating several helpings of the fruitcake with his tea, Frank leaned back and patted his full stomach with a groan. "Oh, brother, you have made a glutton of me," he said quite happily. He glanced at his mother and saw that she was struggling to stay awake. "Mama, I think we've tired you out with all our talk. And it's been a long day. Let's make you comfortable in your room."

"And tomorrow's a big day," Archie added. "After the Christmas service, we are invited to the Welds' home for Christmas dinner. Aunt Angelina has been poorly of late, but she so wants to meet you, mother. I believe she wants to hear about our father from you."

Nancy rose with difficulty, ready to go to bed, but she stopped short when she heard about the invitation. She frowned. "Does she? It was so long ago—I don't know," her voice faded into uncertainty. Nancy shook her head in a kind of sad disgust. "You told me she felt 'shamed of his behavior toward me. What does she know?" she asked, more sorrowfully than angry. "I'm not 'shamed of anything. Your father was mostly good to me—and without him, where would you boys be?" She looked at Archie and Frank with a defiant smile, but she remained troubled by her memories. She had not been forced into her relationship with Henry, she knew, but she had also understood that it would make her life easier. How many times had she asked herself if she had been wrong to love him, or if she should have steered clear of him, knowing her own mixed motivations? But she came back, as always, to the rightness of the boys.

Archie tried to reassure her. "No, it's not like that, mother. She understands. She loved our father, too. I think she just wants to hear that he was a decent man, and how he was towards the end and all." He hesitated before continuing, "And she wants to know you. They've been kind to us—she and Uncle Theodore—and Aunt Sarah, too, before she died."

"Yes, 'course they have—and I thank the Lord for that every day. But those memories—those years—they are hard to think about." With a bitter sigh, she went on, "I guess he loved us, but he was careless 'bout our future. And Montague took 'vantage of that, and the rest of the family didn't do anythin' to make it better. So, it's all mixed up for me."

Frank looked down, then shook his head quietly at Archie, wishing that his brother had not raised painful memories on a joyful day. But he said only, "Let's get you to bed, Mama. You'll have happier thoughts on a Christmas morn. When you wake up, we'll all be here together."

A few minutes later, Frank and Archie sat down at the table again, talking in low voices. Archie drummed his fingers on the table. "I'm a bit worried about how mother will fare here in Boston. Of course, I'm delighted to have her here. But my rooms are so small—and she will not be used to New England winters. I wish I had more to offer," he said regretfully.

"The winters are harsher here, it's true," Frank agreed. "But she is so happy to be with us, Archie! Life in Charleston was becoming impossible for her, you know."

Frank rubbed his hands together anxiously. "In any case, I hope to be settled in Washington within the year. I've been offered an associate position at the Fifteenth Street Presbyterian Church there. Once I'm established and have some income, I should be able to have mama there."

Archie nodded, feeling some relief. "Congratulations, Frank, that is great news!"

Frank paused and looked at Archie shyly. "Did I tell you that I've run into Charlotte Forten several times?"

Archie gave Frank an amused look. "Yes, you did, Frank. Several times. And you told me how pretty she looked—and how nice she is!" He mimicked Frank's sentiments in a high voice. He grinned, happy to have a chance to tease Frank, knowing how long his brother had been "sweet" on Charlotte. "But what does she think of a youngster like you, brother!"

Frank looked serious and a little crestfallen. "Well, not much, I suppose. She's a fine lady, with a good job. She still sees me as that scrawny little jackass!" They both laughed heartily.

"Well, I believe we can fatten you up a bit more over the holidays—like a pig for the slaughter!" Archie chuckled.

Frank rolled his eyes, and changed the subject, "But what about you, Archie? Tell me what's goin' on."

Archie was happy to oblige. It had been such a long time since the brothers had had a chance to really talk and, despite occasional letters, he had felt the loneliness of their separate lives. "The best news is that James Wolff and I started our practice together. He was happy to join with me, and we do well as partners. He's an honest fellow and a good lawyer. We have several clients," he paused with a reluctant grimace, "but we do need to keep drumming up business."

After several moments of dwelling on his financial worries, Archie brightened, and said, "Say, I'd love to show you and mother our offices on Washington Street!" As an afterthought, he said, "And then I have some writing projects I'm working on when I can."

"Do you still hear from Nelly Bradford, Archie?" Frank asked delicately.

"I do" he frowned, "but not as often. She's busy, and well, I haven't responded very promptly. I believe I owe her a letter. I missed her a lot at first, but I got busy, and now—"

"Yes? Now?" Frank probed.

Archie answered testily, "I don't know, Frank. I've been working too hard trying to make ends meet and—well, I can't seem to save anything. I mean—I don't have much to offer her . . ."

There was silence for a moment. Then Frank decided to change the subject again. "Listen, brother, we need to talk about more serious matters."

"More serious than my pecuniary woes?" Archie asked ironically.

"I'm afraid so, brother. I'm so angry about the way the last presidential election ended up. Hayes simply bought the presidency with his promises to Southern Democrats to abandon Reconstruction." Archie listened quietly, trusting his brother's political sense more than his own. "The South was already in dire straits—and now—with no federal protection, no enforcement of the constitutional amendments, it seems like our emancipation is practically meaningless. We have been betrayed!" Frank got up and paced around the room, looking angry and dejected at the thought.

Archie nodded and waited a moment before commenting. "Hmmm. I have a meeting with James Trotter after the first of the year. We are going to discuss the way forward for the colored community. He sees no further use for the Republican Party—but I still believe the party of Lincoln and Grant is the best guarantor of our rights."

Frank lifted his eyebrows and looked skeptical. "Well, I can't think about it much at the moment," he declared. "I need to concentrate on finishing my divinity degree and getting started in the church. But the stories I hear, Archie, they disturb my sleep no end," Frank confessed. "And speaking of sleep—I'm very tired. We can talk more tomorrow," Frank concluded with a worried frown. He rose from the table and carried their teacups to the kitchen.

Archie gave his younger brother a reassuring and grateful embrace before they settled down for the night. He lay blankets on the floor for himself so that Frank could sleep on the sofa. His brother objected at first, but once Frank lay down on the narrow divan, he was asleep before Archie could turn out the gas lamp.

After the morning Christmas service at the Hyde Park Presbyterian Church, Archie showed Frank and their mother around the center of Hyde Park. It was cold and blustery, but there was very little snow left on the ground from the last storm. Nancy seemed well-rested and vigorous, so they agreed to walk across the river and up the hill to the Weld home.

Nancy grew solemn and wary as they drew near to the home of Henry's sister. Archie supported his mother up the steps. Once inside, Susan helped remove the warm coat that Frank had bought for her when she arrived in New York. The Weld parlor was decorated with a few simple, Christmas decorations that Susan had insisted on—evergreen boughs, holly, candles in the window, and a sprig of mistletoe over the doorway to the dining room. Charley was abroad so Theodore met Archie, Frank and Nancy at the door, greeting them heartily, and ushering them into the parlor.

Angelina struggled to rise from her seat to greet Nancy and her nephews, using her cane as a prop. Nancy immediately noticed Angelina's partial paralysis. Somehow Angelina's infirmity reminded her of her own aging body—and it lessened her fear. Angelina shifted the cane to her left arm and took Nancy's hand in both her own as they exchanged greetings and polite inquiries about each other's health. Nancy was still wary, but her reserve softened into a sad smile when Angelina finally asked her about Henry.

Angelina urged Nancy to sit down in a chair next to her and they continued to speak gently and earnestly to each other. After inquiring about Henry's later years, Angelina listened thoughtfully to Nancy's story. She apologized for the injustice of her own family and the code of silence which had kept herself and Sarah unaware of their plight. Nancy could not easily forgive the family for the re-enslavement and mistreatment of her sons, but she believed in the sisters' ignorance of the matter and felt gratified that she was finally listened to and that her suffering was acknowledged.

As their conversation ebbed, Angelina added, "In any case, I must congratulate you on the brilliance and character of your sons. I know the struggles of raising children to be good and thoughtful, and knowing Archie and Frank has made me want to know their mother." Hearing this, the last stone fell from Nancy's heart. If she could not entirely forgive, perhaps she could choose what to remember and what to forget. Her eyes met Angelina's with a well of understanding, and the two women looked over at Archie and Frank fondly.

22

Another Sarah

Boston, 1878–79

THE HYDE PARK HOME of James and Virginia Trotter had a large, comfortable drawing room where a group of guests were gathered for an evening reception. James Trotter had served in the Massachusetts 55th Colored Regiment that had helped to liberate Charleston, rising through the ranks from private to second lieutenant. His wife, Virginia, was a descendant of the Hemings/Jefferson family.[86] In addition to the Trotters and their six-year-old son, William, the group included the young William Lloyd Garrison, Jr., Henry Cabot Lodge, Lillie Buffum Chace, James Wolff, Archie, and five or six other young women and men, both colored and white. One of the young white women, Sarah Stanley, was seated at a piano playing a Chopin nocturne quietly.

Archie was in a spirited conversation with his law partner James Wolff and their host, James Trotter. "But Archibald," Trotter insisted loudly, "this is the great betrayal. After Hayes bought the presidency with our blood, how can we ever trust the Republicans again?"

"The 'great betrayal.' Yes, that is what my brother Frank called it. And I agree, it is that." He continued in a firm and insistent voice. "However, there are still many staunch Reconstructionists among the Republicans, especially in Massachusetts. The Democrats are the party of the white South. Why would we support them?"

"I say, let us judge each candidate by his deeds," James Wolff said, "not by his party. There are Democrats, such as Benjamin Butler, who stood strongly for Reconstruction after the war. And there are clearly

Republicans whose oratory is impressive, but who do nothing for the cause of Negro progress," he pronounced.

"Perhaps," Archie agreed reluctantly, "but I stand with the Republicans at this juncture. We must simply make our voices heard within the party," he insisted.

Virginia Trotter came up to the group and put her hand on her husband's arm, "Gentlemen, enough of your politics!" she chided. "Have you even been introduced to our female guests yet? Come, you must be gallant gentleman and make their acquaintance," she urged them. Archie's eyes traveled to the young woman playing the piano and remained there for several minutes. He was fascinated by this fair-skinned, dark-haired young women intently concentrating on her playing. He judged her to be about six or seven years younger than himself.

In a jocular tone, James Wolff asked, "Mrs. Trotter, you would have us neglect politics for wine, women, and song? I am shocked! But please, lead on." He and Archie followed Mrs. Trotter, who started to introduce the two young men to Lillie Buffum Chace.[87]

"Miss Chace, I beg to present—" Virginia Trotter began formally, then stopped as she saw that Lillie, Archie and James were all chuckling quietly. Lillie spoke in a light-hearted voice. "You are excessively kind, Mrs. Trotter, but I am well acquainted with these gentlemen! I have become a patron of the Harvard libraries, and I am afraid that I first ran into them there. We have spent some amusing hours together. They steal books for me to read."

She paused and smiled teasingly at Archie, "Oh, Archie, don't look so shocked! I know you don't steal them." Then she turned to James and said, "No, it's James that does that." James pretended to look appalled, but they all laughed.

As his sister, Helen, walked over to the group, James said, "Well, here's someone I can introduce. Lillie, have you met my sister, Helen Wolff?"[88]

"No, I haven't had the pleasure. How do you do, Miss Wolff." She smiled easily at Helen and shook her hand. Archie looked at Helen with considerable interest.

"And Helen, I don't believe you've met my law partner, Archibald Grimké yet."

Archie bowed courteously and shook the hand she extended to him. Now that the young people were beginning to mix, Mrs. Trotter moved on to another group.

"I'm very pleased to meet you, Miss Wolff," Archie said. "Your brother speaks highly of you. I hear you are studying at Boston University. How do you find it?"

"Mr. Grimké, my brother speaks of you as well, but I'm never sure whether he is serious or joking," she noted, her intelligent eyes meeting his. "I believe he said you were the only Harvard-educated lawyer he would trust."

"I did, indeed, and that warning includes myself." James quipped. Archie gave a half-smile, and added "James, I fear you dishonor our alma mater."

James turned to Lillie with whom he continued to chat and banter. Helen examined Archie carefully, and deciding he was seriously interested, responded, "Yes, I am studying there. They allow both colored and white women to attend. Like my friend here, I am studying music. Now you must meet her as well."

Helen overcame her initial reserve and gave Archie a quiet smile. She and Archie walked over to the piano as Sarah Stanley was finishing a piece. Archie looked at the young pianist with admiring curiosity. Sarah looked up and smiled at Helen but avoided Archie's eyes. She stood up and murmured, "Helen, thank you so much for inviting me this evening. I was afraid . . . " She stopped, not sure how to finish the sentence.

Helen jumped in, "Sarah, let me present Mr. Archibald Grimké. He is the classmate of my brother at Harvard that I was telling you about. And now they are law partners," she said with satisfaction. "Mr. Grimké, this is Sarah Stanley." Archie bowed slightly and shook the hand she offered him in a friendly manner. Their eyes met for a moment before she looked down shyly.

Archie asked gravely, "What was it that you were you playing just now? It was so lovely!" Sarah was still tongue-tied and uncertain. She looked at Helen for reassurance, then back at Archie before saying, "It's just a Chopin nocturne—Frederic Chopin," she added. "Do you sing or play, Mr. Grimké?"

Archie shook his head sadly, embarrassed at his lack of accomplishments. He looked at Helen and spoke with a touch of defensiveness. "Well, you see, I was raised in Charleston before the war, and I was a slave for much of my youth. I'm afraid that it didn't leave much time for learning to play an instrument." He paused, not wanting to sound self-pitying. "Well, I did have friends who played the fiddle," he confessed.

Helen looked at Archie thoughtfully, admiring his honesty, and nodded her head quietly. Sarah was embarrassed and flustered at her lack of sensitivity. "Of course, I'm so sorry, Mr. Grimké. That was a stupid question. I mistook—" She recovered her composure and spoke more forthrightly. "Well, in truth, most of the colored people I have met in Boston are free colored and were never slaves. But back in Michigan, my father—he's an Episcopal minister—he was involved with the under-ground railroad—peripherally, at least."

Sarah began to speak with more assurance now that she understood the person to whom she was speaking. She continued, "My father was ardently anti-slavery, and I did meet many escaped slaves on their way to Canada before the war. So, I should have known better—I should have known what you suffered. Of course, I was very young then," she said by way of excuse.

"I was very young then, too." Archie smiled, eager to put her at ease. "Well, actually I do sing—in church, at least—but not so's you'd want to listen to me," he assured them. The two women protested laughingly.

Archie continued, "So, Miss Stanley, I'd like to hear more about your life in Michigan and your father's work." Sarah was charmed by his inter-est and eager to please, but she also felt vaguely anxious when asked to talk about herself. She decided to take refuge in her music, and said, "Mr. Grimké," she began formally, "I'd be happy to tell you about my home. But first, Helen, you must come to my aid. Can you help me play that Schubert duet we've been working on?" Helen nodded in agreement and the two women sat down at the piano and began to play together. Archie sat himself nearby to listen to the music and to observe the two attractive women. He wasn't sure which he enjoyed more.

James continued to speak earnestly to Trotter and the younger Mr. Garrison. But when he heard the piano music resume, he looked over proudly at his sister and at Sarah Stanley. He noticed Archie watching both women intently. Behind him, Lillie was speaking with Henry Lodge. Several of the other young people were sitting down and chatting with Virginia Trotter. Conversation quieted and then came to a halt, as most of the room paused to listen to the Schubert Grand Rondo which the two young women played with a quiet passion that entranced the listeners.

The Boston University Music Department was in an older building on Beacon Hill, not far from the Boston Common and Public Garden. Archie walked quickly through the Public Garden, barely noticing the vivid yellows and rusty oranges of Boston's Indian summer. When he drew close to the music building, he stopped and sat on a nearby bench where he could hear a variety of instruments coming from the windows of the practice rooms. He tuned in to a particularly adept pianist, crossed his legs and leaned back, concentrating on the music.

Five minutes later Sarah Stanley and Helen Wolff emerged from the front door of the school. Helen carried a thermos and Sarah struggled with music books in one arm and a hamper in the other. Archie rose and greeted them both with a happy look. They had no free hands to shake. He took the hamper from Sarah who offered a fleeting smile in gratitude.

The trio walked downhill to the Public Garden where they found two benches set at right angles. They poured tea from the thermos into cups that Sarah brought out of the hamper along with delicate sandwiches and pieces of apple. They two women complained about their uncompromising teachers and joked about the miseries of their lessons. Archie asked Sarah to tell him more about her home in Benton Harbor, Michigan and her father's work there. Helen tried to join into the conversation, but Archie's questions were all directed at Sarah. Helen waited for her turn, but she watched Archie and Sarah's animated faces as they spoke, and the truth dawned on her. Sarah's usual studious reserve was nowhere in evidence. She seemed downright gay. Helen looked away sadly as she understood that Archie's interest was in Sarah rather than herself. And, it appeared, that Sarah welcomed and thrived on his attention.

Thanksgiving came and Christmas passed. It was already several months into the New Year when James walked into the office he shared with Archie. Archie was seated at his desk, writing a letter. "Good morning, Grimké" James said in a jovial tone. "Glad to see you're an early bird today. Have you made any progress on the Mackinaw suit?" Archie made an inaudible noise and looked down at the paper in front of him. James paused and gazed at Archie with curiosity. "You look rather glum, old boy. What's the problem?"

Archie stared at his partner for a moment with a frustrated frown. He waved the letter he was writing. "I'm afraid I came in early to take care of some personal business," he confessed. "James, I've asked Sarah Stanley to marry me—and she's accepted." He sat back, wondering how James would react.

James was taken by surprise. "Ooh, boy! I should have seen that coming, but I didn't realize you were so serious." He shrugged and remained puzzled. "Uh, congratulations, I guess. But, brother, you don't look so happy about it."

Archie's mouth turned up briefly in a pained smile, and he said, "Oh, I *am* happy about it. Yes, I'm happy about Sarah. I am certainly in love with her. But I've just written to her father to ask his permission." His face darkened again, and he rubbed his brow anxiously. "Here take a look and tell me if you think it is all proper and well-stated," Archie asked James.

James took the letter and perused it. "Hmmm," he stroked his chin thoughtfully as he read it quickly under his breath.

> I cannot do what I now intend without first seeking to secure your approval. Such approval, sir, would give me great pleasure. Your daughter is the loveliest and most accomplished woman I know, and she must make you proud. She has captured my heart, and to my great astonishment she has accepted my proposal of marriage. I assure you that I will be a loyal and loving husband to her. . .[89]

"Well, I see, Arch. Now you've done it! Are you sure you want to send it?"

Archie was mildly annoyed at James' comment, as it made him question his own resolve. James sat down in the chair across from Archie's desk. "Why, yes, of course I do!" Archie insisted. "It's just—well, Sarah assured me that her father is very liberal-minded and concerned for the progress of our people. But I can't help wondering what his reaction will be. He and his wife have not met me, and—"

"And what will they suspect? Archie, I don't mean to stir things up for you," James said as he studied the pen he had found on the desk. "Sarah is a lovely girl. But have you thought of what this will mean for her, for both of you?" he continued earnestly. "We live in a bubble here in liberal, Unitarian Boston—and we forget what the rest of the country is like. We can't pretend there is no such thing as race prejudice," James said emphatically, "you know that well enough."

"Well, dammit, James! I don't care! I'm sick of my life being run by their rules. Sarah and I can rise above that. We are determined. We love each other, and that's the end of it. I'm going out," he glared, "and I'm going to mail this."

Archie rose angrily, looking at James with a disgusted shake of his head. James knew that the anger was largely because Archie understood the truth of his words. James sat silently and looked down, knowing nothing he said would make it better. As Archie exited with a slam of the door, James shook his head and muttered to himself, "You should have courted Helen, Archie!"

The church office in the front of the Reverend Stanley's rectory shared a foyer with his home. Still in his clerical clothes, he walked from his office to the foyer and picked up two letters addressed to him. He noticed the return address of the first with consternation; he opened the letter hurriedly as he entered the parlor of his home.

As Reverend Stanley read Archie's letter his face grew red with fury. He threw the letter down on a table, stood up and walked around to calm himself, then with shaking hands he took up a second letter in his daughter's handwriting. He sat down again and read the letter from Sarah. He put his hand on his brow in despair; then he stood up and walked to the window with a series of grunts and heavy sighs.

Mrs. Stanley sat at a table in the adjacent back parlor working on some sewing. She looked up with annoyance at her husband's agitation. "Marcus, what can be the problem? You are pacing like a caged lion."

"I fear to tell you the contents of these letters, my dear. My agitation will seem like a kitten's compared to yours. It's about Sarah. And there's one from Sarah herself."

"What? Both addressed to you? Tell me, please, sir!"

"He has proposed to her, Mother! This young colored man who is her friend. He writes to ask me permission. Oh, he has pretty things to say about her and about his own honorableness. But, but—the audacity!" Stanley stuttered.

Mrs. Stanley's face grew rigid with anger and shock. "What! Is he mad? Well, of course it won't be. Sarah has certainly refused him. That's probably why she's written the same day—to reassure us."

Stanley laughed bitterly as he re-read Sarah's letter. "To the contrary, Mother, she writes to tell us she loves him and has accepted his proposal and asks for our blessing."

Mrs. Stanley rose and went to her husband, taking the letters from him in order to read them herself. As she did so, she put her hand to her mouth, letting out an exclamation of horror. Then she sat down hurriedly. "That ridiculous, head-strong girl! I knew when you allowed her to go to Boston—among all those free-thinkers—that it would mean trouble." Mrs. Stanley, began to sob hysterically, her narrow shoulders shaking and her chest heaving. Rev. Stanley looked at her with even greater gloom.

"She's so impressionable—and she has that delicate constitution. It's all those ideas you've put in her head about the rights of ex-slaves and their need to make progress." Mrs. Stanley gulped for air between sobs. "It's your fault, Marcus! Now you shall have to refuse your permission, that is all." Mrs. Stanley's sobs continued more loudly, but less sincerely.

Rev. Stanley looked angrily out the window after this recrimination. But it was his nature to be a thoughtful, moderate man and he struggled to contain his irritation. "I don't know, Mother. I need to think and pray about it."

"What is there to think about? It's clearly against God's law and—and nature!" Mrs. Stanley asserted as her sobs slowed.

"I don't believe that, and I don't think you do either. It is not biblical." He was silent for a moment, frowning as he said, "She has told us he's a lawyer, a graduate of Harvard, and a fine young man. His letter was well-written and proper in every way. I'm sure he's well-meaning, but—"

His wife stopped sobbing and stared at him in disbelief.

"Well, my dear," Stanley continued in a milder tone. "I agree it is heart-wrenching and misguided. I don't think they have any idea of what they would be up against outside of Boston. A marriage between a white woman and a colored man? Why, they will be reviled and insulted every-where." Stanley walked around the room, picking up objects as he went, and rubbing his forehead. "I can't bear to think of that for our darling Sarah. She is our beautiful little girl and our bright light. How can she throw herself away like this?"

"My point, exactly, Marcus. You must refuse him permission, and write to Sarah immediately, before she does something rash." Mrs. Stan-ley stood up, using her handkerchief to wipe the tears from her eyes and cheeks. "I will write to her this evening, myself. But right now, I am feel-ing unwell. My head is pounding. I need to go rest," she said petulantly. Rev. Stanley looked after her sadly, continuing to pace around the parlor. Eventually he came to a decision with a shrug of resignation. He sat down at the table in the back parlor to compose his response to Archie.

The letter reached Archie's rooms in Hyde Park before the end of February 1879. Archie opened it with great trepidation. His face was dis-torted with pain as he read it to himself.

> Your letter was received when I arrived home this evening. I feel
> astonished that this business has come to my attention so late
> in the game. You were right in conjecturing that I knew next to
> nothing of you. You would hardly ask me for a thousand dollars

on such brief acquaintance, and yet you ask me for what is infinitely more precious![90]

Archie felt deeply offended and deflated, but he was also angrier than he could ever remember being. He kicked his furniture and punched the wall, breaking the skin on his hand. He sat down and rubbed his hand as he continued to read.

> I have always, however, believed that the marriage union should be based on mutual fitness and affection rather than on wealth or rank; and I have always had that confidence in the judgment of my daughters, that they would not contract any undesirable alliance.

Archie's face relaxed a bit as he read the next part of the letter.

> I confess to some misgivings in this case, but I do not intend, in this stage of the proceedings, to interpose any objections to your purposes. Both Mrs. Stanley and myself are deeply convinced, that under the peculiar and unusual circumstances of this case, we should have been consulted long ago.
> Very truly yours, M.C. Stanley

"What!" Archie exclaimed indignantly. 'Peculiar and unusual circumstances of this case'! What is peculiar and unusual about our affection and determination to marry? Only that she is white, and I am colored?" Archie shook his head as he pondered the message more carefully. "Well," Archie reflected, "he has not refused us outright. But why could they not celebrate our happiness? They make us out to be secretive, dishonorable and unworthy!" Archie let out disgusted and angry noises as he thought about Sarah's reaction. He knew she was deeply attached to her parents. "Oh, dear God. What will Sarah think?" he muttered.

The next day was Sunday and Archie and Sarah arranged to meet just after noon at a secluded bench in the Common. Sarah arrived early and was re-reading her father's letter to herself. She was stone-faced.

> It has been flung at me scores and perhaps hundreds of times in years past when I have advocated the rights of the colored race; but little did I dream it was an arrow that would pierce my heart. I have advocated every measure for their full enfranchisement and civil and religious liberty—the opening of our schools and colleges for their education and culture.

Sarah looked up in angry dismay at this point, then shook her head emphatically as she read on.

> But amalgamation always seemed unnatural and revolting. Toward them I cherish none but philanthropic feelings, but to give them my beautiful and accomplished daughter for a wife seems perfectly abhorrent, and that you should be willing to throw yourself into his arms for a husband is a surprise and grief . . . "

Sarah's anger gave way to a desolate grief of her own, and she couldn't hold back her tears of hurt and frustration. She forced herself to read on:

> Oh, my dear daughter, you are bewildered by the bad influence of the society into which you have thrown yourself. It is an old adage: "There is but a step between the sublime and the ridiculous." You were sublime—do not take this wretched step. I feel too sorrowful to write more. With the sweet remembrance of the past, and in the fullness of love for you,
> I remain your affectionate Father

She sat in rebellious silence for several minutes, biting her lip as a few hot tears rolled down to her chin and dried there. After a few moments she looked around and saw Archie hurrying toward her. Sarah wiped away the remaining tears with her handkerchief and daubed at her red eyes. She rose to hurry toward Archie.

Archie looked at her intently from the distance between them, trying to gauge her feelings. He sighed with relief as she drew near and threw herself into his arms. He returned her ardent and desperate embrace. Archie separated himself from her reluctantly, realizing they were in a public place, and eager to prevent any further embarrassment for either of them. But he held her hand tightly as they walked back to the well-hidden bench. Archie pulled out her father's letter to show to Sarah, and she did the same. They exchanged the letters to read.

"His letter to you is kinder than mine, as you can see," Sarah commented with a confused look. "He pleads with me, but he has not absolutely forbidden our marriage. See, he says that he will not interpose any objections to our purposes."

"Yes, he does say that," Archie agreed with a slight loosening of the tightness in his chest. "But his distress—his misgivings seem enormous. And his letter to you—ah, you must find it heart-wrenching!"

Archie took her hand in his own and looked tenderly into her eyes. He glanced down for a moment, hesitant. "I—I should release you from your promise, Sarah. I cannot ask you to be indifferent to your parents' evident sorrow and distress, even if it is unjust and unfounded," he added with just a trace of bitterness.

Sarah had trouble finding her voice. She was still agitated and close to tears. "He finds me ridiculous, Archie! Oh, that is the cruelest part." She surveyed the park surrounding them and it answered her with a brief glimpse of harmony. She gazed back at Archie, taking his other hand and saying in a determined voice, "But, no. I shall not withdraw my promise, and I hope and pray that you shall not either! I know this insulting and hypocritical tone must anger and disgust you."

She paused again, trying to ignore the rush of conflicting feelings. Above all, she dreaded the prospect of ending their engagement. "Archie, we are better than this," she insisted. "Will you still have me? Or is it too much to ask?" she continued. "You know, if he had absolutely forbidden it —well, I'm not sure what I would have done. But he hasn't. And I think that is a sign that he knows in his heart that his feelings are wrong."

Archie looked at her intently again. He was still doubtful, but he agreed with her reasoning about her father's position. He allowed himself a quick smile and was about to speak when Sarah broke in again. "You know I'm angry with him at the moment, and with mama as well. Especially with her. But he is a good man, Archie. And I know once he gets to know you, he will understand your worth—and love you as I do."

Archie looked at Sarah tenderly, "Then, am I to understand that you wish to proceed?" He managed a slight smile as he said, "Oh, my dear girl. You have such courage!"

"Yes, my love, I do. Please, please say you will still marry me!"

Archie nodded and murmured his assent, "Of course I shall!" as he took Sarah in his arms again for a long, consoling embrace.

There was little comfort, though, in knowing that they would continue to face disapproval, if not outright opposition, from Sarah's family. It made the young couple sober as they rose and walked out of the Common onto Beacon Street with Sarah's hand in Archie's arm. Sarah looked up at him every few minutes, giving Archie her brave and adoring smiles. Archie returned those hopeful smiles, eager to reassure her. But as they approached Charles Street, he looked at the families out for a Sunday walk, and his face darkened. He was certain that he understood the challenges ahead of them far better than she did.

When Lucy Stone heard of the engagement, she wrote to Sarah advising her to put off the wedding until her family had been given time to know Archie, but Sarah resisted any delay. Lucy knew she could not change Sarah's mind, so she offered her support and the loan of a wedding dress. About seven weeks later, Archie stood in the garden of a friend's home at 32 Mt. Vernon Street which they had gratefully accepted to use for their small wedding. It was Saturday, April 19th, 1879, the day the first shots of the Revolutionary War had been fired 104 years earlier in nearby Lexington. Revolution was not on the bride's or groom's mind, although some, perhaps Lucy Stone among them, viewed it as a revolutionary occasion.

Archie was dressed in a new, formal suit as he stood at the near end of the garden awaiting his bride. Sarah was dressed in her borrowed white brocade dress with a front-laced bodice, and a gently draped overskirt. But what Archie noticed as she stepped into the garden, was her radiant smile and how her bronze curls contrasted with the delicate fairness of her face.

The small gathering included Theodore Weld, Wendell Phillips, Lucy Stone, James and Helen Wolff, Lillie Chace, Cyrus Heizer, Nelly Bradford, and a few other close friends.[91] Nelly had recently returned to the city.[92] Angelina was too ill to attend. The notice was short and the cost too great for Frank or his mother to make the journey.

Archie took Sarah's hand, and they walked forward together toward the minister. They exchanged vows and rings, concluding with a hymn sung a capella by the small congregation. Helen Wolfe's rich alto and her brother James' baritone carried the other voices along. The guests gathered around to kiss the bride and congratulate the groom, and to join them for refreshments.

Two days after the wedding, Sarah and Archie arrived at a small summer house on Marblehead Neck, lent them by friends as a wedding gift. Since it was already late in the afternoon, they left their belongings and went out for a walk along the nearby beach. On their return, Archie guided Sarah into the bedroom by the hand. They looked at each other for a moment, then began to laugh. Archie sat down in an armchair and Sarah came and sat on his lap, kissing him on his brow, then on his neck, then on his mouth. He responded with equal ardor. It was not their first time together, so all awkwardness had vanished.

After several moments Sarah murmured to him, "Oh, my love, my lord, my husband! Can you believe we have done this? I feel that I no longer have a separate being from you![93]

"No, I can't believe it," Archie said with a laugh. "It is a fairy tale. And you are my princess. I will kiss you, and my magic kiss will dispel all evil and take us to our happy kingdom." He gestured around their simple beach house. "You see, we are already in our happy kingdom!"

Several weeks later Sarah sat at the table in Archie's Hyde Park rooms writing to her new husband who had left three days before on a work trip to New York City.

> My dear husband,
> Why are you gone so long? Without you I cannot tell who I am, nor what I should be doing here! My soul is gone and only a dull machine moves about these rooms or on the streets and Common of Boston. All is an unmeaning haze until my prince returns and revivifies me with his breath and magic touch.

Archie was seated on the train back to Boston. He had received Sarah's letter just before he left New York City, so he had only glanced at it briefly. The train jostled him back and forth, making reading difficult, but undeterred, Archie read on,

> Last evening, I took our usual walk through the Common and the Public Garden, then I came home and tried to straighten out my accounts, but my cash would not balance. Finally, I went to bed.

Archie smiled and shook his head at this remark. Sarah's flightiness was, to him, still a part of her charm.

> All that I do and all that I dream includes thee. I am counting the seconds until your return. Yours, SSG

Archie looked over the letter for several moments, then folded it and put it in his breast pocket. He looked out the window with a contented countenance, barely noticing that they were passing through the ugly backside of Providence.

23

Another Passing

Hyde Park, Massachusetts Fall 1879

ANGELINA LAY IN HER bed, aware that she was close to death. She was weak, but she began humming a familiar melody. What was it, she thought? Ah, yes, the new Shaker hymn? Or was it something else? She couldn't remember the words, nor could she speak them since language had nearly deserted her. But it comforted her and helped her bear the pain she felt almost continuously.

Theodore came in to make her comfortable before going to sleep for the night. After he had arranged her covers, turned her on her side and plumped her pillows, she resumed her humming. But she looked more peaceful than usual, so he decided to sit down across the room for a while.[94]

When he was out of her line of sight, Angelina called out to Theodore in a weak voice, "Theo, Theo, my dear—." Her words would have been barely recognizable to anyone else. She continued to hum the song as he rose to see what she needed. She stretched out her arms to Theodore, who laid down beside her and carefully took her in his arms. After a few minutes, Angelina became agitated and seemed to be having a bad dream. She murmured somewhat incoherently, "No, no! Please sir— oh, no! Are you not a Christian? How can you? Look, look at his . . . !" Theodore could only make out about half the words, although her dream speech sometimes seemed clearer than her waking speech.

Then, "I am singing to the dear Father—happy—happy—happy!" she murmured quite clearly. Her humming stopped, but she continued to mouth the word "happy" for several minutes until she fell off to sleep. Theodore lay on the bed next to her, thinking about their years together. He remembered the hurts, the anger, the resentments and the failures. But those seemed so distant and meaningless now. What he felt most was harmony—a fugue of two melodies interwoven with the occasional dissonance that always seemed to resolve itself into a more complex chord. Soon he fell asleep beside her.

The 30th of October was a bright, but frosty fall day in Hyde Park. Mourners came out of the Congregational Unitarian Church behind Theodore, Charley and his fiancée, Anna Harvell, and Sissy Weld Hamilton. Sissy held the hand of her seven-year-old daughter, Angelina Grimké Hamilton.

Archibald and Sarah Stanley Grimké came out just behind Sissy. Sissy turned her head and smiled at Sarah, noticing that her exquisite blue crepe dress fell loosely over her normally petite waist, somewhat concealing the pregnancy that was now in its fifth month. Sarah managed a weak smile in return and glanced appreciatively at little Angelina. Sissy noticed her pallid complexion and suspected that occasional nausea still dogged Archie's wife. Archie looked contented, but a little tired, Sissy thought.

Strains of organ music from the church followed the crowd outdoors. Sissy, daughter in hand, turned and joined Charley and her father as Wendell Phillips came up to offer condolences on Angelina's passing. He was followed by John Whittier. There were so few of the early abolitionists that were still alive.

Lucy Stone came up to Sissy, who was delighted to see her again. The two women chatted briefly before others approached. She found her eyes tearing up as she greeted these cherished family friends, although she had not yet shed many tears for her mother. Angelina had been ill for so long, Sissy wondered if her death were not a blessing for her mother, as well as for her father who had been devoted to his wife's care.

The younger Will Garrison approached them, saying, "Mr. Weld, our family offers you deepest condolences. My father often spoke of how touched he was by Angelina's first letter to him at *The Liberator*." Theodore nodded, patting this son of his fellow abolitionist on the shoulder in acknowledgment of his words.

Elizur Wright and his daughter, Ellie, approached Theodore and murmured their condolences, and he responded with a quiet smile.

"Thank you, my friends. You know, the waves of sorrow do not overwhelm me. How can I mourn her generous life!" He spoke with gentle serenity. "Indeed, you see, I have no sorrow at all. It is all swallowed up in a great, abounding joy in her deliverance. Her exceeding gain is all mine." His eyes glowed ethereally from their deep-set sockets.

Sissy bent over and whispered to her daughter her appreciation for her good behavior, promising a treat later. Theodore leaned down and swept up his granddaughter fondly, turning back to the Wrights, "You see how blessed I am, with my beautiful daughter here, and Charles and Anna, and this dear young namesake of my wife," he said as he tickled his granddaughter's cheek.

Young Angelina giggled and pulled at her grandfather's unruly white beard, but she soon squirmed and wanted to be set down. "I believe she has inherited my Nina's independent spirit," Theodore said lightly, but with a worried frown.

Sissy laughed as her daughter ran off. "Yes, independent for certain, Father," Sissy sighed.

The Wrights walked on to visit with Charley and his fiancée. Sissy took the moment's interval to speak to Theodore from her heart. "Father, I want to say something to you—I don't often tell you. But Mama's death reminds me that I must not wait," she paused, feeling shy, but certain of her words. "You have the happiest heart that I have ever known, and I know that your happiness comes from always helping others." She looked at her father's crinkled eyes and added, "I hope to catch the sunlight from that same wellspring of light and joy in the world!" Sissy reached up to hug him, and he returned her embrace as she finished her little speech, "I thank God that you live—that you have lived—and I wish that you would live forever, dear Father!"[95]

Theodore held onto her gently, whispering, "Thank you, Sissy. You soothe my aching heart!" Despite his declared peace at Angelina's passing, Theodore allowed himself to feel his grief. He wiped away quiet tears.

24

Frank and Lottie

Washington, DC, November 1879

THREE DAYS AFTER ANGELINA's funeral, Frank Grimké, now a young associate pastor, ended his sermon at the Fifteenth Street Presbyterian Church, a mile due north of the White House. The congregation stood to sing a rousing hymn. Midway back in the church Charlotte Forten stood, watching Frank intermittently as she sang. Frank looked up from his hymn book, and his eyes met hers. He was taken by surprise, and he could barely conceal his pleasure at seeing her there.

After the service Frank stood next to the pastor shaking his parishioners' hands as they exited the church. But he found himself scanning the crowd in between greetings. Charlotte chatted with a few other church members as she waited for him to finish. When the crowd had thinned, Frank looked over at her and gave her a signal with his hand. They smiled and walked towards each other.

"I've missed seeing you here the last few weeks," Frank said. "I thought for sure you disapproved of my preaching."

Charlotte looked at the young minister with amusement. "Well, even if I did, I still would have had to be in Philadelphia on family business this past month. I believe I told you I was going?"

Frank looked sheepish realizing that he had indeed forgotten what she had said. "Oh yes, now I do recall that," he said with his most disarming smile. "So, Philadelphia was your excuse to miss my sermons? And I designed them specifically to address your most glaring shortcomings, Miss Charlotte."

"More's the pity! Well, I'm beyond redemption in any case," Charlotte declared with a sad look of mock despair. Several nearby parishioners looked over with curiosity, noticing their friendly banter and laughter.

"Frank, I did hear about your Aunt Angelina's passing. I am so sorry."

Frank's feelings about it were unclear even to himself. "Yes, I had to be here to preach," he said, "so I couldn't make it up for the funeral. In any case, I didn't want to leave mother. She's too frail to travel much." His expression became thoughtful rather than sad. "Aunt Nina has been sick for many years—and Uncle Theodore has been an angel of mercy for her. He will miss her terribly, of course, but I suspect he will rejoice that her suffering is over, and that she is in a better place."

Charlotte nodded. She had seen enough suffering during the war to know that death was often preferable. But she had also watched the loneliness of aging widowers among her own family, and she felt sorrow for Theodore although she had never met him. Her thoughts were interrupted as Frank spoke again, "Did I tell you that Archie went and got married about five months ago?"

Charlotte's eyes widened and she looked at Frank with a disbelieving laugh, "What! No, I don't believe you did. Well, my heavens!" She shook her head for a moment, then smiled broadly, realizing that this was not an unexpected turn of events. "Congratulations to him. And who, may I ask, is the lucky woman?"

"Her name is Sarah Stanley," Frank said. "She's white." He waited to see her reaction but could read nothing in her face. "They seem very much in love if one can judge by his mushy letters." He rolled his eyes at Charlotte, and she threw back her head and laughed wholeheartedly.

However, thinking about the news, Charlotte grew serious. "It's brave—I hope it goes well for them."

The two walked over to a bench in the church garden where they could continue their conversation more privately. They sat down. Frank said slyly, "Well, all this—it has made me think, Lottie. Life is short. Perhaps I should marry, too."

Frank looked sidewise at Charlotte to gauge her reaction. She looked vaguely annoyed. "Hmmph," she looked through a tree up at the sky, noticing that clouds were thickening. "Do you have someone in mind—or is this simply a matter of expediency? You know—fulfilling your station as an up-and-comin' associate pastor?"

Frank looked away for a minute to summon up his courage. All his wit seemed to desert him. He pressed on "Well, Lottie, I do have someone in mind. Someone I admire and like immensely. But she's a bit older than me. She might think that I'm too much of a youngster and an upstart."

Charlotte tried to hide her smile as she answered tartly. "So, I guess if you don't ask her, you'll never know, will you?" Charlotte looked back at him seriously and expectantly. Frank took her hand in his, feeling uncertain but unable to restrain himself. He was encouraged that she didn't draw it away.

"Lottie, well—I hadn't planned this for today! But I've thought about it very seriously for a long time. I just didn't know—well, if I stood a chance." He looked down, but Charlotte waited patiently for him to say more. Their eyes met and she gave him a teasing smile. "Lottie, you are my best friend," he choked out. "We've shared so much—we believe in the same things. And on top of that I've been crazy about you since I was fifteen. That's nearly half my life!" He looked at her with reckless eagerness. "I—I really have hoped you would consent to be my wife. Am I being very foolish?"

Charlotte burst out laughing at his earnestness, but also in delight. "Oh, Frank! I guess that's a proposal of sorts. And if it were, I suppose I'd have to say yes! Because I'm near as foolish as you." Frank was a little stunned at her answer. He'd expected her to put up more objections. With a crazy chuckle he reached for her other hand in gratitude and joy. Charlotte offered it willingly.

"I've been waiting a long time, too, you know!" Charlotte reminded him. "And in all these years I haven't found a better man—nor one I'd rather spend my days—and nights—with. So yes, my dear, brave Frank! I believe we will do well together."

Despite his amazement, Frank managed to pull Lottie close to him and kiss her tenderly on the brow. He took her small, wise face in his hands and kissed her on the lips. She looked at him wonderingly, stroked his face, then returned his kiss wholeheartedly. They pulled back and laughed shyly at each other, both astounded at the step they had just taken.

25

Birth and Politics

Boston and Washington, D.C. 1879–1880

SARAH STANLEY GRIMKÉ, FIVE and a half months pregnant, climbed the outside stairs to the second-floor rooms she and Archie were renting. It was an unseasonably warm fall day, and she paused halfway up to catch her breath. She and Archie had decided to take rooms in central Boston to be closer to Archie's office, to her piano teacher, and to their friends. To conserve space in the very small living room, they had agreed to sell Sarah's melodeon. She could arrange to use the practice rooms at the music department, she told Archie.

Sarah left the produce she had bought on the kitchen table and hurried to a chair, feeling fatigued and nauseous. Suddenly she got up and ran to a basin where she lost her meager lunch. She washed her face with cool water, ate some crackers, and sat down again, her head between her knees.

She heard Archie coming up the stairs and entering their small apartment. "Whew, it smells in here," Archie scowled. Then recognizing the odor, he looked at his wife sitting with her head down. "Oh, my, Sarah, are you unwell?"

She raised her head and answered sharply, "Yes, you dodo, I'm unwell! As you can see. And yes, it smells—I didn't have the strength to clean it up."

"I'm sorry, Sarah. I didn't realize—here, I'll take the basin down. You go lie on the bed for a while." Archie carried the basin down to the waste bin in the back garden and washed it out with a bucket of water he found nearby.

He climbed the stairs again, sweaty and tired. As he entered the bedroom where Sarah lay, he went over to soothe her. She was pale, and her face was tight with nausea. "I'm so sorry, my darling. What can I do?" Archie touched her belly gently. "Is it the little one making trouble? I thought you'd feel better by now."

"Well, I don't! I know it's tiresome, Archie, but I can't help it. I don't choose to be sick you know." Sarah's misery made her irritable and impatient, although she knew it wasn't Archie's fault. Archie looked away, hurt by her tone. Sarah reached out her hand to pull him towards her. "Oh, Archie, I'm sorry to be cranky. I just need to be loved. Please hold me!"

Archie lay down beside her and took her in his arms, soothing her as best he could. "I'm sorry, Sarah. My mother was sometimes a midwife, but I'm not very well-educated on these matters. I wonder if it's worse for white women?"

Sarah pulled back and looked at him with incredulity. "I don't believe so, Archie. I know you think colored women are stronger and better—but from what I know, it's the same for most women," she said defensively.

"No—I didn't mean it that way, Sarah, not at all!" He tried to soothe the waters, but Sarah wasn't placated. "It's our baby growing in there— and I —I just wish we could be happy about it," Archie said with a defeated shrug.

Sarah softened and smiled wanly. "Of course, I'm happy about the baby, Arch—it's just that I feel so awful. Not all the time, but some of the time—and this warm spell just makes it worse—and the smells around the kitchen. Ugh! You have no idea!" she sighed. "Anyway, tell me about your day. It will distract me."

Archie sat up on the side of the bed and turned around to face her. "Yes. I do have news— from Frank. He's going to marry Charlotte Forten. I told you about her, didn't I?"

Sarah nodded her head weakly, looking curious. "But I thought— well, isn't she much older than Frank?"

"Yes, she is. She helped us when we first came to Boston—and she was already a grown woman. But she was a wonderful friend to us." Archie smiled to himself at the memories of that difficult time. "Truthfully, I am amazed," he chuckled. "I could see he was smitten with her already—at fifteen! I guess she was willing to wait until he grew up." Archie shook his head in wonderment at Frank's good fortune. "So, that's the good news. He says Frederick Douglass has been to dinner several times—and he is going to come to their wedding."

Sarah looked at him anxiously. "Will you go, Archie? I hate it when you're gone, but—"

Archie's brow furrowed as he thought about it, then he looked at her reassuringly. "No, I don't believe I will. I'd like to, but the baby will be almost due. They aren't getting married until December. And there's my work here."

Sarah was relieved. "Oh, I see. Well, good. I'd be so afraid, Archie! I need you here." Archie stroked her cheek tenderly for a moment. "But there's bad news, too, Sarah. Frank spoke in his letter about how dangerous things are getting in the South. He hears story after story from those who make their way north to Washington—and then show up at his church." His voice darkened with distress and impatience. "Booker Washington keeps telling everyone it will all be fine. He says we just need to keep teaching the young ones the basics and help them learn manual skills so they can better themselves."

"But I thought you agreed with that, Archie? You and Frank, too."

"I don't disagree—but I don't agree either," Archie said. "He makes it sound like there are no colored people worthy of a full higher education. That's a failure of vision, Sarah. It's a failure to see our potential—to insist that we have a right to the same educational opportunities as our countrymen." Talking about it made Archie realize how it angered him. "In fact, now that I think about it, that's what almost happened to Frank and me when we first arrived in New England. If it hadn't been for my mother's insistence, and Frances Pillsbury's intercession—and a little help from Charlotte—Frank and I would be factory workers and farmhands to this day."

Sarah was having trouble following the conversation. The waves of nausea were less frequent than earlier, but she was sleepy. She said softly, "I didn't realize that, Arch. And what does Douglass think? He seems to be the leader these days."

"Yes, I think he's a true visionary. He wants all opportunities to be open to us. And he believes we need to organize ourselves to advocate for them." Archie got up from the bed, suddenly craving action. "I don't know, Sarah. I'm tired of fighting—but there's so much to do. I still believe the Republicans are on our side—but there are many colored, like James Trotter out in Hyde Park, who feel our future lies with the Democrats. I can't see it."

He stood and went to the bedroom window, staring out at the busy Boston street. "The rottenness of that last presidential election—it worries me. I fear that monopoly and money are becoming the power behind government, just when we most need it to be honest." Archie looked around and saw that Sarah had fallen asleep. He stroked his new mustache and tried to ignore the restless anxiety he felt. He went into their kitchen and put the produce Sarah had bought into the vegetable cupboard.

A few days after Thanksgiving, Sarah made her way out to Hyde Park for a long-delayed visit with Uncle Theodore. He had only recently regained some of the vigor that had briefly deserted him after Angelina's death. She accompanied him on his daily walk into the center of Hyde Park. Her morning sickness had disappeared a few weeks earlier and she felt vigorous and happy. She was charmed by the tickling movements of the child within, and she was thrilled to sit for long periods watching her belly for the visible signs of the baby's movement.

Theodore held onto Sarah's arm for support and chatted with her in a fatherly way. He paused for a moment as they crossed the river into town, pointing out his favorite birds flittering along the banks. He was a calming presence to her, Sarah thought, and he reminded her of her own father whom she missed.

An exchange of letters after the wedding and the news of her pregnancy had softened her father's attitude considerably, and he had expressed an eagerness to meet his son-in-law. Her mother was civil but reproachful, and Sarah was burdened by the weight of her displeasure.

The little girl arrived in late February of the new decade. Labor was long and exhausting for Sarah, but the delivery was uncomplicated, and Archie's relief was nearly as great as Sarah's. There were the usual post-partum anxieties as Sarah worried about her milk coming in, and about whether the baby would eat properly. But within a few days after the birth, Sarah sat in a rocking chair, feeding her newborn in the early morning light, and humming a happy melody.

Archie came out of the bedroom, looking very tired, but immediately refreshed by this scene. He came over and knelt in front of Sarah and the baby, stroking the baby's forehead, and resting his arm on Sarah's knee. "Isn't this astounding, Sarah! Look what we have made together." Sarah smiled and held out their honey-toned baby for Archie to see. Archie asked, "Have we settled on a name for her yet? We can't call her "beautiful baby" forever."

Sarah answered, "No, you are right. She needs a proper name. Perhaps once we name her, she won't keep me awake for most of the night,"

Sarah yawned. She was still deeply fatigued from childbirth but was contented, nonetheless. "I've been thinking about your aunts, Archie," Sarah said thoughtfully. "We can't name her after Sarah. There are too many Sarah's in the family already. But I'd be very happy to name her after Aunt Angelina and perhaps after Uncle Theodore as well. So how about Angelina Weld Grimké? How does that sound?"

"I think it sounds marvelous." However, as he thought about it his brow wrinkled, and he bent his head thoughtfully. "Well, Angelina is a mouthful, though, and Sissy's daughter is also Angelina, you know, Angelina Grimké Hamilton. That could be confusing within the family."

Sarah puzzled at these complications, and asked, "Well, what can we call her then? Not Angie—I don't care for that. Let's see. Nina was your aunt's familiar name, wasn't it? But how about Nana? It sounds a little like your mother's name—Nancy!" Sarah looked at her daughter happily, pleased at this solution.

"Ah, what a diplomat you are, Sarah. We'll please both sides of the family that way. I agree. Angelina "Nana" Weld Grimké, it will be." Archie gave Sarah a half-smile. "With a name like that I shudder to think of the burden of history that she carries." He looked down at his daughter fondly. "But she looks like she will have broad shoulders. I believe she will be up to it." Sarah rose and laid Nana in the cradle nearby. Archie stretched his arms around Sarah and encircled her from behind as they gazed contentedly at their little girl.

In Washington, D.C., things did not go as well. That same year, Lottie gave birth to a daughter, and they named her Theodora.[96] But the baby was sickly and never thrived. Despite Frank and Lottie's night-long vigils and constant care, she died less than five months after her birth. When it happened, Lottie insisted that she be allowed to hold the still warm but lifeless body of her little girl for nearly an hour before their housekeeper carried her away.

She was laying on her bed, cradling the child in her arms, and weeping when Frank rushed up from his office. He sat on the bed, caressing the dead child's forehead and sharing Lottie's grief. "Oh, Frank, I'm so sorry. I was so hopeful. Am I too old? I thought she was getting better until this past week." She began to sob in a way that broke Frank's heart. "I so wanted a daughter," she sniffled between sobs. "I wanted this baby so much, Frank! For you—and for myself."

"Shhh, Beloved. Just rest. You have done all you could for her." Frank didn't know what else to say. His own sense of loss was so keen that he could barely imagine how it must feel to Lottie who had carried and given birth to the child and cared constantly for her since then. Tears trickled down Frank's cheeks. After a long pause, he added, "I won't pretend I am not sad or that I didn't love our little one. But we did everything right, my dear. There is no reason for blame." Frank looked at his wife with tenderness. "And thank God, you are alive, my love. I could not have borne it if you had been taken from me."

Lottie nodded her head, trying to accept their fate with grace. When the housekeeper came in and took the child away, she sobbed afresh. Very slowly the sobs ceased. "I'm just so tired, Frank," she said as she turned her face away.

"Yes, my dear, sleep." Frank put his hand on her brow and slowly murmured a psalm as she fell asleep.

> His anger endureth but a moment; in his favor is life.
> Weeping may endure for a night, but joy cometh in the morning.[97]

26

The "Good Fairy"

Boston August 1882

ARCHIE WALKED OUT HIS office door, carrying the first issue of *The Hub*, published just the day before. He glanced at the lead headline, wondering how it would play with his audience.

**Few in Colored Community
See Much to Admire in Butler**

As Archie emerged from his office, he started walking up the street heading north. Nelly Bradford and her husband, Solomon Stebbins, were approaching the office from the opposite direction. They had married a year and a half previously. Seeing Archie's back, Nelly called out to her old friend. When Archie turned around, she waved.

Solomon Stebbins, a handsome man of short stature, was twenty years older than Nelly. He smiled broadly at Archie as the couple approached at a rapid pace. Nelly said breathlessly, "Archie! So glad we caught you. We were coming to say hello and congratulate you on the first issue of *The Hub*. We're heading down to the shore tomorrow and might have missed you." She walked quickly up to Archie and shook his one available hand. He greeted her warmly and she offered her cheek for him to kiss.

Archie turned to greet Solomon whom he knew slightly. "Nelly, Solomon! So good to see you! It's been a long time—marriages, children and all." Nelly and Solomon chuckled and nodded, keenly aware of how all their lives had changed.

"Yes, our little George is six months old, already. And your baby—Angelina—how old is she now?" she asked, "And how is Sarah?"

"Why, I suppose she's nearly two and a half already," he said, doing quick calculations. "Yes, she's running all over the place—and chattering like a magpie." He hesitated slightly before adding, "And Sarah's fine. They are in Michigan with her parents for another few weeks. It's a good thing, since this first issue of *The Hub* has been—well, a massive headache, really!" he laughed feebly, able to do so now that the ordeal was nearly over.

"Undoubtedly," Solomon agreed. "But, Archie, I knew you and Mr. Wilson[98] were the ones to carry the Republican message forward. You've done a great job with this first issue," Solomon said, waving his own copy, "I believe your influence on this state's colored community will outweigh Trotter's inroads."

"Thank you, Solomon—and thank you for helping me to get this editorship. I'm not fond of the current political fray. I like Trotter, but I believe he and his friends are wrong on this election. Right now, I'm headed over to speak to Wendell Phillips who is thinking of switching his support to Butler. I must convince him to stay with the Republicans."

"Oh, well, we mustn't keep you from that," Nelly exclaimed, looking at Archie with a rueful smile. "Give our greetings to Mr. Phillips, will you?" She started to turn to her husband, but then glanced back at her old friend. "But please, Archie, before we go, tell me how is your Uncle Theodore? I so miss our chats with him, and with your dear Aunt Angelina, of course."

"Theodore is as hardy as ever. Nearly eighty years old and barely slowing down. But I am sure he still feels the loss of Aunt Angelina." Nelly gave a nearly imperceptible nod as she and Archie shared a moment of nostalgia and grief.

Archie shook hands with Solomon and then with Nelly as they prepared to head off in opposite directions. "Write to us, Archie!" Nelly said as she turned to go. "We'll be in and out of town for a few months, but we want to know all the news and the details about Sarah and your little Angelina!"

"By all means," Archie assured her. "And I'll write to remind you how critical this election is," he said, including both Solomon and Nelly in his earnest smile. But as his eyes met Nelly's, they held just the slightest shadow of regret.

Just before Sarah and Nana left for Michigan, the family had moved back to new rooms at Mrs. Leverett's house in Hyde Park. A few weeks after his encounter with the Stebbins, Archie sat in the living room of their new quarters, writing a letter. He completed two pages, but as he was finishing the second page a drop of ink fell on it, creating a large blot. "What the devil!" Archie complained out loud. He shook his head in disgust and recopied the second page. He set the ink-blotted second page in the desk drawer.

The letter was addressed to Nelly and Solomon Stebbins, and the last sentence with the offending blot over the word "both," read:

> You have been a good fairy to me—encouraging me to be my best self and to reach for higher goals than just day to day existence. For that I am eternally grateful to you both.[99]
> Affectionately, A.G.

Mackinaw City, Michigan August 1882

In July Sarah and Nana had traveled to the Stanley household in Michigan for a visit of several weeks. As they came up from the beach and across the dunes on the Lake Huron side of the point, Sarah stopped and adjusted Nana's sunbonnet which barely covered Nana's full head of brown, wavy hair. Once it was set aright, they resumed their walk along the beachfront path. Nana was holding tightly to her mother's hand, her other hand clutching white pebbles she had found on the beach.

When Nana saw a seagull, she ran off to chase it, bending over and laughing hilariously as the bird flew away. Two women passing by glanced at Sarah, and then at her copper-skinned daughter, with puzzled looks. The older woman looked sidewise at her companion with raised eyebrows. Sarah, busy watching her daughter, remained oblivious to their reproachful attention.

They neared the house where she and Nana were staying with her parents and her sister, Ida. From the end of the road Sarah saw that her mother was busy pulling weeds from the flower bed. Sarah felt vaguely annoyed with her. She understood that her mother was doing her best to accept her marriage as a fact despite her inner resistance. Mrs. Stanley seemed genuinely fond of her grandchild, Nana, but Sarah sensed that in public her mother couldn't shake off her embarrassment about the child.

As they came in the gate, her mother stood up and stretched her back. "Sarah, you've been out a long time. You'd best go inside. All this sun is not good for you—nor for Nana! She is dark enough already," she chided.

Sarah rolled her eyes in exasperation at her mother's ill-chosen words. "She's fine, Mother. Nana, go show Grandma what you have found." Nana ran over to show the pebbles to her grandmother. Mrs. Stanley scooped her up affectionately and exclaimed over the pebbles. Nana soon slithered out of her arms and ran into the house to find her grandpa.

"Any letters for me, Mama?" she asked. "It seems like weeks since Archie has written," she frowned. "I know he's busy with the magazine and all, but you'd think he'd find time."

"Yes, there is one, dear. It looks like his hand. He's written you just about every other day, Sarah," Mrs. Stanley reminded her. "You ask a lot, you know."

Sarah ignored this remark and hurried inside to find the letter. She sat down and opened it quickly. She had just begun to read it when Reverend Stanley entered hand-in-hand with Nana, who pranced around happily and restlessly. She ran to climb in her mother's lap, then scurried off as quickly to look at some books that caught her eye.

"So how is your husband, my dear? It sounds like he has been working hard," he said approvingly.

"Yes, an admirable trait you may think, unless perhaps he neglects his wife and child," Sarah said sourly.

"I would hardly call three letters a week neglect, my dear! You are a lucky young woman. I confess I thought you were headstrong and unwise to marry Archie, especially when you were so young." Rev. Stanley seated himself facing Sarah. He leaned forward, with his arms on his knees and his folded hands pointing to his chin as he spoke with gravity. "But now that I have gotten to know him, I can see why you fell in love with him. He is a young man of deep intelligence, good character, and warm affections. Who could ask for more? I'm sorry that his race blinded me at first to seeing the propriety of your choice, Sarah. I hope you have forgiven my bitter words."

Sarah nodded and gave her father a tentative smile. "Yes, but I don't think Mama has forgiven me yet. Even though she loves Nana," she said.

"Well, Nana has won us all over. Your mother struggles, but she is coming to accept the marriage—so long as you are happy."

Sarah looked away for a moment, her expression troubled. "Archie has only written two pages. He is worried about the upcoming election for governor of Massachusetts. Mr. Trotter—I've told you about him. He's supporting the Democratic candidate, a Mr. Benjamin Butler, and Trotter is trying to win colored votes for him. Butler is a defender of reconstruction in the south, but Archie doesn't trust him—or any of the Democrats, for that matter."

"Yes, I can understand that. But the Republicans have largely abandoned reconstruction, have they not?"

Sarah shrugged uncertainly. "Ever since Archie took over *The Hub*, he's been involved in this controversy. It's his job to rally the colored community for the Republican candidates. Generally, their support for Republicans is a given, but this year Trotter and his friends are making significant inroads," Sarah sighed. "Oh, I do wish Archie would just practice law and avoid all these politics. He works so late—I feel like I never see him," Sarah complained.

"But aren't you proud of him?" Rev. Stanley asked, looking at his daughter with some consternation. Before Sarah could answer Nana ran up to her grandpa and distracted him. Sarah looked at the letter with a discontented sigh.

27

Marriage

Hyde Park Fall 1882

By that fall, Sarah and Nana were back in the apartment above Mrs. Leverett's home in Hyde Park. Sarah carried a drowsy Nana into her bedroom and put her to bed. She returned to sit by a window that overlooked the quiet town center. The poplar and maple leaves had blown haphazardly across the square, settling into a neat pattern of yellow and red stripes. The colors were burnished by the flickering gas lights. Sarah noticed them abstractly, but they failed to improve her despondent mood. The remains of her and Nana's supper were on the table.

She heard steps on the stairs and glanced up at the mantel clock which read 8:45 pm as Archie came in the door. Looking preoccupied, Archie hung up his overcoat and came over to Sarah "Good evening, dear," Archie said as he bent down to kiss her. Sarah responded coolly and Archie detected the chill. Looking around for his daughter, he asked, "Is Nana in bed already?"

"Why, of course she is. It's nearly 9 o'clock." Sarah's look was blank, but her tone was accusatory. "I thought you said you'd be home by six. I had supper ready for you—it's all cold now. And Nana missed seeing you, but she couldn't stay awake any longer."

Archie was taken aback. "I'm sorry, Sarah. I did say I expected to be home earlier—but I also said that my time was unpredictable these days. It's our deadline, you know." He shook his head and looked away, momentarily at a loss for words. Then he looked at her appealingly. "The printer didn't bring the proofs until 5:30 pm and I had to read and correct it so it could go to print tonight. I hurried through it as best I could. I probably missed some errors as a result."

Sarah's voice was acidic. "Oh, I know there's always a good excuse, Archie. But it keeps happening."

Archie fought down his irritation and said quietly, "My dear, don't you think that's unfair. I *want* to be here with you and Nana more than anything. I hate missing our evenings together. But this election—it is so critical, and Trotter is making significant inroads in the colored vote. We are putting out an extra edition next week, right before the election."

Sarah rose to put away Nana's dishes that she had left on the table, her body stiff with resentment. Her voice was chilly and edgy. "So you say. But, Archie, do you ever think what it is like for me? You have your work—and it seems to be all you care about. I'm stuck here with Nana all day. Now that it's dark early I can't go out much after 4 pm."

She fiddled with her hands, then looked up at him angrily. "And you know—well, maybe you don't know—I was up twice with Nana last night. She was sick again. But you slept right through it, and you were gone before we woke again this morning." She paused. "I hate this!" Sarah turned away and sat down. Her voice broke with a sob, "And I don't even have my melodeon to play!"

Archie moved a chair to sit close to her, taking her hands and trying comfort her. He spoke softly. "I'll try to do better, Sarah. Please, dear. Be patient with me. I want more than anything to spend time with you and Nana. It will be better after the election. I promise. But if I don't do well at this—well, it's our income, and I don't have extra time for clients, so I must make this work."

Sarah sniffed and wiped her eyes. She was not appeased, but she was distracted by another grievance. She drew her hands away. "Oh, that reminds me. I talked to Mrs. Leverett this morning and she said you'd only engaged these rooms until December. Do you mean for us to move again in the middle of winter? I thought we had agreed to take the rooms for the whole year?"

Once again Archie found himself on the defensive, and he was hurt by Sarah's assumption of the worst. "No, no. I meant to talk to her very soon. I only engaged the rooms for six months because our income was so uncertain at the time. But now, yes, I must do that. I'll talk to Mrs. Leverett in the morning."

He frowned and scratched his head, then continued, feeling like he was losing ground. "Well, no, I mean—uh, probably I can speak to her in the evening. I need to leave very early tomorrow morning so I can pick up the paper from the printer and get it in circulation."

Sarah gave a hopeless shrug and spoke in the same sarcastic tone she had used earlier, "Of course you do." She stood up and started toward their bedroom.

Archie got up and followed her, reaching for her shoulders and turning her gently towards himself. He looked at her anxiously. "Please, Sarah let us not quarrel. I'm sorry, truly I am!" He drew her close to himself, and she relaxed into his embrace reluctantly, but with some relief.

They held each other for several moments until Sarah drew back and said quietly, "Come and eat something, Archie. I'll sit with you—if I can stay awake." She smiled wanly at her husband and led him toward the table.

Several weeks later Sarah and Nana, dressed in their winter coats, mufflers, and hats, walked with Theodore from his home back toward the town center. Theodore and Sarah chatted amicably as Nana pranced along close beside them. Theodore took Nana's hand to guide her across a road, then watched her with delight as she skipped along. When they crossed the bridge, he took her hand again and bent over to point out some birds and ducks along the riverbank. Sarah found she could speak frankly to Theodore and even tell him some of her discontents and complaints about Archie's absorption in *The Hub*. She knew she sometimes sounded petulant, but Theodore seemed able to listen without judgment, although he often pointed out Archie's viewpoint to her. It wasn't like having a woman friend, but Theodore's mixture of candor and compassion soothed her and seemed to restore a measure of contentment.

In December, the snows came in earnest, and Sarah found herself staring out their living room window at a blizzard. Nana was sniffling from a cold and acting restless and cranky. When she couldn't reach her art pencils, she pulled some books from Archie's desk and threw them on the floor in a tantrum. Sarah rose from her chair and grabbed Nana roughly. "Nana, what are you doing? Those are papa's books. Look what a mess you've made."

"I—just—I want my pencils," Nana sobbed. "Mama, why can't I go outside? I want to go outside. It's too hot in here. And you won't play with me! I want to go see Uncle Theodore." Nana started to cough and sniffle through her tears. Her mother looked at her helplessly. "Nana, it's snowing very hard and freezing outside—and you have a bad cold," she said with annoyance. She immediately regretted her irritation and added, "But listen, darling, I'll read to you. Here, come and cuddle up with me and we'll read some poems."

After a few more sniffles, Nana relented and came to crawl into her mother's lap. As Sarah read to her, she fell asleep. Sarah gently carried her into her bed for a nap. Then she looked around, restless like Nana, for something to do. She sat down for a moment, then remembered the basket of apples that Mrs. Leverett had given her. She set to work peeling and paring the apples, rolling out pie dough and lighting the oven. An hour later, covered in flour, she pulled two pies out of the oven. Both pies were burnt on the top, but one was only slightly so. Unthinkingly, Sarah touched the crust with the apple filling bubbling up from the inside and burnt her finger badly. She shook her right hand in pain, grabbed a potholder and managed to get the pies out of the oven. Her finger hurt and the crust of one pie was mostly blackened and unappealing. After spreading some lard on her sore hand, she sat down in frustration feeling defeated and depressed.

To distract herself, Sarah went over to tidy up the books and papers on Archie's desk. She opened the drawer to put some papers inside and her eyes rested on the discarded second page of Archie's letter to the Stebbins from the previous summer. Taking the letter out of the drawer, she perused it for several minutes, her eyes falling on the middle of the page.

"You have been a good fairy to me—encouraging me to be my best self and to reach for higher goals than just day to day existence. For that I am eternally grateful to you . . . "

She stopped at the ink blot, unable to read the rest of the sentence. There were several more blots that made it difficult to make sense of the rest of the letter, although she could clearly read her husband's signature at the bottom.

Sarah turned the letter over and back, trying to discern to whom it was addressed. She quickly realized it was only the second page of a longer letter. She searched anxiously through the drawers hoping to find the first page but found nothing. At first Sarah was more puzzled than bothered by what she had read. She put the page back in the drawer as it was. Then she moved to a chair by the window and sat there, frowning and introspective, as suspicions began to arise.

She muttered to herself, with growing alarm, "'You have been a good fairy to me . . . ' Hmmm. Good fairy, indeed! Who can it be? A woman, of course!" She rose and walked around the room, stopping at another window. She could hear Nana beginning to stir in the adjoining bedroom. "So much for being his princess," she thought. "How can I compete with a 'good fairy' when I can't even bake a pie!" That was her first thought. Then she thought about how easy it was to be a "good fairy" when you didn't have to live with someone. She knew she had often blamed him when he was trying hard to please her. Yet she felt neglected and angry at his constant absence for work and his apparent indifference to her loneliness. As these fleeting, inchoate thoughts battled for supremacy in her mind, her imagination flew quickly to the worst interpretation. But at that moment, Nana began calling insistently for her Mama. Sarah put aside her dark thoughts and went in to pick up her daughter.

A few days before Christmas Sarah went down the stairs hand in hand with Nana, both dressed for the winter weather. They stepped out the front door of the house as Mrs. Leverett was about to come in. Their landlady was saying good-by to another woman friend.[100]

"Oh, hello, Sarah! And Miss Nana—how do you do?" Mrs. Leverett shook Nana's hand in a kindly way, treating her as a small adult. Nana returned the handshake solemnly, clearly pleased. "Sarah, I'm so glad you appeared just now. I've been wanting you to meet our new neighbor, Mrs. Stuart. Mrs. Stuart, this is our young tenant, Mrs. Sarah Grimké. I believe I've told you about her and her husband?"

"Mrs. Grimké, I'm delighted to make your acquaintance. And look at your darling little girl!" she oozed in a velvety voice that approximated the pronunciation of the Boston elite, but somehow fell short. "What pretty brown eyes you have, my dear!" Nana hid her face in her mother's skirt in shyness. At nearly three she already intuited the condescending manner of certain adults, and she disliked it.

"Why, thank you, Mrs. Stuart. I'm very happy to meet you as well. You live down at the corner, I believe?" She smiled and turned to her daughter, "Nana, can you say, "thank you" to Mrs. Stuart?"

Nana was still hiding in Sarah's skirts, but she managed to look at the ground and to whisper "thank you" in a dull voice. Mrs. Stuart gave her a thin smile. When Sarah turned and spoke to Mrs. Leverett for a moment, Mrs. Stuart stared at the child with obvious distaste. As they were about to set off, Mrs. Stuart asked, "Are you going towards the square, Mrs. Grimké? Let me walk with you for a bit. Oh, and please, call me Penelope."

Sarah was flattered by Mrs. Stuart's attention, noticing that she was a stylish woman, a few years older than herself. Naturally reserved and busy with Nana, she had made few friends in town other than Mrs. Leverett and the Welds.

"Why, thank you, Mrs. Stuart—uh, Penelope," she corrected herself with a shy smile. "We were just going that way."

She turned to her landlady. "Mrs. Leverett, I'll see you later this evening. I believe Archibald wishes to speak to you about fixing our door."

Mrs. Leverett was mildly annoyed at the prospect of another needed repair, but said only, "Of course, dear. I'll expect him. Good-by, Nana!" She waved at Nana who flapped her hand in return, not at all shy with Mrs. Leverett. Sarah took Nana's hand again and they walked along with Mrs. Stuart.

"So, my dear—may I call you Sarah?" she asked, and without waiting for an answer, she continued her inquisition. "Tell me about yourself. How do you happen to be in Hyde Park? Are you from Boston?"

"No, ma'am, from Michigan, actually. Benton Harbor. But I came here for school at Boston University, and I met my husband—and well, here we are! Do you know the Welds? Do you know about my husband?" Sarah asked, equally curious to know what Mrs. Stuart had heard through the town gossip network.

The two women continued to chat animatedly as they walked into the town square. They walked around the square once, then Mrs. Stuart shook Sarah's hand in farewell saying, "Now you must come to tea at my house very soon! Perhaps next Monday? I'm so happy we shall be friends."

Sarah was gratified to find a friend to talk to in Hyde Park. "We'd be delighted! That is, well, may I bring Nana? I don't—" Her voice trailed off, reluctant to confess that she had no household help to watch her daughter.

If Mrs. Stuart was taken aback by this request, she managed to hide it well, and she replied smoothly, "Indeed, yes. Such a—an unusual child!" She patted Nana on the head, with a condescension that made Nana turn her face away. A sour look briefly crossed Mrs. Stuart's face as she turned to head toward her home. As they parted from Mrs. Stuart, Sarah and Nana turned around to look in some shop windows. Sarah pointed out some dolls in which Nana showed a fleeting interest. She skipped ahead of her mother and looked curiously in other shop windows, fascinated particularly by the shoemaker's display.

They walked into a bakery, and when they came out Sarah carried a loaf of fresh bread wrapped in brown paper. Nana had crumbs on her face and a half-eaten cookie in her hand. Sarah looked up at the gas streetlamp and showed Nana the slow, graceful descent of the thick flakes that were beginning to cover their coats. Sarah tightened Nana's muffler, then her own, and they strolled contentedly toward their apartment at Mrs. Leverett's house.

28

Darkness

Hyde Park 1883

SARAH LAY ALONE, LISTLESSLY, in the bed she shared with her husband, coughing and sneezing from an illness she had had for several days. It was a Saturday and she realized it was already after midday and the apartment was quiet. She called out in a weak voice, "Archie! Are you there? Nana?" There was no answer.

Earlier that morning Archie had been concentrating on some work when he looked around and saw that Sarah, who had been up briefly, had gone back to bed. Nana was restless and he knew that he was unlikely to get any work done with her in a pestering mood, so he decided to take his daughter for an outing as Sarah had suggested. Once outside he hoisted Nana onto his shoulders, much to her delight. Behind them he pulled a makeshift sled he had fashioned. When they arrived at a nearby park there were seven or eight neighborhood children playing and sledding on the small hill.[101] Conditions were perfect, Archie thought. There was abundant snow, and the sun was shining.

Sarah struggled to get out of bed, shivering in the cold. She found a heavy shawl and wrapped it around her, then hobbled toward the kitchen to make a cup of hot tea. Feeling forlorn, she sat down on a hard chair as she waited for the water to boil. She looked around wearily at the untidy kitchen, then carried the tea back to her bedside, crawling under the covers and curling up in misery.

Archie took Nana down the hill on the sled several times, enjoying her squeals of fear and delight. He pretended to chase his daughter through the snow, then caught her and swung her around, both of them falling into a snowdrift.

They built a snowman, and they were just finishing it as Virginia Trotter stopped by to watch. "Archie Grimké, is that you? Hello, Miss Nana!" Nana looked around and waved her hand but continued to concentrate on forming a nose on the snowman. Archie walked over to shake hands with Mrs. Trotter.

"Mrs. Trotter! Good to see you. How are you? How is James?" Archie asked.

"He's well, At least I see more of him now that the election is over and done! Perhaps we will see you and Sarah now, too." She smiled kindly. "How is she? I've wanted to invite her over to play our piano. She plays so beautifully."

"She's feeling poorly at the moment—just a bad cold, I believe." He looked at his pocket watch worriedly and added, "Hmmm. We need to get home to her soon." He looked back at Mrs. Trotter and with a wry grin said, "But yes, now that Butler is governor, James and I will have nothing to fight about. I was disappointed, of course, but it was a fair fight." He paused and added enthusiastically, "We would love to see you all again."

"And look how Nana has grown! She's a lively one, isn't she?" Mrs. Trotter glanced benevolently at Nana who ran up to her father, and tugged at his hand, eager to continue their play. Mrs. Trotter spied her twelve-year-old son, William coming down from the sledding hill.[102] "And here comes William. I was hoping to find him here. You've met him, haven't you, Archie?"

She waved at her son, who came over to greet them. William shook Archie's hand in an awkward but friendly manner. "Of course. Good to see you, son! But I believe you were only about eight when we last met—you've grown up."

William response was quietly polite, and just a shade shy. "Yes, sir. Uh—I'll be starting high school next fall." He turned toward his mother as he started to move away. "Ma, I need to say good-by to Tom. I'll be home in a few minutes."

"Yes, you'd best be home soon, Will. You've got chores to do." She shook her head resignedly as he ran off and spoke confidingly to Archie. "Will's a good boy—but I think you are lucky to have a daughter. My Maud is much easier."

Archie laughed genially, watching Nana who had returned to their snowman and was trying to put her own mittens on his stubby arms. "I'm pleased with our Nana—there's no question. But Will looks like a very promising young man." He turned back and called out, "Come, Nana, we must get home to Mama."

"So nice to see you, Mrs. Trotter," he said in farewell. "We'll get together soon, I hope." Archie scooped a mildly protesting Nana up on his shoulders again and carried her back toward their rooms.

Sarah rose to sit on the side of the bed as she heard Archie's heavy footsteps, and then, Nana's faint ones, coming up to their apartment. She felt miserable and wrapped herself in a warm shawl again. Archie and Nana arrived at the top of the stairs, laughing and shaking off the snow on their outer clothes.

"Archie? Is that you and Nana? Where have you been?" Sarah's throat felt dry and croaky, and her tone was irritated. She coughed violently after she spoke. Nana ran into her parents' bedroom as soon as she had her coat and boots off. She came up to her mother with great excitement.

"Mama, Mama—we slided—I mean sledded and—and we builded a snowman. And I put a funny nose on the snowman!" she said, putting her hands on her mother's knees. Sarah looked at her daughter blankly at first, then took one of her hands, and smiled weakly at Nana's enthusiasm.

"Why we've been having a wonderful time in the snow. Haven't we, Nana?" Archie added as he came into the bedroom, doing his best to ignore Sarah's unhappy tone. "Oh, and we saw Mrs. Trotter. She'd like you to come over and play her piano sometime."

Sarah glared at Archie bitterly, not mollified. "But Archie, you left more than three hours ago! I've been here all alone—and sick—and I needed some tea, but I had to make it for myself. What were you thinking?" She looked out the window at the early twilight and said accusingly, "It's almost supper time."

Archie looked at Sarah uncomprehendingly, "But Sarah, you said you'd rest better if I took Nana out for a walk. I thought that's what you wanted."

"A walk, Archibald, not an expedition. I thought you'd be back in thirty or forty minutes. Why don't you think of what you are doing! You only think of yourself—never of me!"

Archie looked startled at her vehemence. He tried to answer her mildly, but his voice was aggrieved as he responded. "I think that's a disservice, Sarah," he said in a soft, cool voice. "I was trying to make it easy for you to rest. And Nana was having such a wonderful time. You know

I only have Saturdays to really enjoy her." He paused and added "It was such fun," although it felt like Sarah had taken the joy out of it.

Sarah sat stone-faced and began to cough again. He went over and sat by her on the bed. "I'm truly sorry, my dear. I misunderstood. Let me get you another cup of tea—and perhaps some soup for supper? I'll feed Nana and myself."

Nana, sensing the tension between her parents, had gone off to a far corner to look through some picture books. Sarah remained only partially appeased. "No, don't bother. Well, maybe just some tea." She reached for a handkerchief. "I'm going to try to sleep again. I kept waiting for you to come in, so I didn't really rest much after midday." She bent her head to one side and with a reproachful frown, she asked, "And how can I go to the Trotters to play the piano when you are at war with Mr. Trotter? You've made enemies of our neighbors, Archie."

"Not at all, Sarah! Mrs. Trotter seemed sincerely pleased to see me, and she gave us both a very warm invitation to visit them. James and I don't always see eye to eye politically, but I still consider him a friend—and a mentor. Anyway, now that the election is over, we agree on many issues."

"Hmmm." Sarah crawled back into bed, looking tired and defeated.

"I'll get you that tea, Sarah—before you fall asleep."

In March the frozen streets and snowbanks had melted away to mud, and cloudy days predominated over sunny ones. It had felt like a long, dreary winter to Sarah, particularly when she was ill. She was finally well enough to once again venture out to Penelope Stuart's home for tea. Mrs. Stuart gave Sarah a formal kiss on the cheek as she welcomed her into her home. Nana trailed behind her mother, but Mrs. Stuart largely ignored her. The two women chatted easily as a housekeeper served them tea. Mr. Stuart came in to meet Sarah and speak with her for several minutes; then, having done his duty, he left the women alone. Nana sat on a large armchair and was engrossed in a picture book that Sarah had brought for her.

When Mrs. Stuart inquired about her husband, Sarah drew the letter she had found in Archie's desk out of her handbag discreetly and put it in her pocket. She started to speak with some embarrassment.

"I don't believe in speaking ill of my own husband, Mrs. Stuart—I mean, uh, Penelope. But since you ask, I must say I am sometimes sorely disappointed in him. He seems so pre-occupied with his work. He is away such long hours. I don't believe he thinks at all of what it is like for Nana and me." She looked away, confused and ashamed of her complaints. "Of course, I try to do the best I can on his income, but we always seem to be short. And it doesn't bother him at all! I haven't had a new dress—nor new clothes for Nana—in nearly a year." Sarah shook her head, unsure if she should confide in Mrs. Stuart, but needing desperately to tell her worries to someone.

"Hmmm, so he's not providing well for you," Mrs. Stuart said in a tone that concealed smugness under a veneer of concern. "And how are you feeling, dear?"

"I'm still not truly well. You know I was very ill a few weeks ago, and now I still have headaches and I tire easily." Sarah looked over at Nana who was turning the pages of her book with undisturbed concentration. "And I must attend to Nana all day," she added in a low voice.

"Yes, that must be very trying!" Mrs. Stuart sympathized in a simpering voice, but her air quickly changed to one of authority. "You know my conviction, don't you, Sarah? I believe all illness is due to some fear. And I believe your illnesses are grounded in your relationship—your fears that Archibald has taken over your life.[103] Men can be so selfish and lordly, can't they, dear?"

Sarah felt vaguely uncomfortable with this, and her first reaction was skeptical. "Well, yes, I do sometimes feel that I have become invisible to him—that he does not hear me or see my situation." She frowned thoughtfully, wanting to be fair. "However, I have had a weak constitution since my childhood. I don't know. It doesn't seem quite right to blame him for my illnesses. He does try to do things for us. It's only that I wish he would care for me more. His work—"

Mrs. Stuart looked at her with a pitying, condescending smile. "Well, think as you will. But there's something else, isn't there, my dear? I sense you have more to tell me." Sarah put a hand to her eyes to wipe away some involuntary tears as she nodded. She took the page of the letter that she had found out of her pocket and handed it to Mrs. Stuart.

"I found this in his desk. Well, you see, I wasn't looking. I was just arranging his books and papers, and there it was. He didn't even bother to hide it from me. You see the part at the end, just before the ink blot?"

Mrs. Stuart took the letter with a satisfied look on her face, read it, and appeared to choke with horror. "Oh, my dear Sarah," she exclaimed reaching over to pat Sarah's hand. "Oh, what you must be suffering! These infidel men! Can none of them be trusted?"

Sarah's fledgling suspicions were vastly amplified by Mrs. Stuart's reaction. She uttered a cry and her eyes filled with tears that she tried to hide. Nana looked up from her book with alarm. She stared at her mother but remained very still.

"Oh, Penelope—do you really think?" she continued, "Do you really think it means he's been unfaithful? I mean it's just a phrase, 'my good fairy.' Perhaps—well, it's disturbing, but perhaps I am reading too much into it?"

Mrs. Stuart shook her head sadly, not wanting to be too obvious in fueling Sarah's fears. Nevertheless, she relished the taste of a scandal in the making. "Well, who am I to say? Of course, you could read it innocently. Or perhaps it is best just not to think about it." She paused ominously, letting Sarah's anxiety grow. "Still, I believe in facing reality firmly, myself." She gave Sarah a pitying smile, shaking her head and adding in a near whisper, "And in my experience—well, of course, I have nothing against colored men—but their appetites! I don't know if they understand their marriage vows as we do!" She sat back with poorly disguised satisfaction. "Well, no wonder you feel sick, my dear!"

Sarah was deeply bothered by Mrs. Stuart's apparent certainty that Archie was blameworthy, and she still she felt the need to defend him. "Oh, but Archie is not like that. Not at all, Penelope!" she said emphatically. "I mean, he's a good husband. He has failings—but not like that! There must be another explanation—I thought perhaps—" Her voice trailed away, unable to articulate her defense of Archie in face of Mrs. Stuart's definiteness.

Mrs. Stuart reached out to take Sarah's right hand in her own two hands, saying in a silken voice, "Of course, my dear, you do not want to believe such a thing of your own husband. Why it makes you wonder how you have come up short!" She shook her head doubtfully, "It's just that I have seen these cases before, and—" She hesitated and looked over at Nana. "Oh, and what will become of your poor child, Sarah? Yes, perhaps it is best just to pretend you never saw it, my dear. Such upheaval to a family!"

Sarah grew wildly alarmed at this. "But what are you saying, Penelope? It can't affect our dear Nana, can it? I shall certainly take care of her, whatever happens!" Mrs. Stuart just looked at her sadly, letting her venomous insinuations do their work. Sarah wiped her eyes, put away the letter, and called to Nana as she rose.

"Come, Nana," she said, walking over to take her by the hand. She turned back to her host and said coolly. "Well, I'm afraid we must go, Mrs. Stuart. I must think it over, but I believe I will just speak to Archie. Honesty is best."

Mrs. Stuart rose to escort Sarah out, answering her with just a trace of sarcasm. "And of course, he will tell you the truth." She smiled sardonically.

Sarah gathered up her things and put on Nana's coat and hat. "Thank you, Mrs. Stuart," Sarah said formally. She hurried towards the entryway, eager to get away.

"My dear, know that Mr. Stuart and I are at your service if we can do anything to help," Mrs. Stuart called after her.

Archie was home by seven that evening, and although Sarah was very quiet during their supper together with Nana, Archie was too preoccupied to think it unusual. While Sarah washed the dishes, Archie got Nana ready for bed and read her a story until she fell asleep. He tucked her in and kissed her on the forehead before coming back to their parlor. Sarah was sitting silently on the couch. Archie came over to sit near her, and he quickly realized she was out of sorts. "You have been very quiet all evening, Sarah. Please, tell me what is wrong, my dear."

Sarah glanced quickly at him with fear and hurt in her eyes. Then she looked away, trying to summon the courage to speak. Her words burst out harshly. "Archie, are you unhappy with me? Am I not a good wife to you? I try very hard. I don't know what else to do—"

Archie looked at her with astonishment. "Sarah, what can you mean? Of course," he waffled a bit, "I know you try hard to be a good wife." Well, you *are* my wife, and I am happy for that. And I know I am not always a perfect husband." He frowned, "Of course, sometimes we see things differently but, I'm afraid I don't understand. What are you asking, Sarah?"

Sarah seized on this opening, and her anger spilled out, "No, you are not a perfect husband, are you? Perhaps you are not a true husband at all!"

"Sarah! What are you insinuating? Have I not been devoted to you in every way? I know I do not provide for you as well as I would wish— but that will improve with time." Archie brightened as he remembered something to please her, "Oh, I talked to the owners, and I believe I can buy back your old melodeon for a fair price. And next year things should be better." He shrugged, "I have clients who owe me."

Sarah retorted, "So now you will buy my affection, will you? You think you can do whatever you like, and then try to appease me." Sarah couldn't bring herself to voice her real suspicions. Archie found it hard to hide the hurt he felt when this most recent effort to please her was mistrusted. He recoiled within himself and felt a wall being constructed in his heart.

Sarah plunged ahead. "I saw Mr. and Mrs. Stuart today. And Mrs. Stuart helped me to see that I must confront the question."

"But what question, Sarah? I don't know what you are talking about," he pleaded. Their raised voices had awakened Nana. She tiptoed to her bedroom door, which was just slightly ajar, and peered out at them with alarm. Her parents did not notice her, and after several minutes she sneaked back into bed, clutched her stuffed bear and fell into a troubled sleep.

"The question of your 'good fairy Archibald,'" Sarah responded coldly. "Who is this 'good fairy' who seems to have replaced me in your affections?"

Archibald was now more confused than taken aback. He barely remembered his use of the phrase. "What? What are you talking about, Sarah? 'Good fairy'?" He furrowed his brow and scratched his head. "Why yes, now that I think about it, I suppose I did use that phrase, but only to mean their kindness to me—it's not—"

Sarah had become too enraged to hear Archie's response. She got up and walked across the room. "So, you admit it! Don't try to fool me with your excuses! This 'good fairy'—whoever she is—she is no more than an evil genius. She is prompting you to seek fame and power, instead of peace and goodwill. And tempting you to renounce your marriage vows. Who is it, Archie? Is it Lillie? Is it Helen? No—don't tell me, I don't want to know!"

Archie's hurt suddenly turned to anger at these unaccountable accusations. He got up and walked to the opposite side of the room from Sarah, beside himself. He could only think of the injustice of it. After a moment he blurted out, "Sarah, have you lost your mind? What are you saying? What are you thinking? You don't trust me? After all I have done to try to make you happy and comfortable here. After all my devotion to you and Nana! And when it comes to trust, why were you reading my letters, in any case? Do you really think I would . . .?" He stopped unwilling to name the unthinkable.

Sarah interrupted him. "Devotion? Hardly! Do not lie to me, Archie. I see it all now. These late nights—your indifference to my feelings! Clearly it doesn't matter what I think—or what I feel. What does matter is what I am going to do about it. Am I going to stay here and let you deceive and neglect me, or am I going to depart?"

"Depart? Sarah, have you taken complete leave of your senses? You are my wife! And what about Nana?" Archie felt deeply alarmed by her words, and yet he judged it out of character for Sarah. After several moments' reflection, he spoke up, "Oh, I think I see! It is your friend Mrs. Stuart who has convinced you of this, isn't it? Lately you have seemed entirely under her control."

This notion gave Archie some degree of hope and he tried to soften his manner to reason with her. "Well, at present you are in no condition to view this matter dispassionately, Sarah. You've misunderstood, but you won't listen to anything I say. And you only see your side of the picture— a very distorted side which you have presented to her, if I may say so. And she has sown the seeds of suspicion in your heart." He reacted to this realization with deep disgust, "What a despicable woman!" he said, under his breath.

Sarah's manner remained icy. She was determined to have it out with Archie. She mistrusted her ability to withstand any gesture of affection on his part and had decided to head off any attempts at reconciliation. "You may say what you like, but she is my friend, and she has only helped me to see the truth—the bitter truth!" Sarah turned and headed toward their bedroom. "Do not come near me tonight," she said stonily as she closed the door to their bedroom firmly.

Sarah leaned her back on the door she had just closed against her husband, her face crumpled with deep pain and fierceness. She swiftly took off her dress, put on nightclothes and crawled under the covers as deep but quiet sobs shook her body.

Archie remained standing in the living room, unable to fully grasp this turn of events, much less know how to respond. Eventually he sat down on the couch, leaning his elbows on his knees and burying his face in his hands. In his mind he turned over every event—every disagreement or misstep— of the previous few months, trying to determine where his fault lay. It was several hours before he found a blanket and slept.

At five p.m. the next day, a horse-drawn delivery wagon drew up to the Leverett house. Archie jumped out and gave directions to two delivery men who removed Sarah's old melodeon from the wagon.[104] The two men grumbled and swore, but with Archie's awkward help they eventually got it up the outside stairs and into the Grimké apartment in Mrs. Leverett's house.

"Sarah, are you here?" he called out, "Nana?" It took only a moment for him to understand that they were not at home. It worried him, but he assumed that they were on an outing. Archie moved an armchair and a small table, and the three men situated the melodeon in the far corner of the living room. He paid the men and shook their hands as they left. Archie looked around in disappointment and sudden consternation. He walked over to the dining table and found a note from Sarah. With a growing sense of dread, he picked it up. It was very short.

Archie,
Nana and I are going away for a few days. I need to decide what to do. We will be staying with Mr. and Mrs. Stuart.
Sarah

"What the blazes?" Archie cried out as he paced around the room—kicking the wall at one point. He collapsed onto the couch, covering his eyes as he wept inconsolably. The struggles of his earlier life seemed as nothing compared to this threat to his dream. Those struggles had involved objective evils and clear villains, but this went to a vulnerability at his core. He had believed wholeheartedly in the love and contentment he had found in his life with Sarah and Nana. He wanted to scream in protest, but he merely whispered under his breath, "Sarah, what has possessed you? How could you do this?" He held his aching head and asked himself in desperation, "What has happened to our love?"

29

Another Wedding, and Stories from the South

Washington D.C. 1884

ON JANUARY 24, 1884, Frederick Douglass, widowed for two years, stood in the rectory parlor of the Fifteenth Street Presbyterian Church in Washington, D.C. with his fiancée, Helen Pitts. They were ready to begin their small, private wedding. The 66-year-old Douglass brushed some lint from his otherwise impeccable wedding suit. His bushy hair was greying on top, nearly white in places. Helen smoothed the skirt of her wedding suit of cream-colored satin with lace around the high neckline and cuffs. But she was focused on listening to the hymn that Lottie Forten Grimké played as a prelude to the private celebration of their vows.

After the couple pronounced their vows and exchanged rings, Frank beamed at them and said, "Frederick and Helen, I now pronounce thee husband and wife. May God bless and keep thee both in his love, dear friends!"

Frank and Lottie hosted a small but lively dinner party for the couple before they left for their wedding trip. Late that night after the Grimkés had retired, a series of loud knocks on the rectory door aroused Frank from his bedtime reading. Lottie was already drifting off to sleep, tired from the excitement of hosting a wedding and a dinner. Frank wrapped himself in a dressing gown and went downstairs to open the door, annoyed but worried that it might be someone in serious need.

Crowding around the door were five or six reporters, all but one of them colored, and all shouting out questions at once. "Reverend Grimké, why did you agree to marry Douglass to a white woman?" one reporter called out from the back of the group.

"What do you really think about a leader of the negro community marrying a white woman?" a second man called out before Frank could answer.

Frank waved his hands to try to quiet them down, as a third man asked, "Have you heard reports of Douglass courting colored women here in Washington? Why did he choose to marry a white woman?"

Frank's patience was thin to begin with, and he felt real anger rising in his chest. "How dare these people make these judgments based on hearsay and gossip," was his first indignant thought.

"Isn't it true that Douglass doesn't think a colored woman is good enough for him? Aren't you ashamed of performing their marriage?" another reported taunted.

Frank's effort to reply civilly required summoning the full reserve of self-control he had striven to achieve over the years. In a quiet voice he said, "Gentlemen, I have nothing to say about these matters, other than to avow with all my heart, that I believe any man and any woman has the right to marry whomever they choose, regardless of their race." He shook his head, and added with a stern frown, "These questions betray the harsh prejudice that infects our society. I bid you goodnight!"

Frank stepped back inside, finding Lottie there. She looked at her husband as he shut the door, knowing they shared a mutual understanding of the events of the day. Frank looked at her gratefully. He stepped forward and embraced his wife, glad for the comfort that made his discouragement bearable.

About a month later, on a windy day in late February, the congregation of the Fifteenth Street Presbyterian Church was emerging from the front doors after the Sunday service. Families and friends were chatting with each other and with their neighbors. Most of the congregants were dressed well in their Sunday clothes, but some among them seemed to have arrived at the service in the only clothes they owned: worn-down shoes, old jackets, and sweaters, barely adequate for the chill of early spring in Washington, DC, much less for the winter they had just survived.

Frank and Lottie stood just outside the main door, greeting their congregants as they came out. At a pause in the line, a shabbily dressed, tired-looking young man in his early twenties approached Frank to greet him.

"Good mornin', Reverend Grimké," he said shyly. "Thank ya' for yo' words in there. Good to know someone understan.'"

"Thank you, young man," Frank said with a curious look, "I don't believe we've met yet?" He could tell that the young man was freshly arrived from the South. From his slow drawl, Frank guessed he was from Georgia.

"No, sir. Ah jes' get to town last night. Ah'm Albert. Albert McDougall, sir." He corrected himself, "Reveren', Ah mean." He shook Frank's extended hand.

Frank did a quick assessment and decided others in his congregation could wait while he gave this youngster his full attention. "Welcome, Albert! But tell me—I see you lookin' pretty tired. Was it a hard trip?"

Albert was grateful for the inquiry but felt almost too worn down to speak at length. "Oh, sir, Ah don' know what to tell ya. Ah'm so glad to be here. Ah was runnin' scared the whole way—e'en though Ah didn't have any reason to be. Well, you see, down there in Georgia—uh, that's where Ah'm from. Well, things are gettin' rougher and rougher. Last week a hog went missin' and they 'ccused my cousin a-takin' it."

"He din't a'course," Albert added quickly, "but they came and got him anyway." Albert tried to suppress the sob that welled up with the memory of his previous week, and the fear he had endured. "Lynched him. Strung him up from a tree and let him hang. No trial, nothin'.

Between deep sobs he managed to choke out the words, "He my favorite cousin!" He wept more deeply, although he was clearly embarrassed and turned away to hide his face from the cheerful Sunday church crowd. Frank took him aside with an arm around his shoulder, while Lottie continued to greet the few remaining congregants. As they walked away, Albert calmed down a bit, but he was still visibly distraught at the week of terror he had survived.

"Albert, son, I'm so sorry for that. I'm so sorry," he repeated. "What can we do to help?"

The young man wiped away his tears with a dirty sleeve and answered, "It's just—Ah'm so tired—and Ah was so scared coming up here on the train. They got a negro section now—but Ah kep' thinkin' they'd come and throw me off—even though Ah paid my fare. Ah couldn' sleep."

Frank nodded quietly. He'd heard this kind of story before, but it still angered and grieved him. In fact, it brought back memories of his own nights of terror on the several occasions he had run away. Albert continued with a note of hope. "Ah guess—well, Ah do need a place to stay, but Ah ain't got much money—jest a couple a' dollars left. And a job, a' course. Ah need work. Ah got me a girl cousin here, but cain't really stay with her. She's livin' with 'nother family.

"Albert," Frank said carefully as he led Albert toward the back of the churchyard, "I'd like you to sit right here on this bench for a few minutes. Just rest. My wife back there, Lottie Grimké, she knows all about how to get you some help here." Frank smiled at a sudden memory, "Would you believe that she helped me when I first came north—right after the war? Well, you be too young—probably don't remember much a' that." Frank realized, with mixed feelings, that it had been nearly twenty years since the end of that horrible time.

Mrs. Grimké will do whatever she can for you, Albert. But what's important, brother, is that you are one of us now—you are not alone." Frank gave him a firm squeeze on his shoulder, then went over to ask Lottie to see to Albert's needs while he chatted with some of the members of his congregation who were still milling around in front of the church waiting to ask him something. Albert sat with his head in his hands, sniffing and still wiping tears from his cheeks. He looked up hopefully as Lottie approached him. Her calm cheerfulness reassured him that all would be well.

Another month passed before Frederick Douglass and Helen Pitts Douglass returned from their honeymoon. Frank and Lottie had invited them to come to dinner again on their return. After responding to inquiries about their wedding trip, Helen spoke about how Frederick's grown children were not reconciled to their marriage. "It was painful," she said sadly.

"Yes, it was disappointing," Frederick agreed. "I've always felt close to my children, but they see our marriage as somehow an offense to their mother, Anna." He shook his head in puzzlement. "It's not as though Anna is still living and able to be my wife." He turned and took a seat with the others, looking dejected. "I believe my daughter, Rosetta, is resigned to it, but the boys don't seem to understand at all."

"I'm sorry, Frederick," Frank said softly. "And the press has not been gentle either, have they? Perhaps I wasn't as surprised by their reaction as you were?"

"No, I didn't see it coming. I've told them that my first wife was the color of my mother, my second is the color of my father," he smiled.[105] "But I don't think that will quiet them down."

"My brother and I could almost say the same. As you know, Archie's wife, Sarah Stanley, is white, the color of my father, and my Lottie here is the color of my mother. If emancipation means anything, it should mean that every person has the right to choose their own social relations. I am adamant about that, and I declare it often from the pulpit."

As they walked into the dining room, Frederick moved the conversation toward politics. "I see that Archibald is editing *The Hub* up in Boston. It was disappointing that Trotter and his friends supported a Democrat for governor—it may have swung the vote in his favor."

"So, you disapprove of Trotter's political activities?" Lottie asked.

"I don't disapprove of his political activity among the Boston colored. But I do disapprove of his choices." He frowned, "I am a Republican, a black, dyed-in-the-wool Republican, and I never intend to belong to any other party than the party of freedom and progress. Despite its recent backsliding, most elements in the Republican party give better hope for the success of the colored people's cause than those of the Democratic party," he declared, although his demeanor indicated that the question troubled him.

Helen intervened to steer the conversation into safer waters, "Frank, I've heard how many of your congregation here have recently arrived from the south. It appears that conditions there are becoming deplorable—truly unsupportable. What can we do?"

"We must protest loudly!" Frederick interjected in a fierce voice. "If there is no struggle, there is no progress. Those who profess to favor freedom and yet deprecate agitation, are men who want rain without thunder and lightning."

With calm courtesy but a slight tartness Helen replied, "Frederick, dear, I was asking Frank his opinion."

Frank was amused by the exchange and answered with equanimity. "Well, I am generally a man who loves peace, but I agree with Frederick on this point. I have seen how it is when good men—and women—sit back and do nothing. There is too much pain at stake." Frank shook his head slowly thinking of the stories he had heard from many of his new church members. Then he looked around the table. "But what about you women? There is a struggle ahead for you as well."

Lottie and Helen looked gravely at each other. Then Helen looked admiringly at her new husband. "You know what first made me love my husband? It was when I saw how he stood up for women's suffrage at Seneca Falls. He was nearly alone among the men there, and even many of the women felt that asking for the vote was going too far and would make them ridiculous."

Lottie nodded her head vigorously in agreement. Frederick said with an almost imperceptible smile, "Well, you know what I say, dear. 'One and God make a majority'"[106]

Lottie gave him a skeptical smile, and quipped back, "Yes, and if we could just read God's mind all the time!" Helen and Frank acknowledged the dilemma with regretful nods. Although the conversation turned to more personal matters, the foursome knew from experience that their public and personal lives were painfully and inextricably interwoven.

30

Archie's Heart

Hyde Park Spring 1884

MRS. LEVERETT CAME HALFWAY up the interior stairs to meet Nana, and to take her out for the walk to the bakery that she had promised that morning. After seeing Nana off, Sarah returned to the bedroom where she was sorting her clothes and Nana's into neat piles on their bed, preparing to pack. Archie got up from the table and followed her there. He stood in the bedroom doorway, looking unhappy and distraught.

"Please, my dear—my dear Sarah. Can we sit down for a moment and speak? We've hardly spoken since your return from the Stuarts last week. I don't really know what is happening. I don't know how to please you. You never even mentioned the melodeon!"

"No, I didn't." Sarah stopped her folding for a moment, holding one of Nana's dresses to her chest. "I thank you for the thought," Sarah said formally, "but it's a little late, isn't it? I can hardly play it when I am in Michigan."

"So, you are determined to go visit your parents so soon?"

Sarah sighed and walked reluctantly out of the bedroom. She sat down in the living room, her eyes contemplating her feet. Archie followed, taking a seat across from her. As she spoke, her manner was cold and edgy. "Yes, that is exactly what I'm preparing to do, as you can see."

Archie's wound was deep, but weeks of reflection had humbled him and made him willing to admit to some failures on his part. Yet, in honesty, he could not say that he alone was to blame. "Sarah, I have never meant to hurt you. I do realize now that I have often left you alone—and perhaps not always understood your needs," Archie repeated what he had attempted to say multiple times during the previous days.

Sarah's voice was cutting as she said, "Not always? I'd say almost never!"

Archie stiffened and took a deep breath, struggling to remain contrite. "As I have said, Sarah, I recognize that I have been at fault, and I ask your forgiveness for those times. I—well, perhaps I should have included you more in my professional life—and the social relations it involved. You were busy with our little girl—I didn't know you wanted that."

"So, you left me alone with Nana and led your own life? Even when I was sick?"

"Is that fair, Sarah? I had to work—and I came home to you every night!" He felt anger rising in him at the injustice of her accusations. "I know I have not been a perfect husband. But my dear, don't you see that this trouble has two sides? Have you not been too much used to getting all and giving nothing in return. I think upon reflection you will see our marriage in a truer light."

"How is that? You've accused me of failing to pay debts which I never incurred."

"Sarah, please! If you are referring to the issue with the Karr's, I cannot see how you could accept money from them as a gift, and not understand that it was a debt that needed to be repaid. And if you had asked me . . . "

Sarah waved the issue away dismissively. "Well, it doesn't matter now. We are leaving for Michigan tonight."

"And when are you coming back?" Archie looked down, dreading the answer.

"I don't know," Sarah said with an indifferent shrug.

Archie's clenched his fist and bit his lip to stop from answering in anger. Instead, he rose and paced around the room, determined to make his last plea. "Whatever wrongs I have done you, I hope soon you will see the absurdity and groundlessness of the main charge which you have brought against me."

Sarah stared at him coldly, unwilling to consider his appeal. "Well, I trust Mrs. Stuart," was all she could say.

Archie's voice reached a forte and it trembled with indignation, "And you don't trust me? Your husband? I speak the truth, Sarah! *She*—this vile woman—has manipulated your mind beyond comprehension."

Sarah set her lips in a hard line but made no retort. Archie knew he was defeated, and after this he said nothing for several moments. He put his head in his hands and sighed in miserable resignation. "Well, it seems as though a temporary separation is for the best," Archie forced himself to say. "You must have time with your parents to come to your senses. However, I swear to you," he added darkly, "if you come back to Massachusetts and not to me—if you go to the Stuarts—I shall be sure to take Nana from you! I could never let them . . . "

Sarah interrupted with a fearful cry, "You shall never take Nana from me!"

Archie immediately regretted his words. In a calmer voice, he said, "No, I shan't—not if you are with your parents and can care for her properly. But if you were to expose her to the Stuart's malign influence—"

"Don't threaten me, Archie! it is unworthy of you." She glared at her husband, then looked blankly into the distance. "I must go pack. I think there is nothing further to say for the time being." Sarah rose and went to the bedroom. Archie put his head in his hands, utterly discouraged. When he lifted his head again, his face was drawn in grim despair and pain.

Rev. Stanley sat at his desk in Mackinaw, looking over a letter from Archie. He took out writing paper and began to write his response.[107]

> My dear son,
>   I received your letter on Saturday. I also received a letter from Sarah about two weeks ago which surprised me beyond measure. All the time she was with us last year there was not a word, or a hint of domestic infelicity. Sarah is in Detroit with her mother, and I have not seen her yet. When I do, I'll be better prepared to write. Meanwhile you can write me as freely as you wish.
>   Affectionately yours, MC Stanley.[108]

Several days later, Archie stood by a window in his office re-reading the note from his father-in-law that he had received in the previous day's post. *The Hub* was at the printer, and he had a half-hour to himself. He sat down, took out a piece of stationery, and began scribbling his response from his office desk.

> My dear Father Stanley,
>   Your very kind and welcome letter has just been rec'd. I can assure you that I thank you very much indeed. My heart truly goes out in filial love and reverence toward you, my good father.

I would give much to be able to sit down and talk with you face to face and open all my heart's sorrows and secrets to you.

Archie rubbed his forehead and stood up; his mind full of confusion that he sorely needed to sort out. Gradually some thoughts came, and he returned to his desk to set them down, knowing that clarity might come as he wrote.

I have always felt that the unusual character of our union imposed upon me additional obligations to make my wife happy and contented. I have endeavored to meet and discharge them by an unusual degree of devotion to my family. I can truly say that I have spared no attention, no exertion, no expense—in anticipation of my wife's wants. I appeal with confidence to Sarah herself for the truth of this statement—not to Sarah angry and dominated by the will of another, but to Sarah sober and unbiased and clothed again in her right mind.

Archie sat back and fiddled with his pen, struggling to say exactly what he meant. He did not merely want to justify himself. He wanted to understand his own behavior and his wife's. He needed clarity, and he hoped his father-in-law could help him see reality with some objectivity. He frowned and began to write again.

Pray do not understand me to say that I am not to blame—for I say with equal candor—that I am to blame. I do not desire to shield myself. What I mean is that my failures were not what she believes them to be, and that in the future when she is calm, I shall stand wholly acquitted from what to her appears now to be the real cause of our unhappiness and separation.

He hesitated, unwilling to speak ill of his wife to her father. Yet he felt he needed to speak truthfully of his own experience of the marriage. He chose his words carefully.

When I first saw this side of Sarah, I began to feel that perhaps she regretted our marriage—at least, the unusual consequences of our union. Because of that, I grew sensitive and watchful, which I know now was a bad thing. We lived very happily together for more than a year after Nana was born. Then Sarah's health began to fail—and with it, of course, her happiness began to go, too.[109]

Archie put down his pen and stretched his cramped fingers, remembering the beginnings of that painful time of Sarah's illness and discontent. He looked out the window of his office at the budding tulip trees with afternoon sunshine filtering through and realized that what had recently seemed magically beautiful to him no longer did so. He looked down at the page in front of him with a troubled expression as he continued to write.

> I took entire charge of Nana for many weeks—I did everything I could for Sarah and the baby—I washed the dishes, emptied the chamber pots, swept the rooms, brought in the laundry—everything. Then I made investments and sustained heavy losses. The future looked gloomy indeed. And Sarah seemed to be more exacting and more helpless.
>
> Finally, this Mrs. Stuart entered the picture and convinced Sarah that her illnesses were due to some fear, and that the causes of her ailments were grounded in her relations to me. I called her attention to the fact that she had been sick before she knew me at all—You remember, too, that her doctor and your wife— her own mother—said she was not strong constitutionally.

In Mackinaw City, Rev. Stanley had read Archie's long letter up to this point. It was getting dark, so he got up from his chair and turned on a gas lamp. He continued to read; his heart gravely saddened. He could perceive the pain underneath Archie's careful and judiciously phrased prose. But there were parts of the story that puzzled him as well. He read to the end of Archie's letter:

> Briefly, after I prayed for her forgiveness, it seemed that tenderness returned for a moment, but Mrs. Stuart, hearing that Sarah was irresolute whether to go away or return, wrote her a pack of falsehoods. I do not know, my dear father, whether the breach can be healed or not. My yearning, my empty days, my desolate nights, I can endure if my wife and daughter are happy and contented.
>
> In much love, good Father Stanley, I am your son, AMG

Reverend Stanley sat back down in his chair, running his hands across his mouth and along his chin as he reflected on his daughter's history, her choice of marrying Archie, and the written evidence of Archie's broken heart. He didn't doubt that there had been failures on Archie's part, but he also wondered why Sarah seemed unwilling to admit to any failings, or to accept her husband's declared desire to love and please her. It mystified him, and she was not yet there to ask about it. He picked up his pen to write.

Archie, my dear suffering child—most dearly do I love you and sympathize with you. I wish you were here with me this evening that I might embrace you, and counsel with you with perfect freedom, for I feel that you are both magnanimous and forgiving.

You are to me as a very dear child whom I love as my own. Do not, I pray you, allow yourself to fall into the dark clouds of despondency but summon up all the manly resolution of your truly noble nature and continue to hope.

He was going to end the letter there, but he felt that he owed Archie honesty as to the state of Sarah's health.

I think you are correct as to the cause of all: poor health and her extremely sensitive organization. She went to Boston an invalid, and it is as ungenerous as it is unjust for Mrs. Stuart or Sarah or anyone to charge you with her poor health. So please stick that arrow in the fire and never let it prick you again. You did what you could to make her happy. Let that comfort you. You must not humble yourself but treat her as an equal and love her like a strong and good man.

Your father, M.C. Stanley[110]

Back in Boston, Archie received his father-in-law's letter with the other post at his office. He read it quickly and found considerable comfort in Reverend Stanley's empathy, but it brought no hopeful news of Sarah's disposition. That was what he had hoped for. He needed to take a walk and mourn, but a colleague came to his desk with some papers for him to look over. Archie folded up the letter and put it slowly into his inside breast pocket.

Archie had let go of their rooms at Mrs. Leverett's house in Hyde Park, and again taken two small rooms close to his office in Boston. He was farther from Uncle Theodore, but closer to Wendell Phillips with whom he walked regularly. Occasionally, Theodore would come to Boston on the warm summer evenings and the three of them would walk together around the Common and the Public Gardens and sometimes down to the Charles River. They talked intently about current politics, the state of the South, and the competing views of how to achieve progress for the Negro communities in both north and south. They also talked of Shakespeare and Thoreau, and of women's suffrage. Although they talked rarely of Archie's marital troubles, Archie treasured their friendship and sane advice, finding in it a stellar substitute for the biological father he had barely known.

After one summer walk with his elder friends, Archie came home to find a letter from Sarah. He read the letter, shaking his head sadly at her words. He picked up one of Nana's dolls that had been left at Mrs. Leverett's and that he had brought with him to Boston. He held on to it tightly as he sat in his armchair, forlorn and undecided. Then he moved to his table to write back to Sarah.

> My dear wife,
> Your long-looked for letter has just been received . . . .You have spoken plainly, and it would seem sincerely. But dear, you know I cannot acknowledge charges which you make against me when they are not true—whatever you believe of me, my wife, I shall continue to believe that the highest and best in you, which is your true self, will yet be felt and seen.

Archie stopped writing to hold his aching head and to wipe away the tears that had begun to blur his vision.

> My heart! Oh, my wife. My love runs out to thee and pants after our child. Let there be no strife between us, dear, forevermore, for her sweet sake. Believe me, my wife, that I love thee and truly repent of my sins. I have loved you as I have loved no man or woman. Please tell me your plans and what you intend for our little girl. You know the door here is open and you always have a home for yourself and Nana here.
> Will you kiss my child for her papa? God bless you and me, too—your husband forever and always, AG[111]

Archie sat back in his chair, emotionally spent. He was determined to do his part for reconciliation, but he knew better than to be hopeful.

31

Separation

Detroit, Michigan 1884

THE SUMMER HAD COME and gone when Sarah walked through a park, carefully holding Nana's hand. At first, she didn't notice the passers-by who stared at Nana, or who turned around to look at them after they passed by. She didn't see the women who gave each other disapproving or even horrified looks as the pale mother and her honey-toned, dark-haired daughter walked serenely along.

But eventually, Sarah noticed the undisguised stares of one group after another. She turned and looked back at them with an expression that signified both challenge and disdain. She gathered Nana into her arms and carried her for a short distance until they were close to her family home.

After supper with her parents, Sarah put Nana to bed, reading to her and saying goodnight with an especially tender kiss. She moved to the desk in their bedroom to write to her husband.

> Dear Archie,
> Thanks for your note just received and for the opportunity you kindly offer to express my wishes in regard to our little girl. I believe it is best that we stay here, and that you and I live separately.

Sarah paused to summon her courage to say what she needed say.

> I wish to be assured that you fully relinquish your claim to Nana, and freely entrust her care and education into my hands. And

further I wish to know whether you would still consider it a
pleasure as well as a duty to assist in her maintenance. If so, I
should be glad to know just how much by the year you would
deem proper and consistent with your means.

Sarah glanced at Nana who was sleeping soundly in her bed. Her
look was full of pride and affection, but there was anxiety in it as well.
She wanted to care for Nana, but she was also uneasy about her ability to
protect and nurture her child. She added to her note:

She is, as you well know, a child of unusual promise, and I wish
very much to be able to attend personally to her education . . .[112]

By the time Archie received Sarah's letter that fall, he thought he was
resigned to the inevitable. But he felt an unexpected shock of despair at
her cool, formal language. He read the letter seated by his office window
in the last light of the evening. He was sad and lonely without Sarah, but
it was the thought of not seeing his daughter for an unknown time that
contorted his face with grief. He acknowledged her right as a mother, but
he could barely restrain himself from shouting out, "Damn you, Sarah!"
Instead, he wrote back as civilly as he could,

Dear Sarah:
    I desire to say that I consider your claim to Nana higher
than my own; that your wishes and intentions for her and her
education take precedence of mine in all respects. It shall be my
pleasure as well as my duty to do all I can toward her support.

In a melancholy reverie Archie recalled carrying Nana on his shoulders through the snow and hearing her giggles of joy and terror as she
rode in front of him on the sled down the snowy slopes in Hyde Park. He
picked up a photograph they had had taken of Nana at about age three.
Fortunately, Sarah had left it in the apartment, and now he kept it on his
work desk. He examined it carefully, a little smile creeping onto his face
at the thought of his precocious daughter. His words to his wife were
business-like, betraying little of the echoing pain of this amputation.

I have won a public position and reputation which I hope, before long, will enable me to do for our child all you may desire,
and all that my own heart longs to perform. Can you give me
an idea as to what the minimum sum for Nana's maintenance
should be?
    I kiss Nana's picture and pray for you both.
    Sincerely yours, A.H. Grimké

During the three years that followed, Archie's desolation at the loss of his wife and his daughter abated only slightly. It was, indeed, as if he were missing a limb. Gradually a numbness set in, and the worsening conditions for negroes in the South, as well as a crushing of their hopes for rapid progress in the North, occupied him both professionally and personally. As he was drawn into the public world of law, writing and politics, his reputation as a leading voice of the colored community in the North grew, and that overlay of a rising professional reputation brought superficial relief of the unhappiness beneath.

In Michigan, three years had brought little of the peace that Sarah Stanley had hoped for. She continued to struggle with poor health but had managed to do some successful writing and lecturing in between bouts of sickness. She felt anxious and constrained, and finally she had come to a wrenching decision.

Seven-year-old Nana, sat curled up, reading a book in a comfortable chair in the bedroom she shared with her mother. She got up and walked over to her mother's desk to show her some pictures and to ask about a word. Sarah hugged Nana lovingly around the shoulders as she helped her sound out the word. As Nana trotted back to her chair, Sarah looked at her with longing and anguish before she continued to write. Her face was pale and fatigued, and she coughed deeply.

> Dear Archie,
>   I have come to realize that it is not for the best good and happiness of our little girl to be brought up under divided claims.[113] I now realize that it is far better for little Nana's well-being that she should go to you at once. She is so very happy at the prospect of going to see her papa that I am quite reconciled to resign her to you (at least for the present).
>   Sincerely, SSG

32

Reunion

Boston April 1887

THE POST HAD ARRIVED when Archie returned from a luncheon outing. He picked it up and walked up the stairs to his office with several letters in his hand. Seeing the letter from Sarah, he tore it open quickly and read it. He scanned the letter again, checking the date, to make sure he had read it correctly. He hesitated to trust the lightness he suddenly felt. "Oh, my dear little girl—are you truly coming back to me?" he said out loud.

Archie's colleague, Butler Wilson, overheard his exclamation and looked at him with interest. Archie found that, despite his uncertainty, he needed to share his joy. "Excuse me, Butler, but I've had astounding news. It appears that Sarah is sending Nana back to me for the present!"

Wilson got up and shook Archie's hand in a gesture of kindly congratulations. He had never seen Archie with a wider grin in their three years of partnership. Archie sat down in his desk chair to finish reading Sarah's explanation.

> She needs that love and sympathy of one of her own race. My own family, kind and anxious as they are to do right, do not. Neither is it possible for them to give her the love she needs to make her both good and happy, and a child cannot be good unless it is also happy.
>
> She is now getting old enough to see and feel the thoughts of others which the difference in race and color naturally engenders regarding her.

Archie grimaced and shook his head in momentary disgust. "Oh, Sarah" he said to himself, "what has possessed you? I hope it is not too late for Nana." He wasn't sure what he meant by this—too late for her not to be harmed by other people's rejection? Or too late for her to bond with him and his family in a new situation? How must she feel about her mother sending her away—even to her beloved Papa, he wondered. He read on,

> My present plan is to send her on to you by express from St. Louis or Cleveland. I am thinking of spending the season at the northern lakes or in Canada. My health demands a radical change.[114]
>
> For some considerable time, I have seriously thought that, in the best interests of both of us, the legal ties which bind us should be severed. Our marriage relationship exists only in name and can never be otherwise.

Archie looked out the window from his desk for several moments, absorbing the finality of this pronouncement. Explaining his sudden departure to Butler, Archie left the office and walked to the omnibus that would take him to Hyde Park. He found Theodore at home and rather than walk into town, they walked along Theodore's favorite path bordering the river. Archie relayed the sweet news and the bitter news. He spoke hesitantly, feeling an embarrassment and shame at the impending divorce despite his gladness about Nana. Theodore listened to him attentively, nodded sagely, and was delighted at the prospect of Nana coming back to Boston. When Archie spoke of Sarah, however, he was overcome with grief, and Theodore caught him in a fatherly embrace until his long-repressed sobs subsided.

It was a long sixteen hours alone on the train from Cleveland to Boston for seven-year-old Nana. The seat next to her was empty. After her mother left her on the train in the conductor's care, she had tried to feel brave and excited about this adventure, but she couldn't shake a chilling unease about the way her mother had said good-by. Wouldn't they see each other again in a few months?

She had distracted herself by gazing out the window as they passed along the banks of Lake Erie on the way to Buffalo. But enroute to Albany, as it grew dark, a deep fatigue came over her and she curled up in her coach seat and fell asleep. When he passed through the car, the conductor threw a warm blanket over her. She slept soundly through the stop in Albany and the change to tracks that would take them to Boston. A train whistle woke her up from her deep slumber as they passed through a western Massachusetts town. She rubbed her eyes and retrieved the book that had fallen off her lap. She was lonely, but she was used to that.

Then a restless boredom set in. She reached for the second lunch her mother had packed and ate it slowly to make it last. As her hunger subsided, her mood improved. She remembered that she was on her way to see her Papa after more than three years of separation. As the train neared Boston, the sights along the way again caught her interest. She noticed that among the children playing in the backyards close to the train tracks, there was occasionally a family of colored children, a sight she had rarely seen in Michigan. She settled back into her seat, thinking eagerly of meeting her father again.

The kindly conductor who had covered her with a blanket, came to her seat as they approached the station. He reached up and pulled her small valise down from the luggage compartment. As the train slowed to a stop, he took her by the hand to help her get off the train and safely into her father's care.

Archie hurried along the platform, looking in each window, as the train pulled into the station. He was still near the front cars as the conductor and Nana get off from one of the back cars. Nana looked up and down the platform, pulling away from the conductor as she spied the man she was sure was her father. She ran towards him, weaving through the crowd as she waved her hands and called out "Papa, papa! It's me—your Nana!"

Archie turned to see her just as she was almost upon him. He grabbed her and swung her around in his arms, then drew her close to his chest. When he put her down, he gazed in wonder at this taller, less familiar version of his daughter. They walked back to get her bag from the conductor and tip him. He took her valise, and they walked out of the station, Nana's hand firmly in his own. His daughter smiled up at him quietly, as though they were sharing a long-held happy secret. There was much to say, but for the moment words seemed unnecessary.

33

Fast Friends

Hyde Park Spring 1890

AT TEN YEARS OF age, Nana had the round face and stocky figure of a girl who had not yet stretched out to her full adolescent height. Her curly dark hair was pulled into thick, unruly braids that were constantly coming loose. She was re-braiding one of them as she came out the door of the Weld home. When she finished, she took Theodore's hand.

On Theodore's part, holding his grandniece's hand was as much for his own support as for her safety. At eighty-six, he walked with a cane, but he stood erect, and his stride was still energetic. The two companions walked down the hill from the Weld home and across the river to Hyde Park center. Nana swung Theodore's hand gaily as she walked, and as always, Theodore pointed out his favorite trees, birds, and other sights along the way. Nana paid only occasional attention.

Theodore stopped to chat with friends as they got close to the town center. Nana ran away from his side to look in some windows, and then returned, pointing at a delicately decorated copybook in the stationer's window. Theodore gave Nana an affectionate squeeze around the shoulders as they looked in the window. They continued to walk together until they reached their destination, the new Hyde Park Library which Theodore had helped to found.

This was paradise for Nana. She hurried to the young people's section and spent an hour there poring over her favorite authors and choosing the one book she was allowed to take home. This time it would be *Eight Cousins,* since she had already finished *Little Women, Little Men, and Jo's Boys.* Theodore filled the time reading the available newspapers from New York, New England, and London. He had made sure the library had subscriptions to these.

Nana had received occasional letters from her Mama, but they seemed to grow less frequent over time, and Nana had stopped asking when she would see her mother again. She was happy with her Papa, with her school in Hyde Park, and with the chance to spend time with the Weld family. If she felt the hole in her life where a mother should be, she plugged it with ardent attachments to both classmates and familiar adults, with devotion to her father and great uncle, and with the stories and poems that she was beginning to write.

On Christmas Day, 1893, shortly after midday, the doorbell rang at the Weld home and Charles opened the door to let in Archie and Nana.[115] They shook the damp snow off their coats and took off the overshoes they had wisely put on in order to trudge the mile from their rooms on the other side of Hyde Park. Charley shook hands with Archie and gave Nana a hug. Charles had married the same year that Nana was born, and his son, Louis, was two years younger than Nana.

Theodore rose from his armchair with difficulty as Archie and Nana took off their coats, hung up their hats, and came to wish him a Merry Christmas. Nana stealthily laid a few small gifts under the Christmas tree. It had not been the Weld family custom to have a tree but Charles' wife, Anna, had insisted on it for the past few years, arguing that it was primarily for the children—their son, Louis, and Nana. Theodore still thought of it as a pagan tradition, but he tolerated it for Anna's and the children's sake.

Anna appeared from the kitchen where she had been helping Susan prepare Christmas dinner. She removed her apron and Nana saw that she was dressed in an emerald velvet dress with a pleated bodice, a high collar, and sleeves that puffed above the elbow. Nana gaped in awe at Anna's understated elegance, now that adolescence had made her occasionally conscious of such things.

"Welcome, welcome—Merry Christmas!" Anna called out as she came into the room. She kissed Nana, and Archie pecked her on the cheek. She looked approvingly at Nana who had blossomed into a slender, well-proportioned thirteen-year-old, still awkward with her gangly legs and arms, but vivacious and eager to please. She had a youngster's unconventional sense of fashion, Anna thought. But Anna predicted that her smooth, copper skin and wavy dark hair would give her an exotic beauty when she reached maturity.

Nana, of course, was oblivious to this generous evaluation, and said merely, "Oh, my—it's so nice and warm in here. Freezing as the bottom circle of Hades outside!"

"Nana!" Anna exclaimed disapprovingly, although she was mildly amused. "You must watch your language—you are a young lady now!" Nana sighed resignedly at Anna. She turned away and rolled her eyes at Uncle Theodore who laughed as he leaned on his cane.

"Has your father been reading you Dante, Nana? When did you learn that Hades is not a pit of fire but a frozen wasteland?" Theodore's eyes twinkled below his bushy eyebrows. "Come over, my dear child, no frozen greetings here—I want a proper Christmas kiss."

Nana reached up on tiptoe and planted a warm kiss on his forehead. "You look just like Saint Nicholas, Uncle Theodore." He chuckled, "So they say."

Nana saw her cousin Louis coming in from another room, and she called out to him, "Hi, Lou! Merry Christmas." Louis came up next to her and began poking her in the side in an eleven-year-old boy's show of affection.

"Yeeh—don't tickle me, you rascal!" she said as she pushed him away. "Did you come from the kitchen? Oh, let me go say Merry Christmas to Susan, too." She peered into the dining room where Susan was setting out some fresh rolls for dinner. As Archie, Theodore and Charley settled down to chat, Nana went to greet Susan. Louis tagged along, and she seized the opportunity to return his tickle and roughhouse with him a bit. They disappeared into the kitchen with Susan.

Theodore turned to Archie and said, "Well, well—Archie. You have done us proud once again!" His eyes scanned the room with a frown, "Here—somewhere I have your new books."

"Thank you, Uncle. I tried to—"

Theodore interrupted him, "I am reading the one on Garrison first. You have made some changes since the draft I reviewed. Well done! Important to get the story right." He shook his head with a melancholy look, "Brother William and I had our differences. And as you report, he often lacked tact, and loved to stir up controversy. But at heart he was unequaled in his devotion to ending slavery and—well, he stuck to his guns, too, on the woman question."

Theodore gestured to Archie to take a seat, "But come, come sit down! It's Christmas and we have better things to talk of." Theodore sank gratefully back into his armchair. "How are Frank and Lottie? What do you hear from them?"

"They are well, yes, but both very busy." He folded his arms across his chest and frowned deeply. He looked sidewise at Theodore and said in a pained voice, "But the news from the South that Frank passes on to me—it makes me sick at heart." Archie lowered his voice and spoke quietly to Theodore and Charles, not wanting to shock Anna and the children, although the latter were well out of earshot. "Frank hears more firsthand than we do here. We only hear about the worst of the lynchings—the mobs dragging colored men out of jail. Many are there only because they forgot to step aside for a white man."

Theodore nodded, his face darkening. Archie tried to speak calmly despite his fury. "And then, they are beaten, dragged behind carts, hung from trees, and set on fire. And all while the local sheriffs just 'look away'" Archie lapsed into dark silence, unable to speak more of the horrors he had heard.

Theodore shook his head in despair. "Will all great Neptune's ocean wash this blood clean from our hands?"[116] he murmured, falling back on Shakespeare to acknowledge the guilt of the nation.

Archie sighed deeply, glancing at Charley to gauge his reaction. "Frank hears from those who come to his church" he explained for Charley's sake. "Those who have finally given up on their homes in the South to come north. They are terrified. They have been cheated out of any profits from their sharecropping. They are kept perpetually in debt, even afraid to ask for what is justly theirs."

"And, let me guess," Theodore interjected. "They don't really want to leave the South, but finally, there is a last straw—the Negro school is burnt down, and nothing is done to replace it, or their cousin is lynched. That is when they leave everything and come north. Is that about right, Archie?" He looked intently at his nephew who nodded sadly in agreement. "But to what, Archie?" Theodore asked rhetorically.

Charley had listened intently to this interchange, troubled, but skeptical about the extent of the injustices that Archie reported. "But yes, to what, Father?" Charley asked. "There are no jobs here for people who only know how to pick crops. They have no skills. It's all economics," he said with a shrug.

Archie jumped in, impatient with Charley's evident lack of both accurate knowledge and compassion. He struggled to restrain his indignation. "Well, Charles, you are right that some of them have few skills. But many of them *are* skilled at carpentry or at husbandry or blacksmithing, and now many more have learned to read, and can keep accounts and mend machines."

He looked at Theodore for support. "But the problem is that given a choice between hiring a poorly skilled, and perhaps lazy, white worker and a well-skilled, conscientious black one, who do you think northern employers choose?" Charles looked uneasy, but the men were interrupted before he could answer.

Susan called out, "Christmas dinner is on the table, dearies! Now don't keep talkin' away. Jest come 'n eat!" She placed the turkey in front of Charles' seat. Anna came out of the kitchen with a bowl of gravy and a carving knife in her hand, "Here, Charles, can you carve the turkey?"

Susan turned back to the young people who had just emerged from the kitchen, and commanded, "Nana, can you bring in the sweet potatoes. And, oh, my, I almost forgot! Louis, can you pour the grape juice for everyone?" On her way back to the kitchen, Susan complained to Nana in a voice loud enough for all to hear, "Too bad your great uncle don' 'low a drop a' wine in the house, e'en at Christmastime!"

"I wouldn't trust it within twenty miles of you, Susan!" Theodore said jocularly. Laughing, they all found their way to the table. Once Susan and the children finished putting dishes on the table, they all sat down together.

Theodore led the grace. "Dear Lord," he began in a somber but conversational tone, "we gather in your blessed name with hope and cheer in one another's presence, and we remember our dear Angelina and Aunt Sai, and our Thodie and Sissy who cannot be with us tonight, and—" Theodore sighed heavily as he continued, "We ask your courage and wisdom in the continuing struggle." Theodore paused for a moment, as he often did, and then his voice seemed to brighten. "And we give thanks for all our loved ones and for this Christmas feast!"

"Amen!" Everyone responded.

"Susan—you've surpassed yourself, once again," Theodore said, eyeing the sweet potatoes with particular eagerness. "And Anna, too, of course. Thank you."

The family passed dishes and bantered easily as they began to eat. Anna Weld was eager to assure lighter conversation at dinner, so she asked, "Archie, I hear rumors that your appointment as Consul General to the Dominican Republic may come through at last, now that Cleveland is president again. Is that true?"

Archie threw up his hands in a gesture of uncertainty. "It is possible, but not while the current consul is still there." He frowned, "I really don't know what to think. I have stopped counting on it, but perhaps—"

The food disappeared quickly, and the conversation was casual as they ate. As they were finishing, Archie and Anna glanced over at Theodore who looked as though he were nodding off to sleep. They exchanged an amused smile. Anna, Susan and Nana begin chatting about the cooking and the pies that were awaiting them in the kitchen.

Archie turned his attention back to Charles and said, "Now, Charles—I just wish to say that I think you are right that it is economics that is at the core of the southern problem. We are still in a monumental struggle between two systems—the northern industrial system, and the southern agricultural system which in reality—well, to my mind at least—it is just a throwback to a feudal system—you know, wealthy lords and powerless serfs." Louis listened in to the men's discussion with one ear but found it much more interesting to bother Nana when the opportunity presented itself.

"Yes," Charley agreed, "but the South believes that its agricultural economy cannot survive these changes, and indeed it has struggled. That has barely changed, even in the twenty-eight years since the North won the war."

Archie had spent a lot of time thinking about these issues, and he responded promptly, "I know, unfortunately, that many in the South still believe it can only survive with a system of slavery and class privilege. But that has been proven wrong by many agricultural economies—even in our own northern and western states. Those economies now depend on well-paid labor, better machines, and worker-owned farms. The South has simply refused to progress."

Charley frowned. "In theory you may be right, Archie, but in practice it is difficult for southerners to adjust to a whole new economic system. It will take generations."

Archie scowled and muttered, "Well, we haven't got generations." In a level voice he declared, "Things can change rapidly if the will is there. It is simply a clash of world views, of fundamental beliefs about the equality and dignity of all people versus the need for cheap, productive labor to serve the interests of an unproductive aristocracy." Archie had warmed to his topic, and added darkly, "But then, Charley, perhaps at bottom it is still about the color of our skin. 'Mislike me not for my complexion, the shadow'd livery of the burnish'd sun.'[117] he declaimed in a deep voice. "You see. Even Shakespeare recognized it."

Theodore was suddenly awake again—and piped up in an amused voice, "Archie, you will outdo me with your knowledge of the bard! Othello? No, I believe it's Merchant of Venice, isn't it?"

Archie nodded grimly and murmured, "Some things don't seem to change."

Susan and the children passed around plates of apple and cherry pie and serious conversation resumed. Theodore was alert, but he was tired of the fray. "We struggled so long, and it all seemed worthwhile in '65, but then in '77 we were betrayed again—all the gains of Reconstruction were halted and reversed." He shook his head, then tilted it towards Archie. "You've covered that well in your books, Archie. Both parties sold their souls to get southern votes."

"But then, northern prejudice and indifference can be almost equally destructive to colored people's development," Archie added.

"I agree on that point, Archie," Charley confessed. "I see it all the time, even here in Boston."

Theodore reminisced with a story he had told many times. "Yes, I learned that at an early age. A colored boy came to our school. He was allowed to stay but treated so badly by the other boys and the teacher that I was ashamed for all of us. I was ridiculed when I offered to sit in the back with him."

Nana had picked up the drift of the conversation, and she chimed in eagerly. "Even at my school here in Boston, there are girls who are mean to me, and say I am too smart for a 'nigger.' Can you believe it? What can they mean by that? Should I pretend that I am stupid and lazy?"

"Nana, my dear! You really must watch how you say things," Anna chided faintly.

"She only speaks the truth, Anna, and I hope she always will." Uncle Theodore protested on Nana's behalf.

Archie was disturbed and said, "Nana, you never told me that!" He was dismayed at her failure to confide in him, so he put a hand on hers and said, "But, my sweet child, just be sure you *never are* stupid or lazy. You are my bright star! And the only real harm that can come to you is not to be worthy of your gifts. You must think of your grandma and your great aunts," he said with an encouraging smile.

"Speaking of my dear wife and sister, I see, Archie, that you are taking up women's suffrage issues, too. Bravo! You do us honor."

Archie replied modestly, "Of course, I must do what I can. With Aunt Angelina's and Aunt Sarah's example how could I do less? And that of my own dear mother as well." Archie took a moment to think of Nancy Weston's strength, and how she remained a bedrock of wisdom for Frank and himself, even in her current frailty.

"It will come. The vote will come. And none too soon, for our little Nana's sake," Archie predicted. Anna looked dismayed at the talk of women's suffrage, a point on which she disagreed with the family, and even with her husband. She looked at him to register his reaction, but he was impassive.

"I'm not little anymore, Papa!" Nana protested.

"Ah, so you probably don't care if Saint Nicholas has come," her father answered.

"Papa! Don't tease me. Of course, I care! Anyway, let's go see. I think he left something for you."

The family got up from the dinner table and moved back to the parlor, where they exchanged gifts and exclaimed happily about them. Nana handed her father a hastily wrapped package. "Here, papa. I hid it when we walked over, and you didn't even notice," she laughed.

Archie opened it up, giving Nana a warm touch on her cheek as he saw what it was. "It's *The Last Days of Pompeii*," Nana said eagerly. "I knew you wanted to read it again, and maybe I can read it when you are finished. Uncle Theodore helped me to find it."

Archie gave her a kiss on her forehead, smiling at Theodore as well. "Thank you, child. It's a wonderful gift!"

"Come here, Nana," Anna called out. She handed Nana a present which the girl quickly unwrapped. It was a stylish winter hat, muff, and scarf.

"Oh, thank you, Aunt Anna! And Uncle Charles!" She admired the gift and gave Anna a kiss on the cheek. "Oh, I like them so much!" she said in an excited whisper. "I can hardly wait to wear them to school!"

She turned and looked around for her second cousin, saying, "Lou, that blue one is for you!" He rapidly grabbed the blue package and unwrapped the set of dominoes Nana had found for him.

Louis looked over the dominoes with mild enthusiasm, but a little uncertainty. "Will you play with me, Nana? I'm pretty sure I know how."

"Yes, of course—a bit later," Nana assured him with a friendly look.

After an hour the gift-giving had quieted down, and Nana waited, not very patiently, for Louis to take his turn at dominoes. She picked up a newspaper with a picture of a new two-wheeled vehicle.

Nana waved the newspaper at her father. "Papa, have you seen these? They are called velocipedes—or bi-cycles! Look this one is for women! I want one so much. This is what I want for my birthday." Nana made a play with her last dominoes and said to Lou, more triumphantly than graciously, "There, I won." He was crestfallen but gathered up his dominoes to try another day.

"Yes, curious aren't they," Archie said. "I did try one out several years ago when I was rather more athletic, but it was cumbersome. I nearly fell off. I think perhaps they are better made now." He screwed up his face in disapproval, and asked, "So they have made one for women? Don't you think you already get into enough trouble without that, Nana?"

"But, Papa, look, wouldn't it be marvelous? See here . . . " She leaned toward him to show him the sketch and the caption. See, it says 'Women's Safety Bicycle.' So, it must be very safe. Oh, think of the freedom it would give me. I have heard some women saying, 'This is our freedom cycle'!" She decided to pout. "But you always say 'No'! No to any freedom for me." She was tired and petulant, but she knew better than to wheedle her father.

Anna overheard the conversation and chimed in from across the room, "But my dear, how would women manage their skirts. It looks rather frightening and indecent." She chuckled dismissively, "Perhaps we would need those bloomers like Aunt Sarah and Aunt Angelina used to wear." Archie looked up at Anna with a slight smile, grateful for any ally in trying to raise a proper young lady.

"Well, I would love to wear those," Nana said defiantly. "I think I will find myself a pair—or maybe sew some myself." Anna screwed up her face in distaste.

Nana put aside the newspaper impatiently and turned to her great uncle for support. Theodore responded with a barely perceptible wink. "Come give me your arm, dear, I need some fresh evening air." Nana went to find her winter coat and her uncle's greatcoat and hat.

Theodore rose with difficulty, balancing himself on Nana's arm as he donned his coat. Then he steered her toward the front porch. They stepped outside into a frigid but starry night. Nana stood close by, supporting Theodore under one arm as he pointed out the constellations that were visible. They gazed in silence for several minutes before Theodore said, "Let's walk a bit."

Nana marshalled her courage to ask her great uncle what was on her mind. "Uncle Theodore, I never knew my great aunts. Papa says I should be like them—but how can I be like them when I never knew them? And they were so old! Well, I know they weren't *always* old—"

"No older than I am, Nana," Theodore reminded her with a smirk.

She paused; her brow wrinkled as she tried to imagine them as young women. "Why didn't Great Aunt Sarah marry? You and Great Aunt Angelina married." She asked shyly, "When did you first meet?" She bit her lower lip, and asked her boldest question, "Was it love at first sight?" She paused, a little embarrassed at inquiring about such a private matter. But she pressed on, her curiosity overtaking her sense of propriety.

Theodore looked gruff for a moment as he complained, "Hmmm. So many questions." But his face relaxed as he realized that he was happy to talk about his past. Few people asked anymore. "No, not exactly love at first sight—although she *was* striking when I first met her." He paused, smiling at his vision of the vibrant, clear-eyed woman with thick chestnut hair that had intrigued him.

"More likely love at first word. We'd met for a brief period, and I had heard her speak in public. But then we exchanged letters for many months. She didn't like it when I scolded her and Sarah about speaking out on women's issues. We were sparring before we spoke any words of love!" Theodore grimaced, but Nana saw the tenderness in his eyes.

"Well, if truth be told, I was rather stupid about affairs of the heart." He paused, shaking his head with a sorrowful look. "I was worried that they would weaken the abolitionist cause by confusing it with women's rights."

"But didn't you believe in women's rights, Uncle Theodore?" Nana was perplexed.

"Of course, I did! I agreed completely with their views, but I was afraid it would distract from the power of their testimony against slavery." He scratched his cheek above his long alabaster beard with a thoughtful air. "They rebutted my arguments powerfully." He looked down affectionately at Nana. "In the end, I must admit that Sarah was right to insist that human rights are indivisible. If you are fighting against oppression, you must fight it on every front where it exists."

Theodore pulled out a handkerchief to wipe his nose, then suggested they turn back to the house. "As for Sarah," Theodore continued with a note of sadness, "Well, she passed up her great chance to marry, and I think at times she regretted it bitterly." He looked at Nana to see if she understood." Nana didn't, and she wanted to ask more, but she just shrugged and encouraged her uncle to go on.

"Well, my dear, she was a rare soul—a chosen one. Her inner sufferings were great at times, but she was our quiet, guiding light—a brilliant mind in a tiny body. She had a moral courage," Theodore mused, "and a perseverance—that surpassed the rest of us." Theodore looked up at the stars, with regret in his voice. "I was not always fair to her. Nor was Angelina I think."

His voice trailed off as he began to cough deeply again. The cough frightened Nana, and she was getting chilled as well. She put an arm around his waist and supported him as they headed back into the warm, well-lit house.

34

"God Sends His Teachers Unto Every Age"

Hyde Park February 7, 1895

THE SKY WAS BLUE, but the distant winter sun did little to alleviate the freezing cold and vicious wind blowing on the day of Theodore's funeral.[118] The Unitarian Society of Hyde Park filled rapidly with Theodore's family, family friends, former students, and townspeople, few of them deterred by the sub-freezing temperatures.

Theodore had declined slowly over the fourteen months since that intimate family Christmas. He passed away quietly, in his sleep, a few months after his 91st birthday. None of his original abolitionist band survived him. However, there were at least two generations of those still fighting for women's rights alive, and several of them made it to Theodore's funeral. A delegation of colored friends and admirers from Hyde Park and Boston attended, some of whom had been his coworkers in the fight against slavery.[119]

Theodore's Hyde Park family gathered in the front rows: Charles Stuart and Anna Harvell Weld and their son, Louis, now a 13-year-old. Sissy was ill and could not make the trip.[120] Susan, who had cared for Sarah, Angelina, and Theodore in their final illnesses, sat with the family. She felt Theodore's passing as keenly as anyone. Notably missing were Archibald, Frank, and Nana. Archibald had very recently taken up his post as Consul General to Santo Domingo and had left Nana in Frank and Lottie's care in Washington, DC. Frank could not leave his mother, Nancy, who was very frail.[121]

The pallbearers brought forward the plain coffin covered with floral wreaths. A painting of Theodore in his eighties, with his long and bushy white beard, was set up in the vestibule of the church. After a prelude from the church organist and a brief introduction by the Unitarian presider, William Lloyd Garrison, Jr. strode up the aisle to take the podium. He cleared his throat and spoke slowly and dramatically in a manner that improved on his famous father's gift of rhetoric because it was tempered by his mother's gentleness and equanimity.

> God sends his teachers unto every age, and it was the happy fortune of our friend, Theodore Weld, to be an early teacher in the largest school of the century. Nature fitted him to be a persuader of men. A spiritual nature, a logical mind, a sensitive conscience, moral courage, an eloquent tongue, these were the endowments of Theodore Dwight Weld.

Garrison's words fell on fertile ground as his close neighbors and old friends nodded in recognition. Only a few had known him as the young firebrand with wild hair and shabby clothes whose anti-slavery speeches held audiences spellbound. More of them remembered him as the rigorous but kindly teacher who had mentored them and set an example of a life that combined physical discipline, intellectual rigor, warm affection, and compassion.

The younger among his neighbors knew him as the town elder with a formidable white beard and penetrating eyes who always had time to chat with young people. Garrison continued to tell his story, as their throats choked, and tears fell.

> To be an anti-slavery teacher in his day was to be a soldier—not less heroic because the warfare was not fought with guns, but with tongue and pen. A few brief but exhausting years cover his anti-slavery lectures. But so crucial were the times when he espoused the cause that no history of the abolition movement can be written without including the story of Theodore D. Weld, his wife Angelina, and their beloved sister, Sarah.

Louis, who had never experienced the death of a family member, looked up at his father as he heard him stifle a sob at the mention of his mother and aunt. He had never seen his father cry before and found it alarming. Then he looked at Susan, and saw large, wet drops falling freely into her lap. He had never known his great aunts, but he sensed that with his grandfather's death, the family's glue was coming loose. Bonds he had barely recognized as existing, were now broken. He moved closer to his mother, needing the comfort of her presence. She put an arm around him. He listened more carefully to Mr. Garrison.

> During two years only was Mr. Weld permitted to labor on the platform, his magnificent voice failing through overuse. But with his pen he continued the brilliant and stirring arguments that had characterized his speeches. His harrowing book, *Slavery as It Is, Or the Testimony of a Thousand Witnesses* stimulated Mrs. Harriet Beecher Stowe to the later writing of "Uncle Tom's Cabin." Less well-known were his two seasons in our nation's capital, supporting our noble John Quincy Adams.
>
> Perhaps the most surprising chapter in our friend's history was his marriage to Angelina Grimké. That a despised abolitionist should secure a wife from one of the proudest slave-holding families in South Carolina would be considered improbable in fiction.

Lou tried to imagine his grandfather as the young man whom Garrison was describing. It was even more difficult to imagine a romance between him and his grandmother whom he knew only through the stern photos of her as an elderly woman. He looked down with a vexed countenance, but continued to listen.

> Who can forget his striking and familiar figure as he wended his abstracted way through our New England streets? This great teacher of Shakespeare might himself have been a Shakespearean hero—this man of lion-like courage and appearance.

Louis recognized this last portrait of his grandfather, and suddenly the grief of the congregation took hold of him as well. This was the kindly man who had taken him for walks, encouraged his love of nature, gently corrected him, but always treated him with serious respect as well as deep affection. His lips quivered and the tears fell as he realized what he had lost.

As Garrison wrapped up his eulogy the atmosphere of universal grief was slowly transmuted into a feeling of satisfaction, and even celebration.

> Theodore Weld saw the death of slavery and enjoyed the triumph accorded to most reformers only after death. Yet he has lived long enough to recognize the indignity and misery stilled

heaped upon our colored brothers and sisters, and to mourn the incompleteness of our country's transformation. It was time that this untrammeled spirit should be emancipated. He had no doubt that death was the threshold to a larger life and no man had more reason for assurance.

The funeral congregation understood that this was a life that was complete and good and all that a life could hope to be. As Garrison finished, the gathered mourners stood and began to clap. He knew that it was not for his eulogy, but a homage to its subject, in gratitude for such a life among them.

The pallbearers accompanied the casket down the aisle and loaded it into the back of a hired carriage. Mr. Minnis, Theodore's favorite hackney driver, drove the casket to Mt. Hope Cemetery, where he was buried, as they had planned, next to his wife and sister-in-law.

35

An Awakening

Washington, DC, Late February 1895

NANA SAT AT A writing table in the parlor of Frank and Lottie's home. She nibbled nervously on the end of her pen as she composed her thoughts.[122]

> Dear Mamie,
>
> I do not know how to tell you how much I am thinking about you these days. You ask me, "Angie, do you love me as you used to?"

Nana paused, smiling at her friend's words, and then scribbled feverishly.

> Can I tell you what I really think? I know you are too young now to become my wife, but I hope, darling, that in a few years you will come to me and be my love, my wife! How my brain whirls, how my pulse leaps with joy and madness when I think of these two words, 'my wife.'[123]

Nana sat back, trying to quiet the tumult in her heart and body as she remembered a scene from several months earlier. Nana had been walking with her new schoolmate, Mamie Burrill, in a park. The two of them were in deep conversation, finding commonality not only in politics, but in their love of literature and writing, and in the vast and unfettered breadth of their imaginative lives.

Mamie was slightly taller than Nana. She turned to face Nana and took her hands in her own. The two stood looking at each other with a mysterious excitement. Mamie lifted her hand to brush back a strand of Nana's hair that had come loose. Her hand lingered on the side of Nana's face.

Nana smiled wistfully at the vivid memory, but her smile faded into a frown as she continued to write, "I know you, of all people, understand. No one else does." As she put her pen down Nana heard someone approaching the front door. She sighed, folded up the letter and hid it in her pocket. She got up and lit a fire in the fireplace, wrapping her shawl more tightly about her and then momentarily resting her head on the mantel, still shaken by her confused feelings. Uncle Frank walked into the room, shivering with the cold.

"Brrr. . .my dear girl, are you warm enough? It's a chilly day, and I fear you've forgotten to light the fire soon enough," Frank chided her with a concerned look, as he sorted through the mail he had picked up. "Well, here is something that will warm your heart at least," he said with a smile as he held out the letter. "And where is your Aunt Lottie?"

Nana's mood improved immediately. "Uncle, I'm so happy to see you!" She walked over and reached for the letter eagerly. "Is it from father?" She saw at first glance that it was. "Auntie went to bring soup to the Wilson's—the children have been sick. But I've been so—well, so alone this afternoon. And now I feel cheerful again!" She gave her uncle a distracted kiss on the cheek as she began opening the letter.

"Yes, it is his handwriting and there's a pretty stamp on it from the Dominican Republic. But I don't read your mail, you know." He tweaked her cheek fondly.

"Why wouldn't he take me to Santo Domingo with him, Uncle Frank? I didn't understand at all. Of course, I like being here in Washington with you," she added apologetically. "But I miss him so, and it would have been such an adventure!"

She sighed again, her emotions in their usual turmoil. "Of course, he tells me about everything, so that I feel that I am there. But it makes it worse somehow, because I want to truly be there myself, and see what he sees." She twirled around on the parlor rug and said dreamily, "I want to feel the sweet-smelling winds on my face, and even perhaps swim in the warm ocean."

Frank gave her an admonishing look. "You know precisely why he couldn't take you, my dear. As Consul he has many responsibilities and cannot be worrying about the education and safety of his lovely daughter. There are too many unknowns there, and you are headstrong, Nana. You know that. And you know how much he misses you as well. But he wanted you to finish high school here and prepare for college." Frank gave his niece a troubled look, "And you haven't exactly made that easy for any of us."

Nana ignored the last remark and responded with adolescent ardor, "Safety, safety, safety! That's all I hear from you and papa. At least Aunt Charlotte understands that safety isn't everything! And who are you to speak of living "safely" when you ran away from the house where you had been made a slave—several times I believe!" Nana raised her voice as she continued, "And papa! He was even worse, was he not? He ran away from being a slave, too. Didn't he?" She gave her uncle a challenging look. "Well, of course he did," she said.

"And then, there were my great aunts. Uncle Theodore told me about them. Were they safe when they spoke out against slavery? Wasn't there a new building right up there in Philadelphia that burned to the ground because the women and abolitionists had been allowed to speak there publicly? Weren't Aunt Angelina and Aunt Sarah almost burnt up in it?"

Francis seated himself in an armchair by the fire and took out a pipe to smoke. He tried to listen patiently to Nana's babbling. He smirked at her historical inaccuracy. "No, no, my dear. They were not near the building when it was set on fire. Where did you get that idea?"

Nana ignored her uncle's correction and went on. "And they even spoke for women having the vote someday. It's fifty years ago now, and we still don't have it! And Uncle Theodore did, too," she added. "And you said you believed that, too," she concluded triumphantly.

"Did I? What was I thinking?" He smiled quietly.

Nana stopped, suddenly deflated. She sat down near to her uncle and confided, "I miss Uncle Theodore terribly," she frowned. "He looked fierce, but he was always so kind to me! When I was little, he took me for walks all over Hyde Park and into Boston. He took me past Jamaica Pond and through the Fenway and even as far as the Public Garden one time. We fed the ducks."

Her brow wrinkled as she tried to remember, "Why, I think it was just last summer we did that, or was it the year before?" She grew quieter and more thoughtful again. "And I miss Grandmamma Weston, too, though I only knew her so briefly. I like sleeping in her room now. It feels like she is there with me sometimes."

There was a long pause. Frank sighed deeply, contemplating the very recent loss of his invincible mother—and the uncle who had been like a father to him, and even more so to Archie. "Strange, isn't it, that they both died this month."

Nana nodded, pondering this quietly, but then returned to her theme. "In any case, I do not believe I have been set any good example of living safely."

Frank had to make a serious effort to remain patient with his impetuous niece. "Nana, dear, you are right, of course; none of us have chosen to live our lives without taking risks when they are dictated by our conscience. But that is different from exposing oneself to unnecessary dangers and illnesses for no good reason."

He continued, "A tropical climate with its unhealthy airs, and a beautiful, young woman who is strong-willed and eager for romance and adventure. Can you blame your father for preferring to keep you here among family and books?" Frank sweetened his words with a questioning smile.

Nana looked away. She was mildly embarrassed at her petulance but decided to play the tragic adolescent a bit longer. "Well, I'm not beautiful anyway," she declared, giving Uncle Frank her most truculent look, "Oh, I suppose I am never to know real life. I'll always be kept at home and locked safely away!"

Frank took a different tack and answered sternly. "Nana, you have little cause to complain. Your job right now is to study hard, to do your duty and to stay out of trouble so your father, and your aunt and I don't have to worry. That is the least you can do to help your father." Nana stared at her Uncle Frank, then sank back into her chair feeling guilty, miserably alone, and misunderstood.

Two weeks later, Nana and Mamie Burrill walked home from school together. They held hands and swung them happily as they walked along. Aunt Lottie stopped by an upstairs window and glanced out just in time to see the two girls stop halfway down the block. Mamie leaned over and gave Nana a lingering kiss on the cheek as they parted. She turned down another street and Nana continued toward the Grimké home, smiling to herself as Lottie watched.

Aunt Lottie came down the stairs and took a seat in the front parlor as Nana, looking happily distracted, entered. She dropped her schoolbooks carelessly on a table. Lottie looked uncomfortable as she said "Nana, come and sit down, my dear. I want to talk to you."

"Oh, Aunt Lottie, must it be now? I have a great deal of schoolwork to do, and I'm invited out to the Brown's this evening," she said airily.

"Yes, I'm afraid it must be now, Nana. Besides, you've been out far too many evenings recently. I believe you should stay in tonight."

Nana looked annoyed and screwed up her face in a rebellious pout. "But, Auntie, it's just the Browns, and Uncle Frank said . . . "

"I know what your uncle said, but he's not here at the moment. Sit down, Nana."

"Oh, what have I done now?" Nana looked at her aunt crossly. Then she noticed a notebook of her poems on Lottie's lap. She reacted swiftly. "Why? What have you got there? I believe it is my poetry notebook—how dare you? How could you? It is private!" Nana spoke with both alarm and indignation. She started to reach for the notebook, but Lottie held it away from her.

"Please sit down, Nana—and do not speak to me in that tone!" Lottie did not like confrontation, and she found herself angry that Nana was making this even more difficult than she had anticipated. But she plunged ahead. "I am concerned, Nana," she said in a low voice. "It is one thing that you are self-willed, headstrong and often unhelpful around the house, but now, this!" Lottie waved the poetry notebook in front of Nana. "I don't know what to think, Nana! Your poems, your friendships, your—well, your fantasies. There is something quite unhealthy." Aunt Lottie looked away. She was embarrassed but felt it was her duty to speak. She could not leave this to Frank. He wouldn't understand. "It is difficult for me to speak of such things, Nana, but the evidence is mounting up, my dear."

"What evidence? Are you going to tell me who. . .who I must choose for my friends, or—or what I must feel about them?" she sputtered.

Lottie opened the notebook and began to read from one of the poems:

> I clasp thee close within my yearning arms
> I kiss thine eyes, thy lips, thy silky hair,
> I felt thy soft arms twining round my neck
> Thy bashful, maiden kisses on my cheek,
> My whole heart leaping
> 'neath such wondrous joy.

Nana rose and walked angrily around the room. "What? You use my own poetry to judge me? You have no idea. You don't understand me at all. Nor my poetry!

Aunt Lottie continued, "Then there's this one."

Ah, come and woo me for thine own
Thou wild, weird woman, silent, lone,
And fix me with thy wide, strange eyes
Forever mystical and wise;
And kiss me with thy cold, white lips,
Till all my swooning being sips
Of ecstasy undreamed, unknown.

"What am I to think, Nana?" Lottie shrugged her shoulders in genuine uncertainty, but quickly added, "And then I see you out there with your friend—that Miss Burrill—and your behavior seems—well, extraordinarily intimate." Lottie forced herself to say more. "It borders on an unnatural affection, I believe."

Nana stopped in front of her aunt and stared at her boldly. She was stony-faced. "You don't even understand poetry, Auntie. That last poem is about death! Don't you see! You took it out of context." She folded her arms across her chest angrily. "I cannot sit here and listen to this. You are spying on me. It is reprehensible."

Nana leaned over and snatched the notebook from her aunt's hands. She turned away, intending to leave the room. Lottie let her take the notebook but put her hand on Nana's arm to restrain her from leaving. Her voice was gentler, almost pleading. "Nana, dear, please. Stay a moment." Nana stood still, listening sullenly with her back to her aunt.

"Nana, I don't mean to judge. But your father has left you in our care, and I cannot ignore what I see. I don't—I don't believe you have done anything wrong or sinful, Nana, but I feel the need to warn you. You are still very young and impressionable. You do not have a mother to guide you, poor lamb!" Lottie paused, uncertain how to finish without further damaging their increasingly tenuous relationship. "I only wish to alert you and warn you against tendencies which you may not yourself understand. You must temper these romantic passions lest they lead you astray, Nana."

Nana's chest was tight with anger and hurt. Lottie's reference to her absent mother was like salt in an already gaping wound. But her words expressed her indignation rather than the hurt she felt deep down. "Aunt Lottie, I'll thank you not to invade my privacy again. I do not believe either Uncle Frank or Papa would approve," she said archly. "I find your attitude insufferable—and I do not wish to discuss it further. I do not need you to be my mother!"

Nana gathered up her schoolbooks, placing her poetry notebook carefully on top. "I shall be out at Brown's tonight. Do not expect me for supper." Nana left for her room hastily. Lottie shook her head slowly in frustration, wondering if she could have done her duty more diplomatically. She went to the writing table and took out a piece of paper to start a letter. "Dear Archie," she began.

Once the door was closed to her bedroom, Nana threw herself onto her bed, pounding it in anger, and sobbing uncontrollably. The anger she felt was fierce, but beyond it was a dark cave of loneliness and pain that she dared not enter.

36

Consul General

Santo Domingo, Dominican Republic June 1895

ARCHIE CLIMBED OUT OF the open carriage that had brought him to his small house in Santo Domingo. He turned around to reach up and shake hands with the Spanish Consul who had offered him the ride home. Señor Marquez shook Archie's hand heartily, saying "Your Excellency, I am so glad we have been able to pass a pleasant afternoon together. Congratulations on your success in settling the Republic's trouble with France. A job well done, Mr. Grimké," he smiled at his peer effusively.

"The honor was mine, your Excellency. I have been excessively reserved since I arrived here, but I am grateful for the respect of my colleagues. I look forward to another time together." Archie bowed and smiled, "Good day, Señor Marquez!"[124]

Archie entered his modest, consular residence, walking through the outer office directly to his private quarters. It was hotter and even more humid than Washington at its worst, he thought. He took off his suit jacket and top hat and loosened his collar with great relief. He went back to the office, picked up several letters that had been delivered, and began to read them eagerly.

There was a letter from Lottie with a note from Frank, and a separate one from Nana. He frowned as he read them, putting the letters down on his lap so he could think. After a long meditation he walked to his desk to pen a reply.

> My dear child, I was very glad to get your little letter, but I am
> sorry enough to learn through Aunt Lottie that she does not

feel able to assume the responsibility of caring for you for another year. For although she speaks in the kindest way about the
matter, she has at the same time written me very frankly about
yourself and the evil influence which Washington is exerting
upon you. This news, coming so soon after the death of my dear
mother and your grandmamma, saddened me greatly.

When Nana received her father's reply in late June, she read it with
more sadness and shame than rebellion. She fell into an armchair in
her bedroom and looked out the window with her lips trembling as she
read on.

All that she has written I know is quite true, for I have feared
as much all along. You'll remember my conversation with you
before we parted in October. I had hoped against hope that you
would disappoint this dread of mine and that you would try to
be a comfort and a joy in the home of your uncle and aunt.[125]

Nana threw the letter down in distress and got up to walk restlessly
around the room. She picked up a stuffed rabbit from her bed and threw
it into a corner. She stared out the window for several minutes, then sat
down again and read on.

I know now that you have been neither, my dear child, and that,
on the contrary, you have been the source of unhappiness and
anxiety.
    Mrs. Day, whom you will remember as our dear friend in
Boston and your "fairy godmother," has suggested that you
continue your studies at Northfield Academy in Minnesota
under the guidance of the highly regarded headmistress, Miss
Richardson.

Letting the letter drop into her lap Nana hid her face in her hands
and let out a groan of resentment and shame. "Papa, how could you!" she
cried out loud. "Minnesota! What are you thinking?" She sat still for several moments, letting this news sink in, then shook her head in disbelief.
She had only begun to make friends in Washington, and now she was
expected to move to a new school again. She read the rest of the letter,
hoping for some better news.

You must be brave, and true, and good and do what you must do
henceforth like a little woman. Above all things, do not blame
anyone because of this determination of your dear papa. Blame
only yourself for it, my child, for you are alone responsible for it.

Nana stopped reading to wipe away the bitter tears splotching her face, then pushed on.

> All I want you to do is to turn over a new leaf in your dear young life and begin a noble chapter of achievement in every good thing and work, and a conquest of self. My choicest blessings and love go with you. You are the very apple of my eye. Please try to do your best, not for a little while but all the time. Your loving Papa
>
> P.S. Mrs. Day will be in Washington soon and has offered to help you select new, suitable clothes for your time at Northfield. She believes you will do well to be dressed stylishly and well, as befits our position in life. And showing yourself to be a girl of refined manners, will help to earn you the respect of fellow students.

Nana read this last part with bitter amusement, and her dark mood lifted slightly. She frowned at the obvious bribery, but then a slight smile appeared as she contemplated getting a new, stylish wardrobe for her "exile" to Minnesota. The tension with Lottie was at a level that made her glad for an escape. She contemplated a year at a young women's boarding school in Minnesota and realized reluctantly that worst things could happen.

The next five years were a time of small steps forward for Nana. She survived her year at Northfield, though it was not a time she remembered fondly. Mrs. Richardson looked after her, and thanks to Mrs. Day's advice and her father's position, Nana was accepted by her classmates as their social peer. She made a few friends but missed her father and her old life in Boston sorely.

She returned to the Boston area the next year and finished high school at Cushing Academy. When not at school she lived with the Lees, who were old family friends. For graduation, her father bought her a bicycle and she rode it around their Boston neighborhood and up the Fenway in the summer and fall.[126] She continued her education at the Boston Normal College of Gymnastics, which would soon be incorporated into the Department of Hygiene at Wellesley College. She persevered in writing poetry, and in due time received her teaching certification.

By 1898 her father had finished his time as Consul, and returned to the U.S. He spent some periods with Nana in Boston, but he also spent an increasing amount of time in Washington, D.C. where he and

Frank anguished over the alarming stories of the suppression of rights and terrorism against negroes in the South. The spread of Jim Crow laws institutionalized a regression for colored people throughout most of the country. Under these dark skies, Archie became active with the American Negro Academy which promoted higher education for the colored community as well as carrying on the struggle for basic rights.

His independence of thought often put him at odds with the more conciliatory leadership of Booker T. Washington, and his writings reflected the growing controversy about Washington's emphasis on manual training for negroes. He allied himself briefly with W.E.B. DuBois and the Niagara Movement. His views matured and his insistence on coming to his own conclusions, meant that he continued to be a powerful intellectual voice for bold action and sensible paths forward.

37

A Summer of Unrest

Boston 1903

IN THE SUMMER OF 1903, after her first year of teaching in Washington, D.C., Nana returned to Boston, staying once again at the Lee family home. Archie came back to Boston to stay with the Lees as well, glad to be elsewhere during the oppressive Washington summer.[127] One mid-summer day, Nana sat at her writing desk, which she had situated so it had a view out the window. She wrote feverishly, pausing occasionally to daydream.

> This is my first attempt at a diary. Poor little book to bear so great a burden. But one must talk to someone or go mad—
>
> Dear heart, this is the first time I have written it so and though you are not for me, still, yet still you are dear to me, God knows how dear. Why is it that you must be so much to me? I have tried to crush out all the love but can't.
>
> Dear, I shall never forget our last evening together. We were at Arlington . . .[128]

Nana leaned back and stared out the window as she recalled the evening soiree in Arlington in mid-June. She had been sitting by herself, gazing at a handsome young man of mixed race. She had known him for several weeks and he had spent time at the Lee's home along with their circle of mutual friends. He was playing whist with three other guests. His light blue eyes roamed the room and settled on her. His smile seemed to suggest some secret intimacy between them, and it charmed her.

After a fleeting moment, Nana turned her eyes away with a blush. The young man rose from the table when the game was finished and came over to sit next to her, asking her about her life in Washington, DC, and conversing in a quiet but attentive way. Nana remembered that he made her feel gay and saucy.

As she was about to leave, the young man helped her put on her coat, letting his hands rest on her shoulders a bit longer than necessary. Nana turned to give him an adoring look, but his glance had already been diverted to another young woman in whom he seemed to show equal interest. As she thought about it, Nana still felt the sting of his roaming eye. She had turned and left haughtily with a woman friend, barely looking back to give the young man a withering look. But she had not given up hope. She frowned as she wrote,

> . . . And now you have gone away, and I have had no letter. Nothing! I shall not wait and watch for a letter anymore. I am through. Dear, I wonder if you know how it makes me suffer. Dear, can I give you any more than this, a woman's first ever love? Whether I see you again or not you have made a woman of me.[129]
>
> I have no presents, nothing to remember you by, not even a kiss, and dear if only you had taken me in your arms and kissed me (how my heart leaps at the thought), I should have been happy forever.

A week later Tessa Lee, the daughter of Nana's hosts and Nana's long-time friend, brought the mail into the foyer of their home. Her brother, Howard, rushed past her and bounded up the stairs. Hearing Howard's boisterous entry, Nana and her father looked up from their seats in the nearby drawing room. When Nana saw Tessa with the mail she jumped up and hurried to the foyer expectantly. Tessa handed her a letter, but looked at Nana with pity knowing she would be disappointed. She brought another letter to Archie.

Nana looked at the return address on the letter and tossed it on a table in disgust. She walked to a window at the far side of the room trying to hide her discontent. Archie noticed it and thought perhaps a distraction would help. "Nana, dear, Mrs. Day has four tickets to the theatre for tonight. Wouldn't you and Tessa like to join us? It's a musicale."

"Papa, please. I'm not interested. In any case, it is raining. Tessa, you go if you like," she said off-handedly.

Archie regarded his daughter gravely. He was concerned, but he also felt irritated at her moodiness. He spoke sharply to her. "Nana, I do hope you will shake off this torpor you seem to be in. This young man you are so enamored with—is he worth these black moods? From what I saw of him he seemed a consummate ass, self-absorbed and disingenuous."

Nana turned and looked at her father with furious disbelief. "Why, Papa—how can you say that? You know nothing about him! The first man I could really love, and you hate him!" she said in a tragic voice that only a young person could make convincing. "But you know nothing about me either. You are so—so old-fashioned! You disapprove of all my friends, unless they are your friends, too." She sat down at the far end of the room, her face sullen. Tessa watched them both. She was used to their disagreements, but she was disturbed by the highly charged emotion of this argument between them.

"Nana, you know that isn't true," Archie said, with an effort to be calm. "But I do worry about your—your unusual tastes, and your dark moods." He shifted uncomfortably in his chair. Archie got up, wanting to say more, but he recalled that Tessa was present. Instead, he let out an anxious sigh, and with a shrug at Tessa, he left the room.

After a few moments, Tessa spoke, "Nana, do come here. You look so forlorn. You never fight with your papa like that. What is wrong with you?"

"I know he's not going to write, Tessa," Nana said, her mind still on the object of her infatuation rather than on her father. "Why do I keep looking? I'm sure he received my letter because his landlady told me he had written and thanked her for forwarding his mail."

"Don't give up, Nana. Perhaps it will come soon," she said faintly. "You know, he may just be busy."

"Yes, so busy that he has had time to write to Anita and Maraval. But not to me!"

Tessa stood up and walked over to Nana. She leaned over and took her hand as she spoke. "Come on, Nana, let's go see Hattie. I know you planned to do so today in any case. She's expecting her baby in just about a week now."

Nana hesitated, then nodded reluctantly and followed Tessa to the foyer. Tessa put on a narrow-brimmed straw boating hat that fit neatly above her bun. Nana grabbed her wide-brimmed sunhat with a yellow ribbon that tied under her chin. The two friends walked out onto Columbus Avenue.

"Hmmm," Tessa ventured with a frown. "Did you offend him somehow?"

"I suppose I did—that last night in Arlington. He was being his charming self with the other girls, and I became haughty, and I didn't even say good-by to him." She turned a sad face toward her friend, saying "But, Tessa, I fear friendship is all he ever felt for me. I don't blame him for not loving me. I'm not beautiful or fetching like the other girls. He just found me unusual, and our house here was a pleasant place to kill time."

"Well, that's just not true, Nana," Tessa protested. "You *are* unusual—but you are very attractive as well—don't you see that?" Tessa frowned and added, "And he did seem very friendly."

Nana shrugged and gave her a skeptical look. "Tess, I know that one cannot love someone just because they want to be loved. But he did pretend to be friendly, didn't he? In any case, I see very clearly that if I keep on in this strain, I shall hate him in time. Perhaps that is a good thing." With those words Nana gave Tessa a melancholy smile.

"Well, here we are," she said. The two women climbed up the stoop of a modest row house. The door opened before they knocked and a pregnant young woman, about the same age as Nana and Tess, appeared and greeted them happily.

Tessa and Nana emerged from the house an hour later in the heat of the late afternoon. Tessa arranged her hat carefully as they came out into the sunny summer day. Nana gratefully let her hat, held on by the ribbon at her neck, fall behind her head. She shook her hair free, hoping for a breeze.

"Well, I'm glad we came," Tessa said with satisfaction. "Hattie looks so tired—and almost ready to burst! But she was so happy to see us."

Nana remained solemn and spoke bluntly. "Why she looked terrible, Tessa! She is not at all well."

Tessa nodded reluctantly, "Yes, I noticed that, too. Women certainly pay up in suffering and sickness for all the wickedness they do. Nowadays women are so delicate that motherhood often means death."

"Yes," Nana added sardonically, "perhaps that is a good way to commit suicide—by marrying."

"Nana! You can't mean that! Why motherhood—"

Nana interrupted her in a bitter tone, "Is a curse! Especially for us colored women. Even if we survive it, who knows what will happen to our sons? What a tremendous price we women pay, simply for being female in this world."

Tessa was shocked and she looked away from Nana in dismay. Nana continued with her rant. "Yes, you see I am getting bitter and hard, but there was always more of the devil than the angel in me. No one knows better than I do how devilish I am," Nana declared darkly. "And now I've argued with Papa as well. You see how bad I am, Tessa?" Before Tessa could respond, Nana continued her speech, "I am certain about one thing now. I shall never be a mother, for I shall never marry. I am through with love and the like forever," she said adamantly.

Tessa looked at Nana with even more alarm, but she only said very softly, "You must miss having a mother very much, Nana. And it is so sad the way she died." Tessa knew this was painful territory and she immediately regretted the reference to Sarah Stanley's death several years earlier.[130]

Nana gave Tessa a dismissive shrug as she answered, "I don't understand that word in connection with me. I suppose I am used to not having one. Anyway, I still have Papa, if he hasn't given up on me." She puckered her lips and tilted her head as she reflected, "And I have my writing."

Tessa looked sidewise at her. "Yes, you do have that." Then she looked at the ground sadly. They continued in silence, reaching the Lee home just before dusk.

A few weeks later, after Nana's disappointment in romance had dissipated, and Archie's worries had subsided, they were able to put aside their differences. Their relationship was far too important to jeopardize for long. But a fundamental dissatisfaction lurked in Nana's heart.

It was a warm evening at the end of July, and they were enjoying a welcome evening breeze as they walked along Columbus Ave toward the Zion AME church with their companions, Tessa and Howard Lee. Nana's hand was tucked comfortably into her father's arm, as she chatted about friends and upcoming social gatherings with Tessa. Soon they approached the large church hall where Booker T. Washington was scheduled to speak.[131] They were among dozens of small groups walking toward the hall from various directions. There was a large banner stretched above the entrance to the church hall that announced:

Dr. Booker T. Washington
Thursday Night at 8 pm

Howard Lee surveyed the large crowd anxiously. "My, there's a lot of people! What do you think, Mr. Grimké? I hear that Monroe Trotter[132] and his friend, Granville Martin, have prepared a series of questions for Dr. Washington and Mr. Fortune. I wonder if there will be trouble."

"Hmmm. I don't think so, although young Monroe can be quite hot-headed at times. Much like his father!" Archie smiled and shook his head ruefully.

"I'm eager to hear Washington, and I agree with him on many issues. But I am skeptical about his insistence on primarily manual training for negroes," Archie said with a troubled expression. "He seems downright opposed to preparing qualified students for access to higher academics. That is very short-sighted. We need to expand, not contract, our professional class." He frowned as he thought about Washington's apparent assumptions about the "proper" work for negroes.

"Yes, he is so eager to please and placate white southerners. It seems that he wishes to reassure them that we know 'our place' and will keep to it." Howard said darkly, echoing Archie's thoughts exactly. Archie nodded. Washington's attitude disturbed him but he had not yet worked out how best to counter it.

Frank and Lottie had come up to Boston recently—partly to cool off, but also to engage in the active discussions taking place there.[133] At this point they appeared across the street, having arrived from another direction. Lottie saw Archie's group first and waved at them. Nana waved back. "Oh, there's Uncle Frank and Aunt Lottie. It looks like they are going in the side door. I supposed we will see them afterwards. How long are they here for, Papa?"

"Several more weeks, I believe." He smiled at Nana, in a conspiratorial way, "Lottie and I share a birthday on the 17th, you know!"

"Oh, my! I'd almost forgotten," Nana looked abashed. "Already the end of summer! And then it will nearly be time for us to join them in Washington for the school year again." Nana puffed out her cheeks and let out a long breath loaded with ambivalence at the thought. Frank and Lottie had disappeared into the hall.

They entered the church hall with some difficulty amidst the growing crowd. It was stuffy, and Nana fanned herself as they came in. Archie found them two seats near the back door, close to a window. Howard and Tessa found seats nearby.

"Blazes, it is hot in here! The window gives a bit of a breeze, but heavens! The air is so sultry," Nana grimaced.

At the front of the hall, the presider, Thomas Fortune, was urging the crowd to settle into their seats. "Gentlemen, ladies, here, there are some seats up here," he pointed out. Dr. Washington sat quietly near the podium, looking studiously at some notes on his lap. Most of the crowd settled down, although many were still left standing in the aisles. Nana noted that there were some young men seated near the front. She recognized them as a rather rowdy crowd, and they included a young man she barely knew, named Bernard Charles. To complicate matters an attorney, Mr. W.H. Louis, a man for whom Archie had little respect, stood up front near Fortune and Washington, visibly inebriated.

"Please, ladies and gentlemen, take your seats," Fortune reiterated. "We wish to begin by introducing—"

Before he could get any further, Granville Martin rose to ask a question. Young William Monroe Trotter was seated next to him. Martin said loudly, "Mr. Fortune, before we get started, I'd like to ask the speaker a question which he should address immediately." There was a combination of hisses, and cheers. Some in the crowd yelled out "Sit down!" "Let him speak!" while others seemed to cheer for Martin.

Mr. Louis yelled out in a drunken voice, "Shut up, Martin!"

Martin ignored the interruption and spoke over the objections of the crowd. "Mr. Washington, in view of the fact that you are unwilling to insist upon the negro having his every right, both civil and political, would it not be a calamity at this juncture to make *you* our leader?" Martin asked.

The mixture of hisses, boos, applause and cheers continued, and they alarmed Archie deeply. He looked around with consternation. Martin continued as Louis started to come toward him threateningly. But Louis stopped short, and Martin uttered a stark challenge to Washington. "Is the rope and the torch all our race is to get under your leadership?"[134]

Pandemonium ensued, with many in the church yelling out their approval or disapproval. "Yeah, answer that, Mr. Washington!" one man called out.

"Sit down, Granville!" pleaded a woman's voice.

"Get 'em outta here," several called out.

"Let Mr. Washington speak!"; this sentiment came from a chorus of voices.

Archie noticed that despite the vocal minority, most of the audience were frowning and obviously upset that Washington was not being allowed to present his case, whether they agreed or not. Monroe Trotter stood up next to Martin, attempting to speak but unable to make himself heard. Before calmer voices could prevail, Bernard Charles and several of the Trotter and Martin partisans sprinkled red pepper around and set off stink bombs near the front of the room, escalating the unrest in the hot, stuffy hall.

Thomas Fortune pleaded, "Gentlemen, please desist from insulting our speaker tonight! Have the courtesy—." Granville Martin started to take his seat, but Trotter and many of the other young people were on their feet and he joined them.

Trotter yelled over the noise of the crowd, more loudly as the chaos increased. "Mr. Washington may speak when he answers our questions!" He turned around and faced the audience behind him, asking "Are we to return to a caste system in this country? Are we to be cowed by the racist political power of the South? Is our hard-won right to vote and to participate in the political system to be denied?" Trotter turned back toward the speaker and asked, "Mr. Washington, you said whites and negroes 'can be as separate as the fingers on a hand Do you sanction segregation, then, sir?"

Fortune signaled to several policemen, who had appeared from outside the building, to escort Martin and Trotter out of the hall. "Mr. Trotter, do you take responsibility for this disgraceful behavior? Shame on you. You hurt our cause, sir!" Fortune reprimanded the young man. Four policemen walked over and quickly grasped Martin and Trotter under the arms. They resisted mildly, but the police succeeded in roughly escorting them out.

Nana was watching this scene unfold first with amusement, then with growing anxiety. She put her hand on her father's arm for reassurance. She saw Maude Trotter, Monroe's sister and her friend, leave her seat and follow her brother out of the hall in great distress. As she neared the exit of the hall, Maude's hat was knocked askew and she took it off, holding the hat pin in her hand.

Archie continued to view the disturbance warily. Close to them several men began tussling with each other, pushing and shoving, and several older women appeared to be fainting. Archie stood up, eager to get Nana out of the danger, but Nana had leaned over to attend to an elderly woman next to her who had bent over and covered her ears in distress. A young man on the other side of the woman helped her to walk outside. A few rows away Howard and Tessa were taking care of another anxious and overheated gray-haired woman and helping her to get outside. Out of the corner of his eye, Archie saw Frank ushering Lottie out a side door.

Nana turned back to her father, who grabbed her by the arm and guided her through the crowded aisle out the main door of the church. They crossed the street hurriedly, then looked back to see that the noise and disorder had spilled out of the church onto the street.

Nana turned to her father and pointed at Maude Trotter who was about twenty yards from the church door. Maude seemed to be trying to reach her brother who was still held tightly by a policeman. They saw her holding out her large hatpin as she struggled to get through the crowd. Nana looked away, distracted by the crowd pouring out onto the street. She scanned it to see if she could locate Tessa and Howard.

Meanwhile as Maude got close to her brother, someone knocked her from behind and she inadvertently plunged the pin into the arm of one of the policemen. The policeman yelled out in pain, turned and grabbed Maude roughly, and placed her under arrest as well.

Archie's main worry was still his daughter, and once he had surveyed the scene, he turned back to her and asked quickly, "Nana, dear, are you all right? You aren't hurt, are you?"

Nana turned her gaze back toward her father and said, "No, no, I'm fine—but you, papa! Are you —?" She stopped and looked up when she heard the policeman's yelp. Nana and Archie's attention was drawn back to the commotion across the street. They saw that both Monroe and Maude Trotter were being restrained by the police, along with Granville Martin. Then she noticed that Bernard Charles was under arrest as well.

"Papa, look! They've got Maude, too. Heavens! Why have they arrested her? And Bernard Charles!"

Archie scowled at the whole scene. He was angered at the disruption of Washington's lecture and equally disturbed by the embarrassingly chaotic situation that had been created by the protesters and the unfortunate involvement of the police. He could foresee the next day's news headlines in Boston, and he shuddered at the thought of it. But first, he had the responsibilities of a father.

"I see, Nana—but my concern is to get you home safely. Who knows what will happen with this crowd? I'll go down to the court tomorrow and see what I can do for them," he promised. "Ah, here come Tessa and Howard now," he added. Nana reluctantly followed her father's lead. They joined the Lee siblings for an anxious walk home.

Around noon the next day, Archie came through the front entry and looked in the door of the parlor where Nana and Tessa were sitting. He had left early in the morning and had picked up several newspapers on his way to the courthouse. Nana jumped up to confront him. "Papa, why did you sneak out without me this morning? I told you I wanted to go to the courthouse with you." Nana's voice was steaming with indignation.

"It's no place for a young woman, Nana."

"Papa, how can you say that! I abominate these stupid conventions that won't let women do what men do. You know that!" She turned away from him with an impatient shrug. Then she added, "Well, it's certainly no place for Maude, either." After a moment she muttered, "But tell us what happened, anyway."

"Yes, what about Maude?" Tessa wanted to know.

"Well, fortunately, she was released last night. It was all because of her hatpin sticking into a policeman." Archie chuckled quietly at the absurdity of it. "Here, you can read all about it. Whether it was intentional or not, we'll never know! But in any case, I don't believe she will be tried."

"She was trying to help her brother," Nana protested, "trying to rescue him from that horrible policeman. If I'd been Maude, I would have used more than a hatpin on him. And if anyone had touched you, Father," she said in a fiery tone, "I would have torn him to pieces!"

Archie was amused at her protective vehemence, and murmured, "And, my dear, that is precisely why I got you away from there as fast as possible!"

Tessa took the newspapers that Archie handed to her and began to read the headlines. "Hmmm. Listen to what these say, Nana!" She started to read off several headlines.

Tuskegee Reformer, Booker T. Washington and T. Thomas Fortune Interrupted by Previous Arrangement Chaos Results

Tessa paused, looking confused. "Was it truly all previously arranged?" she asked rhetorically. She frowned as she continued to read.

Three Negro Arrests Police Finally Quell Disturbance

"It makes it sound so awful. And look at this one, Mr. Grimké,"

Two Disturbers Arrested A Woman Digs a Hat Pin into the Back of a Policeman

Tessa burst out laughing as she showed the headline to Archie and Nana. "Oh, my, it just sounds so silly, doesn't it? Who knew that a hatpin was such a dangerous weapon?" Nana's expression softened into amusement as well. She took the newspaper to look at the story.

Archie spoke to the young women sternly, "Well, it is lucky there were no serious injuries. A crowd like that . . . " He shook his head in disapproval. "It's really a disgraceful affair all around. I am sympathetic to Monroe's issues, but it just makes all of us look foolish and uncivil."

"But Papa, think of Garrison, Will's father, and your Aunt Angelina and Aunt Sarah, and even of your old friend, Wendell Phillips. They were hotheads and fanatics, too—at least when they were young. We need men like Monroe. If he is a fanatic, he would be honored to be put in the same class as they."

Archie felt the sting of being considered too moderate and not sufficiently passionate, particularly by his daughter. He was troubled, but said only, "Hmmm. Well, I believe I am temperamentally more aligned with our Uncle Theodore. The power of the word and of reasonable discourse is what distinguishes us as humans. And your great aunts were never violent—they spoke disturbing truths, powerfully, but they were always courteous ladies."

He frowned at his daughter, asking, "Don't you believe that, Nana?" Nana rolled her eyes, but looked tolerantly at her father, "From what I have heard I believe I am more like my namesake, Aunt Angelina. Passionate—and willing to make trouble when it is called for!"

Archie walked over to Nana and gave her a kiss on the top of her head, then stepped back, and smiled at her fondly. She looked up at him with a challenging half-smile. "Oh, my darling girl. I do worry about you," Archie declared. Tessa stood apart from them, absorbed by the news stories. She was less worried now about their frequent arguments and equally frequent rapprochement.

38

"Meek or Strong": Divided Voices

Boston August 1903

ON AUGUST 17TH ARCHIE and Nana joined a gathering of friends and colleagues in the gracious Charles Street home of Dr. George Grant and his wife, Fanny.[135] Dr. and Mrs. W.E.B. Dubois were guests of honor, along with their three-year-old daughter, Yolande. Frank and Lottie were there, and so were Virginia Trotter and her daughter, Maude.[136] Mrs. Anna Julia Cooper, the principal of the M Street School in Washington, and a close friend of the Grimkés, was invited. Archie's friend, Mrs. Day,[137] and several other family friends including Mr. and Mrs. Forbes, Fanny's mother, Mrs. Bailey, and two of Nana's friends, Dirier and Mon, were all present.[138]

Archie and Frank sat down with a group speaking with Dr. Dubois and Dr. Grant. Nana found a place next to Maude Trotter and her mother, and they were joined by Lottie and Mrs. Day. Mrs. Cooper sat on the edge of the two groups managing to listen in to both conversations. Mon did the same. After introducing unacquainted guests to each other, Mrs. Grant busied herself directing her housekeeper and another helper who were passing refreshments.

"Maude, I'm so glad to see you safe and sound," Nana said as she joined the group. "Mrs. Trotter, how is Monroe doing?"

"As well as can be expected, I suppose." She shook her head and gave Nana a melancholy smile. "He wanted to serve his time as quickly as possible. I saw him at the House of Correction last Sunday. He seemed in good spirits, but I think it was a show for me. I wish . . . "

Maude interrupted her mother to say, "He'll be all right, Ma," as she patted her hand reassuringly. She turned to Nana and added, "He's sentenced to six months, but your father says he will be out in three. It has made it difficult to meet deadlines for *The Guardian*, but I'm helping. I think we will manage to keep publishing the paper on time."

"Well, I think he's splendid! And you, too, Maude," she said emphatically.

Virginia Trotter reached over and squeezed Nana's hand, "That's kind of you to say, Nana, dear. But if you were a mother, you would not think it so splendid. His headstrong nature worries me. Of course, we believe in what he is doing, standing up to the Bookerites, but I try to tell him—"

Maude jumped in again, "Mama, Mama, he's grown up now. You can't tell him anything." She laughed ruefully. "Not that we ever could."

The men exchanged small talk for several minutes, but shortly after taking his seat, Archie asked, "Dr. Dubois, what do you make of this fracas we had here to welcome Dr. Washington?" DuBois looked halfway across the room toward Mrs. Trotter, with whom he was staying. Knowing her son was serving jail time for the disturbance he spoke softly, afraid to offend her. Archie thought his tone was rather pompous.

"Well, I admit I find it troubling. I agree with Dr. Washington on many points. I believe, like him, that the negro community must lift itself up must take responsibility for its own betterment."

"Yes, I agree," Frank said. He stroked his graying moustache with his hand as he thought about this. "White men cannot help us except in an indirect way. We have got to work out our own salvation."

"Hmmm." Archie frowned. "I have come, somewhat reluctantly, to believe that on the race question, a white man is a white man. Scratch the skin of one of them, whether a Republican or a Democrat, and you will find race prejudice close to the surface. I don't excuse them, but I don't blame them entirely," he continued judiciously. "They have not shared our experience as slaves and children of slaves, and they cannot truly feel the oppression that our color has earned for us. It takes an effort of imagination—and empathy . . . " He paused and started to say, "And as for Dr. Washington's views on education and segregation—I must express—"

Dubois interrupted him with a wave of his hand, "Mr. Grimké, I anticipate your objections and I heartily agree. This notion that we must confine ourselves to industrial education, that we must kowtow to the white sensitivities in the south, and tiptoe around, being careful not to offend them. Why, this is wrong-headed in the worst way! It is for that reason that I admire the voice of young men like Monroe, although . . . " He lowered his voice again, not wanting to offend the Trotters, "I fear these disruptive tactics only divide us and make us look weak."

Although he was considerably younger than the others, DuBois' tone was didactic. "I do believe that we must educate a colored professional class; men such as yourselves—the 'talented ten percent'—because they will show the way to full equality with the white community. They will be the leading edge that leads our whole race upward. That is how the progress of a society occurs."

Frank looked skeptical. "But don't you fear a kind of "elitism" in this approach? That the so-called "talented ten percent" will run ahead, leaving our more struggling brothers and sisters behind? Personally," Frank said with a modest shake of his head, "I fear that luck played as much a part as talent in bringing Archie and me to our current situations. And we do owe something to our white benefactors—people like the Pillsburys and the Welds."

Archie rejoined, "And let us not forget to give full credit to our women." He turned to his brother, "Frank, where would you and I be without that strength and fierce love of our mother, and without the help of women like Lottie here, or Virginia or Mrs. Bailey, for that matter." Archie and Frank both looked over at Lottie admiringly. She was still engaged in conversation with the Trotters.

Anna Cooper was following the men's conversation from her strategic position between the two groups. She watched the men intently and looked quizzical at several points. She smiled provocatively at this last comment.

"Well, then, don't you think you must give us the vote?" she asked.

Nana, Maude, and Dirier heard this and clapped their hands in approval. "Yes! Hurrah! Suffrage for women!" they called out with lighthearted laughs.

Lottie looked up with a serious countenance and agreed, "Absolutely, we must have the vote! May it come in my lifetime!" Frank and Archie both nodded their support, but Dr. Grant and Mr. Forbes looked more amused than enthusiastic.

"Before I forget to ask, Dr. Dubois, I hope that you will consider an invitation to come and speak to the students and faculty at M Street High School," Mrs. Cooper said. "We have so many talented, and I dare say, hard-working students there, and I think your words would fall on fertile ground."

Dubois gave his assent graciously but formally, "Why yes, of course, I'd be delighted. We will have to check our schedule," he said, turning to his wife.

Nana's attention was captured, and she looked over at Mrs. Cooper. Although she had met her many times at Frank and Lottie's home, she was still in awe of this well-educated woman who had recently been named principal of the highly respected M Street High School. She began shyly. "Mrs. Cooper, you know that I am teaching physical education and hygiene at the Armstrong School, but I would love to come to M Street School sometime. I mean, just to visit perhaps," her voice trailed off doubtfully.

Mrs. Cooper smiled at Nana kindly. "Of course, Nana! I didn't know you were interested. But don't just come to visit, come to teach with us!" Nana was delighted and flattered at this undreamed-of invitation. But she wondered if this was just momentary kindness, or if Mrs. Cooper was sincere.

"Oh, Mrs. Cooper, do you mean it?" Nana almost gushed. "Do you think I could? I mean—I know I *could*, but do you *need* someone like me?"

"We always need well-prepared teachers, Nana. Your father has given me a few of your poems to read. They are quite amazing. You seem to have a gift."

"Why, thank you, ma'am. I don't know quite what to say." Nana took a deep breath and regained some measure of poise. "I would prefer to be teaching English. I think I could do well at that. I've taught some English at Armstrong. And frankly," she sighed deeply, "I'm rather worn out with teaching physical arts to awkward fourteen-year-old girls." She screwed up her face in mild distaste.

Nana's friend, Dirier, let out a low giggle, and Mrs. Cooper chuckled appreciatively. "Well, it is too late to promise you anything for this year, but we should speak of it again next spring. In the meantime, you can come and meet some of our young teachers." She tilted her head quizzically. "Have you met John Love and his sister, Percy Love? They have been boarding at my house, along with a few other teachers. We are a jolly crew. You would like them a great deal, I think." Nana beamed. Her father, who had overheard some of this conversation, looked at Mrs. Cooper gratefully. He and Mrs. Day exchanged swift, approving glances.

It was still summer twilight when Fanny Grant entered the parlor along with her housekeeper and cook, each carrying one of three small birthday cakes with candles lit. She whispered something to Dirier who went to the nearby piano.

"Attention, everyone! In addition to hosting our illustrious visitor, Dr. Dubois, we are celebrating three birthdays on this happy day! Mr. Archibald Grimké, Mrs. Day, and Mrs. Lottie Grimké," Mrs. Grant announced.

"Does everyone know the new happy birthday song?"[139] A few of the young people nodded. Dirier played an introduction as the cakes were placed on tables in front of each of the birthday guests. Mrs. Grant began the singing and was quickly joined by Mon who had a strong baritone voice. Nana, Maude and the other younger guests joined in enthusiastically if not always on key. The guests applauded as the three individuals with birthdays, one by one, blew out the candles on their cakes. The young women rose to help cut and pass the cake around, and the groups rearranged themselves. Dirier began to play a ragtime tune on the piano.

After the cake was consumed, the young people got up and rolled up part of the carpet as Dirier continued to play. They began to dance to the ragtime tunes with great gaiety, and a certain amount of silliness as well.

The following evening was the night that Frank was scheduled to give a sermon at St. Mark's Church in Dorchester. Services were being held in Grove Hall, near the old church, while the congregation's new church was being completed. Archie and Nana were eager to hear Frank preach in this new setting, although Frank was more anxious than eager.

Frank, wearing the new spectacles that attested to the dignified scholar he had become, walked over early to have some time alone before his appearance. Archie, Lottie, and Nana had met up with Anna Cooper and Virginia Trotter as they approached the building. A large signboard announced the event.

Sermon Tonight Given by
The Reverend Francis Grimké
Pastor of the 15th St. Presbyterian Church Washington, D.C.
"The Way Forward:
Are We Called to Be Meek or Strong?"[140]

Nana felt an unexpected pride in her uncle when she read the sign. As the group entered the church, an usher led them to seats reserved for them near the front. The makeshift sanctuary was already nearly full, with latecomers jostling for the few remaining seats. Organ music was playing quietly.

The church's rector preceded Frank into the sanctuary and the organ music ceased. The congregation grew quiet as the rector offered a very brief introduction to their guest preacher. When he finished, Frank walked to the center of the sanctuary and bowed his head in silent prayer for several moments. He then turned to the raised podium that served as the pulpit.

He raised his hands for the congregation to stand, then in a quiet voice he led them in an introductory prayer. "Almighty Father, give us wisdom this day to speak your word of truth and to listen to your voice in our hearts. Amen."

The congregation echoed with a heartfelt "Amen!" They sat down and Frank began in a strong voice:

> Events of the past few weeks here in Boston have forced to our attention a divide in our community that must be healed if we are to move forward together. It is a divide in which well-meaning leaders of our people see our duty in very different ways. How is God calling us in this day? What should we believe and how should we act?

Archie looked straight ahead, not daring to turn his head around to monitor the reaction of the congregation. But Nana managed to look sidewise enough to see that most were listening attentively: some nodding, some frowning, and a few staring down at their hands with worried faces. Frank continued.

> Let us recall some facts.[141] Hundreds of men of our race have laid down their lives on southern soil in vindication of their rights as American citizens. In the past 16 years more than 1700 negro men and women have been lynched here in our United States, rarely for heinous crimes, but more often for insisting on their rights as human beings and as citizens. They have been hanged or shot or burned for "stepping out of line" or for objecting to a white person's abuse.

Frank's voice was quiet but powerful, more filled with grief than anger. The audience looked grim, shaking their heads angrily, or nodding in silent distress. Frank went on in his sober voice, but with growing indignation.

> Now we are being told, by black men as well as white, that the
> sacred cause for which they poured out their life's blood is to be
> relinquished, that the white ruffians who shot them down were
> justified, that it was to be expected, and therefore that we have
> no reasonable ground for complaint.

There was an ominous pause and the congregation listened expectantly. Frank's volume increased and his tone became vehement.

> Away with such treasonable utterances—treason to God, treason to man, treason to free institutions, treason to the spirit of
> an enlightened and Christian sentiment!

"Amen!" someone called out boldly, and several others joined in, "Amen to that, Brother!" Frank stretched out a hand to quiet the audience as he continued.

> I have heard black leaders glibly issue apologies for our race and
> refer to other blacks as "darkies." They seek to gain the respect of
> white America through a shuffling acquiescence to race prejudice. They are betrayers of our rights and enemies of our liberty.

Many in the congregation grew still at the boldness of Frank's words, knowing full well who those leaders were. Some individuals frowned, looking worried. A few shook their heads in grief, and others slowly nodded in certain, if reluctant, agreement. Frank left the pulpit to walk down to the front rows of the congregation to make his appeal more directly. There was a new sense of urgency, and even intimacy with the congregation as he continued.

> My brothers and sisters, we need a new response to race prejudice in this country. I am not counseling violence. I am not saying that it is a wise thing for the negro to resort to violence, but I
> am saying that sometimes violence is the means which God uses
> to arouse the sleeping conscience.[142]

Nana heard a few quiet "amens" behind her. But she sensed that many in the congregation were wide-eyed with surprise at Rev. Grimké's words. It was not what they had expected from this mild-appearing bespectacled preacher.

> My friends, are we not counseled by the gospel, by our Lord
> Jesus, to be meek and to turn the other cheek? Indeed, we are,
> but Jesus also gives us examples of righteous anger. He also

criticized the ruling authorities, both political and religious! The pernicious doctrine of self-effacement does not serve us well.

Frank paused a long time for emphasis, surveying the audience intently. There was silence in the hall.

> A race that permits itself to be trampled upon, a race that goes around with hat in hand, in a cringing attitude, is sure to be an object of contempt.

Holding out his arms, palms upward, in a gesture meant to include all the congregation, Frank concluded:

> Let us here, tonight, one and all of us, before God—in this sacred place, pledge ourselves to eternal hostility to any teaching that would put the negro in such an attitude. Be assured that nothing is to be gained by compromising with evil![143]

Francis drew his hands together and bowed his head in silent prayer, then slowly returned to the sanctuary. The congregation, still stunned by the boldness of the speech, seemed immobilized. But slowly they absorbed its power. A few people rose to their feet with amens and applause, and within seconds, the whole congregation was standing and applauding the speaker enthusiastically.

Archie had known something of what to expect from Frank, but he was moved by the power of his brother's rhetoric. He thought of his mother, who had tolerated no compromise to her dignity, and reflected on how proud she would be of her middle son. Nana looked sidewise at her father with a slight smile as they rose. He nodded his heartfelt approval of his brother's message but did so with a grave expression. Lottie, let out a deep sigh of relief, and Nana put her arm around her aunt's waist in a gentle embrace, smiling more broadly.

The organ began playing "Blessed be the Tie that Binds." Frank and the congregation sang out boldly; some singers adding a rich harmony to the melody.

> Blessed be the tie that binds, our hearts in Christian love;
> The fellowship of kindred minds, is like to that above.
> Before our Father's throne, we pour our ardent prayers;
> Our fears, our hope, our aims are one, our comforts and our cares.
> We share our mutual woes, our mutual burdens bear,
> And often for each other flows, the sympathizing tear.[144]

39

Teachers and Friends

Washington, DC, 1909

SCHOOL HAD BEEN IN session for nearly two months at the M Street High School where Nana had been teaching for five years. It was a Friday afternoon, and the all-colored student body was pouring out of the classrooms into the hallway. There were twice as many young women among them as there were young men.

Nana lingered in her classroom listening to the familiar excuses of two of her students about missing assignments. She responded airily, "Ah, how inconvenient that your essays were due after a warm and sunny evening. I suppose they floated away upon an autumn breeze? But you shall recapture them by Monday, n'est-ce pas?" As they left, she scowled and shook her head at their backs, thinking about the naive disingenuity of youth. After a few moments she followed them out into the hall.

Several of her fellow teachers were gathered down the hallway, among them her teen-age friend, Mamie Burrill, and their former principal, Anna Julia Cooper.[145] After a controversial tenure as principal, and a few years absence, Mrs. Cooper was now the Latin teacher at the school. Mamie saw Nana first and waved to her as she emerged from the classroom. Mrs. Cooper's hands were full of books, but she gave Nana a friendly nod. Nana acknowledged them with a little wave but turned and walked down the long school hallway in the opposite direction from her two friends. She carried her copy of *Merchant of Venice* and another one of *Ivanhoe*. She stepped into the school office looking for the interim principal, Garnet Wilkinson, and found him standing inside with a folder in his hands.

"Miss Grimké!" Wilkinson exclaimed. "I was just going to go looking for you."

"And behold, I appear. It's magic." Nana's manner was tart and a bit sardonic.[146]

"Here, I have your poems that you typed so nicely for me." Wilkinson said with an undecipherable smile. I believe we will get them published in the district journal. This one entitled 'Surrender' in particular. But I have a question."

"Ask away!" Nana replied. Wilkinson walked over to her with the typescript of the poem and pointed out a line.

"Well, this line here: 'Let us forget the past unrest.' Doesn't that seem unnecessary? Perhaps it is unduly negative?"

Nana gave Wilkinson a withering look, incredulous that he was trying to revise her poem. Then she burst out laughing. "Mr. Wilkinson—that is my poem! That is the way it is written. It cannot be written differently—it forms a whole!" Nana paused, trying to digest the motivation of her critic. "Why? Are you afraid it will offend someone? In any case, recall that you asked me for these poems—I didn't ask you to look at them."

Wilkinson was taken aback by her adamant attitude and looked surprised but not embarrassed. Nana continued in a cool tone, "Frankly, I have no feelings one way or the other about whether they are published. But I cannot change a line. Please give the poems back to me."

She reached for the typed pages, but he held them out of her reach and placed them on the desk behind him. At that point Nana's friends and co-teachers, Percy Love,[147] Douglas Haley and Henry Bailey, who had been hovering near the door, crowded into the small office. Henry had the rumpled good looks of a young man who had just gotten out of bed. Douglas wore spectacles and appeared as serious as Henry was mischievous.

Percy was a tall, slender young woman, dressed in a sleek, long jacket over her ankle-length skirt with a pleated high-collared shirtwaist underneath. Her hair was pulled into a bun, but willful curls snuck out, softening her strong features. It was a look that Nana tried to emulate without much success since she was a full six inches shorter than Percy. She marveled that Percy could dress so well on their scant teacher's salary. The teachers carried books and coats for the journey home.

Wilkinson reached for the typescript and gave it to Miss Love to read, holding it high above Nana's head. "Here, Miss Love, tell me what you think. Wouldn't the poem be better without that line?" Wilkinson pointed to the offending line.

Percy read the first stanza aloud as the others listened. Nana was annoyed and turned away to fiddle with her books and papers.

> We ask for peace. We, at the bound
> Of life, are weary of the round
> In search of truth. We know the quest
> Is not for us, the vision blest
> Is meant for other eyes. Uncrowned,
> We go, with heads bowed to the ground,
> And old hands gnarled and hard and browned.
> Let us forget the past unrest,
> We ask for peace.[148]

"No, sir. I don't think so. It's an essential line," Percy said matter-of-factly. She looked at Nana with a slight smile of amusement. As Wilkinson had his back turned to them, Love handed the typescript to Nana who tucked it into her waist. Wilkinson didn't seem to notice.

"Well, I don't understand your stubbornness, Miss Grimké. It's only a line. You are being childish," Wilkinson complained, turning back to face her.

"So, why is it so important to omit it? What are you afraid of?" Then she said under her breath, but loud enough for Wilkinson to hear, "I would like the pleasure of knowing a real man!"

"I suppose that means I am not a man," Wilkinson replied. His smile was meant to convey his amusement at her barb, but instead it seemed almost pitiful. "Why, thank you," he replied sarcastically.

"You are welcome," Nana answered evenly. The others listened to this exchange with some astonishment at her impertinence towards their principal. Nana looked at Douglas Haley and smirked.

"Well, what do you think of that! The young lady treats me as though I am air! But with you, Doug, she is all smiles." Wilkinson was eager to turn it into a joke.

"Don't mind her, Garnet, she is sweet. She doesn't mean anything," Douglas said, adjusting his spectacles nervously.

With a shrug, Wilkinson moved to leave the office and the teachers followed him out into the hallway and toward the building exit. "Doug, what do you think of a lady who would let such a little thing break up a friendship?" Wilkinson queried, unwilling to cede victory in the exchange.

"Perhaps the friendship wasn't worth anything," Nana commented saucily.

"There you are, Doug. Hear that? That's what you call a friend! Think of it, a friend!" Douglas looked uncomfortable at being drawn into the fray especially when he perceived that Nana was increasingly more annoyed than amused. Wilkinson turned and extended his hand to Nana with a slight bow, although his tone was mocking. "Good-by, Miss Grimké."

Nana looked at his hand blankly and refused to shake it. Instead, she said, "Look here, Mr. Wilkinson, if you can't take me seriously, you had better let me alone." Nana grabbed Percy's arm and headed toward the door. She looked over her shoulder at the men and said, "Let's go, Love. My devils are taking over."

Wilkinson shrugged helplessly at the other gentlemen. Douglas, privately embarrassed for his principal, gave him a placating smile. Henry looked away. He was secretly pleased at Nana's uncompromising stance toward their spineless principal, but he worried that her disregard for Wilkinson's vanity could have unfortunate consequences.

"Nana, you'd better be careful," Percy warned gently. "You don't want to be out of his good graces."

"As if his good graces were worth much! Look, it's nearly four and I've ordered dinner for us at Martin's restaurant. We'd better take this streetcar."

Percy wrapped her fur-trimmed winter coat around her more closely as a chill wind came at them. Nana covered her ears and frowned at the insufficiency of the fashionable little hat she had decided to wear that morning.

"This wind is awful. Oh, here's the car," Nana said as the streetcar bore down on them. The women picked up their skirts to manage the big step onto the streetcar, dropping their coins into the farebox. Most of the seats were taken so Nana and Percy stood hanging onto poles. They shivered and pulled their hats and coats tighter as the streetcar moved along at a fair clip.

About a mile down the street, they got off and walked down a side street to a small local restaurant. Martin's Restaurant was unimpressive from the outside, but inside it buzzed with congenial chatter and the familiar aromas of fried garlic and onions and a variety of more mysterious spices.

A slovenly-looking waitress with a grumpy, inhospitable manner led Nana and Percy to a table. Nana rolled her eyes at her friend as the waitress turned away. "That waitress is a horrid thing. I wish that cute young man over there would wait on us," Nana said in a whisper, nodding at the more acceptable waiter. Percy surveyed the handsome young man in question and said with a laugh, "Oh, my, yes. I see what you mean!"

"Oh, Love, I do feel awful about that scene with Garnet. I thought I liked and respected him. But he was so—so ridiculous about the poem! He can be very annoying." Nana shook her head, feeling disgusted with herself as well as with her principal. "I just wish I could hold my tongue and control my feelings when they get out of hand."

"Well, diplomacy is not your strong suit, Nana, but your forthrightness is part of your charm," Percy replied with a sympathetic smile. "And he was certainly out of line about the poem."

"Oh, look. Here comes Henry, and he has Joe Douglass with him," Percy added. Nana was facing away from the door and had to crane her neck around to see their arrival. Percy waved, and the young men weaved their way through the crowded restaurant. They pulled up chairs to join the women at their table near the back.

"Well, Miss Grimké," Henry started in with a grin, "I think you've given Wilkinson something to think about this evening."

"Yes, I hope he sleeps poorly. I'm afraid I shall," Nana grimaced.

Joe Douglass, who had not witnessed the interchange with their principal, was more interested in flirting than serious conversation. He looked teasingly at Percy Love, surveying her from head to toe. "You certainly are good-looking, Love." Percy blushed and her usual poise gave way to a dismissive giggle. Joe turned his charm towards Nana and said, "And Grimké, you are getting better-looking every time I see you. You'll be as good looking as Love soon!"

Nana knew better than to take his teasing flattery seriously, but she couldn't help smiling as she retorted, "And Joe, why I believe you are getting crazier, every time I see you!" They all laughed. Henry reminded them that they were there to eat not flirt so they had better hurry and order before the food ran out. The casual jesting continued as they ordered abundant food—oyster stew, fried chicken with French fries, lettuce and tomato salad, and cake and ice cream for dessert.[149]

As they were finishing the oyster stew and starting on the fried chicken, Joe announced to the group, "I'm going to Boston soon—to attend the Garrison Memorial Meeting."

"Ah," Nana said with an interested glance. Did you know that my father is speaking there? He's on the Committee of Forty that organized it."

"Yes, I thought he would be. I believe Ida Wells-Barnett is speaking, too.

"Well, then, give my love to my father," Nana urged him seriously.

"I thought he had that," Joe teased.

"He has, but I'm sending him a little bit more," she smiled sweetly. "He is staying with the Lees, so you will probably run into him."

"I'll do my best not to run into him. I'll put on the brakes before I do," Joe parried with a half-smile. The meal and conversation went on for close to two hours as the food kept coming and the young teachers indulged their hunger for both food and companionship. They were fully satisfied on both accounts as they got up from the table and headed home.

Nana and Percy walked from the restaurant toward the rectory on Corcoran Street near to the Fifteenth Street Church. Nana deposited her umbrella, books, and the typescript of her poems inside the Grimké home, then rejoined Percy to walk with her toward Mrs. Cooper's house near Dupont Circle.[150] Nana was glad for the chance to walk off the discomfort she felt after the awkward exchange with her principal. Fortified with good food, the women walked along Corcoran to 17th Street and up the tree-lined avenue to a white-washed townhouse.

As they approached the Cooper home, Nana started to say good-by to her friend. "Oh, Love, it's so cold. I'm going to hurry home before I freeze," she declared with a shiver.

"Well, then, you'd better come in and have some tea. I see people in the window. Mrs. Cooper must have guests." Percy smiled coyly. "Let's see who's here."

Nana was reluctant, given her unsettled mood, but she couldn't resist the prospect of interesting company and temporary warmth. "Well, all right. I hope Uncle Frank doesn't worry. I left my things so he may wonder—"

That reminded Percy to ask, "Nana, how is your aunt, Miss Lottie? You know I used to spend evenings with her and your uncle and Anna? Sometimes John and I sang for them."

"Oh, my—that's a story," Nana gazed down at her feet with a troubled look. "Not so well. She's lost her memory and sometimes does the most outlandish things. She's sweet, of course, but when Papa and Uncle Frank are gone—well, it's difficult for me to know how to handle her. We have trying times, and it is sad."

Percy nodded knowingly, and said only, "Yes, I've heard as much. I'm so sorry, Nana." They arrived at the front door of the house and Percy ushered Nana in. They both stood in the foyer for a few moments, absorbing the warmth before taking off their coats and hats. They could hear animated conversation and laughter as they entered the parlor. Mrs. Cooper spotted them and called out, "There you are, Percy. I was beginning to worry. Nana, I'm so glad you've come. There's someone I want you to meet."

Nana surveyed the room and immediately noticed a lovely young woman, about her own age, who was listening to another guest with intense concentration. Nana looked at her with a mixture of awe and curiosity. When the woman looked up, their eyes met, and Nana sensed an immediate connection between them. Nana's face remained impassive, but the woman gave her a friendly smile.

Nana and Percy approached the couch where Mrs. Cooper was seated. She introduced Percy first, then gesturing towards Nana with a smile, she said, "And this is Miss Angelina Grimké. I'm sure you know her uncle, Rev. Francis Grimké, the pastor at Fifteenth Street Presbyterian. And perhaps you know of her father, the Honorable Archibald Grimké?"

"Nana, this is Mrs. Georgia Johnson. She's a writer, too."

Georgia spoke softly with a southern accent, and a diffident manner. "Yes, of course I know of your uncle—and your father. Your family name is one to be proud of." She tilted her head and looked at Nana with interest, "If I'm not mistaken you write poetry. I've seen several in *The Pilot*."

Nana was immediately self-conscious but pleased at the recognition. "Oh, well. They aren't very good—just scribbles really. *The Pilot* isn't too particular, I'm afraid," she demurred.

"Well, I read the one about lynching. What is the name of it? *Beware When . . .*"

Beware Lest He Awakes, Nana said with a pleased smile. She found a seat across from Georgia and sat down. Her pleasure in discovering a beautiful fellow poet proved stronger than her initial hesitancy.

"And I thought it was—well, amazing, really. Powerful and compelling," Georgia continued. She leaned back in her chair, relaxing from their previous formality. "But perhaps I am not much of a critic." She laughed. "I just know what I like!"

Nana gave her a delighted look, "Ah, that's exactly the kind of critic I love!"

Percy took her seat with other friends and Mrs. Cooper got up to see that tea and cookies were replenished. She was pleased that the two women were conversing. "But Mrs. Johnson, tell me about your poetry," Nana continued. "I mean—about your writing. Will you let me read some?"

"Well, yes. I suppose so," she hesitated for only a second before adding, "Yes, I'd be pleased. I think perhaps we are interested in similar themes. I'm haunted by the experience of our brothers and sisters in the South. You know I'm from Georgia? I can't seem to divorce my poetry or stories from those horrors."

"I'm afraid much of my poetry is very self-indulgent," Nana said apologetically. "It's just my nature. But I am also working on a play. It's about the futility of motherhood. I mean the motherhood of black sons, when they are just fodder for white hatred. I'm calling it 'Blessed are the Barren' or perhaps just 'Rachel.'"

"Are you? Well, of course, because 'Rachel' was the barren one in the Bible, right?" She tilted her head and looked directly at Nana. "May I call you Angelina? Please call me Georgia," she interjected.

"Oh, it's Nana, actually. That's what my friends call me. Please call me that."

"Nana, then. Well, it's a disturbing theme, isn't it?" Georgia went on. "But I understand what you mean. I have a play in the works as well." Their conversation grew animated and flowed easily into personal confidences. Normally cautious with new acquaintances, Nana was stunned that she felt no barriers with Georgia.

Guests were beginning to leave, and Percy stood up to say goodnight. Nana took the hint and reluctantly rose to leave as well. Georgia stood and they shook hands warmly, promising to be in touch. Nana said her good-byes to Mrs. Cooper and the few remaining guests. Before leaving, she looked back into the parlor to get a final glimpse of Georgia moving gracefully across the room to thank their hostess.[151]

Nana slept late the following morning, and hurried through her coffee and toast, anxious to avoid even a gentle reprimand from her uncle. Frank wished her a good morning and looked over his eyeglasses at her with concern but continued reading his newspaper. After her hasty breakfast, she went immediately back to her room and sat down at the writing desk, looking dreamily out the window.

She doodled on the edge of the paper she had in front of her, smiling to herself as she silently composed. Finally, Nana dipped her fountain pen and began to write:

Thou art so far, so far
Thou art to me a lone white star,
That I may gaze on from afar;
But I may never, never, press
My lips on thine in mute caress,
E'en touch the hem of thy pure dress, -
thou art so far, so far.

Nana thought back to the previous night, recalling her encounter with Georgia Johnson. She could visualize her looks, her mannerisms, and the intelligence behind her eyes. Nana bit her lower lip and continued with a melancholy smile.

Thou livest in a world apart
Created by thy sinless heart;
There lilies white, and tall, and fair,
Are growing, glowing everywhere,
In gardens wonderful and rare,
          thou art so far, so far.
A sinner, I may only stand,
Without thy white heart's borderland
And kneeling humbly worship thee,
And kneeling humbly pray for thee,
And kneeling humbly long for thee,
          thou are too far, too far.[152]

Nana surveyed the poem with satisfaction, changing a few words here and there. She sat back, sighed deeply, and tucked the poem into the back of her portfolio.

40

On the Cusp

Washington, D.C. 1911—1913

DURING THE SEVERAL YEARS that followed, Nana's writing became more ambitious. She continued her teaching and followed her father's activities with the fledgling interracial organization that would come to be known as the National Association for the Advancement of Colored People. Archie participated in the development of the American Negro Academy as well. Many of their summers were spent together in Boston, where more of his colleagues were, and where Nana had more leisure for writing.

She was on her way to Boston in early July 1911, when the train she had boarded in Washington, derailed and plummeted nearly twenty feet down a hill. Nana was thrown around in the plunging car and badly injured, as were over fifty other passengers. Twelve passengers died in the accident. As she wrote to her father, it felt like the car had gone to pieces. She was pulled from the wreck by an unknown man, whom she later discovered had lost his wife in the accident.

She had broken bones and ugly bruises. She remained in serious pain throughout the summer. Archie, who had planned to follow Nana to Boston later, rushed there to help care for her. It wasn't until much later in the fall, however, that it was discovered that she had fractured her spine. It was a difficult and sobering time for Nana. At first, she had writhed and complained and given in to dark moods. Then gradually she had accepted the slowness of her recovery. It marked the end of her prolonged adolescence.

The convalescence had been a difficult time for Archie as well. He had hated to see her pain and was not always patient with her moodiness. But they had grown closer, and he could see how the near brush with death, and the struggle to heal, had tempered her impetuous—and occasionally self-centered—personality.

On New Year's Eve of that year, Nana was bent over her desk, writing energetically. Her dense, curly hair had, with difficulty, been woven into a thick braid which she had coiled around the back of her head. She wore a sleekly shaped cranberry-toned woolen skirt with a simple, pleated waist of pink silk and a long skating sweater of soft gray wool with a knitted belt. She was rapidly approaching thirty-two years of age, and a new-found serenity and confidence lent her the attractiveness she had long thought impossible.

When Nana finished writing she sat back and stared far out the window at the stripped-down maple tree, admiring the eerie sparkle of its ice-covered branches in the moonlight. She stretched her neck and rotated her shoulders to relieve their stiffness as she began to look over what she had written.

> December 31, 1911
> My prayer for the coming year:
> Dear, beautiful God, come thou close to me day by day. My plea is human. I am evil and my will is weak. Strengthen thou my will. Teach me the habit of conquering myself.
> Make me unselfish, quick to do for and help others. Make me charitable in judgment. Help me to see to the good in each and all. And yet, oh God, keep me alive. Let me not grow into a fossil. Let me keep my sense of humor! Amen.[153]

She read through the remainder of what she had written, fiddling with her pen as she did so. She tilted her head and smiled to herself. When she finally rose from her chair, she grabbed the edge of the desk to steady herself and then walked stiffly toward her wardrobe to exchange her day clothes for her nightgown. Standing at her basin, she washed her face reluctantly with the cold water from her pitcher. To ease some of the lingering pain, Nana bent over and touched her toes holding the position for nearly a minute to stretch out her back muscles. It seemed to help. It was after midnight when she put out the light and climbed into her bed, pulling up her feather comforter and waiting for her body to warm it up.

On New Year's morning, Archibald sat the breakfast table talking to Frank over coffee and buttermilk biscuits that were straight from the oven. At sixty-one, Archie's hair was completely white, giving him the distinguished air of the elder man of letters that he was. Frank's close-cropped hair betrayed his age as well. Lottie, now seventy-four, sat next to Frank, looking frail and distracted. She was dressed strangely with a red dressing gown over her day dress. Frank occasionally reached over and held her hand gently. It was well after nine a.m. when Nana joined them. She came down the stairs with the cane she still used occasionally to steady herself and to relieve her back. She went over to give her father a warm kiss on his cheek. "Happy New Year, Papa!"

She did the same to her Aunt Lottie and Uncle Frank, giving them each a kiss in turn. "Happy New Year, Aunt Lottie. Happy New Year, Uncle Frank. I think it is going to be a good year—better than last!" she predicted cheerfully to all of them. She edged herself carefully onto her empty chair and grabbed two biscuits before pouring herself coffee with an abundance of fresh cream.

"Thank you, my dear!" Frank said. "Your father and I were just talking. So much has happened this past year. It now appears that there will be some peace between the Bookerites and the Dubois factions in our new organization."

"You mean the 'National Association for the Advancement of Colored People'? What a mouthful!" she said with a low chuckle and a roll of her eyes.

"Uh-huh," responded Frank with a slightly reproving smile. "Well, did you know your father was elected to the Committee of One Hundred—the new steering committee?"

Archie frowned. "Yes, but I'm not sure how effective I can be in that role. I'm more interested in forming a strong chapter of the organization here in Washington. We can easily keep an eye on national legislation here." He winked meaningfully at his daughter. "My work with the American Negro Academy is taking up too much time when what I really want to be doing is writing." He glanced at Nana and added, "And just spending some time with you, my dear!" He patted her hand affectionately.

Nana gave her father a whimsical look in return. "Well, you have spent an inordinate amount of time on me since the accident. It's about time we both did something useful!" Archie pretended to be offended and opened his mouth to object, but Nana continued before he could say anything. "But I'm glad for the intention, because I really want to have some time with you today. Can we go for a walk after breakfast?"

Archie looked pleased. "Of course, my dear. But how is your back? Are you up to a long walk?"

"Yes, I'm so much better now. That train wreck—well, being so close to death somehow, it does have a purging effect on one's soul." Nana looked at Frank and then at Lottie, silently admiring her uncle's devotion to his failing spouse.

"People have been so kind," she said reflectively. "I hated being laid up, but as you can see, I'm ever so much better now—just a little pain here and there. I don't think I'll need this silly cane for long."

Around half past ten, Archie and Nana set off straight down Fifteenth towards Lafayette Square. There were patches of snow on the ground, and the breeze was chilly. The low sun in the southeastern sky nearly blinded them as they headed south. Nana was still using the cane to relieve the stiffness in her back.

A scattering of Washingtonians was out on the streets exchanging New Year's greetings and enjoying a leisurely holiday morning, although the cold kept many of them inside by their fireplaces. Nana and Archie walked into the park and found a bench to sit on. Nana drew her diary out of the pocket of her overcoat.

"Papa, I want to read something to you from my diary." She spoke with a slightly embarrassed air, but very earnestly. "I just wrote it last night, but I've felt it for so long." Archie was surprised but looked at her encouragingly.

"I—well, I know you've worried about me," Nana continued. "about my friends, about whom I choose to love, and how my emotions get carried away at times. I know I have not always been wise—or temperate—or good. But I want to be better, Papa. Maybe I've just grown up."

Archie looked at her solemnly. He was touched by her evident sincerity and wanted to hear more. "I see that, my dear. I see how you are trying. And I am proud of you. I'm proud of your writing and your teaching, and of the woman you are becoming. Let's allow those arguments of the past to be forgotten," he said with a grave smile.

"Yes, although I cannot promise I shall never fall or be sinful again. I'm still—well, a bit of a devil." Nana said ruefully. "But here, can I read you this part?" Archie nodded, and Nana opened her diary to her latest entry, and began reading.

> My father—he is so much a part of me. He is so absolutely necessary that sometimes I take him as a matter of course. I know now that I have absolutely no desire for life without him. There

is no father like him and no friend so kind, so patient, so helpful. And I want him to know . . .

Nana paused and looked up at her father shyly.

> . . . I want him to know that I appreciate him to the uttermost. My happiness and my suffering and his are indissolubly bound up together. Words cannot do him justice.

Archie bowed his head—and wiped an unfamiliar wetness from his eye as Nana continued to read.

> My greatest and most beautiful blessing, now and always, is my father. Dear God, make me worthy of him. I hope that I shall never fail him as I know he will never fail me.

Nana looked up expectantly. Archie reached over and drew her into his arms in a fatherly embrace. "Oh, my dear girl. Thank you." They remained like that for a moment, then they rose and walked arm and arm out of the park, each mulling over their own thoughts.

Archie spoke first. "Nana, would you like to take a more active role with the NAACP? You seem ripe for a leadership role."

Nana frowned and looked at him skeptically, but she was intrigued. "Truly?"

"Well, only if you want to, my dear. I've just been asked to take over the chairmanship of the Washington branch and we are recruiting members for the board. I've asked Carter Woodson—your colleague at M street—to join, and I think you'd be an excellent addition as well." Archie lifted his eyebrows and gave Nana a look that was somewhere between a question and a challenge.

"Hmmm. I'll think about it, Papa." She bit her lower lip and looked up at him thoughtfully. "Thank you for asking me. I am flattered," she said softly.

41

Inherit the Dream

ABOUT A YEAR LATER, Nana sat once again at her bedroom writing desk, staring at the manuscript she had just finished. She wrote "The End" with a joyful flourish and put down her pen. She turned the manuscript back to its title page and surveyed it with satisfaction.[154] Nana rose and did a little waltz around the room holding the script to her heart. With a broad smile, she opened the door and waved the script as she called down the stairs, "Papa, I'm finished!"

Archie came to the bottom of the stairs and looked up at his daughter, applauding her proudly. He was glad she had finished the draft of her writing project, but even happier that her health continued to improve, and that she seemed content in their life together.

Nana came down the stairs and received her father's congratulatory kiss. "I'm going to see Georgia," she announced. "I want her to see the final draft—she's been so encouraging, Papa." She reached for her coat and hurried out the door.

At the Johnson home, the housekeeper greeted her with a familiar "Hi, Honey," as she took her coat and led her into the parlor. "Hi Sophie, thanks." Nana murmured. "Is Mrs. Johnson upstairs?" Sophie nodded, but before she could say more, Georgia came down the stairs and appeared at the parlor door.

Nana held up her finished script to show her, "Look, it is done!" She walked over to hand it to her friend.

Georgia beamed at Nana and gave her a congratulatory hug. "Come, let's talk about it—and about what happens next." She put an arm around Nana's waist, guiding her to their favorite corner of the parlor where they could chat. Sophie supplied them with tea and warm biscuits spread with homemade gooseberry jam.

Archie and Nana discussed next steps, too, and Archie suggested that *Rachel* be submitted to the arts committee of the NAACP. The committee helped arrange an initial production for the colored community in Washington, DC. Nana was thrilled at the prospect of seeing her work realized on stage. However, she proved to be a moody partner for the director and actors, alternately finding fault with her script and changing it, or blaming the actors for not bringing her characters to life. She complained loudly to Georgia, and Georgia reminded her that the process would make the play better in the long run. Nana grumpily accepted the truth of that, and eventually resigned herself to what she deemed was a less than perfect result.

The following year, the Neighborhood Playhouse, a community theatre in the Lower Eastside of Manhattan agreed to produce the play.[155] It would be the first production by a colored playwright to attract an integrated audience. On the night of its debut, Archie, Nana, Frank, and Georgia Johnson slogged from their lodging through the April rain and mud of Lower Manhattan to the playhouse. Nana felt alternately sick and agitated with excitement as she saw crowds of New York's colored community coming into the small theater, along with a considerable number of local white patrons.

On the small marquee outside the Playhouse, Nana saw her name in lights for the first time. It read:

Rachel
or
"Blessed are the Barren"
A new play by
Angelina Weld Grimké[156]

The foursome entered the theatre and were quickly waylaid by several of Archie's New York colleagues and some family friends. Nana was too nervous to socialize, so while Frank and Archie chatted with their friends, Nana grabbed Georgia by the hand and fled to find seats in the far back of the theater. She slid in after Georgia, saving the last two seats in the row for her father and Uncle Frank.

Nana felt a headache coming on as she worried about how the production would go, and whether it would be a success. She gripped the arms of her theatre seat tightly as the curtain came up and the first scenes were played. She had re-written a few scenes after the Washington, DC production, and felt more confident of it now, but nothing could truly make her relax.

In the darkened theater, the first act of Nana's play began with the stage set as the living room of a small apartment in a northern city where the pretty and vivacious 18-year-old Rachel lives with her mother, her brother, Tom, and Jimmy, the little neighbor boy, whom she took in when the boy's parents died. In the first act Rachel spoke of how much she loves little children and dreams of having her own. But Rachel's mother reveals to her two young adult children that their father and older stepbrother were lynched in the South when Rachel and Tom were very young. The mother fled north to protect them. The revelation of the lynching in their own family darkens their view of what life holds for colored individuals. Rachel's and Tom's youthful gaiety and optimism have also been dampened by the fact that despite having done well and completed higher education, they cannot find jobs in their professions.

After the first act, Georgia squeezed Nana's hand reassuringly and gave her an encouraging smile. "It's going well," she whispered.

In the second act, set four years later, Tom talks to Rachel's suitor, John, about the disappointments they have faced. John has already told them that although he has a college degree, he could only get a job as a waiter with no prospect of advancement beyond headwaiter.

> TOM: Today, we colored men and women, everywhere, are up against it. Every year, we are having a harder time of it. In the South, they make it as impossible as they can for us to get an education. We're hemmed in on all sides. Our one safeguard—the ballot—in most states, is taken away already, or is being taken away. Economically—we have a slight show—but at what a cost! In the North, they make a pretense of liberality: they give us the ballot and a good education, and then—snuff us out. Each year, the problem just to live, gets more difficult to solve. And how about these children—if we're fools enough to have any?

When Rachel reenters the scene, her face is drawn and pale. She has overheard the conversation and understands its truth. Shortly afterward she hears a harrowing story from a mother whose dark-skinned little girl has been ostracized, isolated, and called "nigger" by her classmates in a local school and church. The teachers also treat her with disdain and prejudice. The little girl is visibly anxious and withdrawn and seems permanently damaged. Rachel tries to reassure the mother that the schools in her neighborhood treat the children better. But the mother says to Rachel, "Don't marry, that's my advice." The crowning blow comes when Rachel discovers that her Jimmy has received similar treatment.

> JIMMY: Ma Rachel, what is a "Nigger"?
> *Rachel recoils as though she had been struck.*
>
> RACHEL: Honey boy, why—why do you ask that?
>
> JIMMY: Some big boys called me that when I came out of school just now. They said: "Look at the little nigger!" And they laughed. One of them runned, no ranned, after me and threw stones, and they all kept calling "Nigger! Nigger! Nigger!". . .
>
> RACHEL: *She sweeps down upon him and hugs and kisses him*: Why honey boy, those boys didn't mean anything. Silly, little honey boy! They're rough, that's all . . .
>
> JIMMY: You're only saying that, Ma Rachel, so I won't be hurt. I know. It wouldn't ache here like it does (pointing to his heart)— if they didn't mean something.

In the final act, Rachel's suitor, John, has come to call and to propose to Rachel. Having heard the heartbreaking stories of continued lynching in the South, of college-educated young colored men being turned away from every job prospect, and of young children, including her own ward, being traumatized by brutal prejudice, Rachel has decided she is unwilling to bring another colored child into the world to suffer.

> RACHEL: I am twenty-two, and I'm old; you're thirty-two, and you're old. Ma dear is sixty, and she is much older than that. We are all blighted; we are all accursed—all of us, everywhere, we whose skins are dark. Our lives blasted by the white man's prejudice. *She pauses.*
>
> And my little Jimmy—seven years old. In a year or two, at best, he will be made old by suffering.
>
> *She turns away from her suitor, and in a pained voice, she explains.* One week ago today, some white boys, older and larger than my little Jimmy, as he was leaving the school called him "Nigger"! They chased him through the streets calling him, "Nigger! Nigger! Nigger!" One boy threw stones at him. There is still a bruise on his little back where one struck him.

Rachel lets that sink in before adding: That will get well; but they bruised his soul, and that—well, that will never get well. . ..And he always awakes in the dark, afraid—afraid of the now and the future! So, John, you see, it can never be, all the beautiful, beautiful things you have told me.

As the play ends, Rachel tells John that he cannot touch her—that they must part. She is adamant in sending him away, but as he reluctantly leaves, she nearly weakens in her resolve.

Rachel runs out into the hallway, looking down the stairwell. Presently she returns. She is composed again. There is a pause until she speaks with infinite yearning:

No! No, John. Not for us. No.

No sunshine. No laughter. Always, always, darkness.

And my little children! My little children!

There was silence for several moments until the cast came out to take a bow. Nana was petrified. But as the unnerving spell of the play broke, the audience clapped enthusiastically through several curtain calls. The play's director came out and called Nana up to the front. She walked down the aisle gingerly, afraid of stumbling in her high-heeled boots. But when she got to the stage and saw the large bouquet of red and white roses awaiting her, she allowed herself to enjoy a moment of triumph and the unmixed thrill of her creative project coming to fruition. She waved happily at the audience as the clapping continued.

Archie and Frank watched Nana's newfound poise with pride. Georgia, however, thought about the long hours of struggle and uncertainty that had brought her friend to this point, and she felt satisfaction on her fellow writer's behalf. She knew that Nana intended the play to be a way to convey to a mixed audience the despair that the lynching in the South, the de-humanizing prejudice in the North, and the failure to provide economic opportunity to eager and ambitious young men, engendered in the young heroine. "Will we really choose to be barren?" she wondered sadly.

Nana soon found that she was back into the mundane routine of her teaching, although her greatest satisfaction came from the hours she could steal to write. She loved those quiet hours to herself, and they nourished her. But living with her father and Uncle Frank did not allow her to be oblivious to the larger world and its issues. Their conversations at the dinner table, her NAACP work and her teaching colleagues, kept her abreast of the currents of the second decade of the twentieth century. On her way home one day, a newsboy waved a paper at her, calling out "Women strike! Read all about it! It was enough to make Nana dig out some coins to pay for the paper, although she knew her father would probably bring one home as well.

When she got home, she found him sitting quietly by the fire absorbed in a book. With little warning she thrust the paper in front of his face so he could read the headline.

Women Strike for Better Wages and Conditions in Massachusetts

"Look, Papa! Today the factory women of Lawrence are going out on strike. Finally, working woman are standing up for their rights. What do you think will happen?"

Archie was taken aback by the interruption, but he smiled indulgently at Nana's excitement. "I think they will win," he said with a judicious stroke of his chin. He put down his book and asked, "And what do you think, my dear?"

Nana's face darkened. "Does it really do any good, though? Striking I mean? Nothing seems to change much. Look, we women haven't even got the vote yet!"

Archie acknowledged this with a nod, but added, "Well, some things do change, or I would still be Montague's houseboy in Charleston." He gave his daughter a lopsided grin. "But yes, it is painfully slow and sometimes things seem to go backward." He frowned and added, "In fact, as you well know, they do go backwards." He looked at Nana with a deeply furrowed brow and said, "But we can't stop trying, Nana, each in our own way." It wasn't a very satisfactory answer, Nana thought, but it stuck with her, nevertheless.

At the end of February 1913, Mamie Burrill and Anna Cooper were pinning up a large poster just inside the entrance to the M Street School. The poster advertised the Women's Suffrage Procession to be held on March 3rd. There was a colorful picture of a woman in battle dress riding a white horse that made her look like Joan of Arc. The woman carried a blue flag and she was followed by a small army of women dressed in white. Percy Love emerged from her classroom and joined the others.

A moment later, Nana strode down the hall toward them. "This looks like a dangerous crew," she teased.

"Look here, Nana!" Mamie responded, ignoring her remark. "You've heard about the Women's Procession, haven't you? It's going to be glorious; thousands and thousands of women marching for the vote." She turned back to finish pinning up the poster. "It's right before Wilson's inauguration," Mamie added, taking some thumb tacks from Anna. "It is meant to send a message to him and to Congress that we won't be silent any longer."

Nana scowled and looked doubtful. "Thousands of white women, I'll wager! What does it have to do with us? They don't need us."

Anna Cooper looked at Nana quickly, "I understand your skepticism, Nana, but it's about the vote. We *must* be there. We can't let this moment pass us by. Alice Paul has said all women are welcome. Many colored women are planning to participate."

"I heard that Mrs. Terrell is organizing the Delta Sigma Theta sorority to all march together—you know, from Howard," Percy added. "Some of our former students will be among them. And Ida Wells Barnett is definitely going to march." She gave Nana a mockingly indignant look, "You can't *not* come, Nana."

"Ask your father and uncle, my dear, I believe they'll wish to march as well," Anna suggested. "You can't argue with that. Anyway, you know Mrs. Barnett from the NAACP. She said she'll be marching with the Illinois contingent." Anna smiled slyly, as if she were hammering the last nail into the coffin. "And I think I've convinced Georgia Johnson to come as well."

Nana made an incredulous face. "Really? You think Georgia will come? I didn't think she went in for this kind of public demonstration much." She frowned slightly and said, "Hmmm. I'll ask her. And I'll talk to Papa and Uncle Frank. I wish Aunt Lottie could come, but she'd just be confused, I suspect. Well, maybe we'll all go together." She sighed wistfully. "I do admire these women who stand up and march and make things happen. I'm just distrustful. It always seems that we colored women are the last in line," she grumbled. "Almost an afterthought."

The women continued to chat excitedly as they finished with the poster and walked back down the hall together. Mamie took Nana aside. "Nana, you really must come. This is our chance. It's what we've all been waiting for."

Mamie gave Nana a meaningful smile. Nana stared at her skeptically, but after a moment's thought, she managed a grudging nod, with a roll of her eyes. "Mamie, I never could resist your manipulative charm!" They both laughed. "But I'm making no promises," Nana added tartly.

On the morning of March 3rd Pennsylvania Avenue was a raucous scene.[157] Thousands of women, as well as smaller groups of men, tried to organize themselves into dozens of different marching groups. Some of the marching groups were organized by geography—state and country delegations—while others represented professional groups such as teachers, librarians, and supportive members of Congress. The latter were, of course, all males.

It was a spectacular tableau with marching bands, banners, women dressed in white, and the labor lawyer, Inez Mulholland, mounted on a white horse to lead the parade. Alice Paul, the moving spirit behind the procession, and her lieutenants did their best to coordinate the groups, but the vast distance between her place at the head of the parade and the rear guard made this impossible.

A greater problem was the rowdy crowd of unsympathetic onlookers who succeeded in blocking the street in front of the parade. The police looked on with grins, seeming to encourage the rough group of opponents who shouted insults and spit upon the women marchers. They did little or nothing to clear the street, and Alice Paul was forced to drive her automobile down Pennsylvania Avenue in front of Miss Mulholland and her steed, to clear a path for the procession.

The chaos was still apparent when Nana, Mamie, Anna Cooper, and Percy Love approached Pennsylvania Avenue from a side street near the head of the parade. The colored women paused, amazed at the scene, but also discomfited by the overwhelmingly white crowd. They began to push their way upstream, through the throngs on the side of the avenue. They were headed toward the back of the parade. A few minutes after their arrival, the front part of the parade began to move and one of the bands began playing.

"Here, girls, I think we need to walk further toward the back," Anna said. "Mary Terrell said she would meet us there and we could march with the Delta Sigma Theta group."

"So, they *have* relegated us to the back—just as I suspected," Nana complained. "Not only behind the white women, but behind the men as well!"

"I'm afraid you are right, Nana," Mamie acknowledged. "I heard there was pressure from the southern women. They said they would withdraw and not march at all if we were integrated into the white groups. So, putting us colored folk in the back was a compromise."

"Some compromise!" Nana wanted to pound her fist with anger, but she had no place to pound it, and she had learned a modicum of restraint. In any case, she had a back-up plan. "Well, I spoke to Mrs. Wells-Barnett last night and she said she was marching with all the Illinois women, white and colored together."

Mamie looked pleased, and said, "Hurrah for her! She's got courage."

"By the way, where is Georgia?" Mamie asked.

"She wasn't feeling well," Nana said with a shrug. "But she said she would try to join us later. We'll see."

The women continued their walk toward the back of the procession as the crowds lining the street grew larger. Mixed in among the sympathetic groups of onlookers, and the merely curious, were loud protesters whose only goal was to heckle and harass the marchers. A few of them carried signs. As Nana and her friends walked by, they saw a group of young men pushing some of the women marchers from the side, calling them names and spitting at them. A few of them stuck out their legs to trip the women.

The women, who were in high spirits, largely ignored the heckling and the annoyances. A few looked at the hecklers with disdain. Mamie pointed to the policemen standing by, and another one sitting on horseback. "Look, ladies, the police are doing next to nothing to protect the women from abuse." Percy added, "They are laughing at those hoodlums. How disgusting!"

A few moments later Nana spotted a large group of white women and men holding a banner announcing, "Washington Teachers March for the Vote!" She poked Mamie and Percy. "Here are the teachers from the District. That's *our* group! Why not join them?" She grinned at the brilliance of her idea.

Anna Cooper smiled at their boldness, but said, "I'll go on to find Mary Terrell and the sorority. They're expecting me. But you girls go ahead." Mamie and Percy hesitated, but Nana grabbed them by the hand and the three women joined in towards the back of the group. They fell into step, marching forward with the other teachers. The white teachers nearby looked at them curiously. Nana saw a woman raise an eyebrow at her companion, but no one discouraged them.[158]

Nana felt a surge of defiance rising inside her. Then, two white teachers marching just behind them tapped the women on their backs. When they turned to look, the teachers smiled at their colored colleagues, and they moved forward so that they could link arms with Mamie, Percy and

Nana. Nana's defiance softened and was replaced by a new feeling: an exuberant solidarity that made her beam like the brilliant sunshine of that spring day.

From a birds' eye view, Pennsylvania Avenue appeared packed full, with marchers and onlookers for nearly a mile as the procession slowly progressed toward the Capitol. From a half-mile back, Nana's group could just barely see the shape of Inez Mulholland on her white horse, and the group of women leaders, dressed all in white, who carried the banners at the front.

Far back in the procession, the Delta Sigma Thetas, also dressed in white, were accompanied by several other groups of colored women. Anna Julia Cooper and Mary Church Terrell were at their head. Near the middle of the procession, closer to the DC teachers, there was a group of women factory workers from Lawrence, Massachusetts. One of the marchers spoke to the leader of the band behind them, and in short order the band began playing the women workers' anthem, "Bread and Roses."

The factory workers began singing the words with the band, and soon the singing spread up and down the parade route until virtually all the women were singing along. Nana and Percy looked at each other happily as they started singing the familiar words. Mamie knew that she usually sang off-key, but she joined in just as enthusiastically.

> As we go marching, marching, in the beauty of the day
> A million darkened kitchens, a thousand mill lofts gray
> Are touched with all the radiance that a sudden sun discloses
> For the people hear us singing, bread and roses, bread and roses.
> As we come marching, marching, we battle too, for men,
> For they are in the struggle and together we shall win.
> Our days shall not be sweated from birth until life closes,
> Hearts starve as well as bodies, give us bread, but give us roses.
> As we come marching, marching, un-numbered women dead
> Go crying through our singing their ancient call for bread,
> Small art and love and beauty their trudging spirits knew
> Yes, it is bread we fight for, but we fight for roses, too.
> As we go marching, marching, we're standing proud and tall.
> The rising of the women means the rising of us all.
> No more the drudge and idler, ten that toil where one reposes,
> But a sharing of life's glories, bread and roses, bread and roses.[159]

As the singing continued, the group of DC teachers drew close to the intersection where Nana and her friends had first arrived.

"Look!" Nana shouted over the singing, pointing to the intersection. Archie and Frank stood there, supporting Lottie between them. Lottie was wrapped up in warm blankets, and she looked aged and frail, but she was waving a small suffragette banner that Frank had supplied for her. At the same time, Nelly and Solomon Stebbins arrived at the corner from another direction accompanied by several other Boston women. Seeing Archie, Frank and Lottie they come over to embrace them. Georgia Johnson, unable to stay away, was standing nearby. Seeing the Grimkés she walked over to join the group.

Nana left her companions and ran over to her father and the others. She managed to pull them in to march the last few blocks with the teacher's group. Archie and Frank made a seat between them with their arms so that they could carry Aunt Lottie. Her thin frame seemed light as a feather to them. With a full heart, Nana took Georgia's arm and whispered, "I so glad you came."

The march continued and the singing grew to an immense chorus. Preoccupied with carrying Lottie, Archie had paid little attention to the song, but as he settled into a comfortable stride, he was struck by the words of the third verse:

> As we come marching, marching, un-numbered women dead
> Go crying through our singing, their ancient call for bread . . .

Archie looked up into the bright sky and in the few, scattered clouds he seemed to see a silhouette of his aunts, Sarah and Angelina, in faint outline. The thought of them drew him into a reverie; he felt a wild elation as he recalled the men and women who had passed away but who shared in the unfinished glory of this day.

He closed his eyes and imagined his Uncle Theodore, and his aunts' friends, Lucretia Mott, Sarah and Grace Douglass, Elizabeth Cady Stanton, Abby Kelley, Mary Parker, Maria Weston Chapman, Lydia Child, Harriot Hunt, and Harriet Beecher Stowe. His mind moved to the couples among them: Frederick Douglass and Helen Pitt, Bronson and Abby Alcott, Gerrit and Ann Smith, and their daughter, Elizabeth Smith Miller. He opened his eyes and stared at the clouds again. This time it was a profile of John Quincy Adams that he saw. From Adams his mind travelled to William Lloyd Garrison, John Greenleaf Whittier, and Archie's wise friend and mentor, Wendell Phillips. Rising above them all, he saw his own mother, Nancy Weston Grimké.

THE END

Epilogue

NANA'S PLAY RACHEL PLAYED at the Neighborhood Theater in New York in 1917 and at Brattle Hall in Cambridge, MA the following year. It was well-reviewed and was among the works that inaugurated the Harlem Renaissance. She continued writing and publishing poetry and drama throughout the 1920s, as did her friends, Georgia Johnson and Mary (Mamie) Burrill.

Charlotte Forten Grimké died in 1914, leaving Uncle Frank bereft. However, Francis continued as pastor of The Fifteenth Street Presbyterian Church until 1928, serving there for nearly fifty years. He died in Washington in 1937. His photo is still prominently displayed on the outside of that church .

Archibald was president of the American Negro Academy for many years, a vice president of the national NAACP, and the president of the District of Columbia branch of the NAACP. In 1919, he received the Spingarn Medal, awarded to him for a long lifetime of service to his race. Archibald died in 1930 after spending his last years writing addresses and pamphlets on the race question and fighting racial injustice wherever it was found.

Shortly after the death of her beloved father in 1930, Nana moved to a home in New York City, where she lived quietly and obscurely for the rest of her life. It is unclear if she ever found the love she longed for. She died in 1958.

Endnotes

1. John Grimké, Archibald and Francis' younger brother did go to Lincoln University for a brief time, and the Grimké sisters helped pay his way. However, at some point, he decided to return to the South, where he lived in Florida for most of his life. Not much is known of his life, although the brothers seemed to be occasionally in touch with him, particularly when their mother, Nancy, died.

2. The Amistad was a Cuban schooner that was carrying 53 Africans to slavery on a Caribbean plantation. The Africans seized the ship, killed the captain and cook and tried to get the Spanish slave traders to sail back to Africa. When the ship ran aground off the coast of Long Island, NY, the US government imprisoned the Africans and returned control of the ship to the slave traders. President John Quincy Adams agreed to argue that the Africans had been illegally taken from their free state in Africa and were never subjects of Spain. Although the Supreme Court was dominated by southerners, they accepted Adams' argument, and the Africans were returned to freedom in their homeland.

3. Perry, *Lift Up*, 187. "Charley. . ..was raised according to the principles laid down in Andrew Combes *Physiological and Moral Management of Infancy*, one of the standard child-rearing texts of the era. He was fed, laid in his crib, and bathed by the clock. But the infant was not healthy and suffered from colic until Sarah intervened. She ignored Combes's advice that infants be fed only five spoonfuls of formula at each feeding and allowed the child to eat his fill, whereupon he grew fat and happy."

4. Elizabeth Cady Stanton to Angelina and Sarah, 6.25.40, Barnes and Dumond, *Letters*, 845.

5. Lumpkin, *Emancipation*, 180—181. This offer did indeed come to Weld from Joshua Giddings prior to the winter of 1841 session of Congress. However, this is not verbatim from his letter.

6. Theodore to Angelina, 1.1.42, Barnes and Dumond, *Letters*, 883. The letter mentions Calhoun of MA, Joseph Lawrence, James Irvin, Thomas Henry, William Simonton, Robert Ramsey, and James Russell in addition to Gates, Giddings, and Leavitt.

7. Theodore to Angelina, 1.1.42, Barnes and Dumond, *Letters*, 883.

8   This would be the copy of the "Landsdowne" full-length portrait of George
      Washington by Gilbert Stuart which was purchased by the U.S. government for
      the White House and rescued when the White House was taken by the British in
      the War of 1812.

9   Louisa Adams was born in England where she met John Quincy Adams. Her
      mother was English and her father, American, but she had lived in France during
      her childhood. She would have been about 66 at this time, and 8 years younger
      than her husband. She appears to have been a beautiful woman and a very good
      hostess during their White House days.

10   Theodore to Angelina, 1.1.42, Barnes and Dumond, *Letters*, 888.

11   The guest list for dinner is unknown other than Leavitt and Weld, but I am imag-
      ining them to include Giddings, Seth Gates, Rep from NY, William Simonton,
      Rep. from PA, and his wife, Martha Snodgrass Simonton. Gates and Simonton
      also lived at Mrs. Spriggs with Leavitt, Giddings, and Weld.

12   Governor Benjamin Smith of North Carolina was indeed related to the Rhett's
      (who were cousins to the Grimkés) but it is not clear if he was directly related to
      Angelina and Sarah's mother Mary (Polly) Smith Grimké. She did have an uncle,
      Benjamin Sr. Smith, and both he and Governor Smith were born in Charleston,
      SC. However, it appears that Mary Smith Grimké's uncle was born in 1746, while
      Governor Smith wasn't born until 1756. The similarity of names may have led to
      this confusion.

13   Theodore to Angelina and Sarah, 1.23.42, Barnes and Dumond, *Letters*, 899.

14   Letter from Louisa Adams to Sarah Grimké, 1838, *Beehive Archives*. Louisa Ad-
      ams wrote a long letter to Sarah Grimké echoing some of Sarah's arguments in
      her *Letters*.

15   At this time, the Library of Congress was housed in the Capitol Building.

16   Sarah to Elizabeth Pease, Weld-Grimké Family Papers, Clements Lib. Sarah
      writes "In speaking of the case, T remarks, 'The effect on the slaveholders has
      been perfectly confounding. They have resorted to every artifice and device to
      put him down, threats and fury, questions of order, motions to lay on the table,
      refusals to adjourn in order to tire him out, starting up with explanations and
      under the pretext of explaining going into harangues, invectives and accusa-
      tions against him, etc. but all in vain. The Old Nestor has cast all their counsels
      headlong, turned all their guns against themselves, smiting the whole host with
      dismay and discomfiture. The slaveholders feel that their end draweth near.'"

17   Charley would now be about 26 months old, while Thodie is not quite one year.

18   Perry, *Lift Up*, 204—205. Perry notes that on one occasion, Angelina had locked
      Charley in a closet, and hearing of it, Theodore had wondered at the loss of her
      temper. He recommended trying to subdue Charley's temper, but knew that it
      would not be helpful for Angelina to lose hers. He was also concerned about
      Charley "handling himself" and Angelina responded by sewing up the front flap
      of his pants.

19   Theodore to Angelina and Sarah, 1.15.42 and 4.17.42, Barnes and Dumond, *Let-
      ters*, 884, 892. This response from Theodore draws from parts of these two letters
      he wrote.

20   It seems that this is the same Stephen who had been a slave in the Grimké house-hold when Angelina and Henry were young. Although he had been freed, Anna and later, the Welds, seem to feel responsibility for providing a home for him.

21   Gerrit's wife was Ann Fitzhugh, but usually went by her nickname, Nancy.

22   Sarah to Jane Smith 2.19.1847 (year is difficult to read), *Weld-Grimké Family Papers*, Clements Lib. New Addition Box 1:17. This entire scene is drawn closely from her lengthy description in this letter.,

23   Sarah to Jane Smith, Weld-Grimké Family Papers, Clements Lib. New Addition Box 1:17. Sarah's describes their effort to reach the house through the snow and the welcome of their hosts in detail.

24   Sarah to Jane Smith, Weld-Grimké Family Papers, Clements Lib. New Addition Box 1:17.

25   Letters to Harriot Hunt 8:22.1948 and 10.19.1848, Weld-Grimké Family Papers, Clements Lib. Box 9. The essence of this fictional conversation is contained in several letters that Sarah wrote to Harriot around this time.

26   Letters to Harriot Hunt 8:22.1948 and 10.19.1848, Weld-Grimké Family Papers, Clements Lib. Box 9. Several times in letters Sarah refers to matters that she doesn't feel free to speak of. It is not clear what those were, but earlier Theodore had complained of Charley "handling himself" and seemed to have a typically puritanical attitude to this. This attitude may have affected Thodie as well, or Thodie may already have shown symptoms of whatever psychological distress later afflicted him. But it could have been a variety of private family issues.

27   Letters to Harriot Hunt. 10.19.1848, Weld-Grimké Family Papers, Clements Lib. Box 9. Sarah does broach this subject in her letter to Harriot, using similar language.

28   Lerner, *Grimké Sisters of SC*. Ch. 18, Loc 3473–81. Gerda Lerner mentions vis-its of Bronson Alcott, Henry David Thoreau, Nathaniel Hawthorne, and Ralph Waldo Emerson to the Weld's later school Eagleswood, at Raritan Bay, NJ. That would have been in the mid-to late-1850s. There is no mention of them visiting the Belleville School, but I have transposed their later visits to Belleville in 1850. Thoreau helped with some surveying at Raritan Bay, and "participated in . . .. one of the Saturday dances, for which everyone—children, parents, teachers and guests—turned out."

29   Sarah to Harriot Hunt, 10.19.48, Weld-Grimké Family Papers, Clements Lib. Box 9. The skating and dancing the Virginia Reel that are mentioned in this chapter seem to have been features of life at Belleville around this time.

30   This is Mary Anna's son, Lew Haskell, not to be confused with Louis Weld, son of Charles Stuart Weld, a generation later.

31   Lerner, *Grimké Sisters of SC*. Ch 18. Many of these sentiments and those that follow were expressed in two unpublished essays of Sarah's, "The Education of Women" and "Marriage" which she wrote around this period or a few years later. They are available at Weld-Grimké Family Papers, Clements Lib. Box 18. "Marriage" also appears in an appendix to Lerner's book.

32   Bronson Alcott's wife, Abigail May Alcott, was the sister of Reverend Samuel May, a fellow abolitionist.

33   Anna Frost's marriage to Llewellyn Haskell ended in divorce. She remarried Joel Hall in 1865. Given the fact that they had nine children together, and given the social stigma of divorce in the late nineteenth century, she must have indeed been very unhappy and/or very liberated in her views of what marriage should be.

34   Sarah to Harriot Hunt 10.19.48. Weld-Grimké Family Papers, Clements Lib.

35   The Weld family seemed to have visited the Smiths in Peterboro, NY several times, since Theodore's brother Greenleaf lived in nearby Cazenovia. In the summer of 1851 the boys are there with Aunt Sarah. In the summer of 1853, the three children were in Saratoga Springs, but I have shifted the events of 1853 back to Peterboro, instead of Saratoga Springs, because more of their "familiar" friends were there.

36   Gerrit Smith and his wife, Ann (Nancy), were among the wealthiest families in New York at the time, although they lived quite simply, and used much of their wealth to support abolitionists and to help re-settle fugitive slaves. Their home estate was a station on the Underground Railroad and the whole Peterboro/Cazenovia area was known as an abolitionist center and a safe haven for fugitive slaves. Harriet Tubman brought ex-slaves there and visited the couple in their home. She eventually settled near Auburn, about 50 miles away.

37   Greene was born in 1842, just three years before his sister Elizabeth Smith Miller's son, Gerrit Smith Miller or Gatty, was born in 1845. So he was just three years older than his nephew. Both boys were educated at the schools run by Angelina and Theodore, and both went to Harvard for a time. Greene became a noted ornithologist, while Gatty had a considerable public career.

38   Passed in 1850, the Fugitive Slave Law required that northern states enforce the arrest and return of fugitive slaves to their owners, even though slavery was illegal in those states. Officers of the law were expected to enforce this return, although many refused. It was highly unpopular in the North, but remained the law until well into the Civil War.

39   Angelina to Sarah, August 1853, Weld-Grimké Family Papers, Clements Lib. Box, 10. This letter is largely verbatim from Angelina's letter.

40   Thodie to Sarah Grimké, 8.53, Weld-Grimké Family Papers, Clements Lib. Box, 10.

41   Angelina to Theodore 9.2.53, Weld-Grimké Family Papers, Clements Lib. Box, 10. This letter is also largely reproduced here verbatim with an occasional paraphrase.

42   Letter from Angelina to Sarah, 9.1.53, Weld-Grimké Family Papers, Clements Lib. Box, 10. Paraphrase.

43   Both sisters continue to wear the bloomer costumes for the next year or two, at least when they were at home or at the home of friends. Sarah wore a regular dress when she was traveling in public areas.

44   Angelina to Harriot Hunt, M.D. 10.10.1853 (year unclear but contents indicate it must have been 1853). *Letters of Theodore Dwight Weld*, Library of Congress. The essential points of this conversation were recorded in a letter that Angelina wrote to Harriot Hunt around this time. It is interesting to note that both Angelina and Sarah treated Harriot Hunt as a confidante. I have put the opinions expressed into this conversation with Theodore.

45   Theodore's mother, Elizabeth Weld, had been sick for some time, as had her husband. She died sometime in the early fall, 1853.

46 Angelina to Sarah, 12.2.53 and 12.7.53, Weld-Grimké Family Papers, Clements Lib. Box, 10.

47 Sarah G Weld to Sarah Grimké, 12.7.52, Weld-Grimké Family Papers, Clements Lib. Box, 10. The basic sentiments expressed here are in Sissy's letter, but it has been paraphrased and expanded considerably.

48 See note 37 about the Fugitive Slave Act.

49 Sarah did publish an English translation of Lamartine's *Jeanne d'Arc* in 1867. However, she had loved this book since her young adult years and it is not inconceivable that she would have started on its translation years before completing and publishing it.

50 Letter from Angelina to Sarah Grimké, 1854, no date, but sometime between March and May '54, Weld-Grimké Family Papers, Clements Lib. Box, 10. Letter has "hypercritical" but "hypocritical" seems to fit her meaning better.

51 Sarah returned home sometime between late March and mid-May 1954. On March 26th, Angelina wrote a letter sharply refusing Sarah's offer to come and watch the children for a time while Angelina went away for a few days or weeks. But by May 31st Sarah is back at Belleville and had visited Raritan Bay for the first time. Angelina's conciliatory letter (there may have been two but only one remains) must have been written between those two events. Sarah's response is not extant either.

52 Perry, *Lift Up*, 206. Sarah to Angelina, date unknown.

53 Lerner, *Grimké Sisters of SC*. Ch 18. The family had not yet moved there but Angelina decided to bring Sarah there to show it to her. There was an existing large house where they were staying with friends (probably the Springs, founders of the Raritan Bay Union). There was construction going on for the new stone school building, which was to include family flats, student dormitory, classrooms, dining hall and parlors.

54 Micah 6:8. *Bible*, King James Version.

55 An article about the school entitled "Manahatta" appeared in *Fraser's Magazine* in 1865. The author had been invited to the July 4th festivities at Eagleswood in 1861 or 1862 and records the essence of this speech as well as many of the colorful details on the school itself, its students, and the young women rowing the barge and swimming in the bay.

56 In mid-1861, the Weld children were all young adults: Charles would have been 21, Thodie or Theo, 20, and Sarah 17. Gerrit (Gatty) Smith Miller would have been about 16. Thodie had been sick for several years and continued to have a mysterious "illness" that seemed to have no permanent cure and left him lethargic and apparently without ambition—continuing through most of his adulthood. We can only guess whether it was a form of mental illness such as depression or adolescent–onset schizophrenia, or some poorly-understood physical disease. This was a great sadness for the family. Charles Stuart was finishing his studies at Harvard and Sarah appears to have been studying music and French and perhaps attending various other lectures in East Cambridge.

57 There does not seem to be any historical record that is clear about Thodie's ailment. Various unorthodox treatments were attempted with little or no success. Whatever it was, it was poorly enough understood that there seemed no obvious

cure. For a period, he worked on a farm in Maine where he seemed more at ease. He lived with his brother Charles for a time but by 1900 was institutionalized at the Westborough Insane Hospital in Massachusetts.

58   *Fraser's Magazine,* "Manahatta," 1865. The essence of this speech by an Eagles-wood student was reported in this article. In 1861, Lincoln still argued that the war was to preserve the Union, not to end slavery, and it would be the following year before the Emancipation Proclamation was even drafted. But northern abolitionists would, nevertheless, have seen the war as a war to end slavery .

59   H. Millard, published by H. de Marsan. In Library of Congress American Song Sheets Collection (public domain). This was a popular national song of the time. The article in *Fraser's* notes that this song as well as the *Star Spangled Banner* were sung by the assembled students and guests at the 1861 celebration that the author attended.

60   The second verse continues:

To all her heroes, Justice and Fame, To all her foes, a traitor's foul name;
Our "Stars and Stripes" still proudly shall wave, Emblem of Liberty, flag of the brave,
United we stand, divided we fall, Gladly we'll die at our country's call.

61   Sarah Grimké to Sissy Weld, 1861. *Weld-Grimké Family Papers,* Clements Lib., New Addition. The ideas behind this exchange, including Sarah's comment about a man not being able to sound the depths of a woman's heart or to write Jane Eyre, are contained in this letter.

62   Gerrit Smith did help abolitionist John Brown financially. It is not clear if he knew or fully understood the extent of Brown's plan for a violent uprising of slaves in order to gain their freedom.

63   Sissy would be about 24 at this time.

64   The name is fictional, but the Weld's did have a single housekeeper who later nursed the sisters as the famIly aged, replacIng Betsy who would probably have died or been infirm by this time.

65   Sarah is wearing spectacles regularly now. She is nearly 75 years old.

66   Perry, *Lift Up,* 228. Text of this letter is verbatim as published with only minor edits . I have added Selina Simmons' and Montague's given names for clarification, and edited parts of the letter for the sake of brevity.

67   Bruce, *Archibald,* 24–25. Angelina and Charles had traveled to Lincoln University to meet the young men at commencement time in 1868. So their visit to Boston in the fall of 1868 was not their first encounter, but Sarah, Theodore and Sissy had not yet met them.

68   Birney, *Grimké Sisters,* 168. Many of the details described in this chapter are recorded by Birney. I have added some details and dialogue and elaborated on the events, but the essential elements are historical. Birney states, "The 7th of March, the day of the election, a terrific snowstorm prevailed, but did not prevent the women from assembling in the hotel near the place of voting, where each one was presented, on the part of their gentlemen friends, with a beautiful bouquet of flowers . . . A number of these gentlemen came over to the hotel and escorted the ladies to the polls, where a convenient place for them to vote had been arranged. There was a great crowd, eager to see the joke of women voting, and many were ready to jeer and hiss. But when the women filed by, led by Sarah Grimké and

Angelina Weld, the laugh was checked, the intended jeer unuttered, and deafening applause was given instead."

69   Sissy and William moved first to Springfield, MA, then to Kansas, and eventually to Benton Harbor, MI where they remained until her death. It appears that after she had Angelina, she had two child die in infancy, then gave birth to her son, Theodore who survived.

70   Bruce, *Archibald*, 28. Archie started at Harvard Law in 1872–73, graduating in 1874. Frank started at Howard about 1873.

71   Bruce, *Archibald*, 29. George Ruffin, another African American, graduated from Harvard Law in 1869, shortly before Archie and James Wolff did.

72   Perry, *Lift Up*, Chapter 11. This scene, like the mock vote scene and Sarah's collecting clothes for the South, are both based closely on real events.

73   Birney, *Grimké Sisters*, 172- 73. Nearly all this letter is verbatim from Sarah's last letter to Sarah Douglass which was indeed dictated to Charles Stuart. It was written in the fall, probably around mid-October 1873.

74   This child was Angelina Grimké Hamilton, another namesake of Angelina Grimké Weld's, who grows up to become a physician practicing first in Idaho, then in Michigan, where she was the main physician at the state mental hospital until her death in 1947.

75   Ellie Wright appears in the Fourth of July scene at Eagleswood as the girl questioning Gatty Miller.

76   Birney, *Grimké Sisters*, 174–75. Most of this is verbatim from Rev. Williams' eulogy on the occasion.

77   Abzug, *Passionate Liberator*, 294. These words and other details of the funeral are described by Abzug.

78   Bruce, *Archibald*, 29. James Wolff was also colored, probably mixed race. He was among the several colored students admitted to Harvard Law at approximately the same time as Archibald. Cyrus Heizer was white. According to Bruce, when a white southern student refused to sit with Archie in the common dining room at Harvard, he "was quickly joined. . . by two other white students, one of whom, Cyrus W Heizer, was to become a lifelong friend, in an ostentatious rejection of their southern colleague's bigotry."

79   Perry, *Lift Up*, Ch. 11, describes Archie as having an active social life at this time, and meeting and becoming friends with many of the people mentioned in this scene, including Frederick Douglass. This is a fictionalized version of one of the "dinners and receptions" he attended during this time.

80   Parker Pillsbury, a well-known abolitionist, was Frances Pillsbury's brother-in-law, so would have known Archie and Frank through their connection to her.

81   Bruce, *Archibald*, 34–35. Ellen (Nelly) Bradford Stebbins (1851–1950) and Archie were romantically involved for several years until her family left Boston c. 1877. She was back in Boston by the time of Archie's marriage to Sarah Stanley and she attended their wedding with Archie's classmate and friend, Cyrus Heizer. In 1881 she married Solomon Stebbins who was 21 years her senior. They had four children. Nelly lived to be 99, and one of her daughters lived until 1981.

82   Bruce, *Archibald*, 34. Although this picnic is fictional, Bruce speaks of Nelly, Cyrus, and Archie spending time in the country together, and Nelly related her memories of a boat trip up the Charles with Archie, Frank and one of her aunts.

83   John Reeve's Presbyterian Church was in Philadelphia at this time, but I've placed it in Washington, DC because that was where Charlotte Forten was working in the U.S. Treasury Department at this time, and where Frank worked at 15th St. Presbyterian Church as young ministry student c. 1876. He may not have run into her until about that time.

84   This is a fictional encounter, but they must have reconnected sometime around this period. It would have been the first time she had seen him in about 8 years and he had grown into a well-dressed, mature-looking twenty-four-year old, now several inches taller than she. She is petite, dressed well, if conservatively, and is lively and animated. Frank Grimké, was 13 years younger than Charlotte.

85   Perry, *Lift Up*, Ch. 12.

86   James Monroe Trotter was a veteran of the MA 55th regiment during the Civil War. He and his brother later married the Isaac sisters and both couples settled in Boston. Virginia Isaacs Trotter, James' wife, was descended from the Hemings family, and was most likely a descendant of Thomas Jefferson through his son. They are the parents of William Monroe Trotter, who was born in 1872 and who continued his father's black activism. However, William was 23 years younger than Archibald.

87   Bruce, *Archibald*, 34. Lillie Buffum Chace, an attractive, intelligent, young white woman like Nelly Bradford, was also a friend of Archibald's in this period, and they spent time together, although it is not clear that there was ever serious romance between them. She was about two years older than him. She had attended the Lewis School for Girls where Theodore and Angelina Weld taught and was the daughter of abolitionist Elizabeth Buffum Chace.

88   Helen is a fictional character. She would be colored but light-skinned (probably bi-racial) like her brother. .

89   Perry, *Lift Up*, 257. The essence of this letter is recounted by Perry.

90   MC Stanley to Archie 2.20.79, Grimké-Weld-Stanley Early Papers, MSRC, HU, Box 39–3:74. This letter is mostly verbatim with minor edits.

91   Bruce, *Archibald*, 38 and Perry, *Lift Up*, 37. The wedding was "a simple ceremony at a friend's house on Beacon Hill." In a later letter Archie refers to it as taking place at 32 Mt. Vernon St. Lucy Stone, Nelly Bradford and Cyrus Heizer attended. We don't know exactly who else attended but this is a realistic guess. There is no record of Frank or their mother, Nancy, attending. It is unlikely that they did, since it would have been a long trip for them. Angelina was still alive but very sick and would die by the following Christmas.

92   Nelly would marry Solomon Stebbins, 20 years older than her, the following year (1881).

93   Sarah uses this language in a letter to Archie shortly after their wedding, 5.29.79, Grimké-Weld-Stanley Early Papers Box 29–3:76.,

94   Birney, *Grimké Sisters*, 311–313 and in Theodore Weld, "In Memory Angelina Grimké Weld" (Boston, 1880) Some of the details of her last few days are recounted in these works. See also Abzug, *Passionate*, 268–269.

95 Note from Sarah Weld to Theodore, Weld-Grimké Family Papers, Clements Lib. New Addition. These words were in a note Sarah sent to her father around this time.

96 Most likely she was named in honor of Frank's uncle by marriage, Theodore Weld. If so, it is evidence of Frank's love and respect for him.

97 Psalm 30:5. *Bible*. King James Version.

98 Archie's partner at the *Hub*, Butler Wilson.

99 Sarah to Archie, 1.11.85 from Detroit Grimké-Weld-Stanley Early Papers, Box 39–3:78. In correspondence several years after their initial separation, Sarah refers to this "good fairy" in the following way. "And allow me, now, to most solemnly warn you that the one you call your good fairy is your evil genius, in that she prompts you to seek *Fame* and *Power*, instead of *Peace* and *Goodwill*. The *Earthly*, instead of the *Celestial*." So, while this letter is fictional, Archie's use of the phrase "my good fairy" is historical. In the original version of this (fictional) letter—which has been placed in the drawer, the "both" is not readable because it and several other words are covered with an ink blot. There is no certainty as to who it refers to, but Nelly is a likely candidate given their friendship and ongoing correspondence. Still there is no evidence to support any illicit affair between Archie and Nelly, or with anyone else.

100 Archibald to Sarah Grimké, undated but c. 1884, Grimké-Weld-Stanley Early Papers, MSRC, HU, Box 39–3:81. Correspondence between Archie and Sarah after their separation indicates that a Mrs. Stuart in Hyde Park had befriended Sarah, that Archie believed Mrs. Stuart had undue influence on Sarah, and that she, for whatever reason, encouraged Sarah's suspicions and unhappiness with Archie, leading to their separation.

101 Most of the children would be white, but a few could be colored or mixed race. Hyde Park was home to the Trotters, who were colored, and it is possible there were other middle-class colored families living in the area as it seems to have been a very liberal, welcoming place.

102 William Monroe Trotter grows up to be an important activist for colored rights like his father, and a leader in the opposition to the conciliatory policies of Booker T. Washington. Although he was more than 20 years younger than Archibald Grimké, they were both friends and opponents in later years, as Archibald had been with his father. Both were instrumental in the early years of the NAACP and in the various movements for colored rights in the early 20th century.

103 Archie's letter to Rev. M.C. Stanley, May 1883(?), Weld-Stanley-Grimké Early Papers, MSRC, HU, Box 39–3:76. Archie discusses his perception of how Mrs. Stuart had influenced Sarah against him using this theory.

104 Weld-Stanley-Grimké Early Papers, MSRC, HU, Box 39–3.78) In a letter to Archibald of 1.11.85, Sarah says she would like to have "the old melodian" indicating that they had one in their home prior to her departure.

105 "Frederick Douglass." Wikipedia. https//en.wikipedia.org

106 Several of Douglass' remarks at this dinner are borrowed from some of his most famous sayings. I have taken the liberty of putting a number of them into this setting. See https://en.wikipedia.org

107   The separation took place in May 1883 and the ensuing exchange of letters took place over several years from 1883 to 1887.

108   Weld-Stanley-Grimké Early Papers, MSRC, HU, Box 39-3:74–81. This and the following excerpts from the correspondence are all largely verbatim with minor edits for clarity.

109   AG to MC Stanley May 1883?(date is unclear), Weld-Stanley-Grimké Early Papers, MSRC, HU Box 39:3:79.

110   Letter from MC Stanley to Archie 5.22.83, Weld-Stanley-Grimké Early Papers, MSRC, HU, Box 39-3:74.

111   Archie to Sarah Stanley Grimké (Not clear where this fits into the previous letter, or if it is a fragment of another letter from earlier), Weld-Stanley-Grimké Early Papers, MSRC, HU, Box 39-3:81.

112   Sarah Stanley Grimké to Archie, 9.22.84, Weld-Stanley-Grimké Early Papers, , HU, Box 39-3:81.

113   Sarah Stanley Grimké to Archie, 1.11.85, Weld-Stanley-Grimké Early Papers, MSRC, HU, Box 39-3:81. The remainder of this letter is from 4.25.87.

114   Sarah Stanley Grimké to Archie 4.25.87, Weld-Stanley-Grimké Early Papers, MSRC, HU, Box 39-3:79. .

115   It is Christmas afternoon about 15 months before Theodore's death.

116   *Macbeth* Act II, Sc. II.

117   *Merchant of Venice*, Act II. scene 1.

118   Abzug. *Passionate,* 300–301.

119   This group is mentioned in the contemporary newspaper account of the funeral in the Norfolk County Gazette, February 9, 1895.

120   It is not clear if Sissy made it to the funeral, although it is hard to imagine her missing it if she had been well. It is likely that she was ill herself. There is no mention of her or her family in the account. Nor is there mention of Thodie Weld, who may have been hospitalized by this time.

121   Nancy died shortly after Theodore, on Feb 23, 1895, at Frank's home in Washington, DC. She was 84 years of age.

122   Perry, *Lift Up,* 313 and Bruce, *Archibald,* 75–76. This scene takes place just a few weeks after the death of Frank and Archibald's mother, Nancy Weston, who was living with Frank in DC at the time. It is also just a few weeks since the funeral for their uncle by marriage, Theodore Weld. Nana is now living with her Uncle Francis Grimké and his wife, Charlotte Forten, at their well-appointed pastor's home in Washington, DC. Nana is already struggling with her sexual identity.

123   Perry, *Lift Up,* 313. These are mostly Nana's own words as written in a letter to a "Mamie." It has often been assumed that this was Mamie Burrill, a close friend, who later publicly identified as a lesbian. However, in *The Grimkés Legacy,* Greenidge indicates it was to a different "Mamie," Mary Edith Karn, with whom Nana had a close relationship while at Northfield Academy.

124   Archie to Frank's household, 1895. Weld-Stanley-Grimké Early Papers, MSRC, HU, Box 39-3:81.

125   Archie to Nana, 6.19.95, Weld-Stanley-Grimké Early Papers, MSRC, HU, Box 39–3:81. This letter is edited for brevity but largely verbatim, with the addition of the suggestion about going to Northfield which is found in later letters.

126   The gift of the bicycle is fictional.

127   By 1903, Nana was 23 years old. Archie was about 54 at this time, Frank about 53, and Lottie around 67.

128   Nana's diary, 1903, Angelina Weld Grimké Collection, MSRC, HU, Diaries, box 38–15, folder 249. Much of this and what follows is verbatim or paraphrased from Nana's diary manuscript.

129   There has been some debate about whether the object of Nana's romantic love at this time was a man or a woman but a careful reading of her diary manuscript makes it almost certain that it was a man, who unfortunately, did not seem to seriously reciprocate her passion.

130   Sarah Stanley died in San Diego, California in 1898, it appears from self-administered poison. Nana would have been about 18, but had not seen her mother since she was seven.

131   Angelina Weld Grimké Collection, MSRC, HU, Diaries, box 38–15, folder 249. Much of this scene was experienced first-hand by Nana and her father and described in her diary of 1903.

132   This is William Monroe Trotter, son of James and Virginia Trotter of Hyde Park, the same young man whom Archie had met as a teen when he took Nana on the sled in Hyde Park. He was about twenty years younger than Archie.

133   Nana's Diary, 6.03 to 8.03, Angelina Weld Grimké Collection, MSRC, HU, Diaries, box 38–15, folder 249. It is not clear that Frank and Lottie attended this event, although Lottie, at least, was in Boston at the time, according to Nana's diary entry of July 22. She mentions going to the Grants' house with Uncle Frank, Aunt Lottie, and her father sometime between August 18 and August 21. I have taken the liberty of placing them at the event.

134   Quoted in Rudwick "Race Leadership Struggle: Background of the Boston Riot of 1903," *The Journal of Negro Education* 31:1, 16–24.

135   Nana's Diary, 6.03 to 8.03, Angelina Weld Grimké Collection, MSRC, HU, Diaries, box 38–15, folder 249. This scene combines several social gatherings that happened in the week of August 14th to August 21st, all of which Nana reports on in her diary. All the guests mentioned were at one or several of these events. One of these was a birthday celebration for Archie and Aunt Lottie on Aug 17th, so I have included that in this scene.

136   James M. Trotter, father of William Monroe and Maude, passed away in 1892, but his wife Virginia survived him.

137   She is mentioned as having the same birthday as Archie and Lottie and celebrating with them. I'm assuming this is the same Mrs. Day that Archie corresponded with while in the Dominican Republic, and who helped arrange for Nana to go to Northfield Academy. Archie called her Nana's "fairy godmother," although Nana doesn't refer to her much.

138   Nana's Diary, 6.03 to 8.03, Angelina Weld Grimké Collection, MSRC, HU, Diaries, box 38–15, folder 249. Dirier, a young woman, and Mon (Monroe?), a

young man, are mentioned several times in Nana's diary with no surnames and no other identifier.

139 It is not clear if this song would have been widely known in 1903. According to Wikipedia, the melody of "Happy Birthday to You" comes from the song "Good Morning to All," which has been attributed to American sisters Patty and Mildred J. Hill In 1893. The combination of melody and lyrics in "Happy Birthday to You" first appeared in print in 1912, and probably existed even earlier.

140 Nana's Diary, 6.03 to 8.03, Angelina Weld Grimké Collection, MSRC, HU, Diaries, box 38-15, folder 249. According to Nana's diary entry of August 18, 1903, Frank did preach a sermon that night at St. Mark's in Boston. The text below however is taken from a set of four sermons he'd given about five years earlier (c. 1898) in D.C. in opposition to Booker T. Washington's accommodationist speech at the Cotton States International Exhibition in Atlanta on May 18, 1895. See Perry, *Lift Up*, Chapter 14.

141 Most of what follows is verbatim from Frank's earlier speeches on this topic, quoted in Mark Perry, *Lift Up Thy Voice*, Chapter 14. See also *The Works of Francis J. Grimké*, Carter G. Woodson, Ed., The Associated Publishers, Washington, D.C., 1942, pp. 247—390.

142 Woodson, Ed. *The Works of Francis J. Grimké*, 254.

143 Woodson, Ed. *The Works of Francis J. Grimké*, 258.

144 John Fawcett, 1782. Public domain.

145 Mrs. Cooper had been forced to resign as principal in 1906 because of controversy over the high academic standards she insIsted upon for the school. Her resignation was fueled by the DC School Board desire to impose a more "manual," less-demanding curriculum on the school, and by rumors of impropriety because of a male teacher who boarded at her home. This was John Love who, along with his sister, were her foster children. Miss Love in this scene is likely his sister, although I couldn't find any confirmation of that, and Nana's diary is confusing, just calling her "Love" and in another place "Love Percy." Mamie Burrill was teaching at the school at this time, but Mrs. Cooper would not have been there in 1909. However, she does return as a Latin teacher in 1910 and remains through 1929. I've taken the liberty of placing her there in 1909. She was about 20 years older than Mamie and Nana.

146 Nana's Diary, 1909, Angelina Weld Grimké Collection, MSRC, HU, Diaries, box 38-15. Most of the two scenes that follow (at school and in the restaurant) are described in detail in Nana's diary, including the dialogue. A student described her as an excellent teacher but sometimes "sardonic and sarcastic." See Robinson, *The M Street High School*, 127.

147 Nana's diary,1909, Angelina Weld Grimké Collection, MSRC, HU, Diaries, box 38-15. In it she refers to her friend simply as "Love." It is evident from Anna Julia Cooper's "Reminiscenes" in *Personal Recollections*, that she was Miss Love, the sister of John Love, who were part of the Cooper-Grimké circle of friends.

148 Angelina Weld Grimké Collection, MSRC, HU, box 38-10, folders. 150—174. Public domain. *Surrender* was later published in *Caroling Dusk*, New York: Harper and Row, 1927 and it is also published in Herron's anthology, *Selected Works of Angelina Weld Grimké*.

149 Nana's diary, 1909, Angelina Weld Grimké Collection, MSRC, HU, Diaries, box 38–15. Nana describes exactly what they ate at the restaurant that night, saying the meal took about one and a half hours.

150 Nana's diary, 1909, Angelina Weld Grimké Collection, MSRC, HU, Diaries, box 38–15. In her diary entry about this scene, she walks Love to her house near Dupont Circle where Mrs. Cooper had her home at 1706 17th Street. Since this was several years after the criticism of Mrs. Cooper for the impropriety of having a male boarder (Percy Love's brother, John Love), it is not clear whether Mrs. Cooper still lived there with them. Later she had a home in the LeDroit Park neighborhood. And in any case, she didn't return to Washington until 1910. So this last scene is almost entirely fictional, except that we know that Georgia Douglas Johnson and Nana must have met around this time, and that they became close friends, both poets and playwrights, interested in common literary themes.

151 Georgia's husband died in 1925 but even before that her home became a "salon" for Washington's wIng of the Harlem Renaissance. Nana and she remained friends for many years. I have not seen any evidence of their having a romantic or sexual relationship, but here she is a "stand in" for the women to whom Nana continued to be attracted and who inspire the imagery in her poems.

152 Nana's diary for 1909–1911, Angelina Weld Grimké Collection, MSRC, HU. Diaries, box 38–10, folders,150—174.

153 Nana's diary from end of 1911–1912, Angelina Weld Grimké Collection, MSRC, HU. Diaries, box 38–15, folder 250.

154 Herron in her introduction to the *Selected Works* writes: "Grimké declared that *Rachel* had been written to educate whites and to correct their attitudes about lynching and its effects on African Americans. The play is about a young African American woman who prefers to forego both marriage and motherhood so as not to provide whites with more black people to destroy through lynching and other racial atrocities."

155 Nana's play, *Rachel* or *Blessed are the Barren,* was produced first by the NAACP in Washington, DC in 1916. It was produced in 1917 at the Neighborhood Playhouse, at that time in the Lower Eastside of New York, and finally in Cambridge, MA. It was the first time a theater in the United States presented a play by a black author with a black cast before an integrated audience. It opened on April 25, 1917. For dramatic purposes I have shifted its appearance to a time preceding the 1913 Suffrage March. Georgia Johnson and Mary (Mamie) Burrill also had plays with anti-lynching themes produced between 1919 and the late 20's, and along with Angelina Weld Grimké, were considered early expressions of the Harlem Renaissance of the 1920s and '30s.

156 A.W. Grimké, *Rachel.* This excerpt is faithful to the printed version but with minor edits for brevity and clarity.

157 "The Woman Suffrage Parade of 1913," Wikipedia. "Officially the Woman Suffrage Procession, was the first suffragist parade in Washington, D.C. Organized by the suffragist Alice Paul for the National American Woman Suffrage Association, thousands of suffragists marched down Pennsylvania Avenue in Washington, D.C. on March 3, 1913 . . . . The march and the attention it attracted were monumental in advancing women's suffrage in the United States. Plans for the

march were threatened when black suffragists announced they intended to participate, which lead white southern suffragists to threaten to boycott the event One solution discussed was segregating the black suffragists in a separate section to mollify white southern delegates. The parade itself was led by labor lawyer Inez Milholland, dressed dramatically in white and mounted on a white horse, and included nine bands, five mounted brigades, 26 floats, and close to 8,000 marchers.

158   "The Woman Suffrage Parade of 1913." Wikipedia. "Some black people did march with state delegations. A group from Howard University participated in the parade. Some sources allege that Black women were segregated at the back of the parade; however, contemporary sources suggest that they marched with their respective state delegations or professional groups."

159   Lyrics by James Oppenheim, "Bread and Roses," *The American Magazine*, December 1911. In the public domain.

Bibliography

Manuscript Collections

Grimké, Archibald, and Francis Grimké. The Letters and Papers of the Grimké Brothers. The Grimké Family Collection. Moorland-Spingarn Research Center of Howard University (MSRC).

Grimké, Angelina Weld. Angelina Weld Grimké Collection. The Grimké Family Collection. Moorland-Spingarn Research Center of Howard University (MSRC). Series G—diaries, box 38-15.

Grimké Personal Papers. Library of Congress. Washington, DC.

The Liberator (newspaper on microfilm) from 1836 to 1866. Library of Congress, Washington, DC.

Stanley, Sarah, and Archibald Grimké. Grimké-Weld-Stanley Early Papers. Moorland-Spingarn Research Center of Howard University (MSRC).

Theodore Dwight Weld Papers. Library of Congress. Washington, DC.

Weld-Grimké Family Papers, 1740–1930 (majority within 1825–1899), including 2012 Addition. The William L. Clements Library. University of Michigan, Ann Arbor, MI. This collection includes correspondence, diaries, personal and published papers, photographs, and memorabilia.

Books and Articles

Abzug, Robert H. *Passionate Liberator: Theodore Dwight Weld and the Dilemma of Reform*. New York: Oxford University Press, 1980.

Adams, Louisa. "Letter from Louisa Catherine Adams to Sarah Grimké, 1838." Massachusetts Historical Society, *Beehive Archives*.

"African Americans in South Carolina." Wikipedia. https://en.m.wikipedia.org.

Birney, Catherine H. *The Grimké Sisters—Sarah and Angelina Grimké: The First American Women Advocates of Abolition and Woman's Rights*. Washington, DC, Lee and Shepard, 1885. Reprint by Greenwood Press, 1969. Reprint by Hard Press, 2014.

Bruce, Dickson D., Jr. *Archibald Grimké: Portrait of a Black Independent*. Louisiana State University Press, 1993.

Barnes and Dumond. *Letters of Theodore Dwight Weld, Angelina Grimké Weld and Sarah Grimké: 1822—1844*. Gloucester, MA: Peter Smith, 1965. Original edition published 1934 by American Historical Association.

Bushkovitch, Mary. *The Grimkés of Charleston*. Greenville, SC: Southern Historical Press, 1992.

Ceplair, Larry, Ed. *The Public Years of Sarah and Angelina Grimké: Selected Writings: 1835–1839*. New York: Columbia University Press, 1989.

Chapman, Maria. "The Times that Try Men's Souls." In Stanton et al., *The History of Women's Suffrage*, quoted in Barnes and Dumond, 91.

Cooper, Anna Julia. "Reminiscences." In Personal Recollections of the Grimké Family. Available in Digital Archive, Howard University.

"Charlotte Forten Grimké." Wikipedia. https://en.wikipedia.org/wiki/Charlotte_Forten_Grimk%C3%A9.

Ferry, Henry Justin. *Francis Grimké*. Ph.D. Diss., Yale University, 1970. University Microfilms, 1992.

Forten, Charlotte. "Life on the Sea Islands." *The Atlantic*, May-June 1864. http://www.theatlantic.com/magazine/archive/1864/06/life-on-the-sea-islands-continued/308759/.

"Gilbert Pillsbury." Wikipedia. https://en.wikipedia.org/wiki/Gilbert_Pillsbury.

Greenidge, Kerri. *The Grimkés: The Legacy of Slavery in an American Family*. New York: Liveright, 2022.

Grimké, Angelina E. *Letters to Christian Women of the South*. New York: American Antislavery Society, August 1836.

——. *Letters to Catherine Beecher*. Boston: Isaac Knopf, 1838.

——. *Appeal to the Women of the Nominally-Free States*. New York: William S. Dorr, 1837 and Isaac Knopf, 1838. (Angelina with Lydia Child and Grace Douglass.)

Grimké, Angelina Weld. *Rachel*. Originally published by The Cornhill Company, Boston, 1920. Reprinted by London: Oberon Modern Plays, 2014.

——. *Selected Works of Angelina Weld Grimké*. Edited by Carolivia Herron. Oxford: Oxford University Press, 1991.

Grimké, Francis. Quoted in "Race Leadership Struggle: Background of the Boston Riot of 1903." Elliott M. Rudwick. *The Journal of Negro Education* 31:1 (Winter 1962) 16–24.

Grimké, Francis. *The Works of Francis J. Grimké*. Edited by Carter Woodson. The Associated Publishers, Washington, DC, 1942.

Grimké, Sarah. *An Epistle to the Clergy of the Southern States*. New York: American Antislavery Society, December 1836. The Cornell University Library Digital Collections, 2014.

——. *Letters on the Equality of the Sexes*. Boston: Isaac Knopf, 1838. Reprinted by Forgotten Books, 2012.

——. "The Education of Women" and "Marriage" Unpublished. Available at *Weld-Grimké Family Papers*, The William L. Clements Library. University of Michigan, Ann Arbor, MI. Box 18.

Hacker, David. "A Census-Based Count of Civil War Dead." *Civil War History*, 2011.

Lerner, Gerda. *The Grimké Sisters from South Carolina: Rebels Against Slavery*. Boston: Houghton Mifflin Co, 1967. Reprinted Chapel Hill: University of North Carolina Press, 1998, 2004.

Lumpkin, Katharine Du Pre. *The Emancipation of Angelina Grimké*. Chapel Hill: University of North Carolina Press, 1974.

"Manahatta." *Fraser's Magazine*, 1865.

Moon, Robert C. *The Morris Family of Philadelphia*. Philadelphia: Philadelphia Historical Society, 1908. Reprinted by Franklin Classics, 2018.

Nickel, Mary. "Incorporating Intimacy: The Evocative Story of Francis J. Grimké." https://scholar.princeton.edu/sites/default/files/marynickel/files/nickel_mary_-_incorporating_intimacy_problem_in_the_field_exam.pdf.

Pastoral Letter of the General Association of the New England Clergy. June 1837 .

Perry, Mark. *Lift Up Thy Voice: The Grimké Family's Journey from Slaveholders to Civil Rights Leaders.* New York: Viking Penguin, 2001.

Pultz, David S. "The Spring Street Church in the Age of Abolition." Masters' thesis, City University of New York, 2018. https://academicworks.cuny.edu/cc_etds_theses/734/.

Robinson, Henry S. "The M Street High School 1891–1916." Available through JSTOR.

Rudwick, Elliot M. "Race Leadership Struggle: Background of the Boston Riot of 1903." *The Journal of Negro Education.* 31:1 (Winter 1962).

Thomas, Louisa. *Louisa: The Extraordinary Life of Mrs. Adams.* New York: Penguin Random House, 2016.

U.S. Census Bureau. 1850 and 1860 Census for Charleston County, South Carolina, and the City of Charleston. http://docsouth.unc.edu/imls/census/census.html

Weld, Theodore Dwight, Angelina Grimké Weld and Sarah M. Grimké. *American Slavery as It Is: Testimony of a Thousand Witnesses,* New York: American Antislavery Society, 1839. Reprinted by Rare Books Club, General Books. Memphis, TE, 2012.

Whittier, John Greenleaf. *The Complete Works of Whittier.* www.gutenberg.org.

Woodson, Carter G., ed. *The Works of Francis J. Grimké.* Washington, DC: The Associated Publishers, 1942,